MIGHTY JACK
and the GOBLIN KING

Ben Hatke
color by Alex Campbell
and Hilary Sycamore

:01
First Second
New York

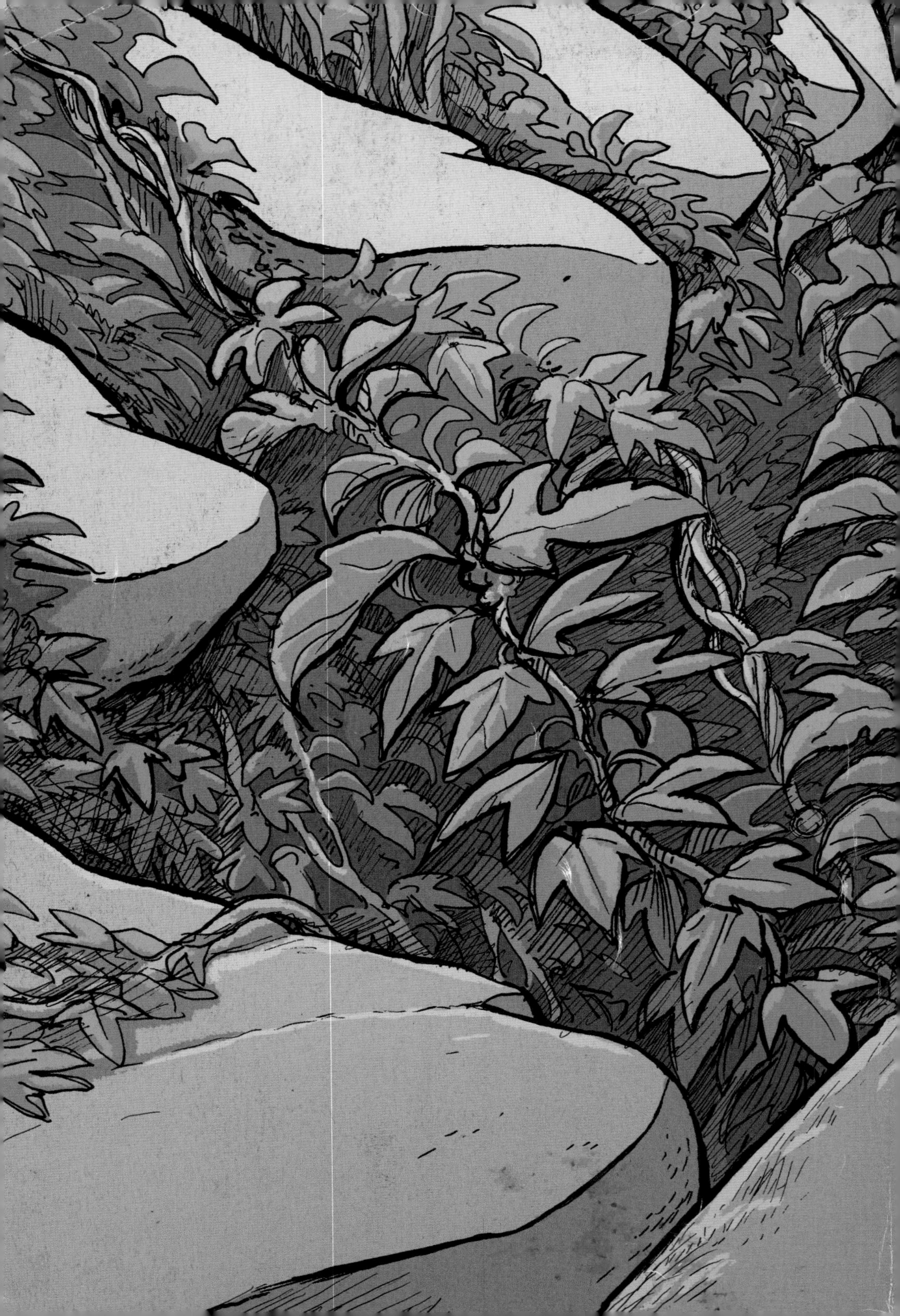

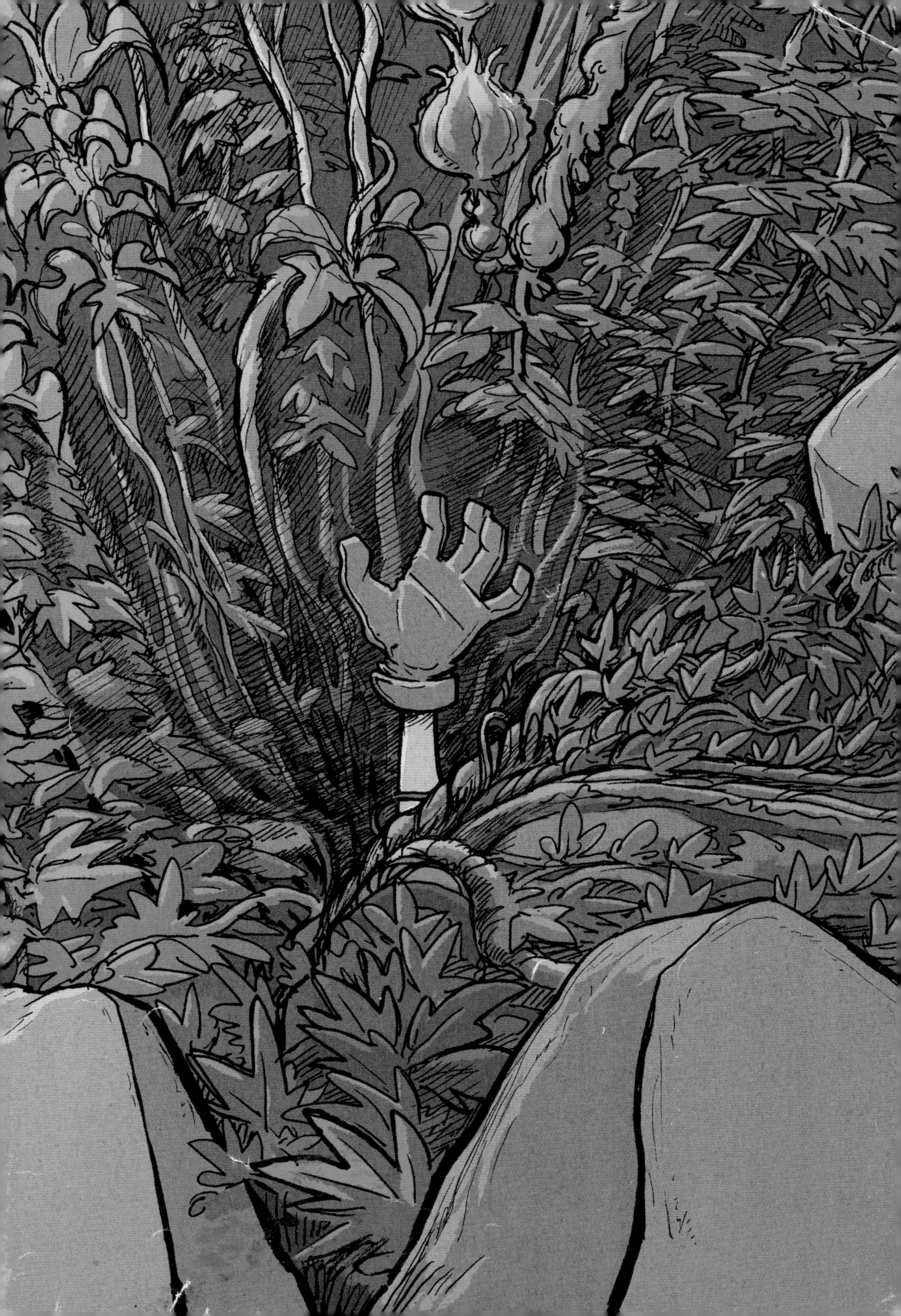

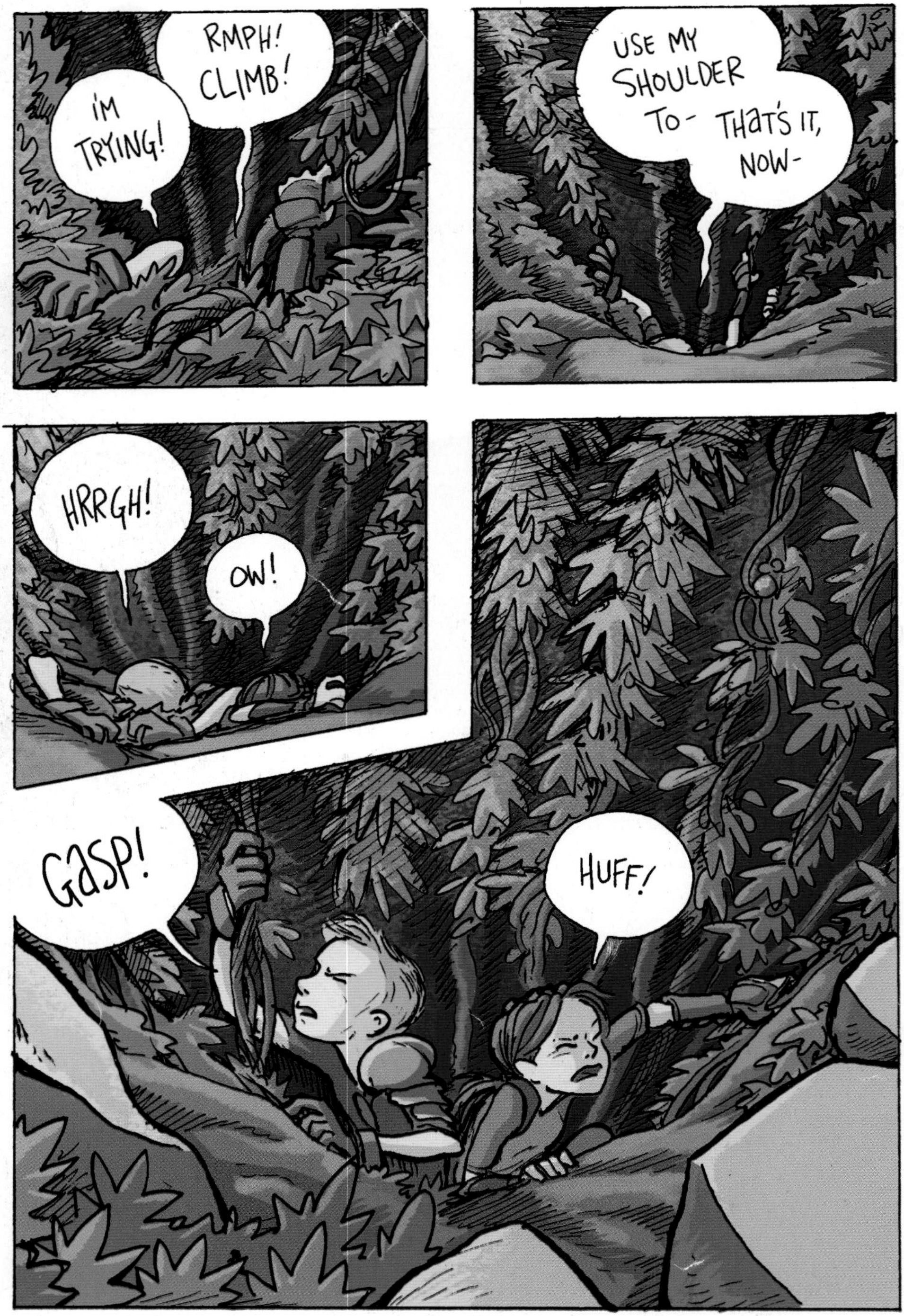
RMPH! CLIMB!
I'M TRYING!
USE MY SHOULDER TO-
THAT'S IT, NOW-
HRRGH!
OW!
GASP!
HUFF!

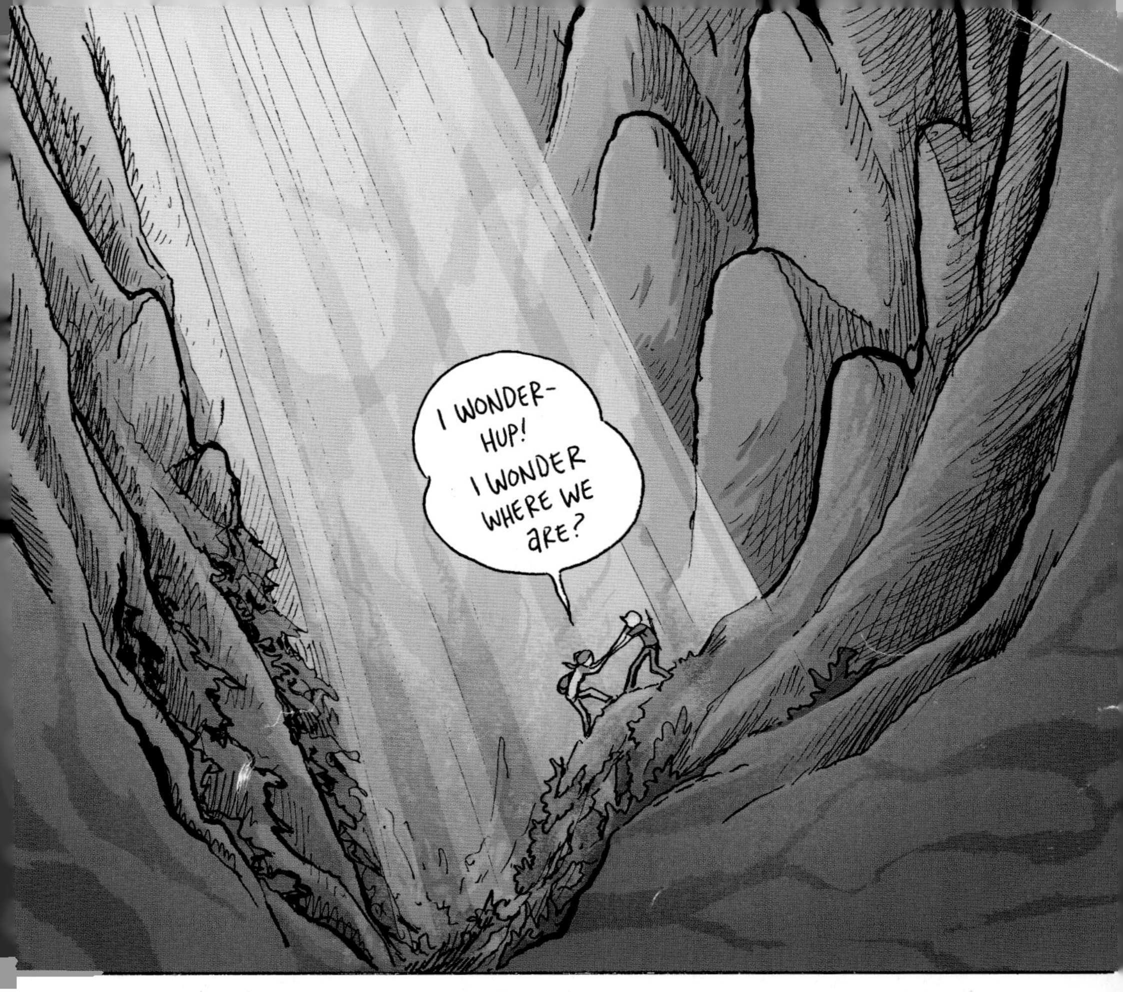
I WONDER-
HUP!
I WONDER WHERE WE ARE?

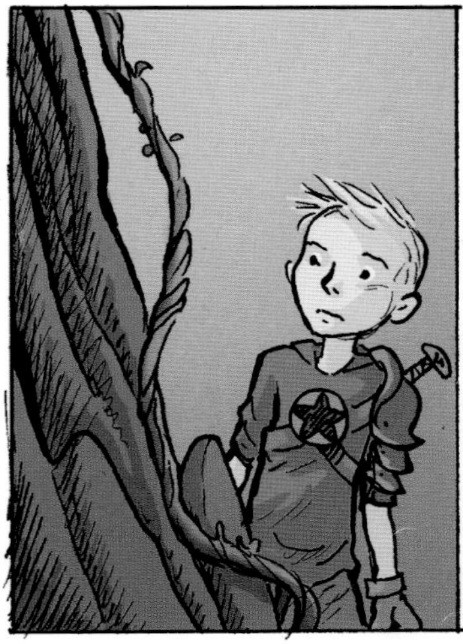

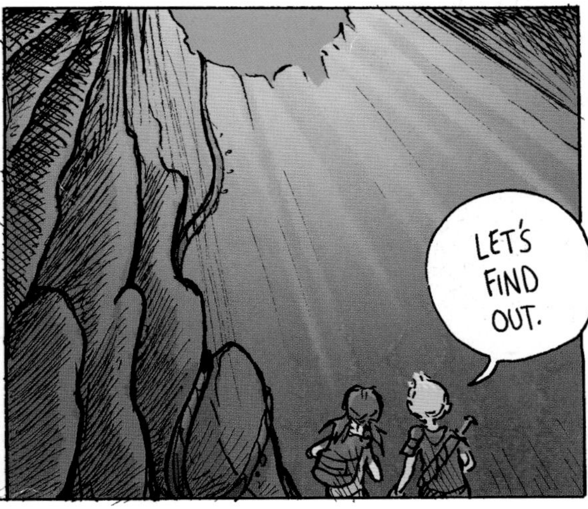
LET'S FIND OUT.

JACK, WAIT!

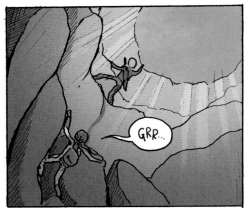

GRR...

JACK, SLOW DOWN!

SLOW DOWN?

LILLY, THAT OGRE THING HAS MADDY!

AND IT ALREADY HAS A HEAD START ON US!

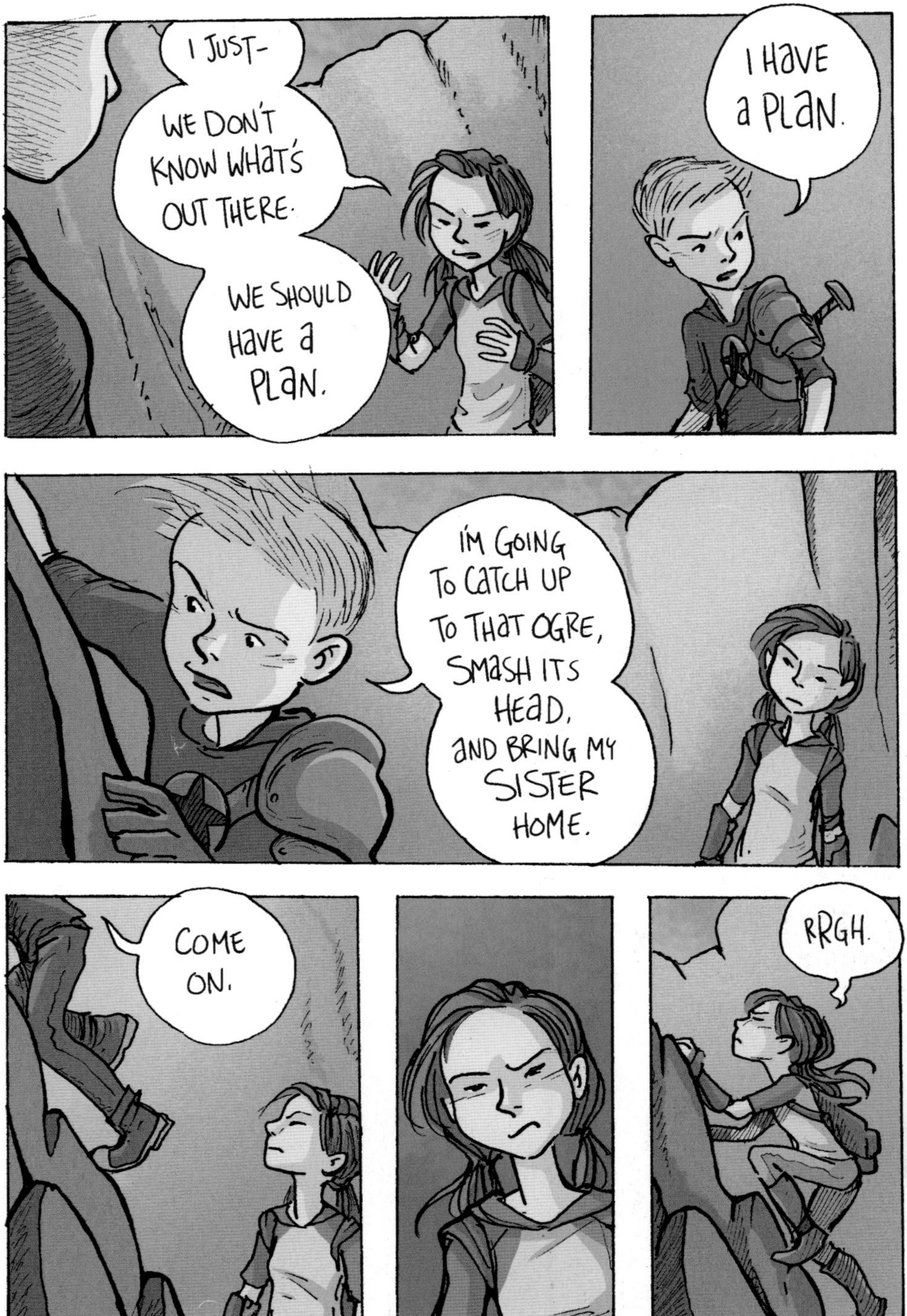
I JUST-
WE DON'T KNOW WHAT'S OUT THERE.
WE SHOULD HAVE A PLAN.
I HAVE A PLAN.
I'M GOING TO CATCH UP TO THAT OGRE, SMASH ITS HEAD, AND BRING MY SISTER HOME.
COME ON.
RRGH.

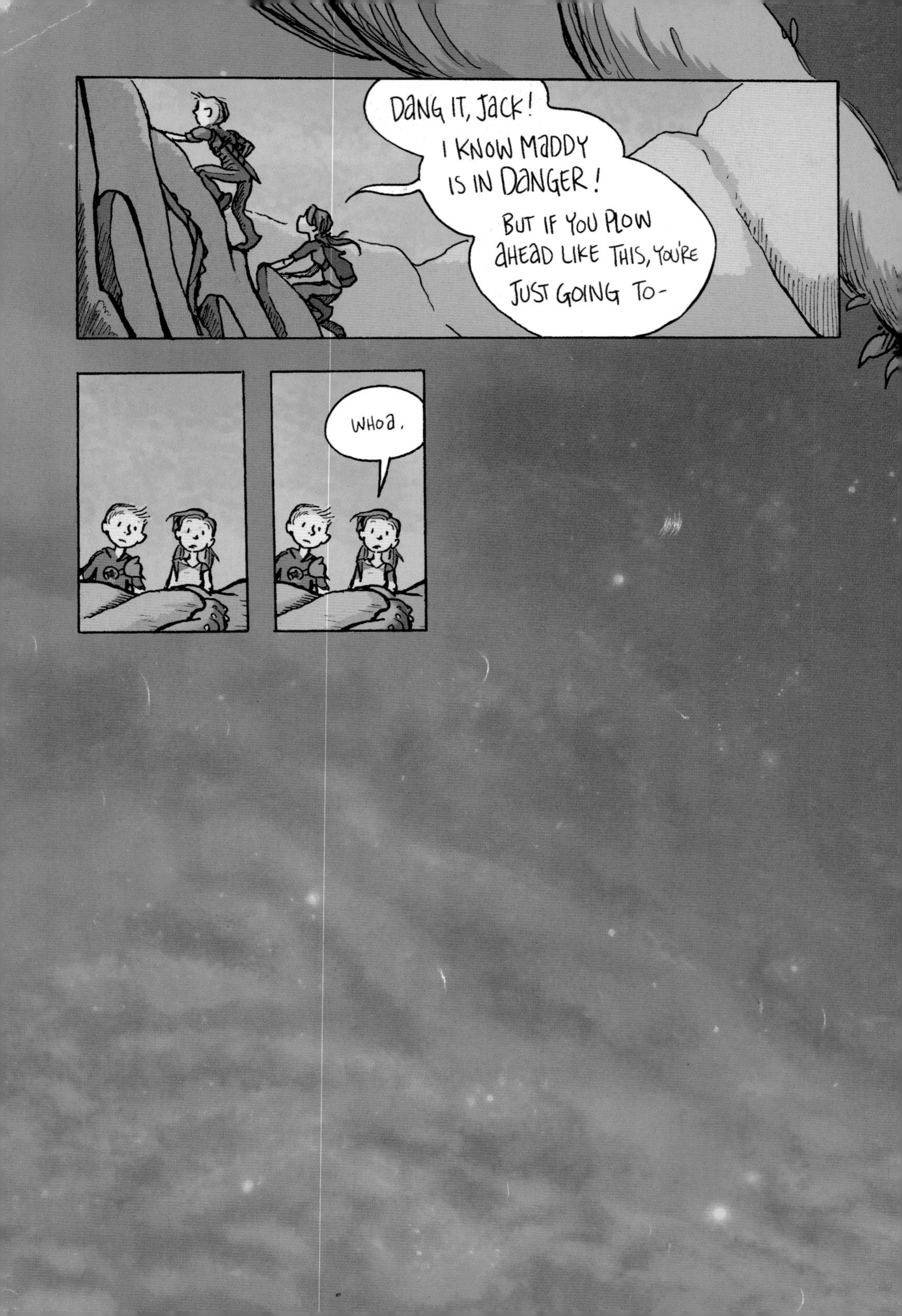
DANG IT, JACK!
I KNOW MADDY IS IN DANGER!
BUT IF YOU PLOW AHEAD LIKE THIS, YOU'RE JUST GOING TO-
WHOA.

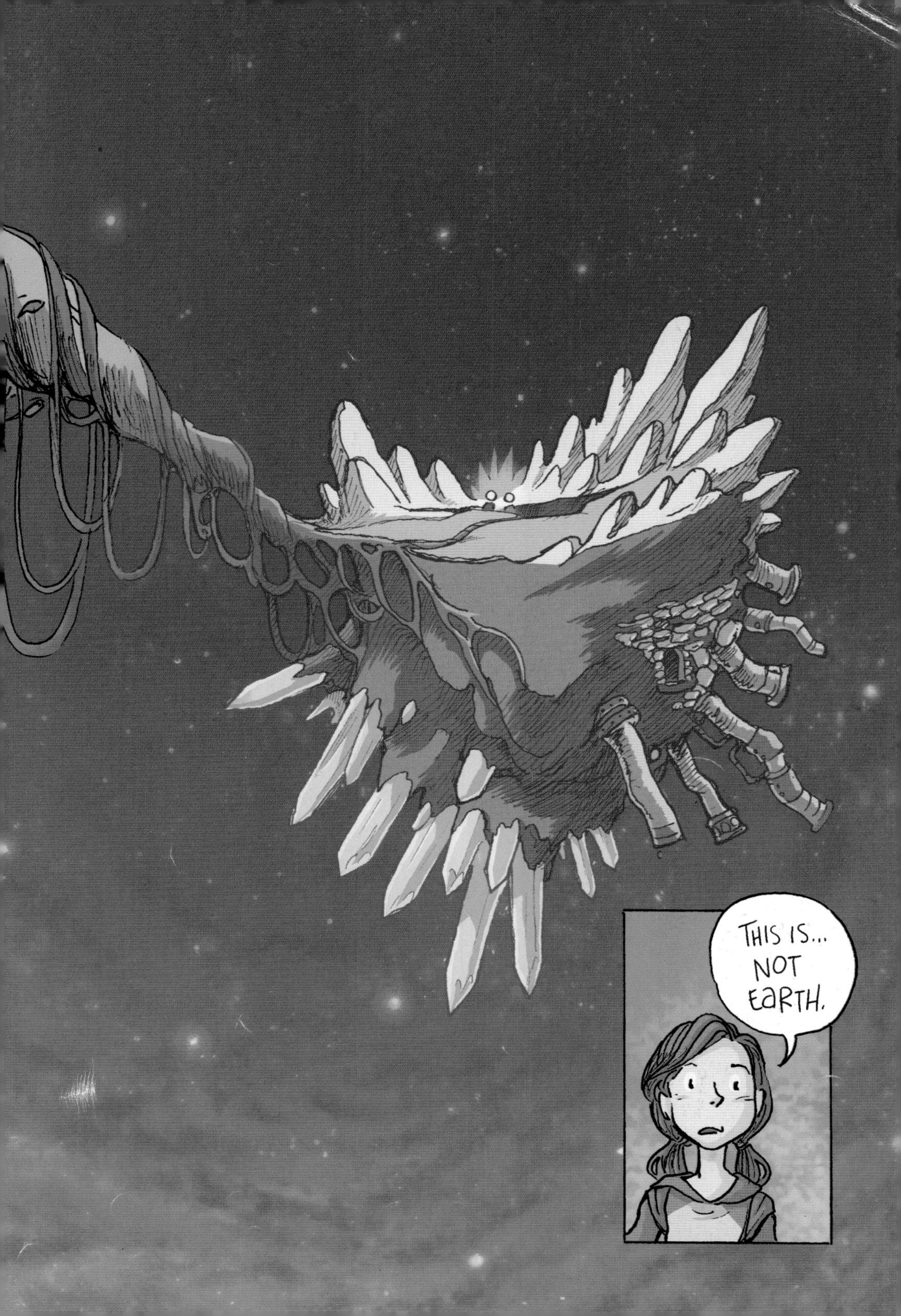
THIS IS... NOT EARTH.

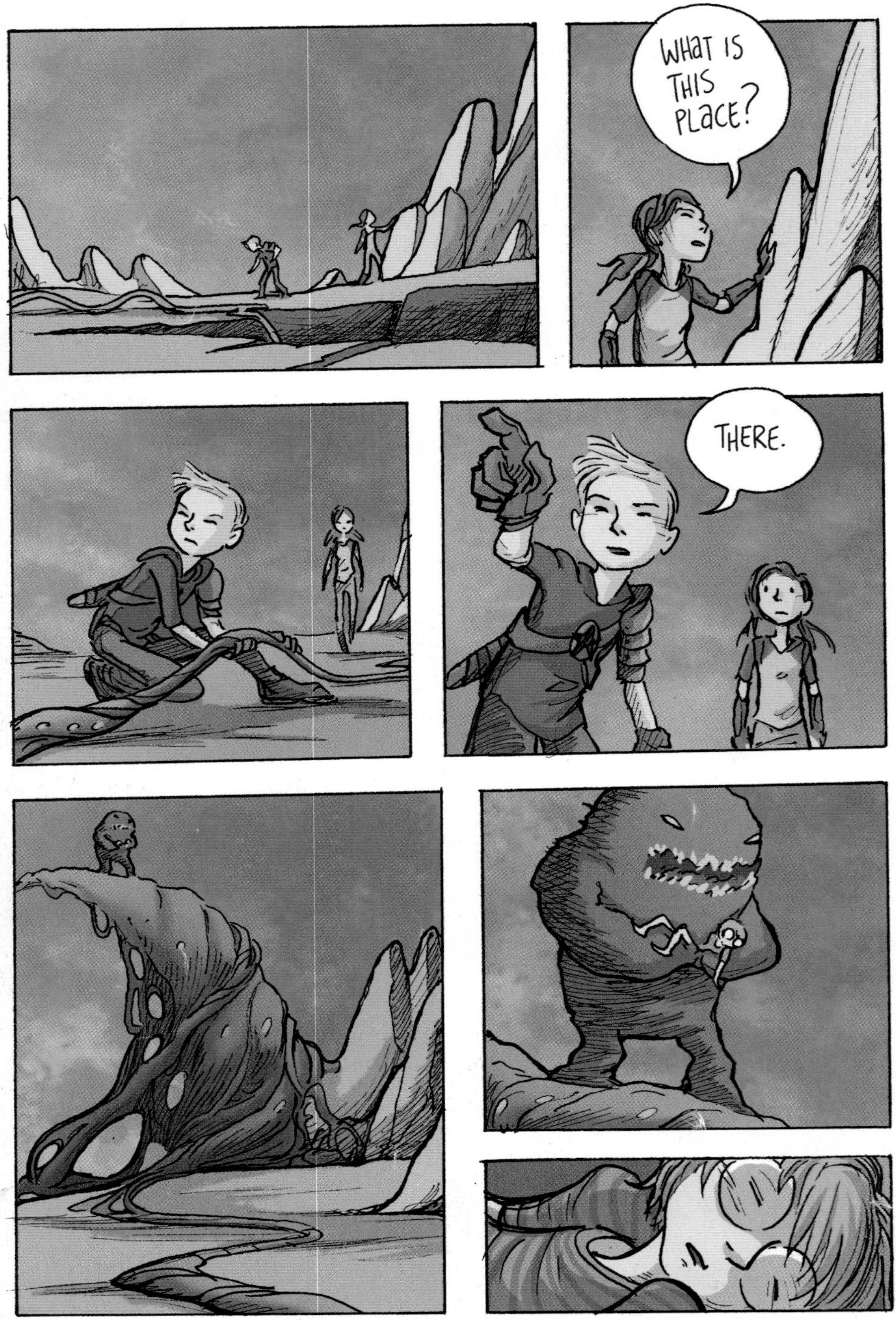
WHAT IS THIS PLACE?
THERE.

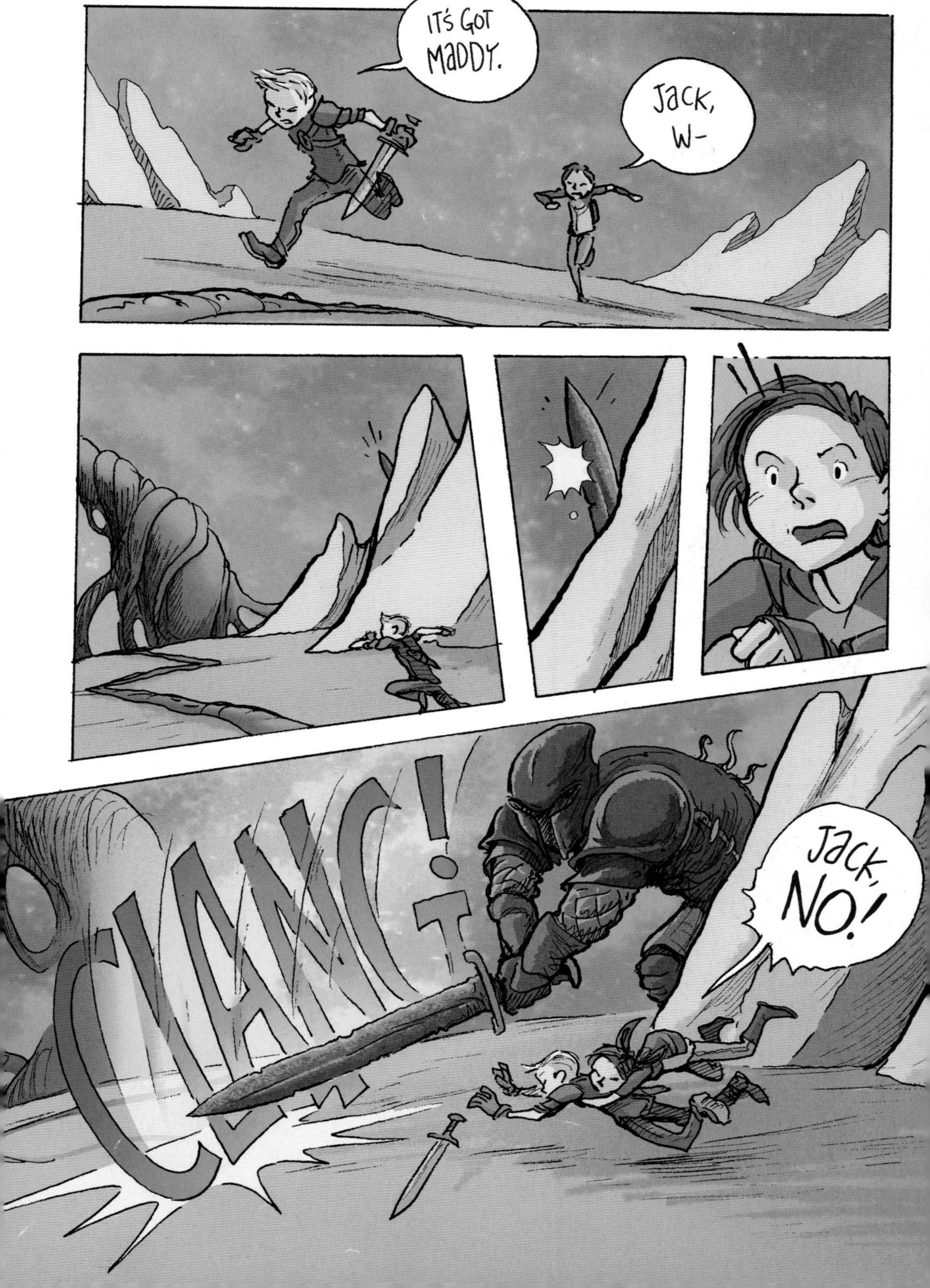
IT'S GOT MADDY.
JACK, W-
CLANG!
JACK, NO!

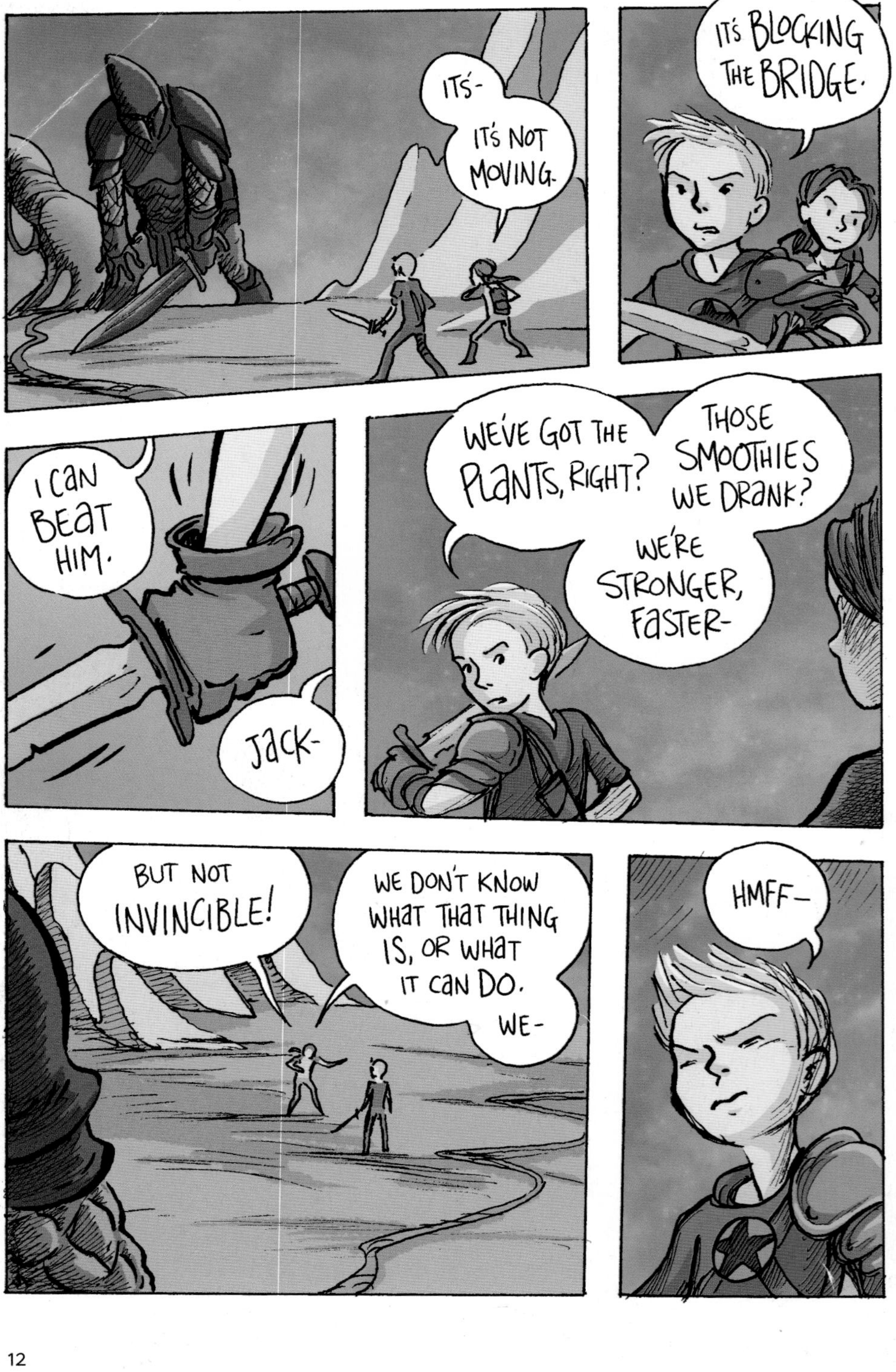
IT'S-
IT'S NOT MOVING.
IT'S BLOCKING THE BRIDGE.
I CAN BEAT HIM.
JACK-
WE'VE GOT THE PLANTS, RIGHT?
THOSE SMOOTHIES WE DRANK?
WE'RE STRONGER, FASTER-
BUT NOT INVINCIBLE!
WE DON'T KNOW WHAT THAT THING IS, OR WHAT IT CAN DO.
WE-
HMFF-

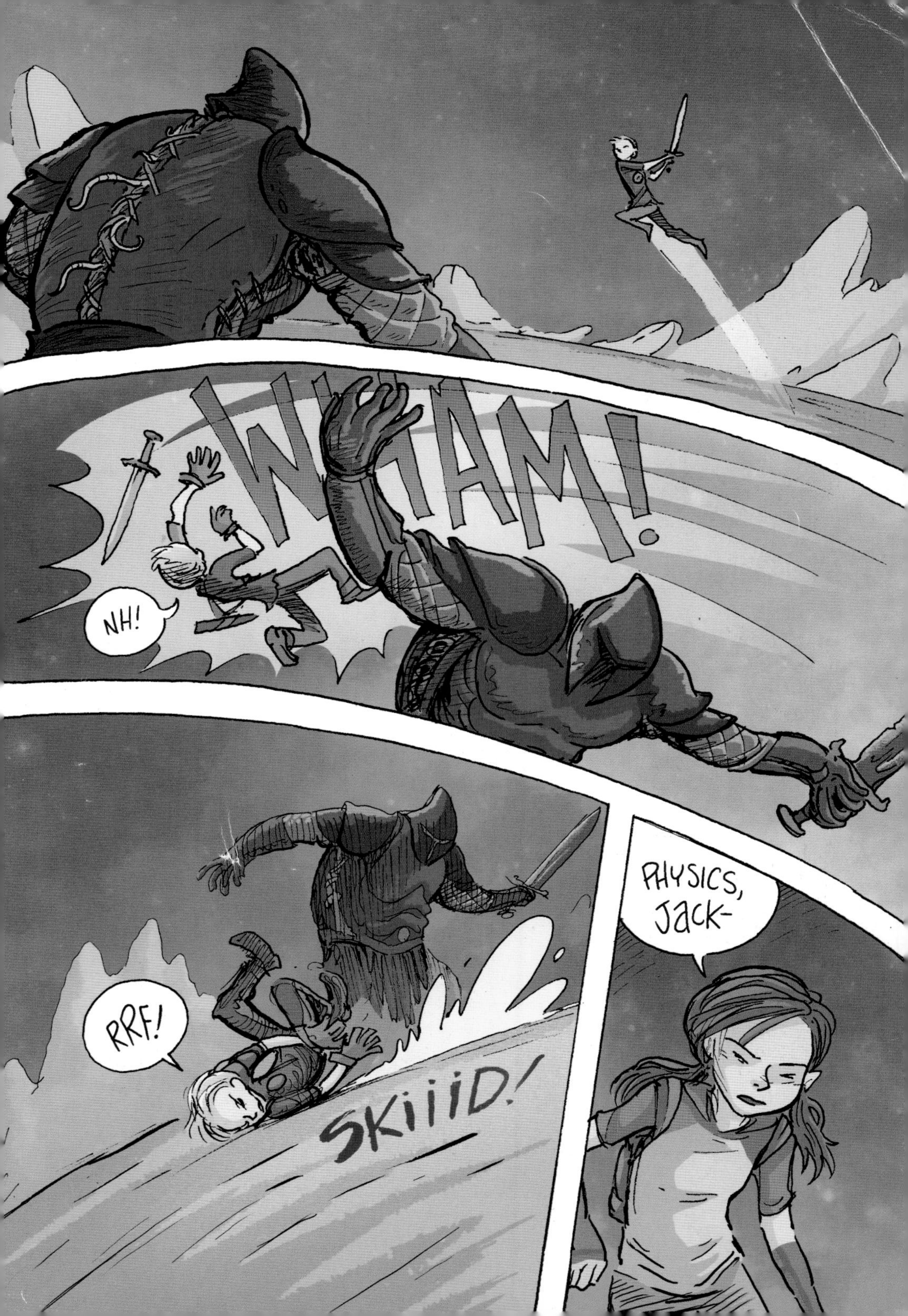
WHAM!
NH!
RRF!
SKIIID!
PHYSICS, JACK-

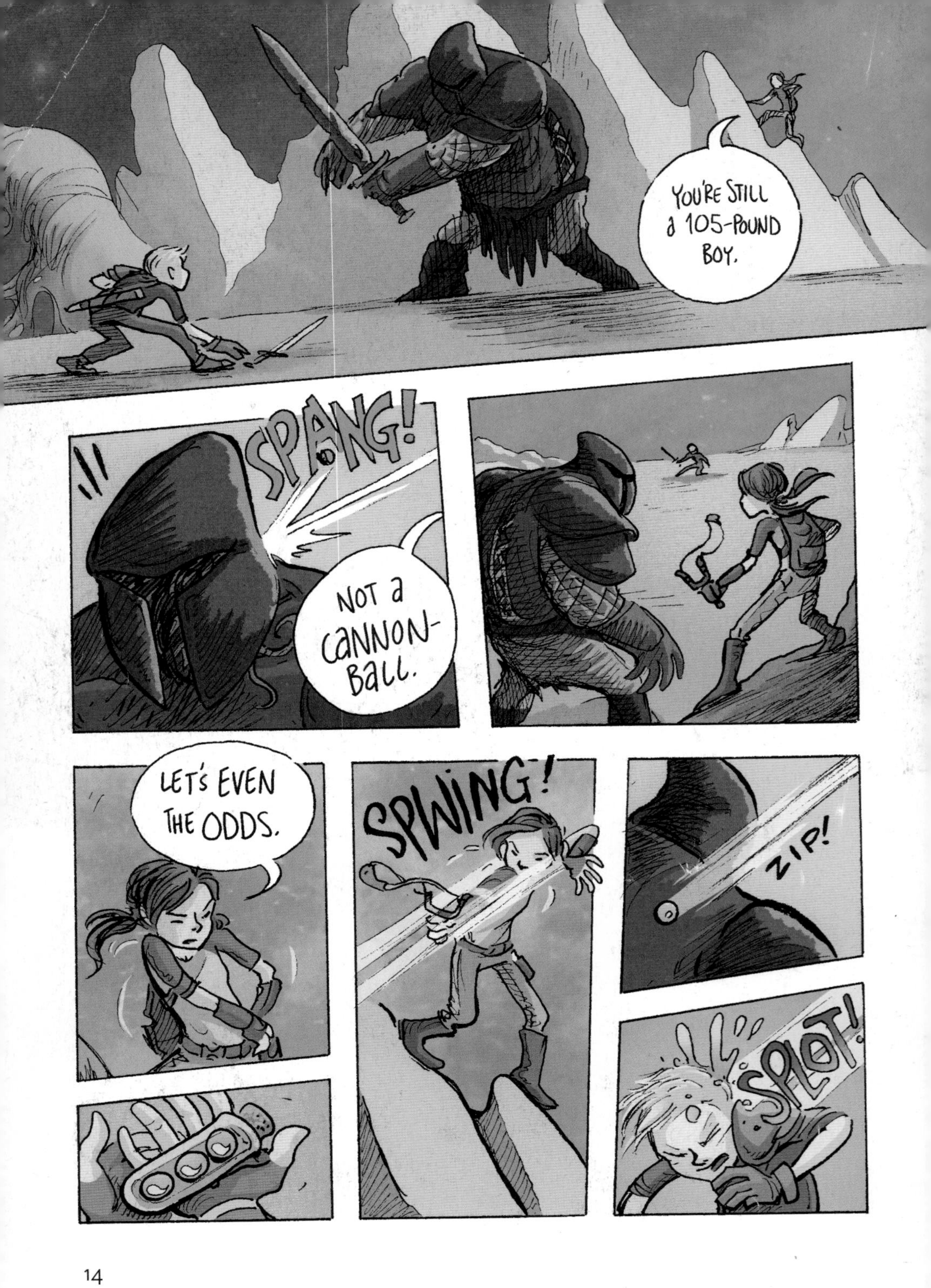
YOU'RE STILL a 105-POUND BOY.
SPANG!
NOT a CANNON-BALL.
LET'S EVEN THE ODDS.
SPWING!
ZIP!
SPLOT!

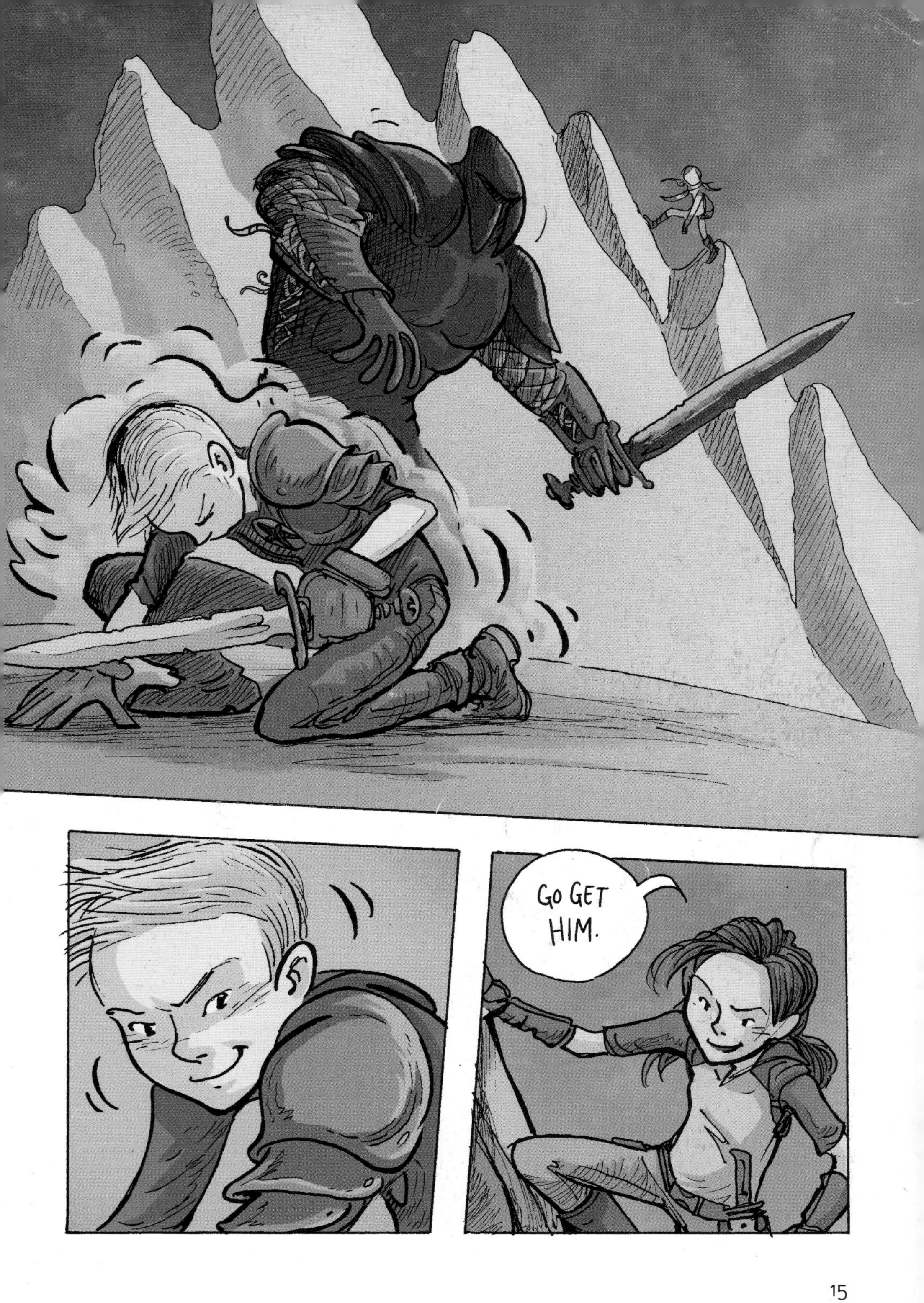
GO GET HIM.

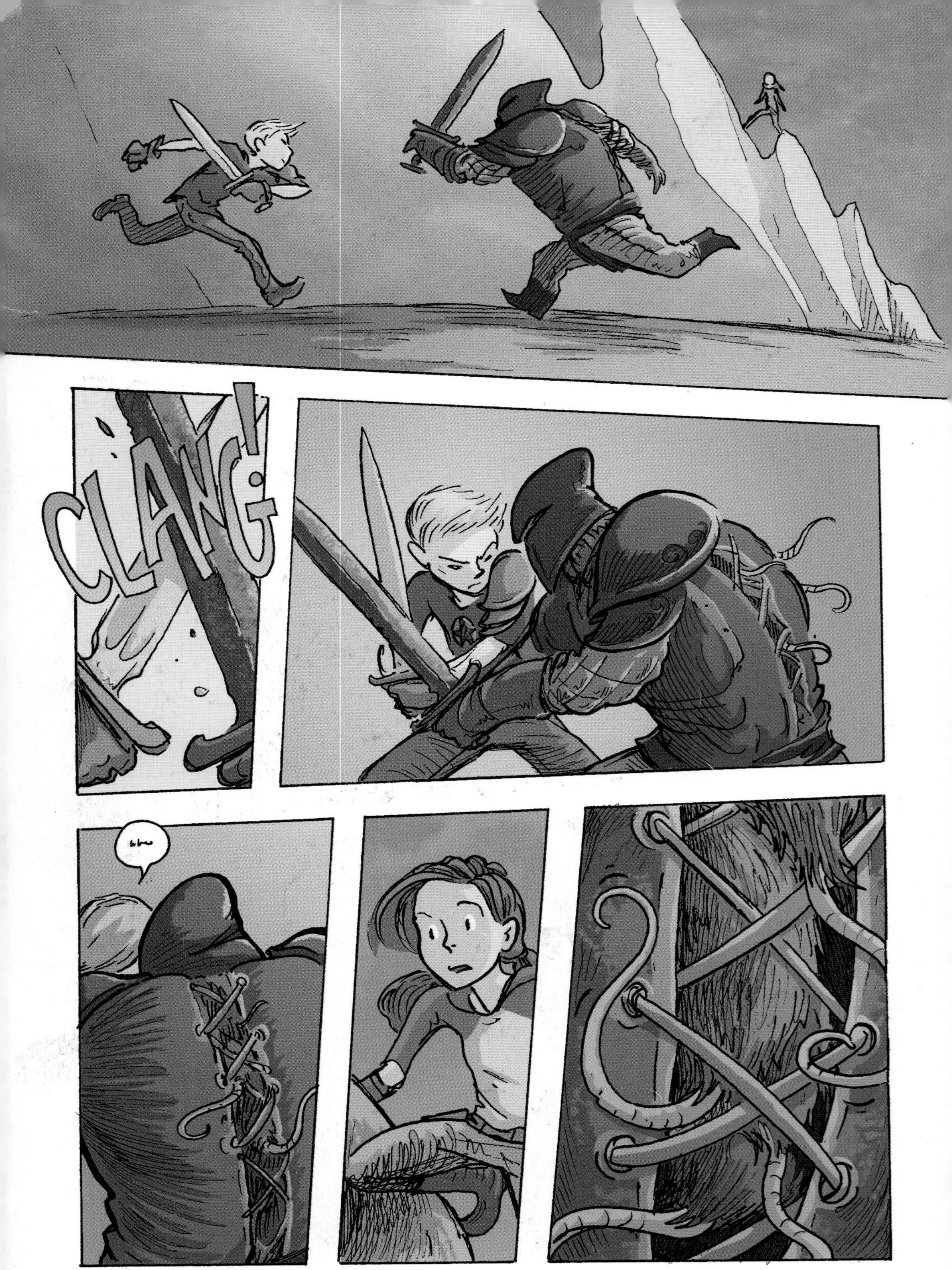
CLANG!

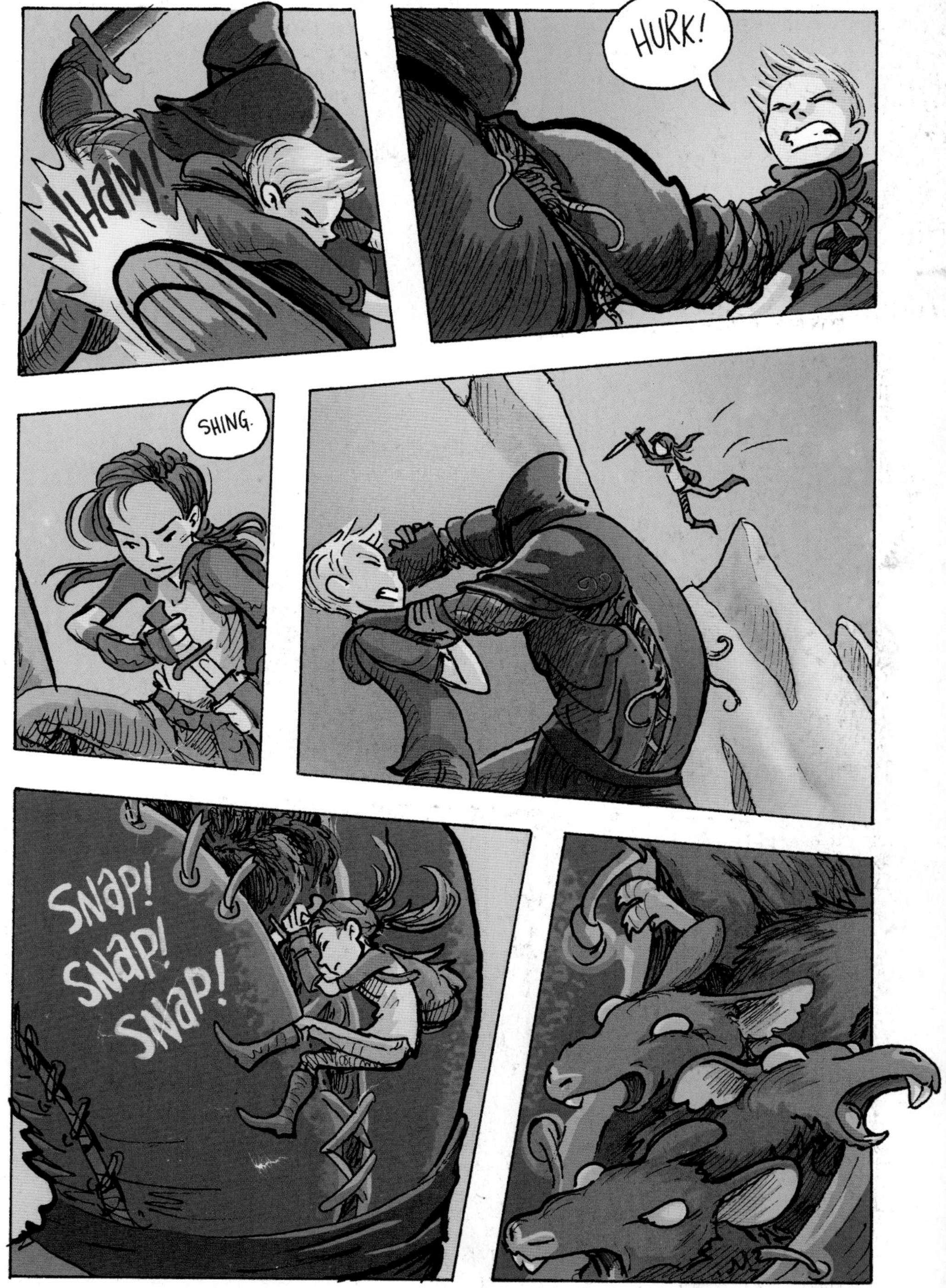
WHAM!
HURK!
SHING.
SNAP!
SNAP!
SNAP!

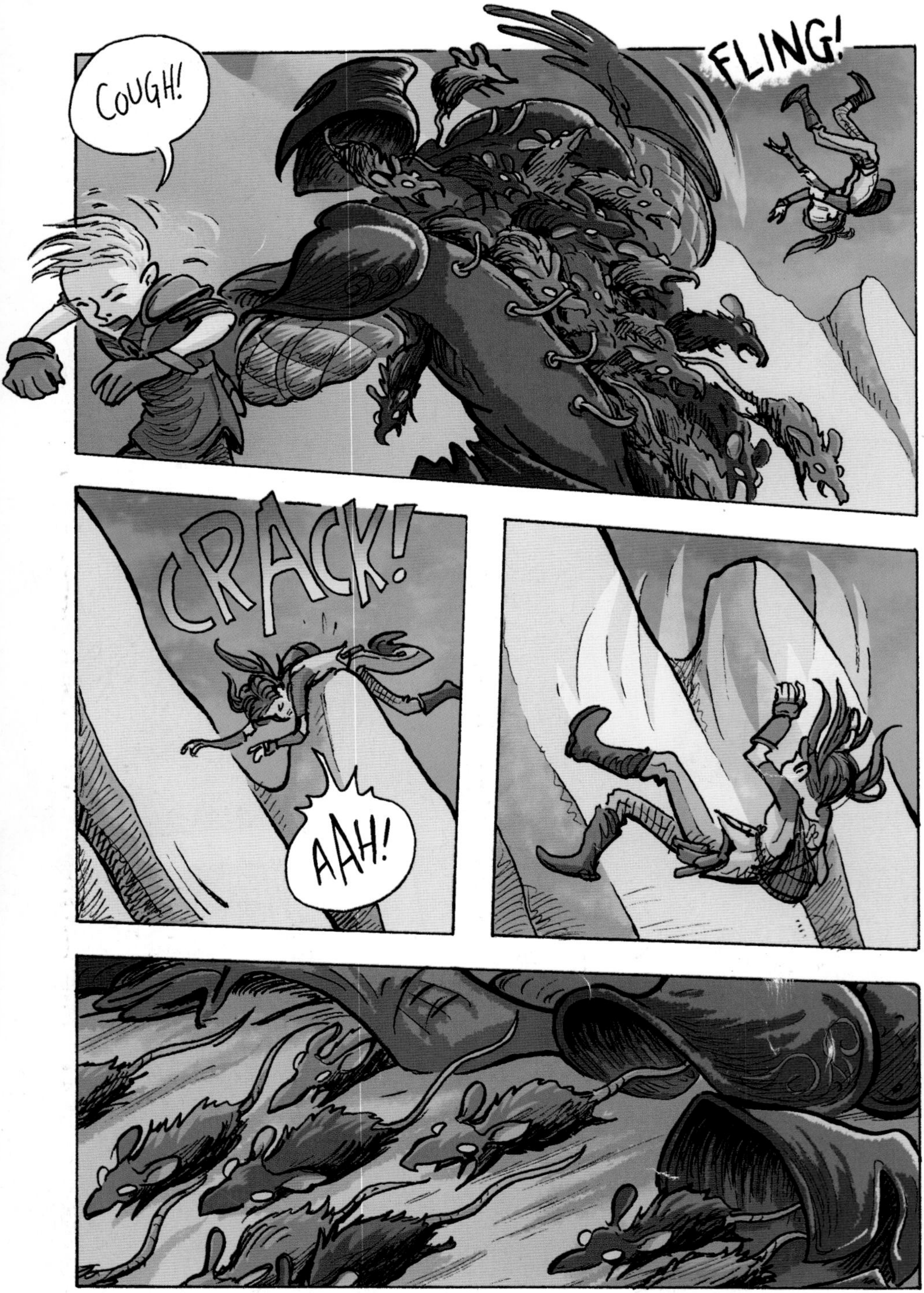
COUGH!
FLING!
CRACK!
AAH!

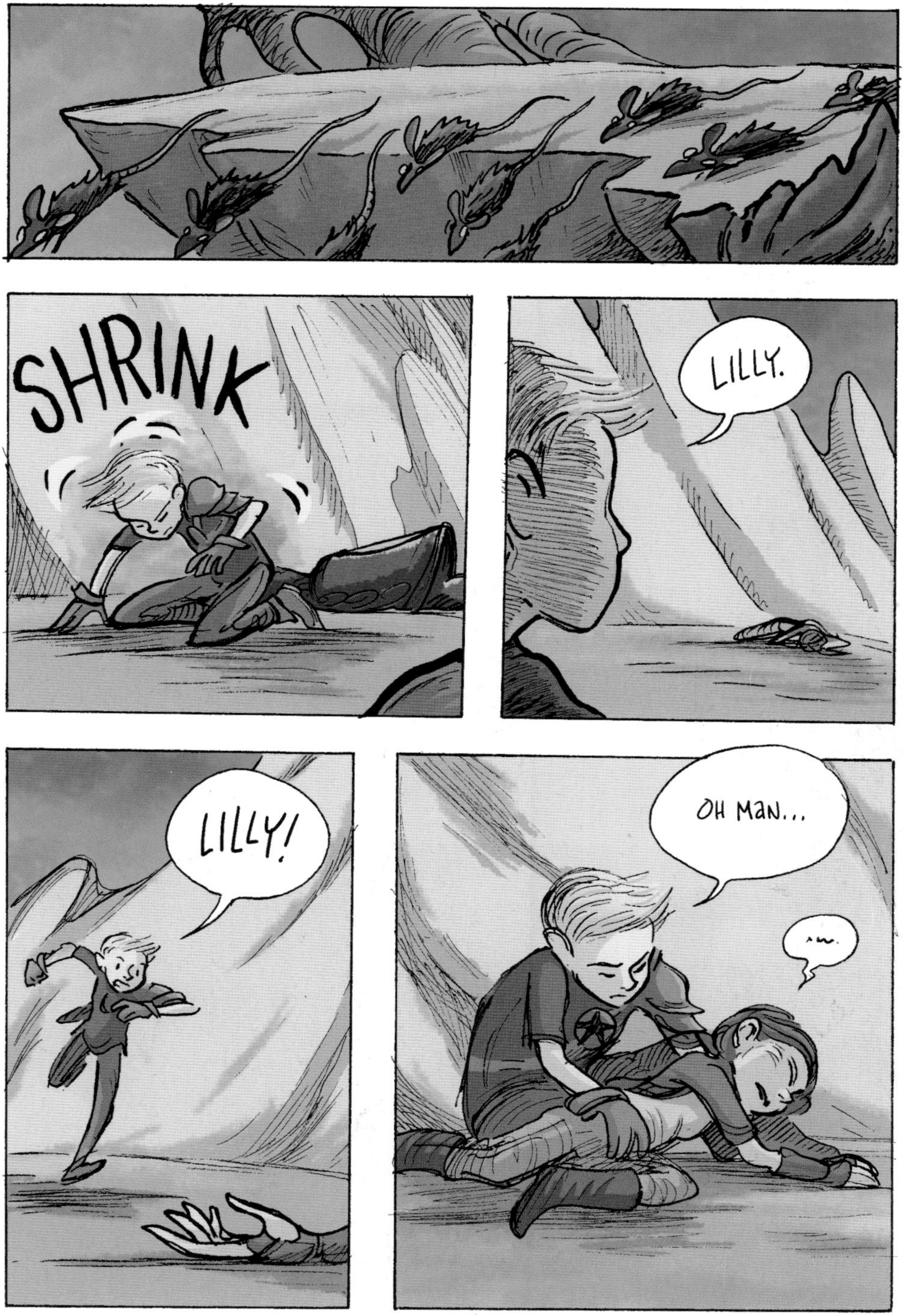
SHRINK
LILLY.
LILLY!
OH MAN...

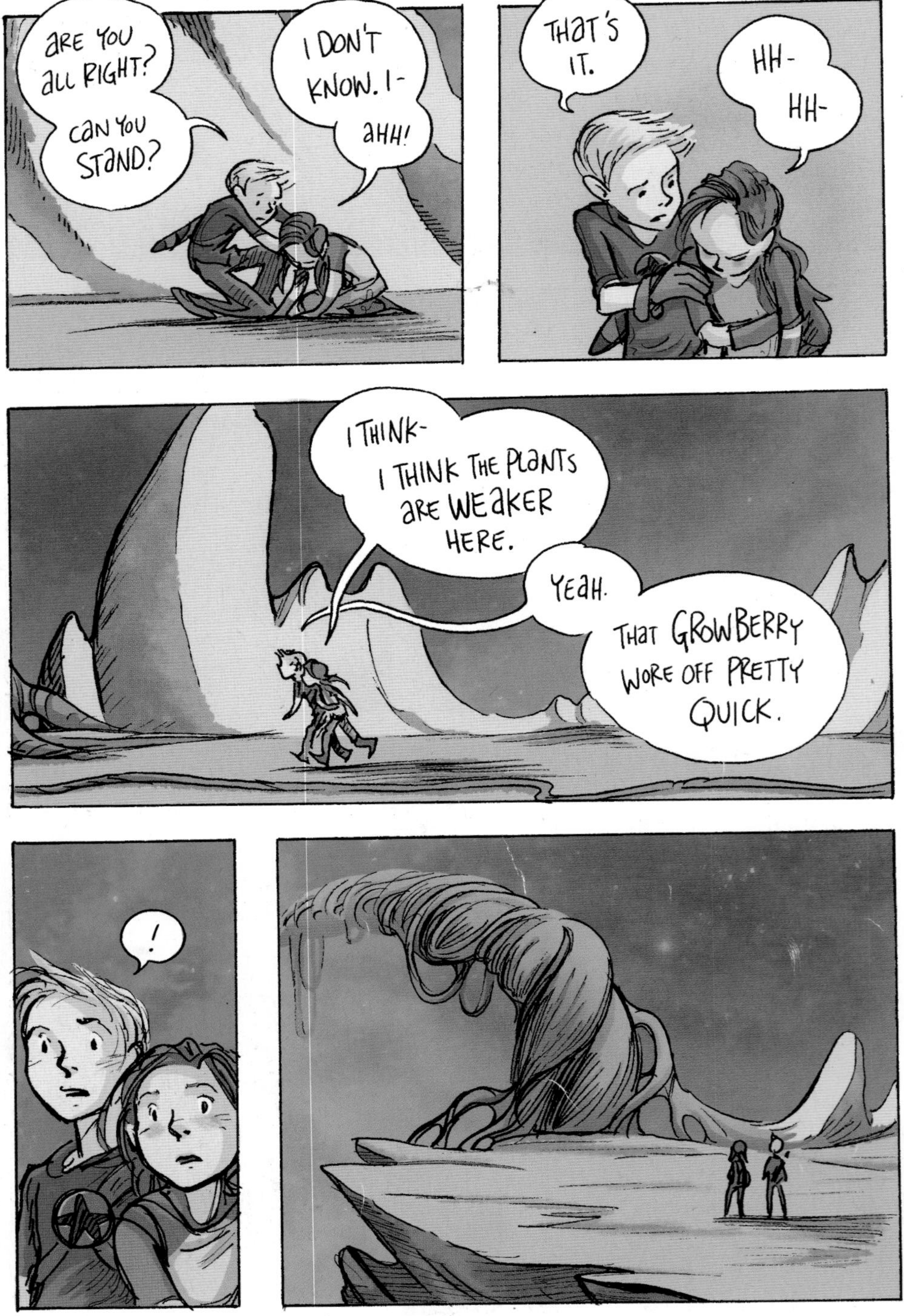
ARE YOU ALL RIGHT?
CAN YOU STAND?
I DON'T KNOW. I-
AHH!
THAT'S IT.
HH-
HH-
I THINK-
I THINK THE PLANTS ARE WEAKER HERE.
YEAH.
THAT GROWBERRY WORE OFF PRETTY QUICK.
!

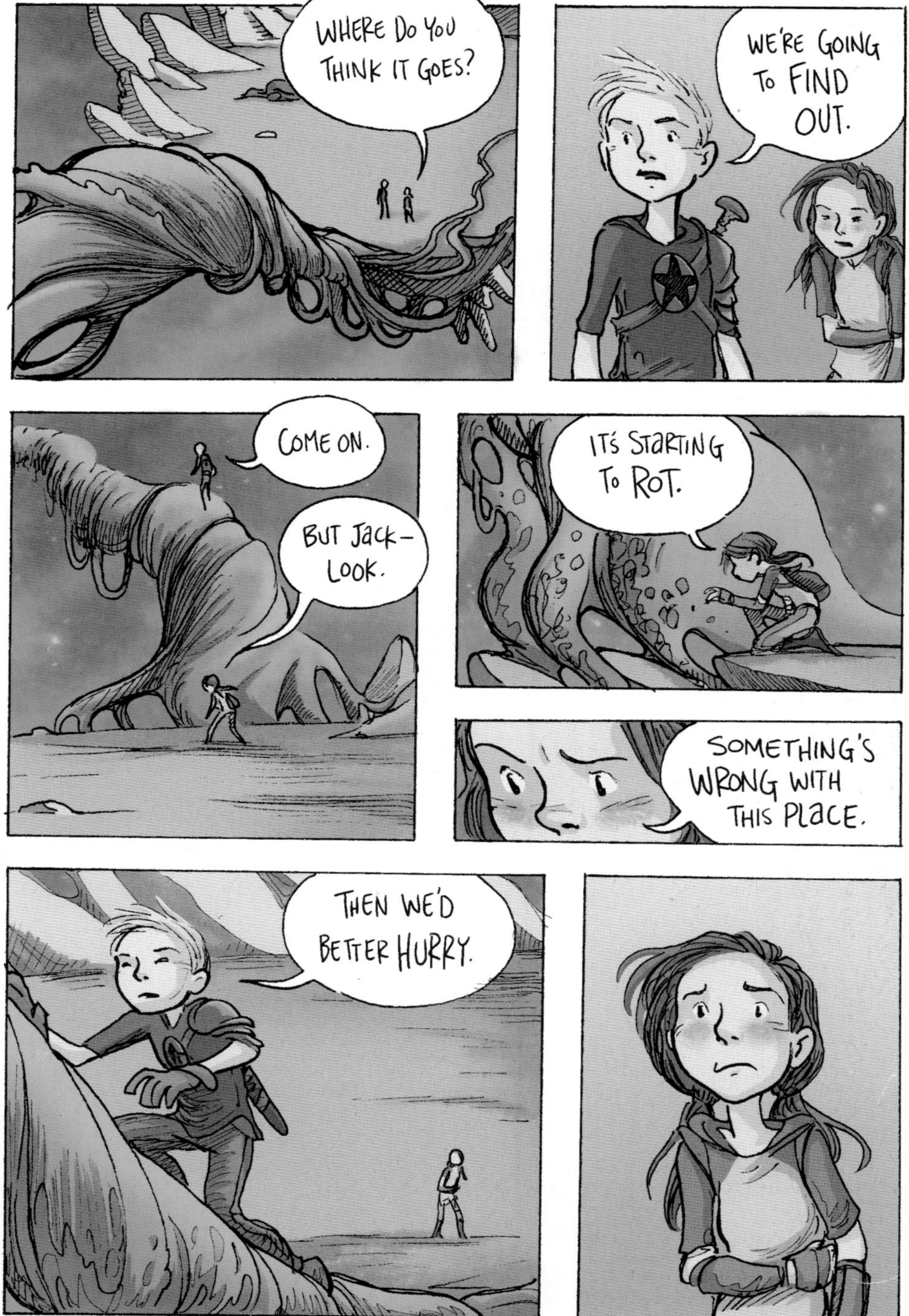
WHERE DO YOU THINK IT GOES?
WE'RE GOING TO FIND OUT.
COME ON.
BUT JACK— LOOK.
IT'S STARTING TO ROT.
SOMETHING'S WRONG WITH THIS PLACE.
THEN WE'D BETTER HURRY.

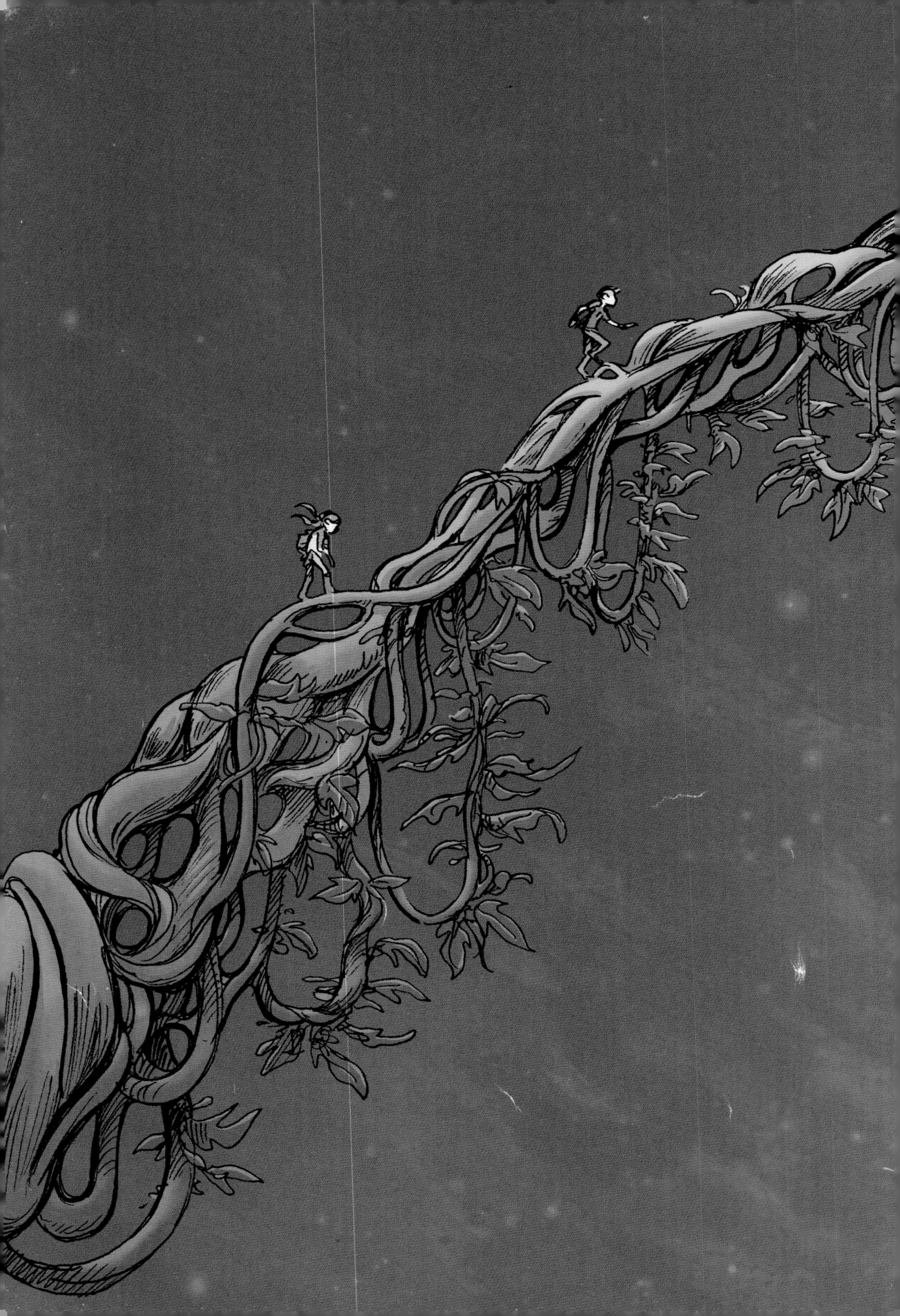

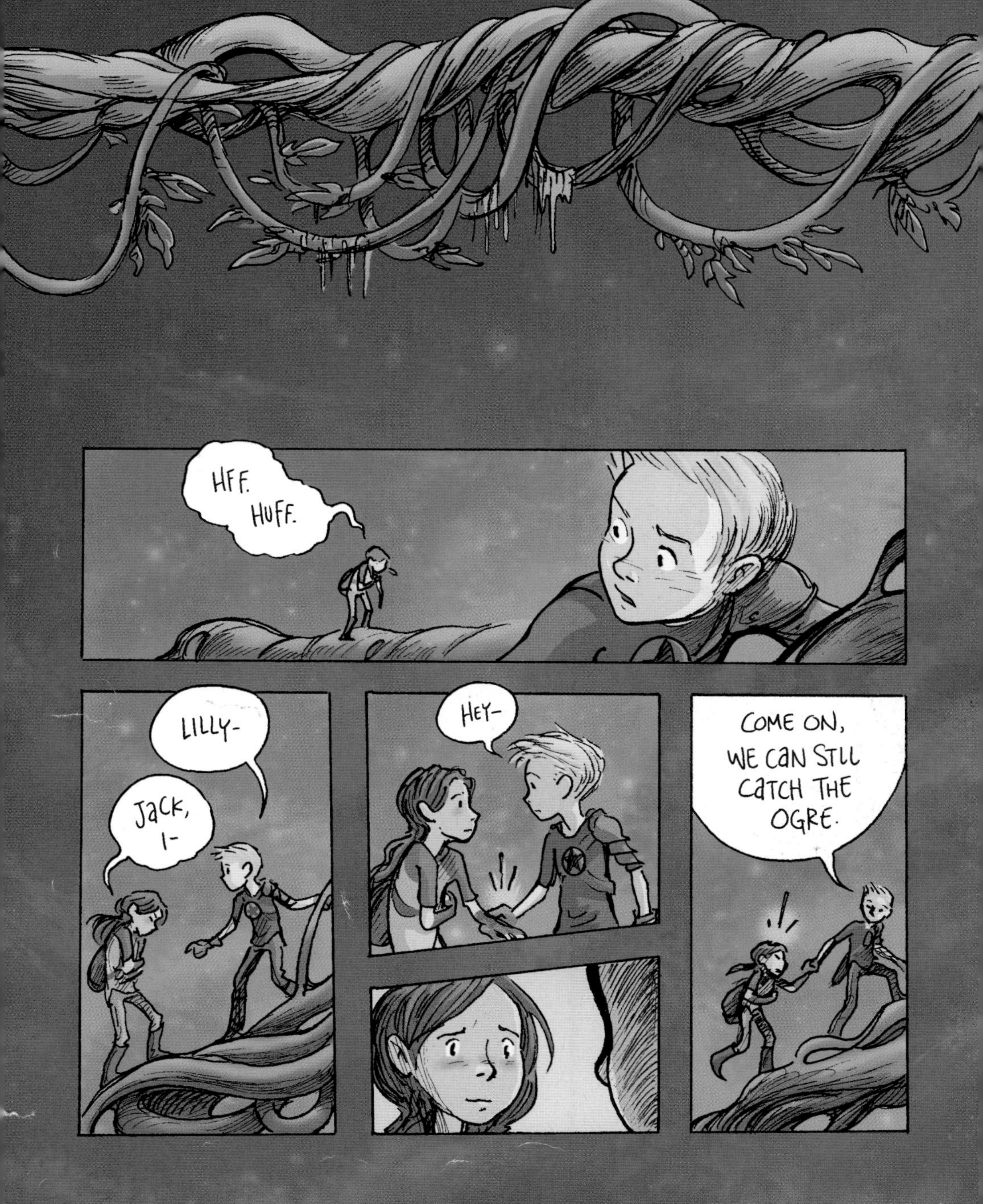
HFF. HUFF.
LILLY-
JACK, I-
HEY-
COME ON, WE CAN STILL CATCH THE OGRE.

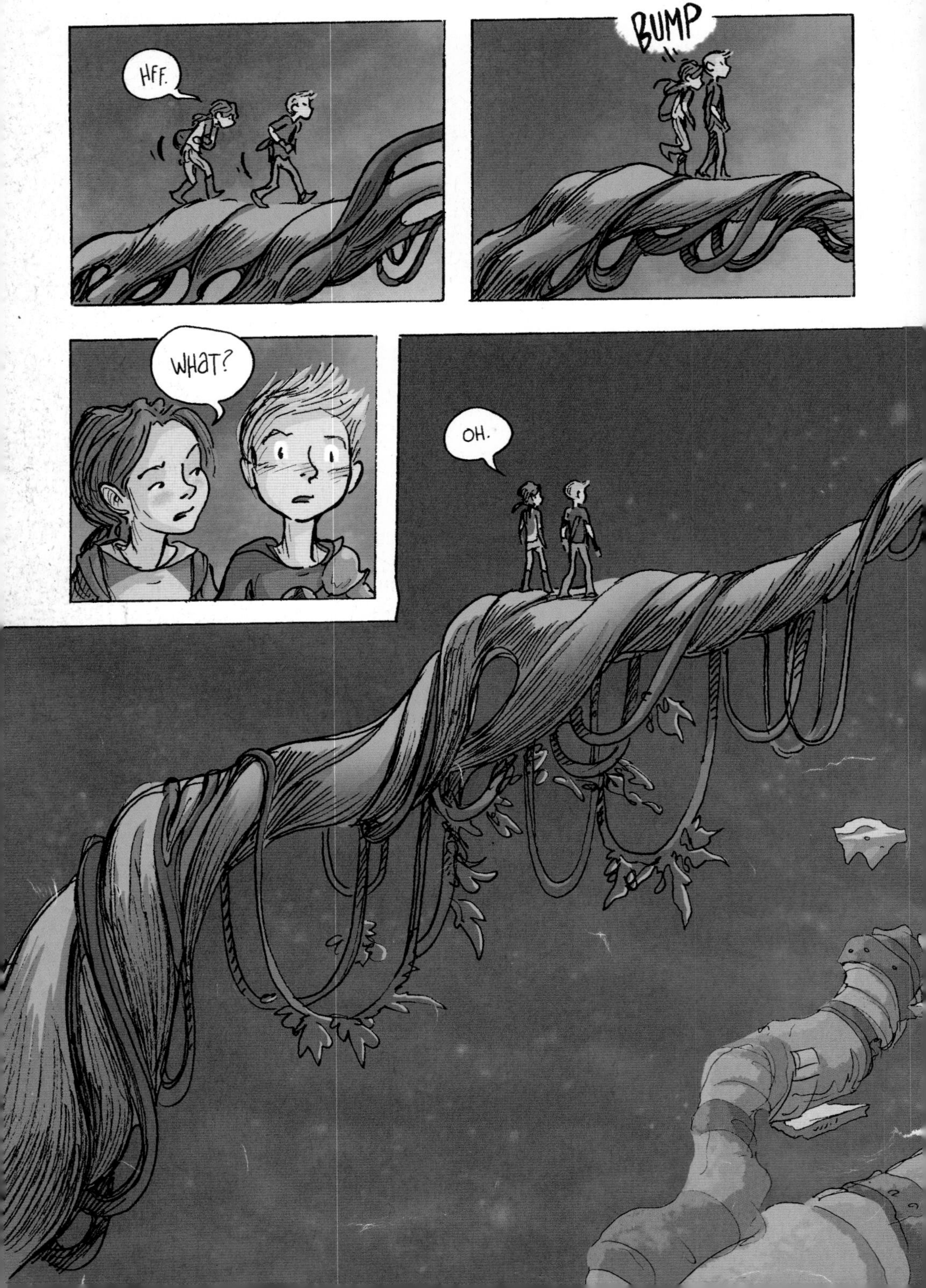
HFF.
BUMP
WHAT?
OH.

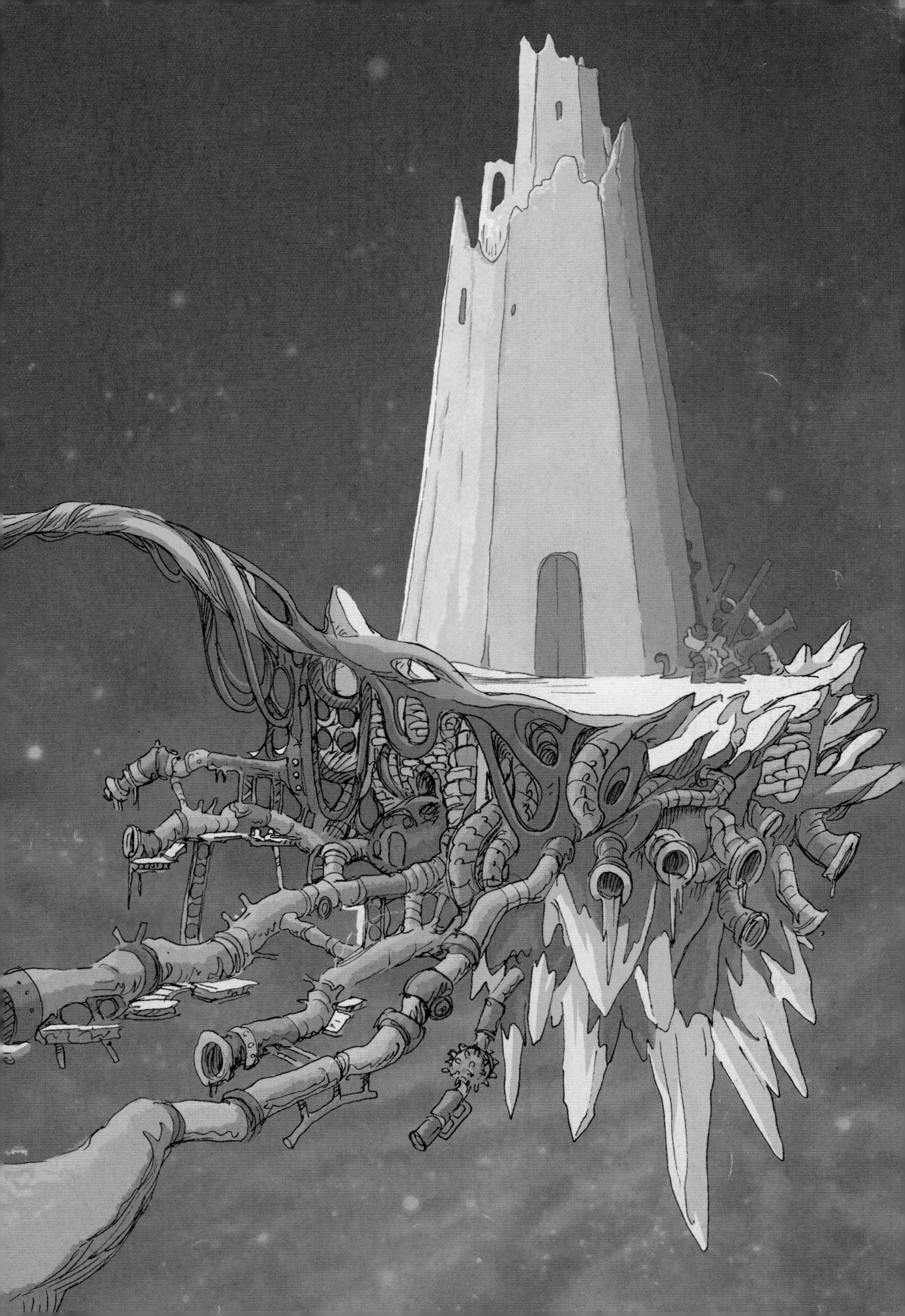

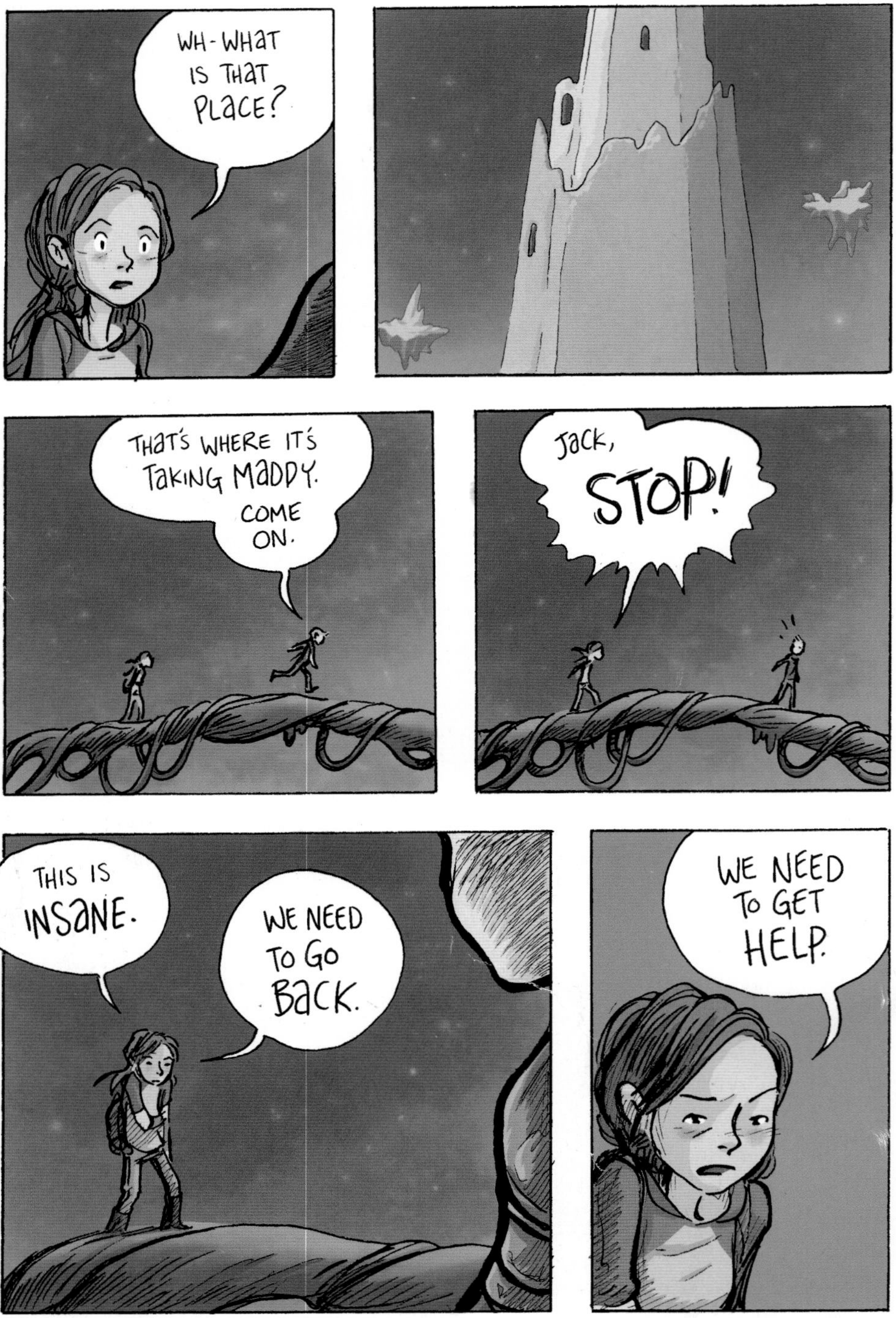
WH-WHAT IS THAT PLACE?
THAT'S WHERE IT'S TAKING MADDY.
COME ON.
JACK, STOP!
THIS IS INSANE.
WE NEED TO GO BACK.
WE NEED TO GET HELP.

HELP? YOU'RE THE ONE WHO THOUGHT WE COULD DO THIS!

I THOUGHT THIS IS WHAT YOU "TRAINED ALL YOUR LIFE FOR."

YEAH. AND LOOK WHERE IT GOT ME.

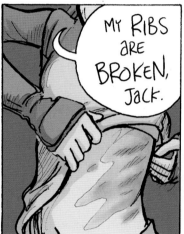

MY RIBS ARE BROKEN, JACK.

WE'VE BEEN HERE, WHAT, TWO HOURS?

I'M OF NO USE TO YOU LIKE THIS.

THOSE PLANT EXTRACTS WE DRANK ARE THE ONLY REASON I'M STILL STANDING.

WE SHOULD GO BACK, GET ADULTS WITH... I DON'T KNOW, GUNS? OR—

NO.

I WON'T LEAVE MADDY.

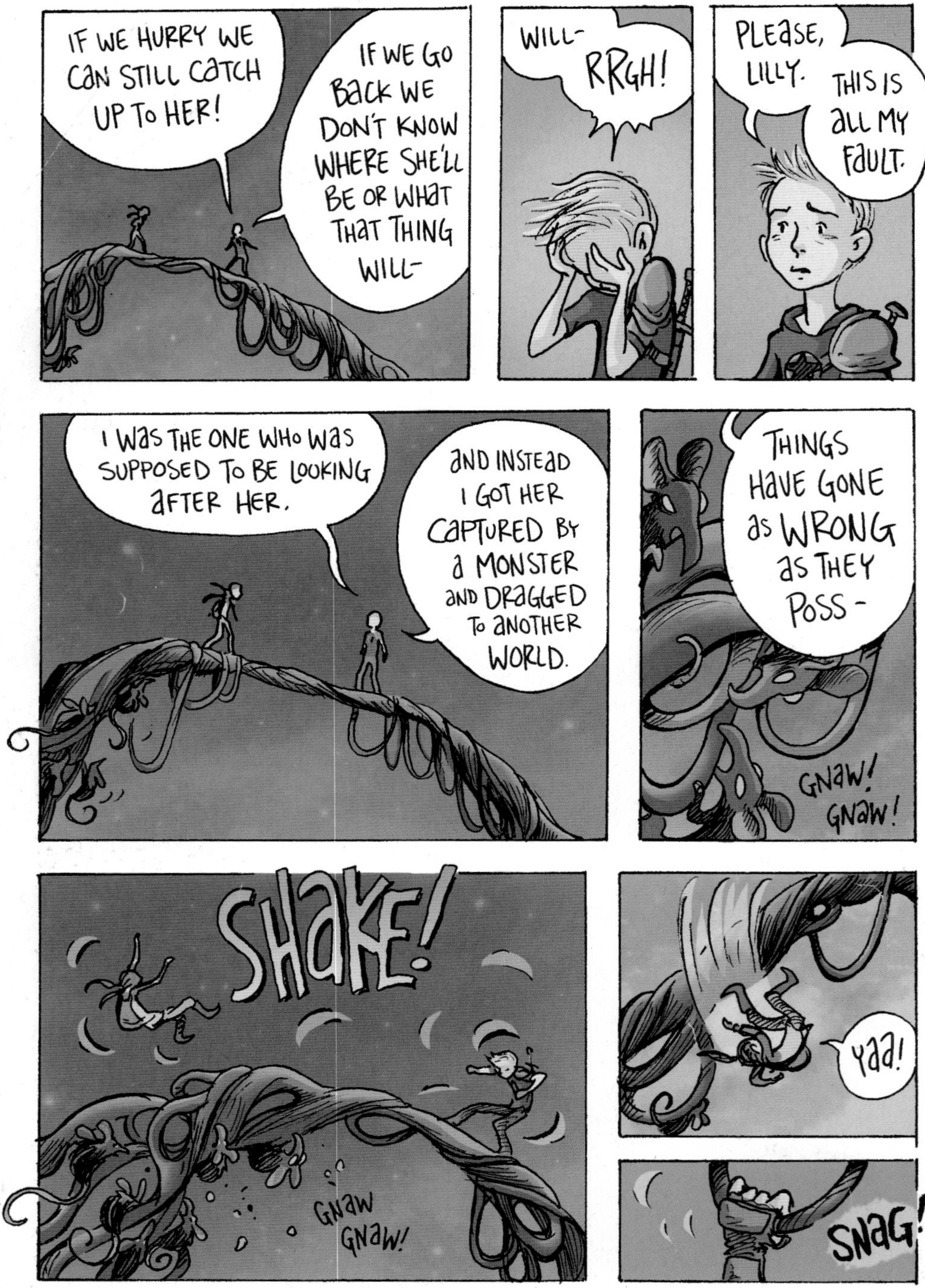
IF WE HURRY WE CAN STILL CATCH UP TO HER!
IF WE GO BACK WE DON'T KNOW WHERE SHE'LL BE OR WHAT THAT THING WILL-
WILL-
RRGH!
PLEASE, LILLY.
THIS IS ALL MY FAULT.
I WAS THE ONE WHO WAS SUPPOSED TO BE LOOKING AFTER HER.
AND INSTEAD I GOT HER CAPTURED BY A MONSTER AND DRAGGED TO ANOTHER WORLD.
THINGS HAVE GONE AS WRONG AS THEY POSS-
GNAW! GNAW!
SHAKE!
GNAW GNAW!
YAA!
SNAG!

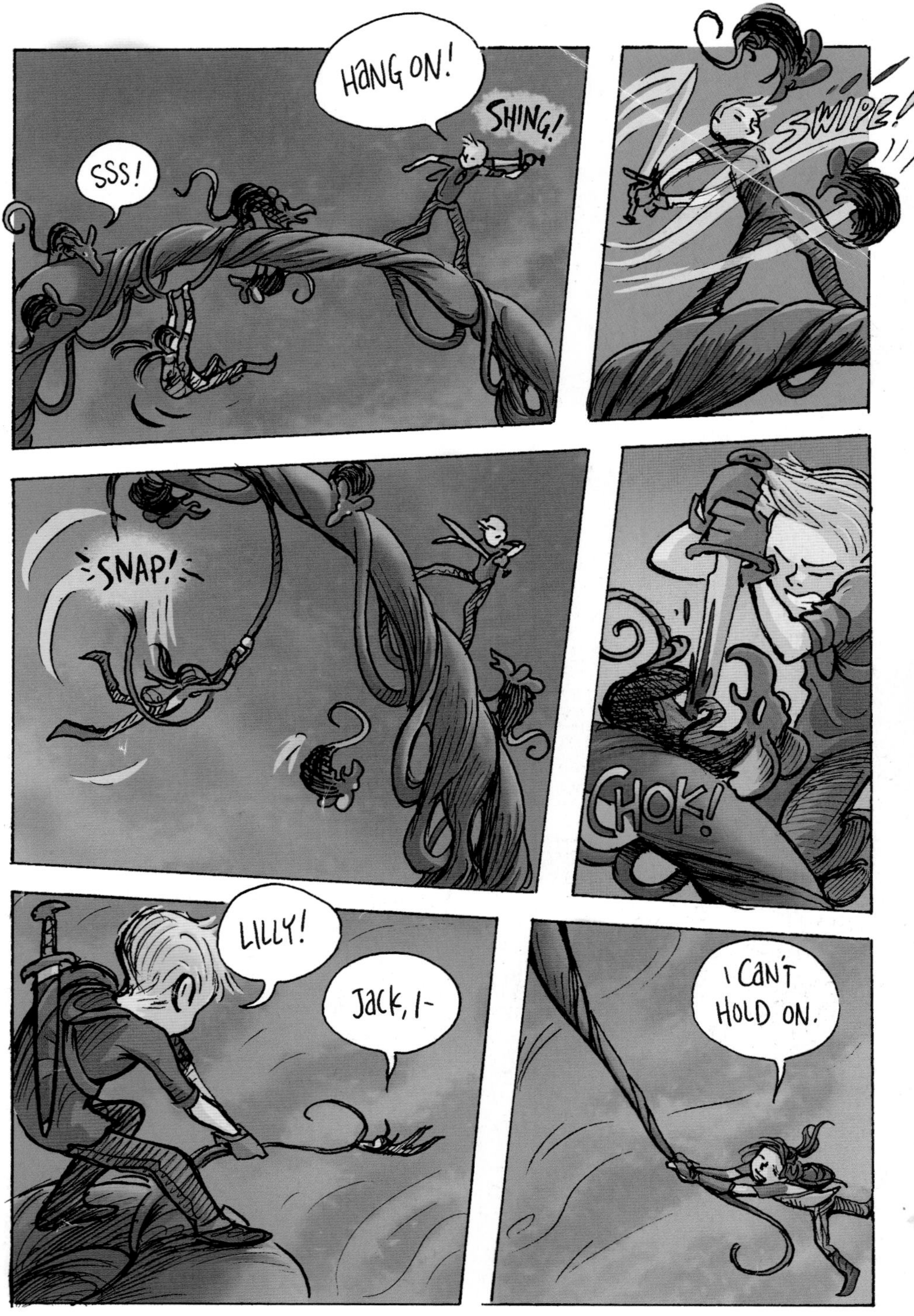
SSS!
HANG ON!
SHING!
SWIPE!
SNAP!
CHOK!
LILLY!
JACK, I-
I CAN'T HOLD ON.

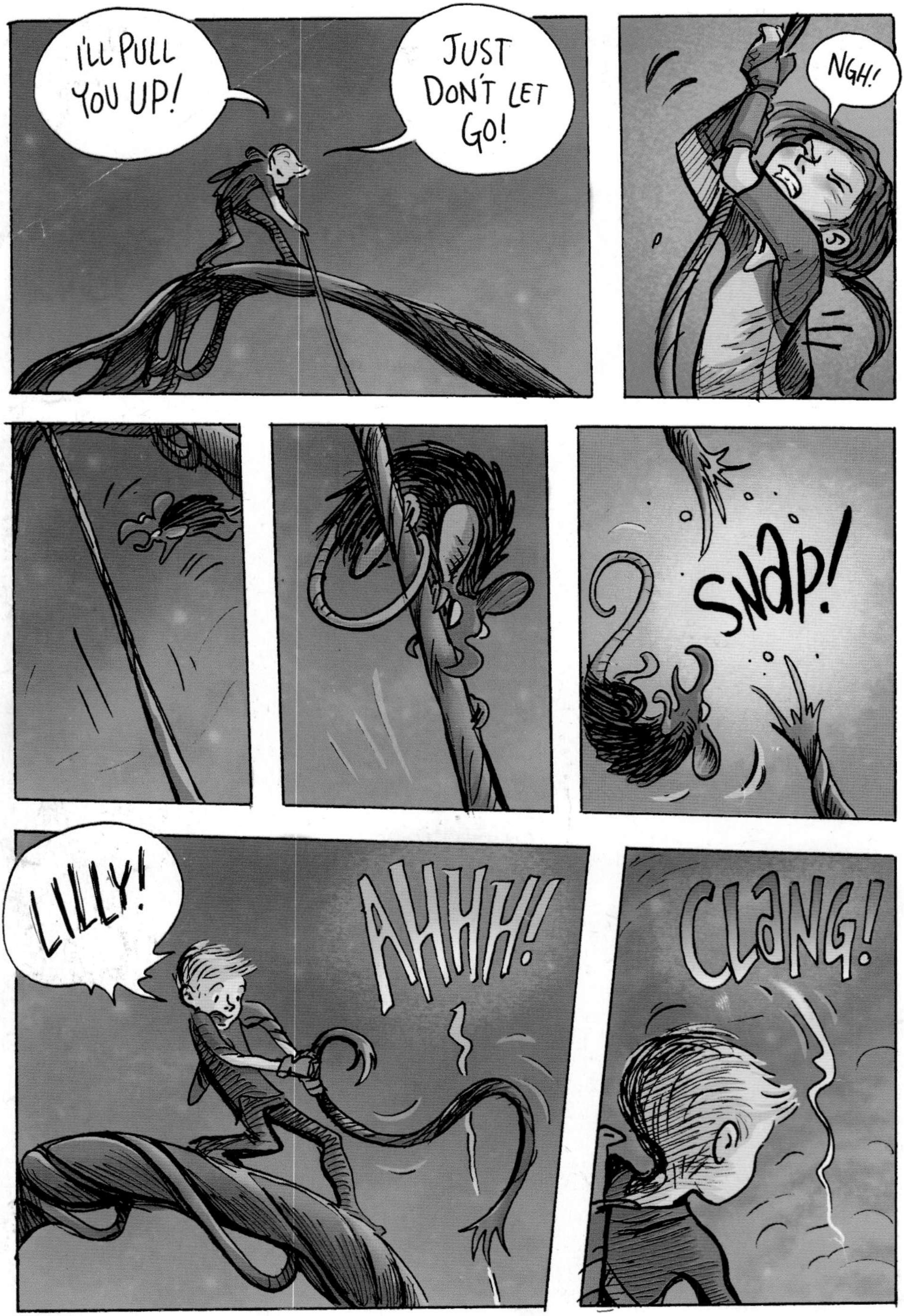
I'LL PULL YOU UP!
JUST DON'T LET GO!
NGH!
SNAP!
LILLY!
AHHH!
CLANG!

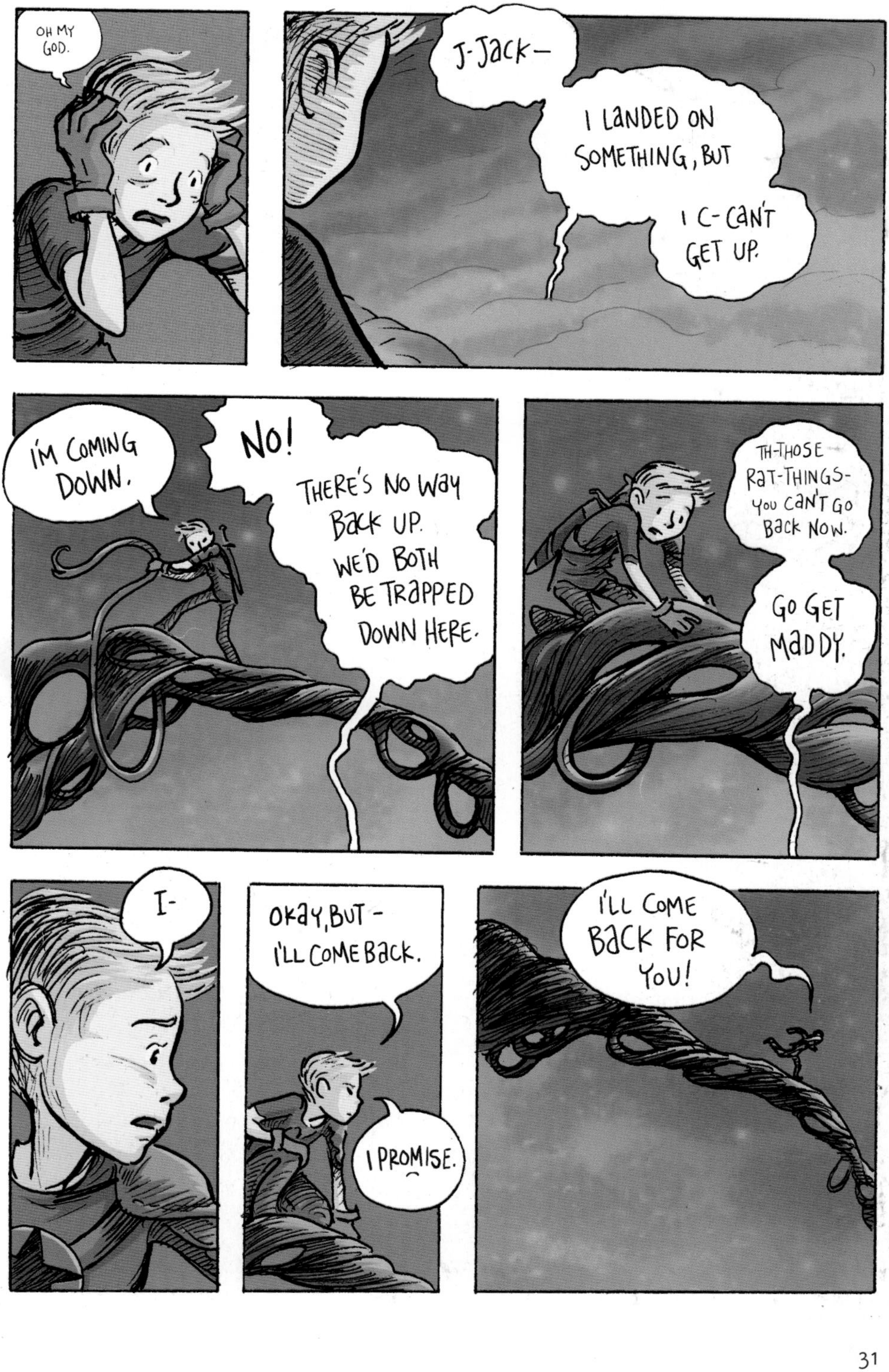
OH MY GOD.
J-JACK—
I LANDED ON SOMETHING, BUT
I C-CAN'T GET UP.
I'M COMING DOWN.
NO!
THERE'S NO WAY BACK UP. WE'D BOTH BE TRAPPED DOWN HERE.
TH-THOSE RAT-THINGS- YOU CAN'T GO BACK NOW.
GO GET MADDY.
I-
OKAY, BUT - I'LL COME BACK.
I PROMISE.
I'LL COME BACK FOR YOU!

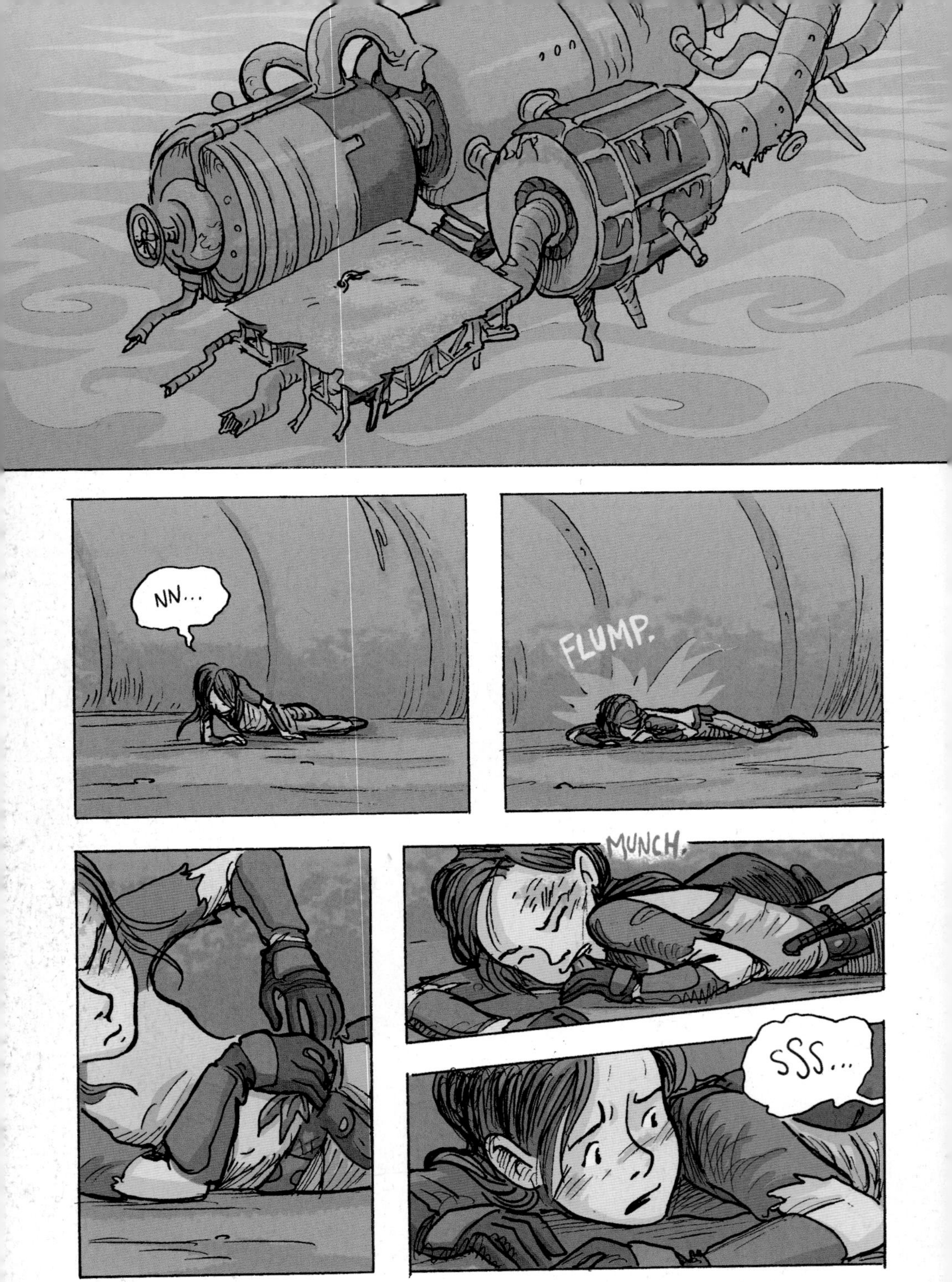
NN...
FLUMP.
MUNCH.
SSS...

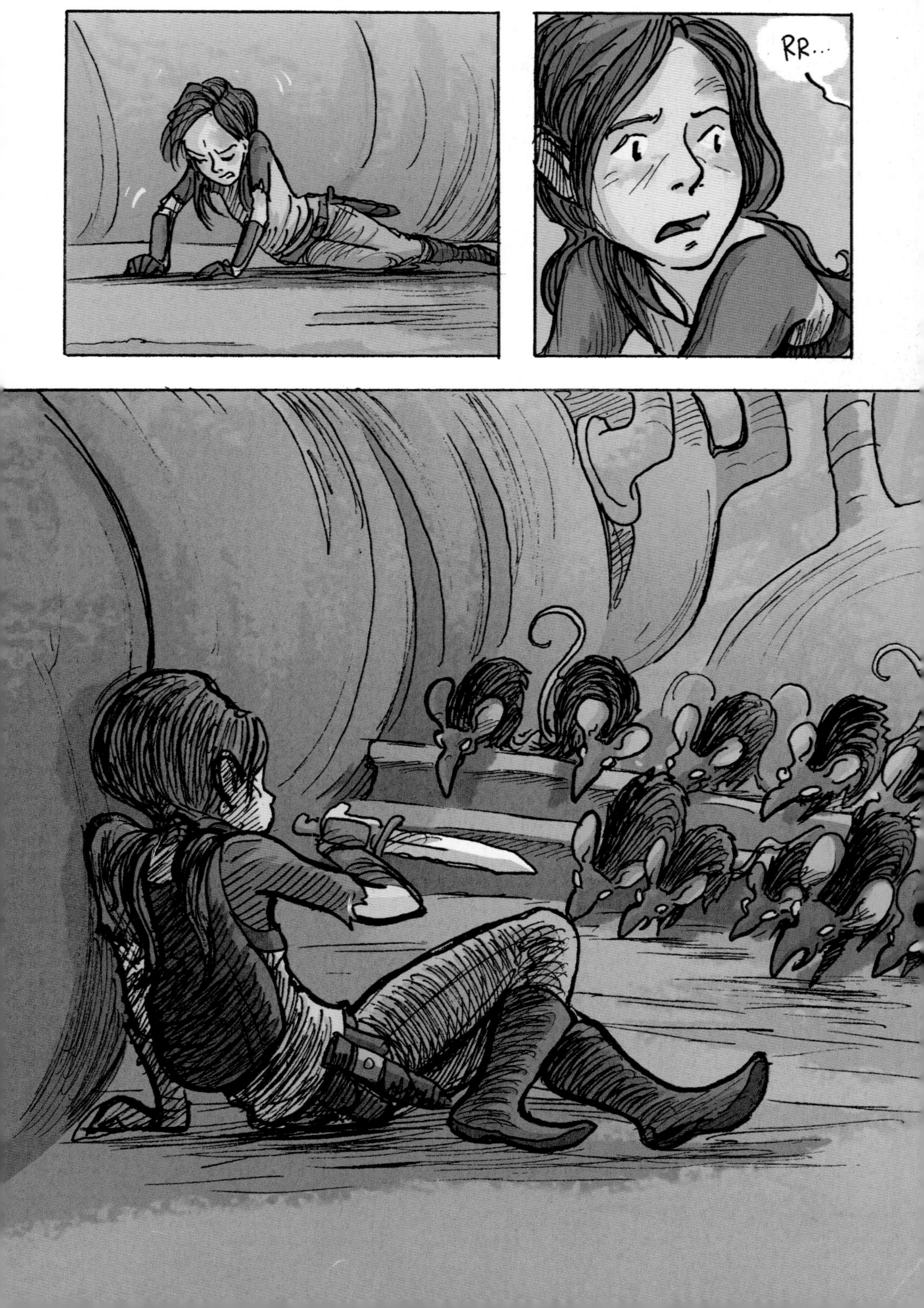
RR...

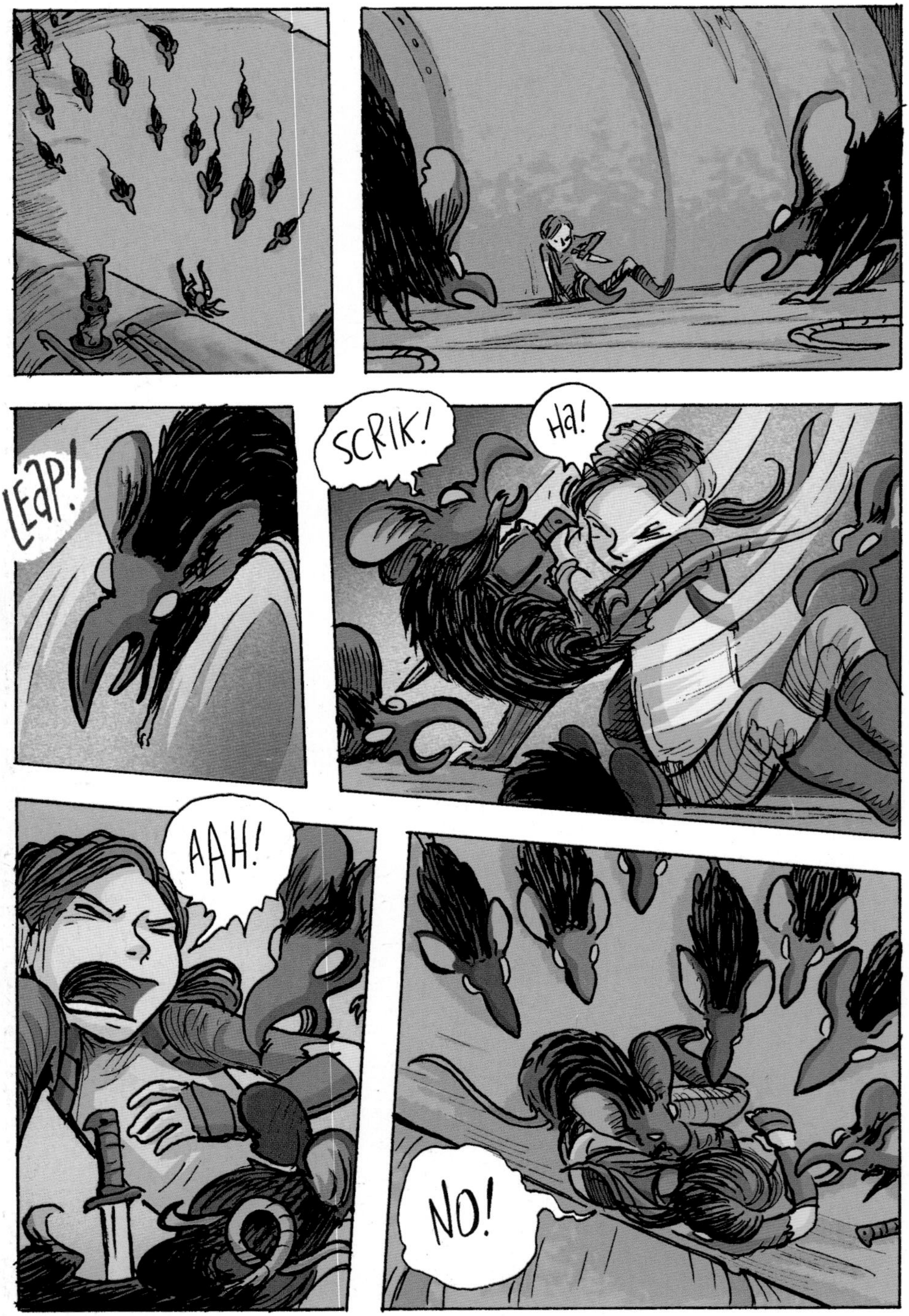
LEAP!
SCRIK!
Ha!
AAH!
NO!

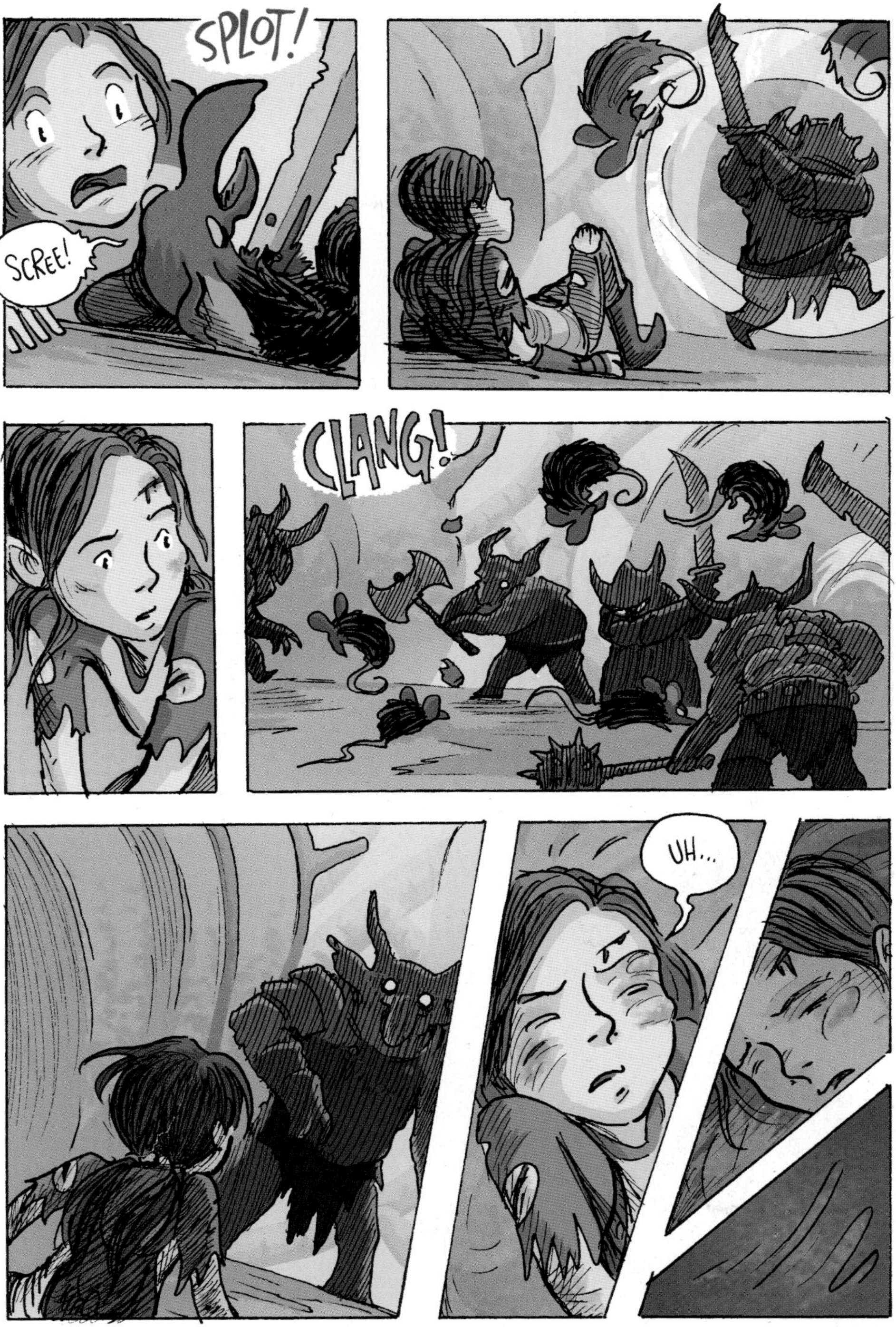
SPLOT!
SCREE!
CLANG!
UH...

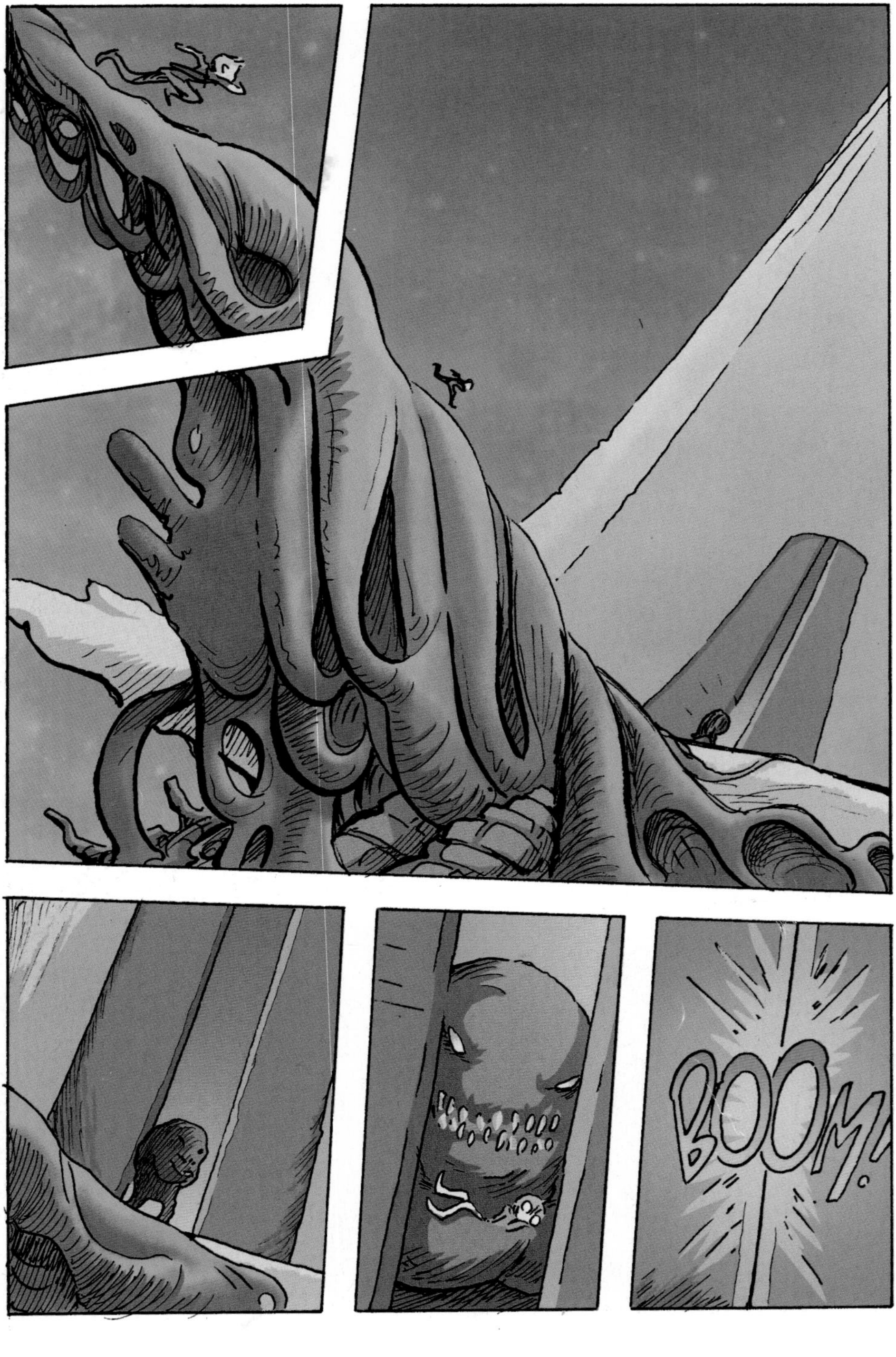
BOOM!

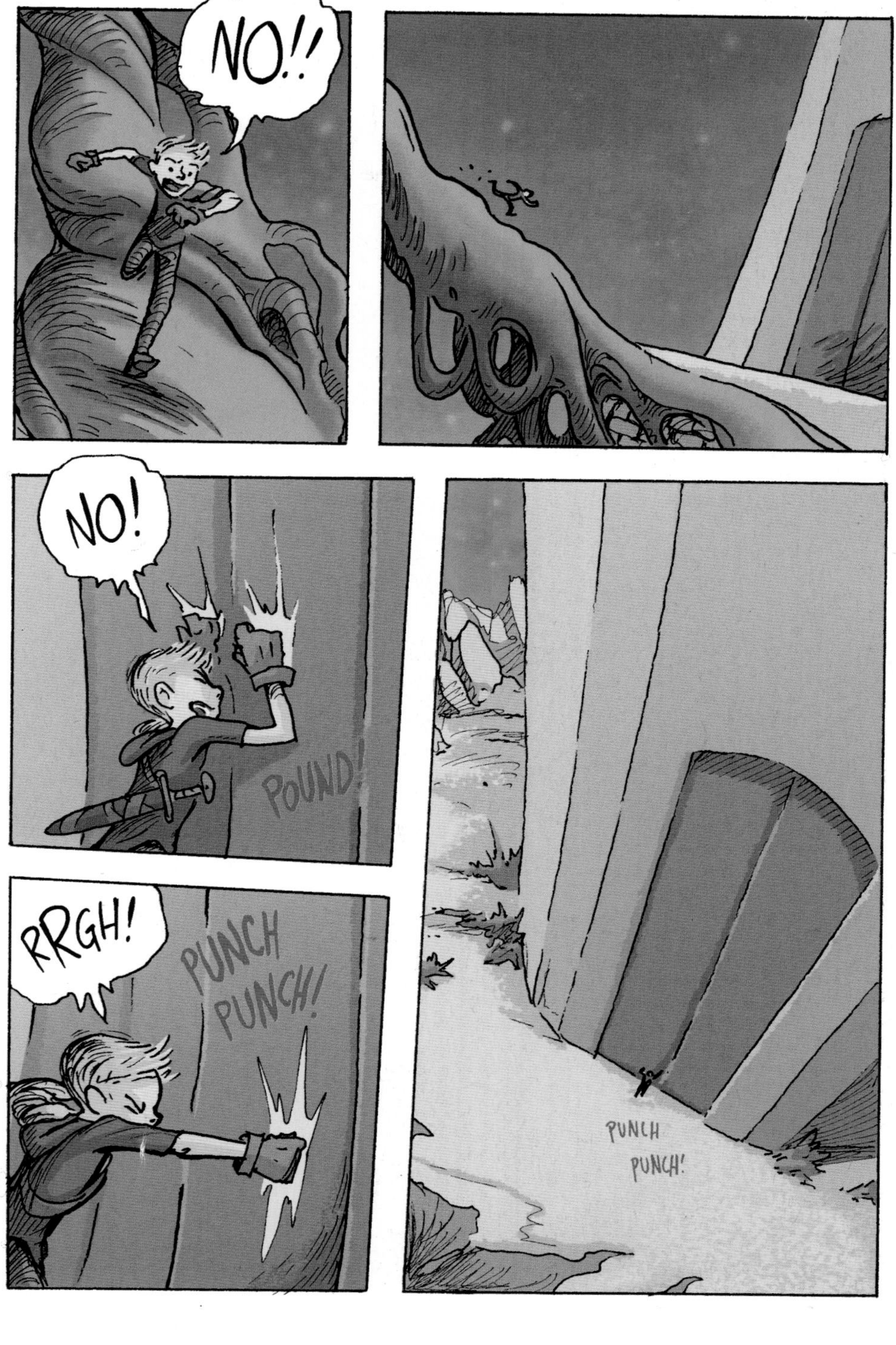
NO!!
NO!
POUND!
RRGH!
PUNCH PUNCH!
PUNCH PUNCH!

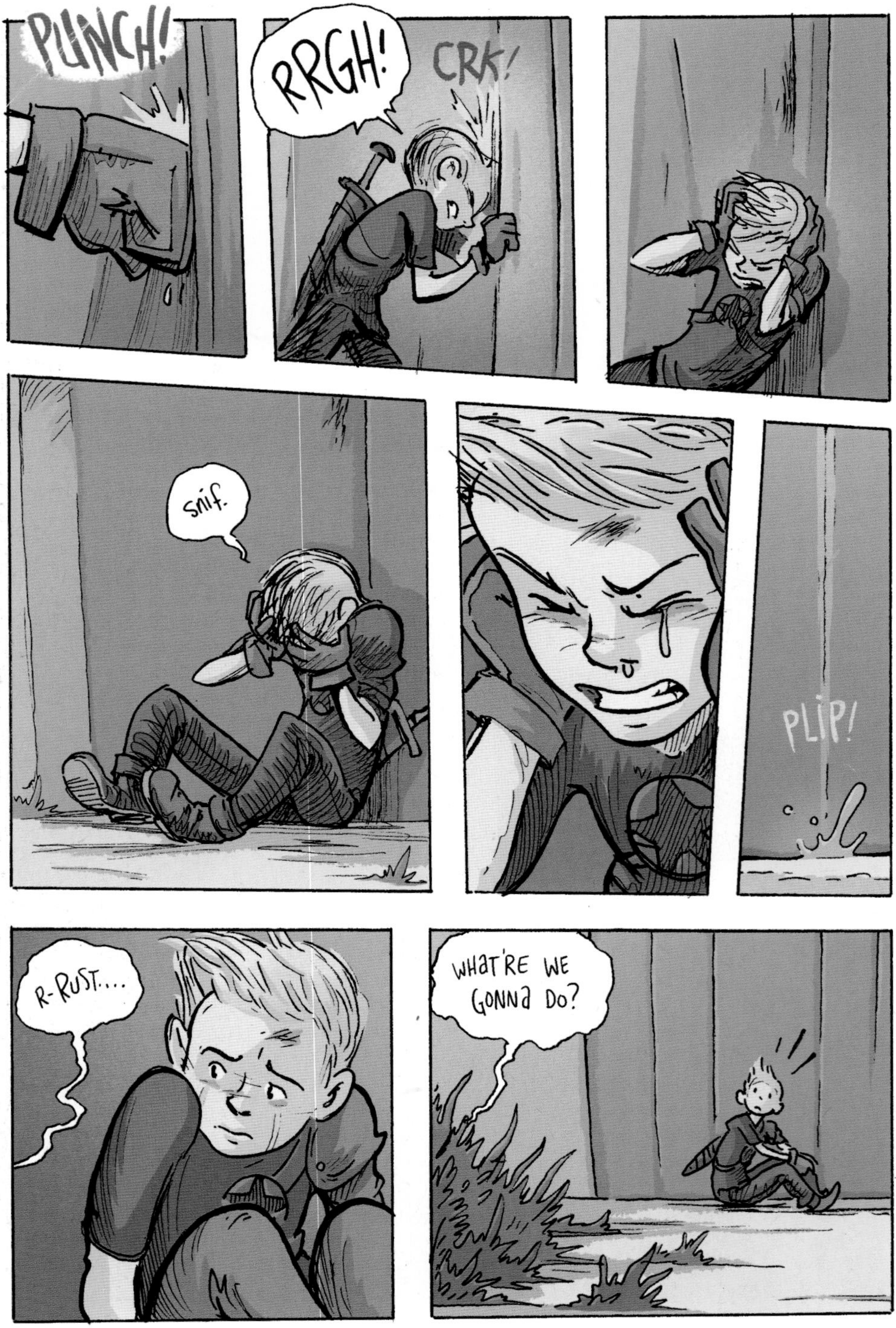
PUNCH!
RRGH!
CRK!
snif.
PLIP!
R-RUST....
WHAT'RE WE GONNA DO?

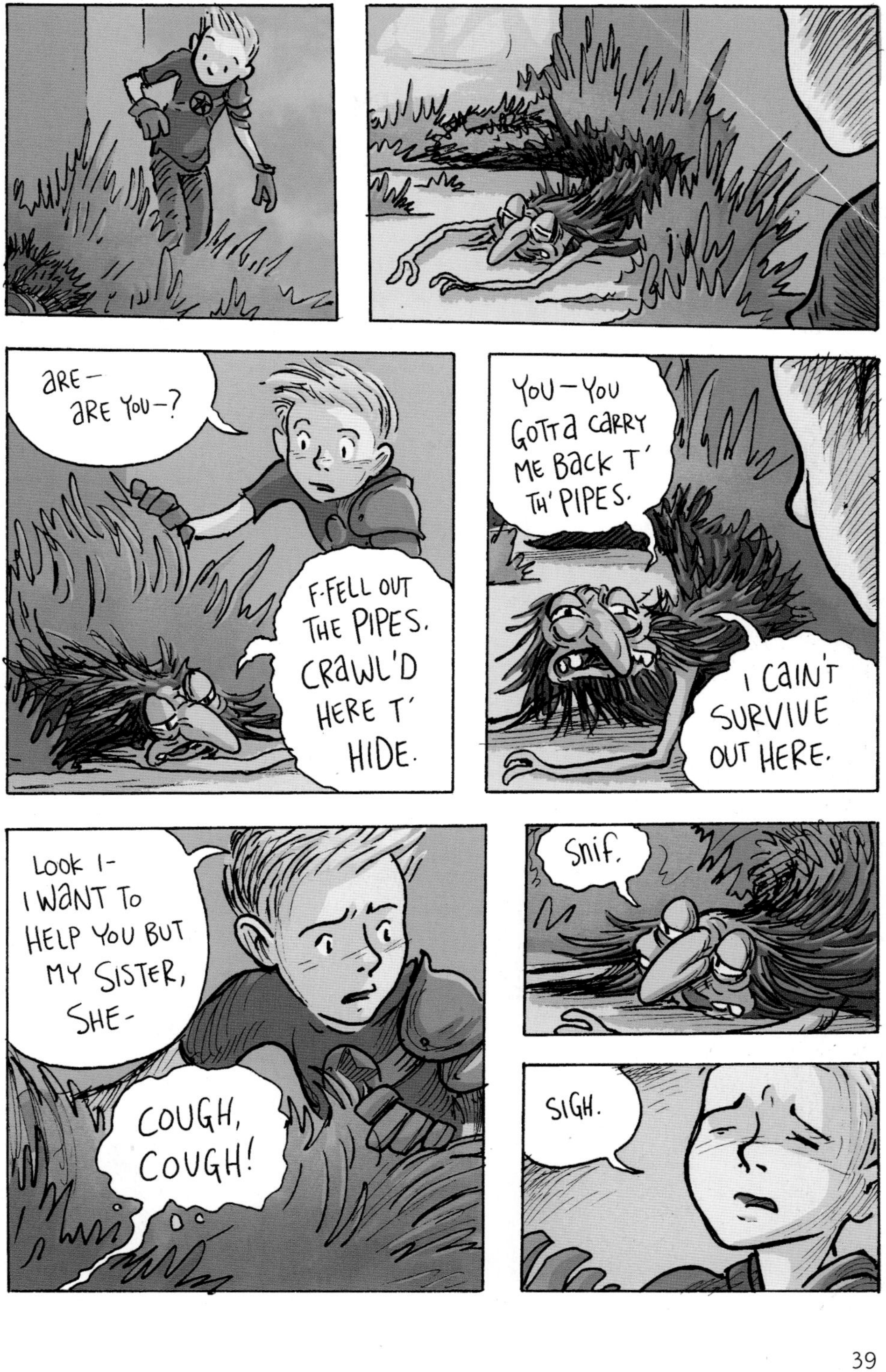
are— are you—?
F-FELL OUT THE PIPES. CRAWL'D HERE T' HIDE.
YOU—YOU GOTTA CARRY ME BACK T' TH' PIPES.
I CAIN'T SURVIVE OUT HERE.
LOOK I- I WANT TO HELP YOU BUT MY SISTER, SHE-
COUGH, COUGH!
Snif.
SIGH.

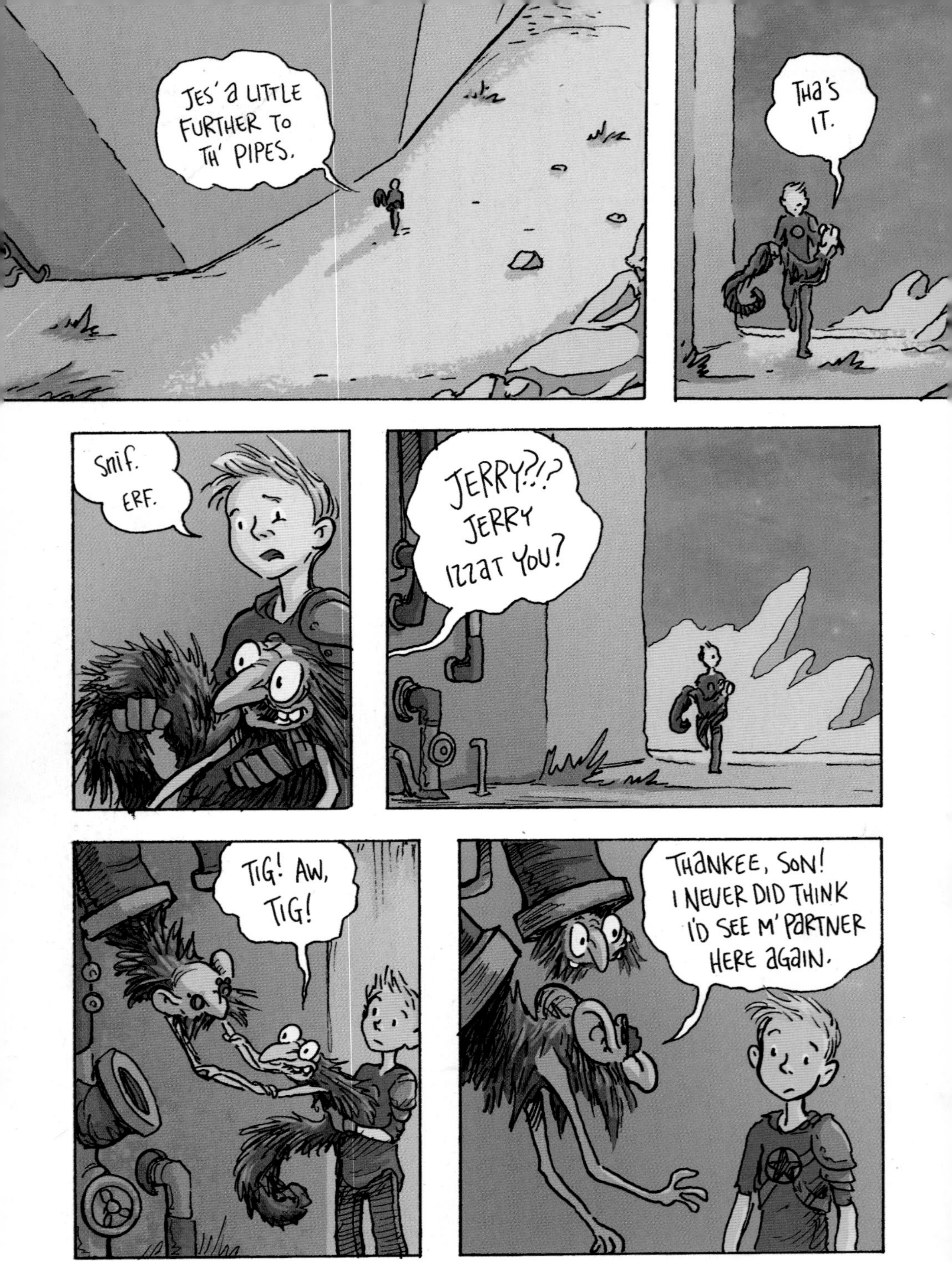
JES' A LITTLE FURTHER TO TH' PIPES.
THA'S IT.
SNIF. ERF.
JERRY?!? JERRY IZZAT YOU?
TIG! AW, TIG!
THANKEE, SON! I NEVER DID THINK I'D SEE M' PARTNER HERE AGAIN.

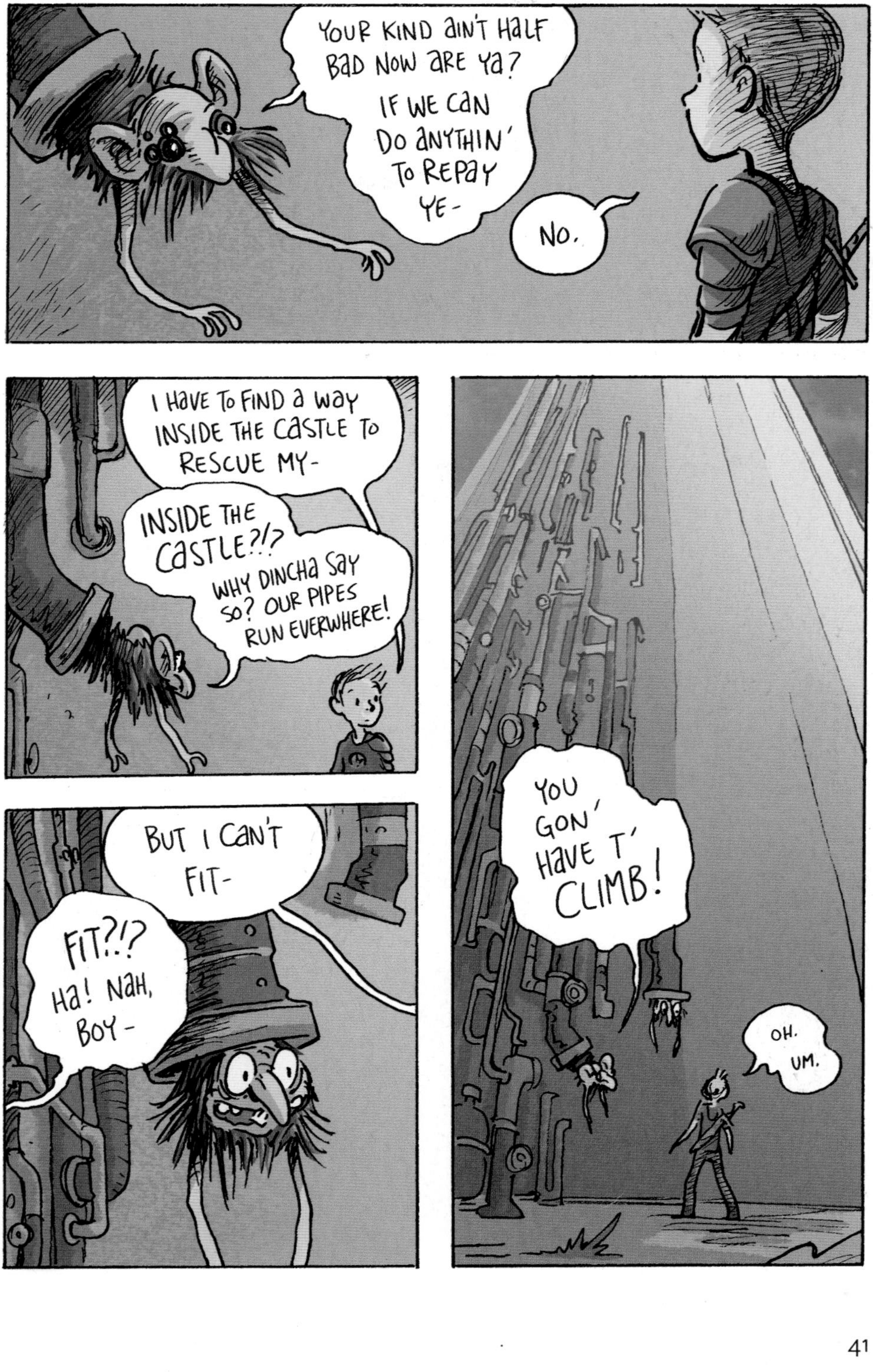
YOUR KIND AIN'T HALF BAD NOW ARE YA?
IF WE CAN DO ANYTHIN' TO REPAY YE-
NO.
I HAVE TO FIND A WAY INSIDE THE CASTLE TO RESCUE MY-
INSIDE THE CASTLE?!?
WHY DINCHA SAY SO? OUR PIPES RUN EVERWHERE!
BUT I CAN'T FIT-
FIT?!?
HA! NAH, BOY-
YOU GON' HAVE T' CLIMB!
OH.
UM.

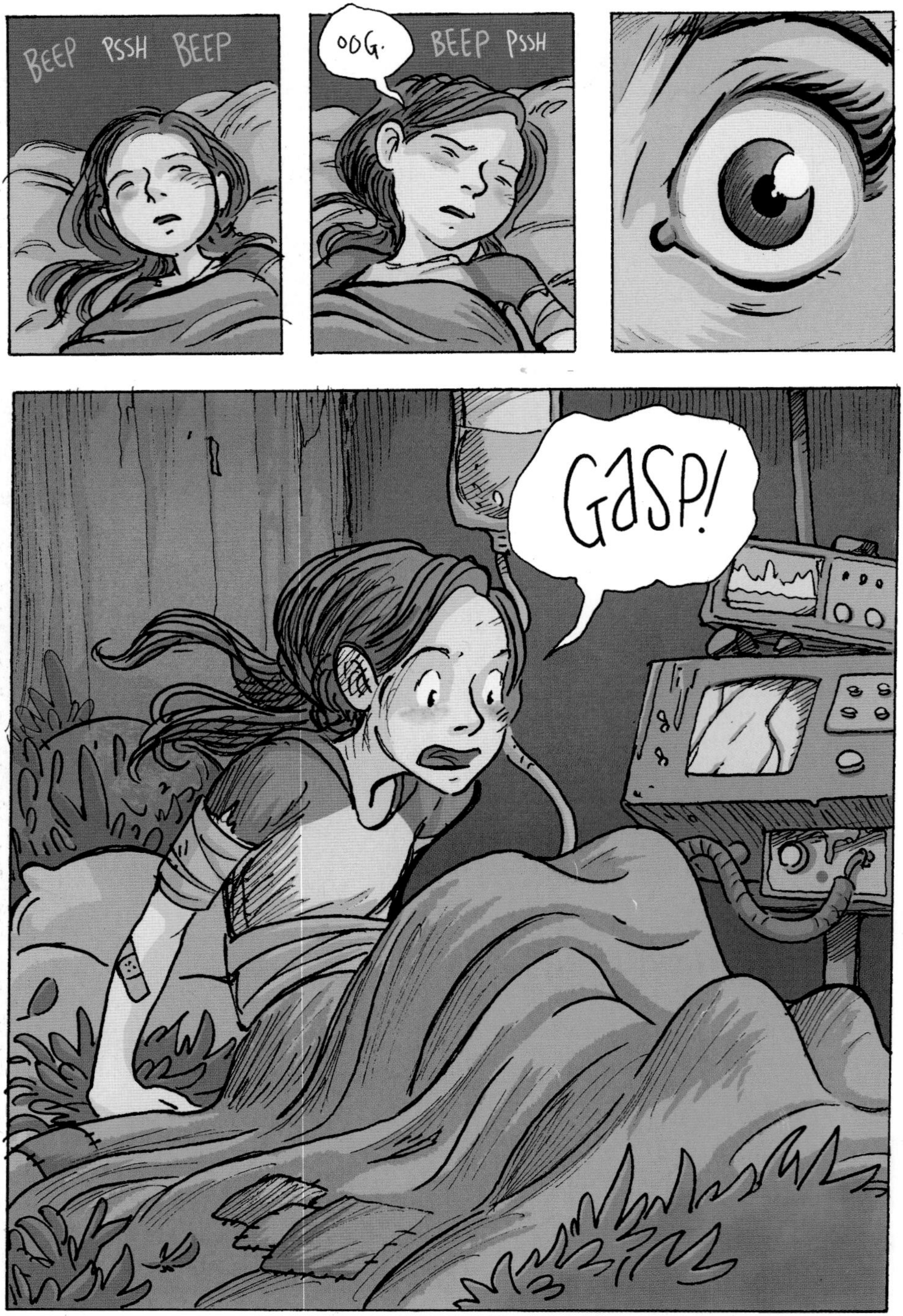
BEEP PSSH BEEP
OOG.
BEEP PSSH
GASP!

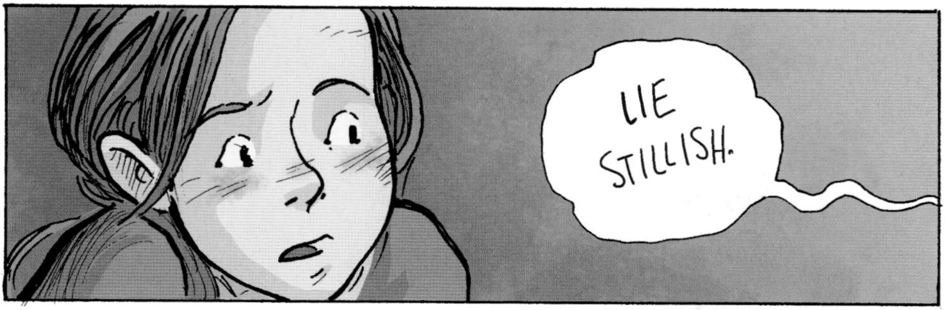
LIE STILLISH.

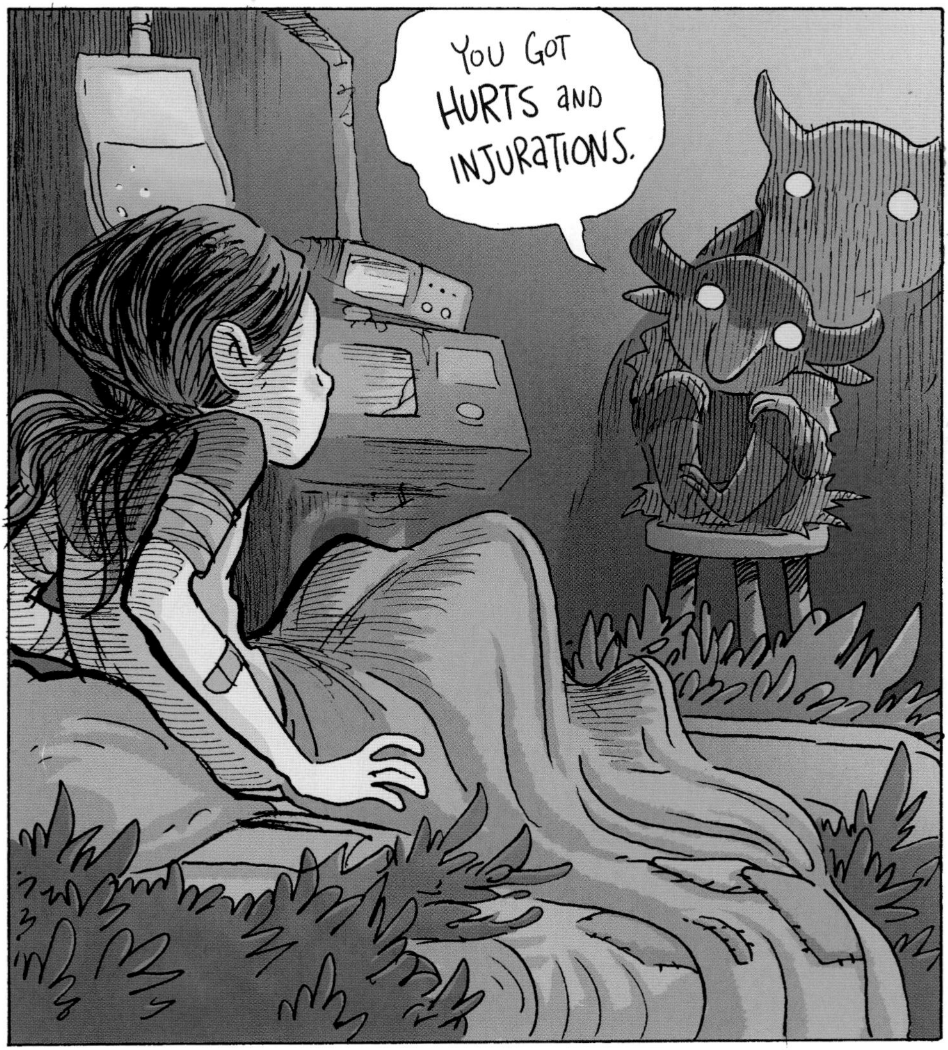
YOU GOT HURTS AND INJURATIONS.

YOU HEALIT QUICK FOR a BEAN.

EXTER QUICK.

BEEP

BUT NEED RESTIT.

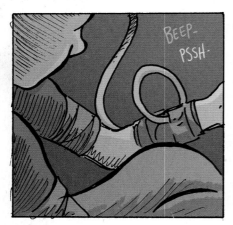

BEEP-PSSH-

BEEP-PSSH-BEEP-

WHAT IS THIS?

WHAT are YOU PUTTING IN ME?

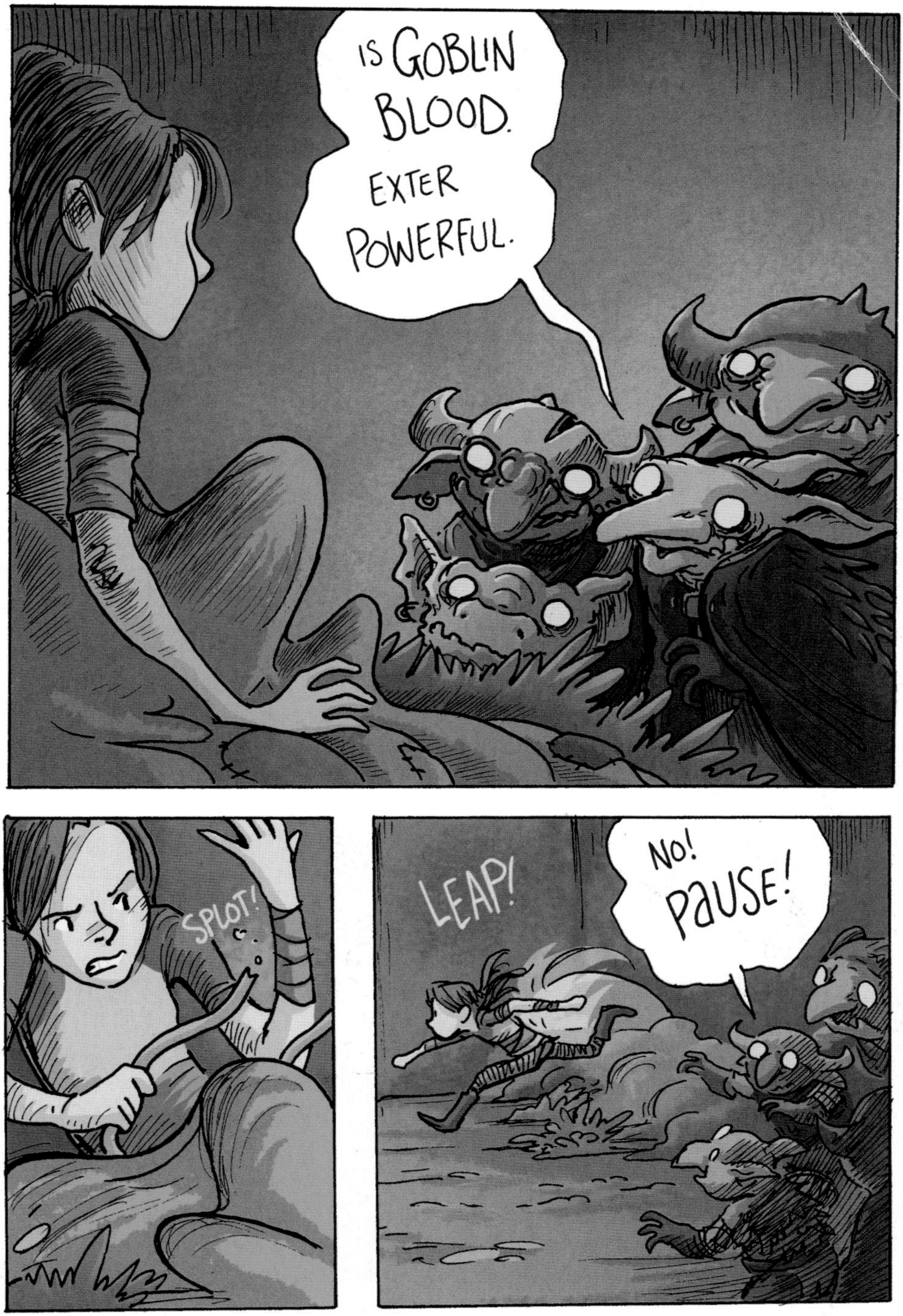
IS GOBLIN BLOOD. EXTER POWERFUL.
SPLOT!
LEAP!
NO! PAUSE!

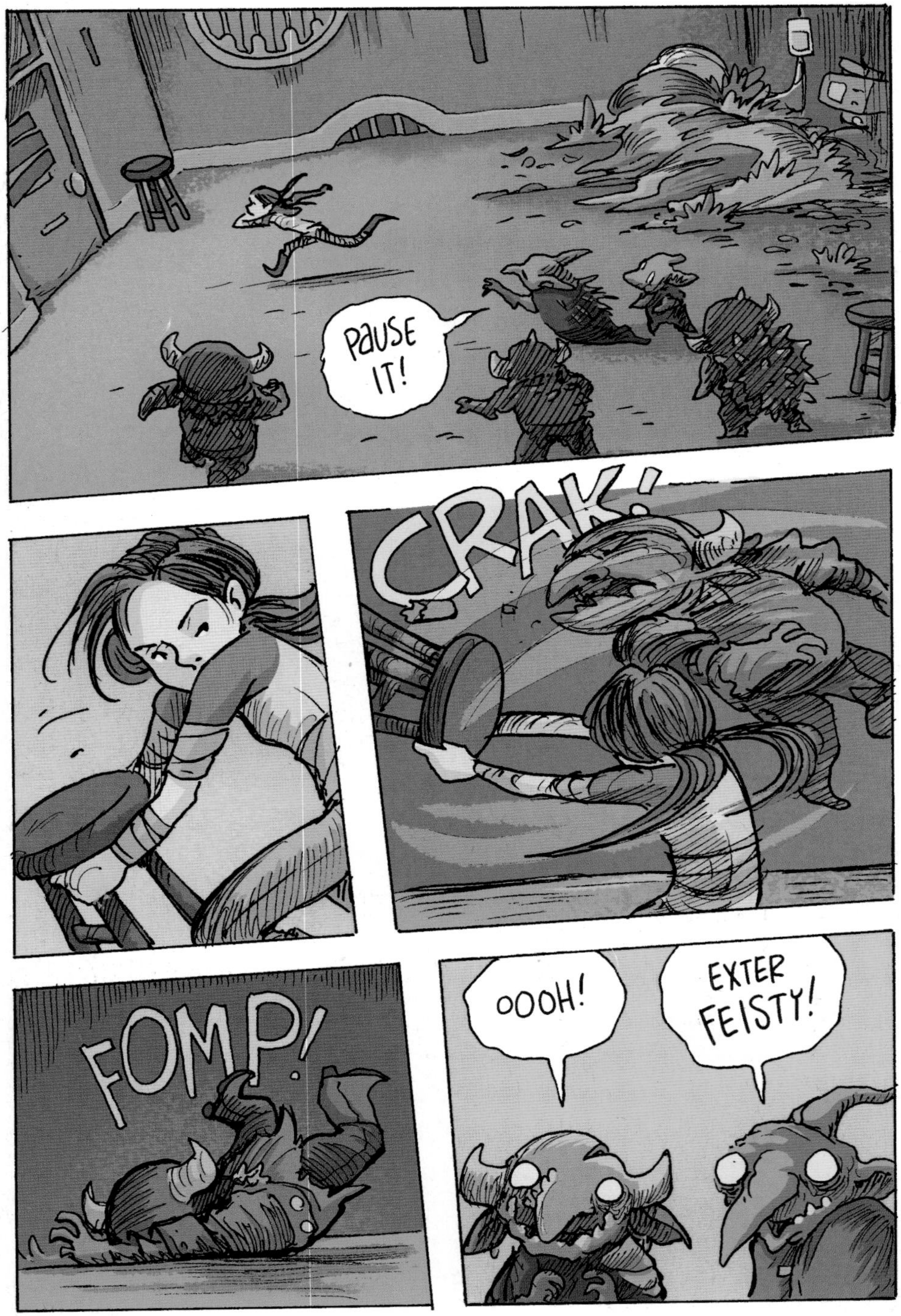
PAUSE IT!
CRAK!
FOMP!
OOOH!
EXTER FEISTY!

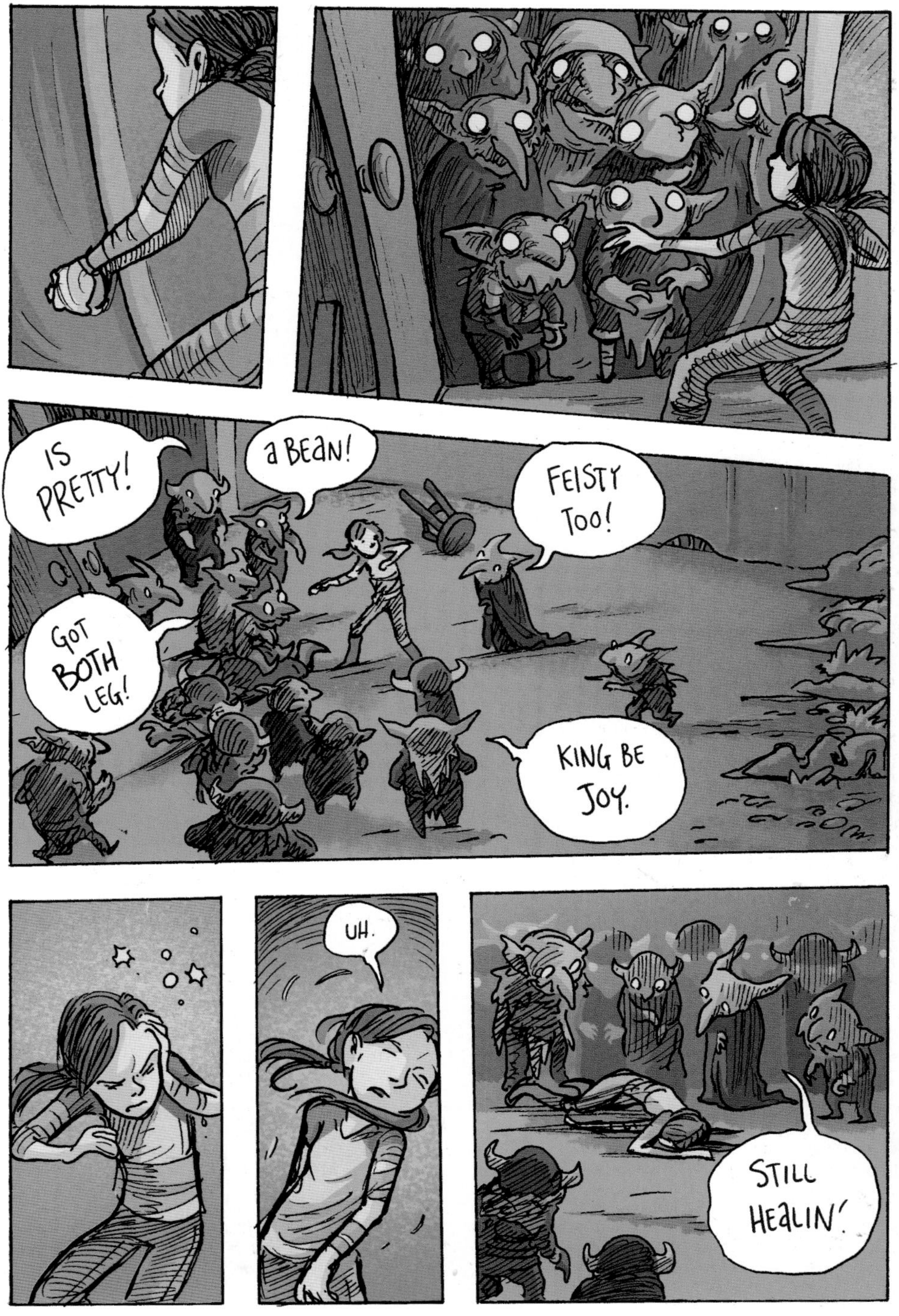
IS PRETTY!
a BEAN!
FEISTY TOO!
GOT BOTH LEG!
KING BE JOY.
UH.
STILL HEaLIN'.

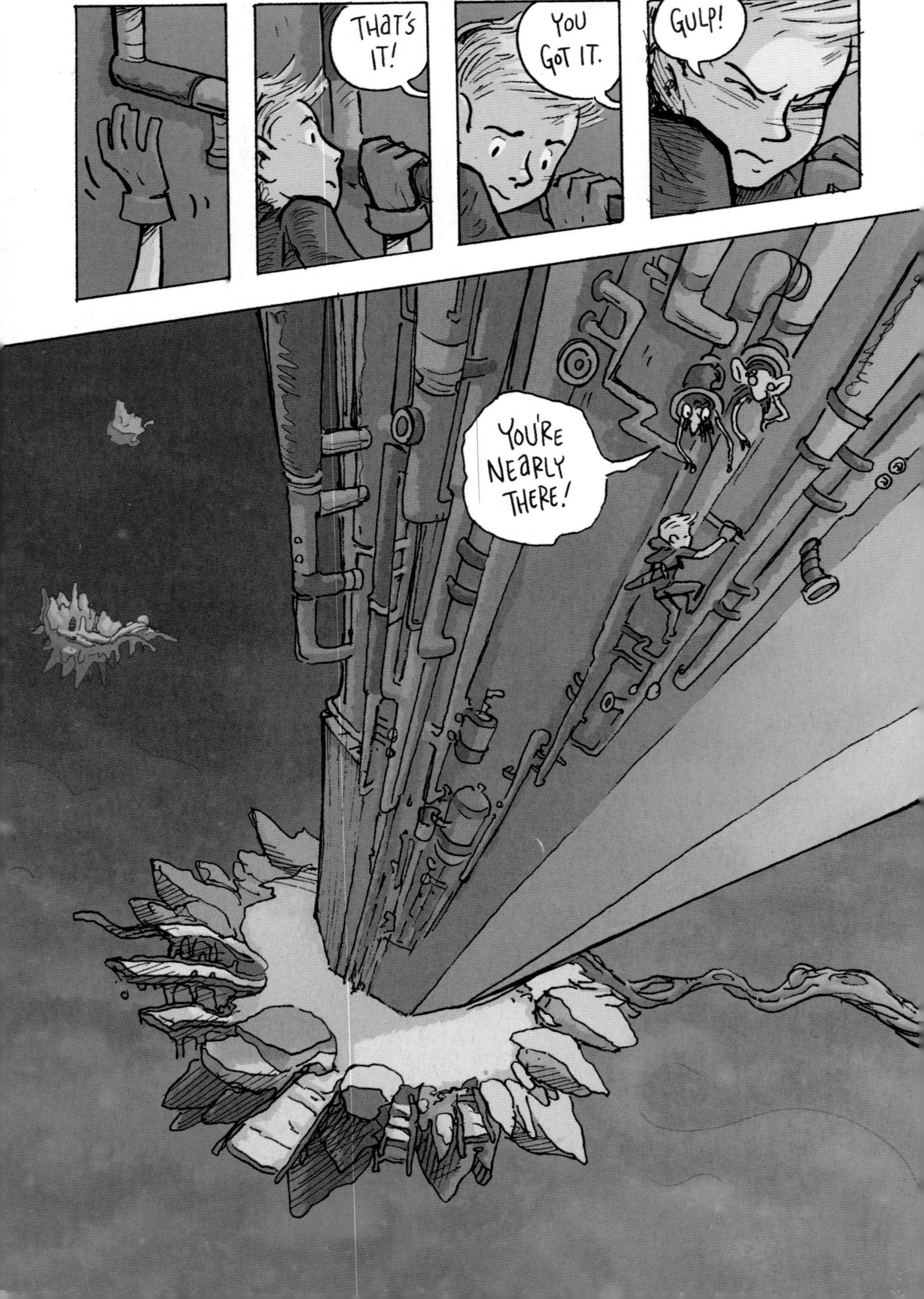
THAT'S IT!
YOU GOT IT.
GULP!
YOU'RE NEARLY THERE!

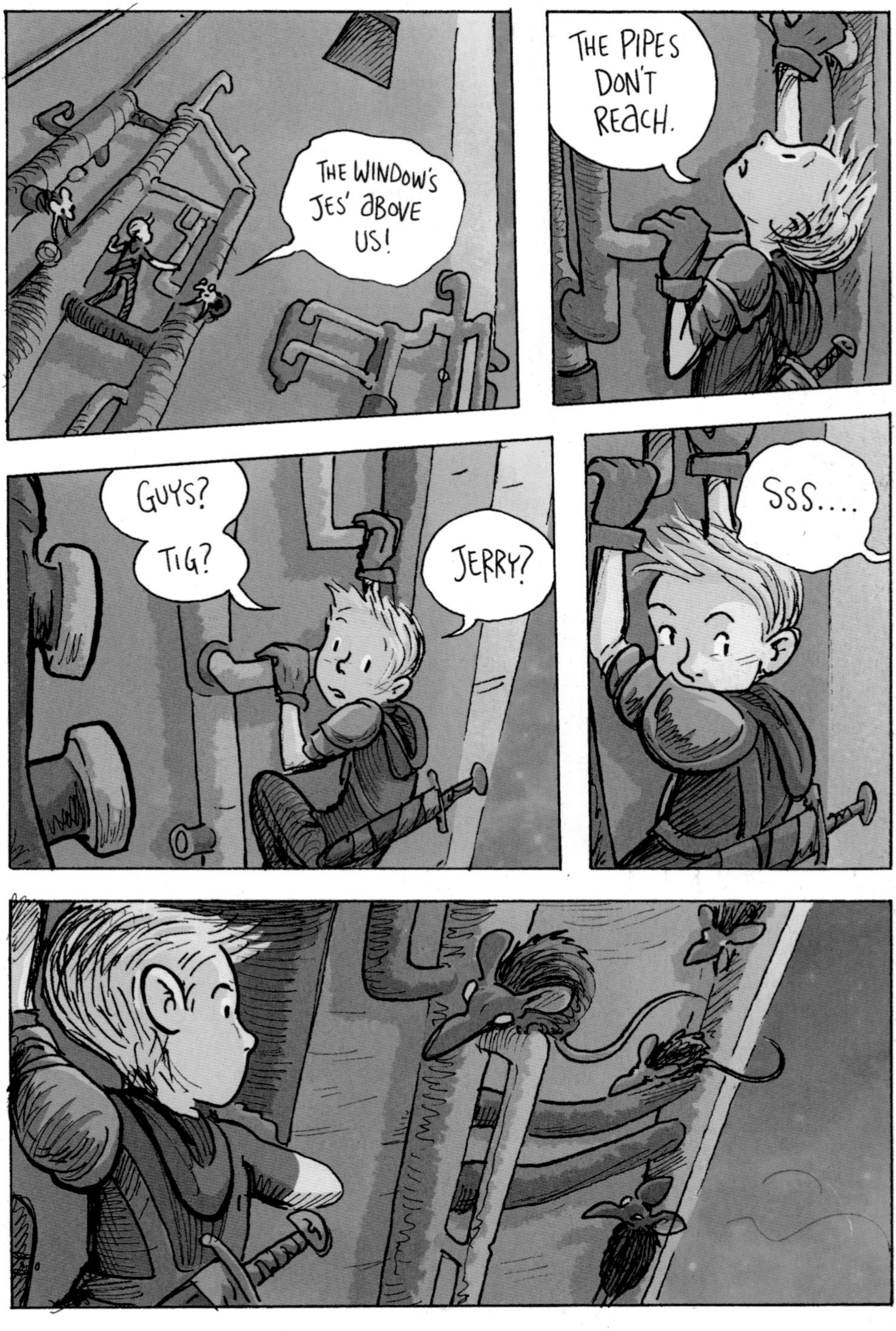
THE WINDOW'S JES' ABOVE US!
THE PIPES DON'T REACH.
GUYS?
TIG?
JERRY?
SSS....

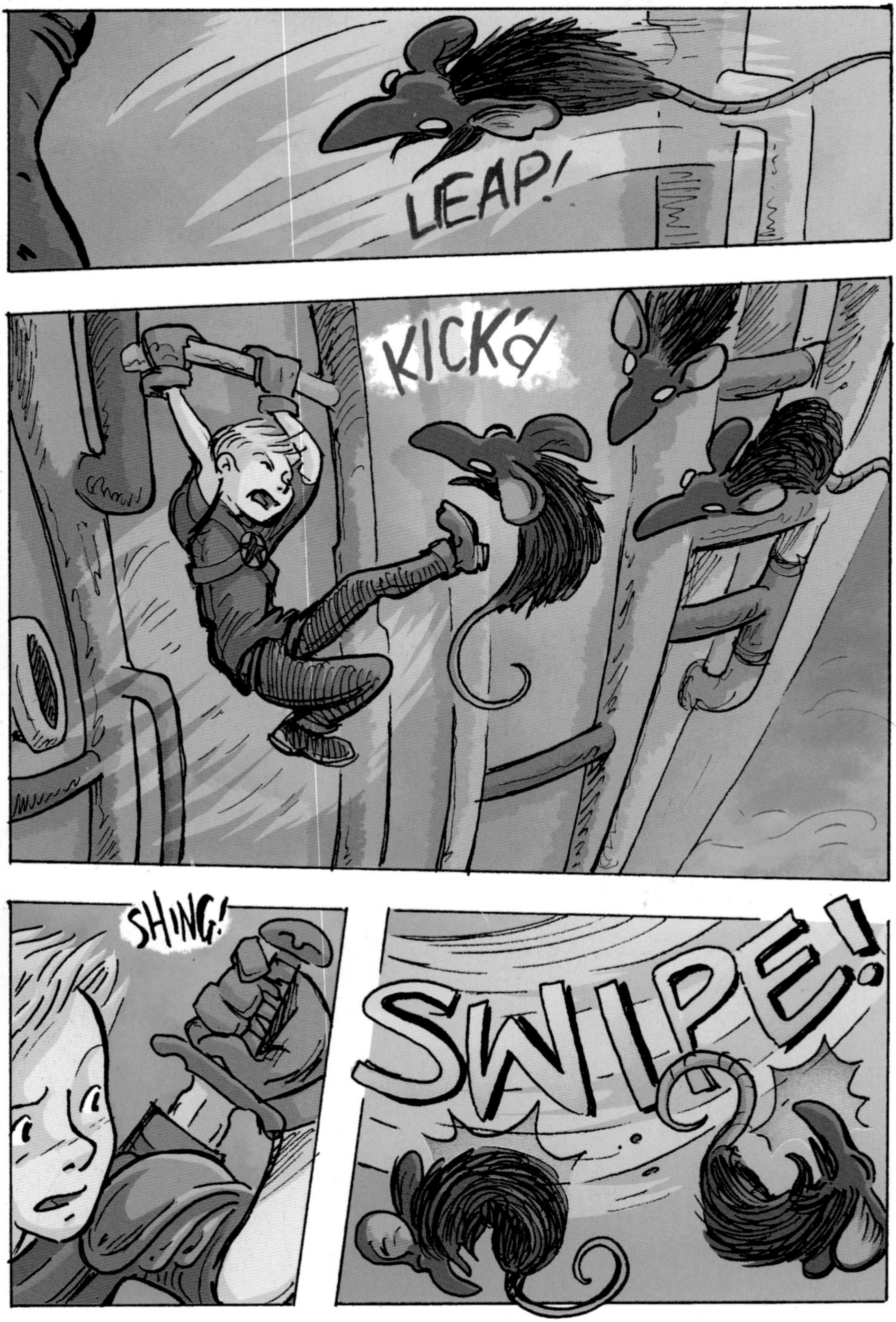
LEAP!
KICK'd
SHING!
SWIPE!

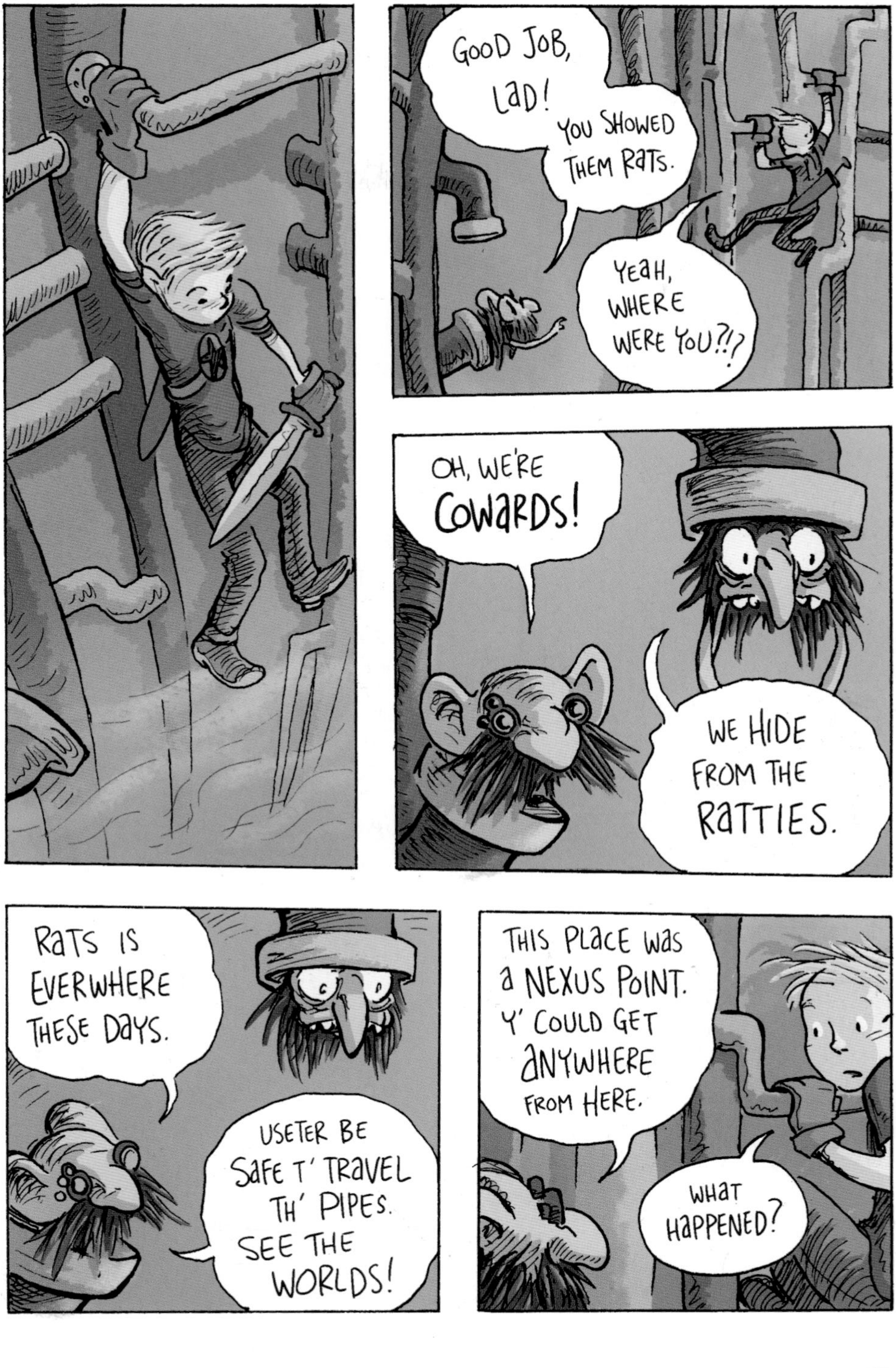
GOOD JOB, LAD!
YOU SHOWED THEM RATS.
YEAH, WHERE WERE YOU?!?
OH, WE'RE COWARDS!
WE HIDE FROM THE RATTIES.
RATS IS EVERWHERE THESE DAYS.
USETER BE SAFE T' TRAVEL TH' PIPES. SEE THE WORLDS!
THIS PLACE WAS A NEXUS POINT. Y' COULD GET ANYWHERE FROM HERE.
WHAT HAPPENED?

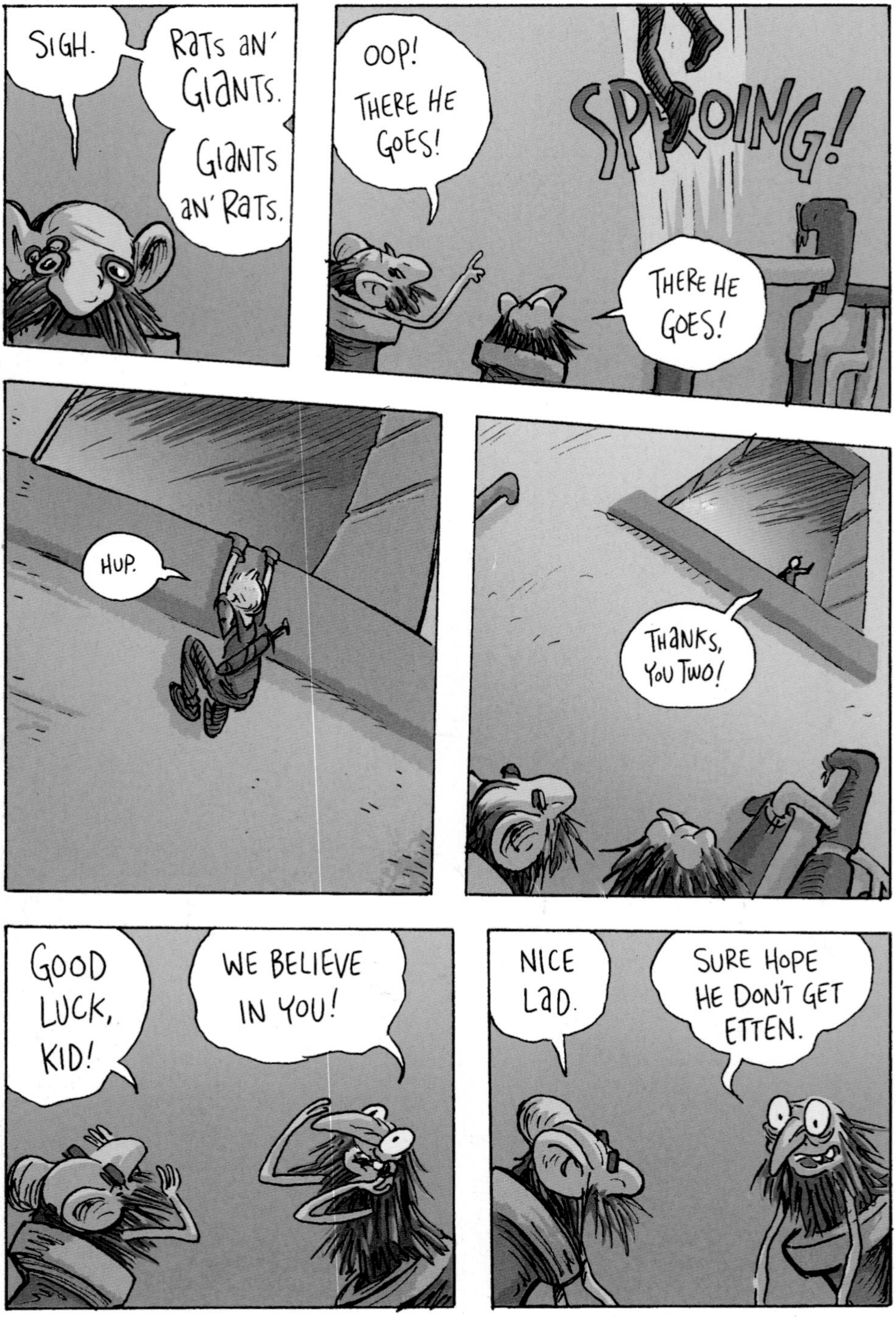
SIGH.
RATS AN' GIANTS.
GIANTS AN' RATS.
OOP! THERE HE GOES!
SPROING!
THERE HE GOES!
HUP.
THANKS, YOU TWO!
GOOD LUCK, KID!
WE BELIEVE IN YOU!
NICE LAD.
SURE HOPE HE DON'T GET ETTEN.

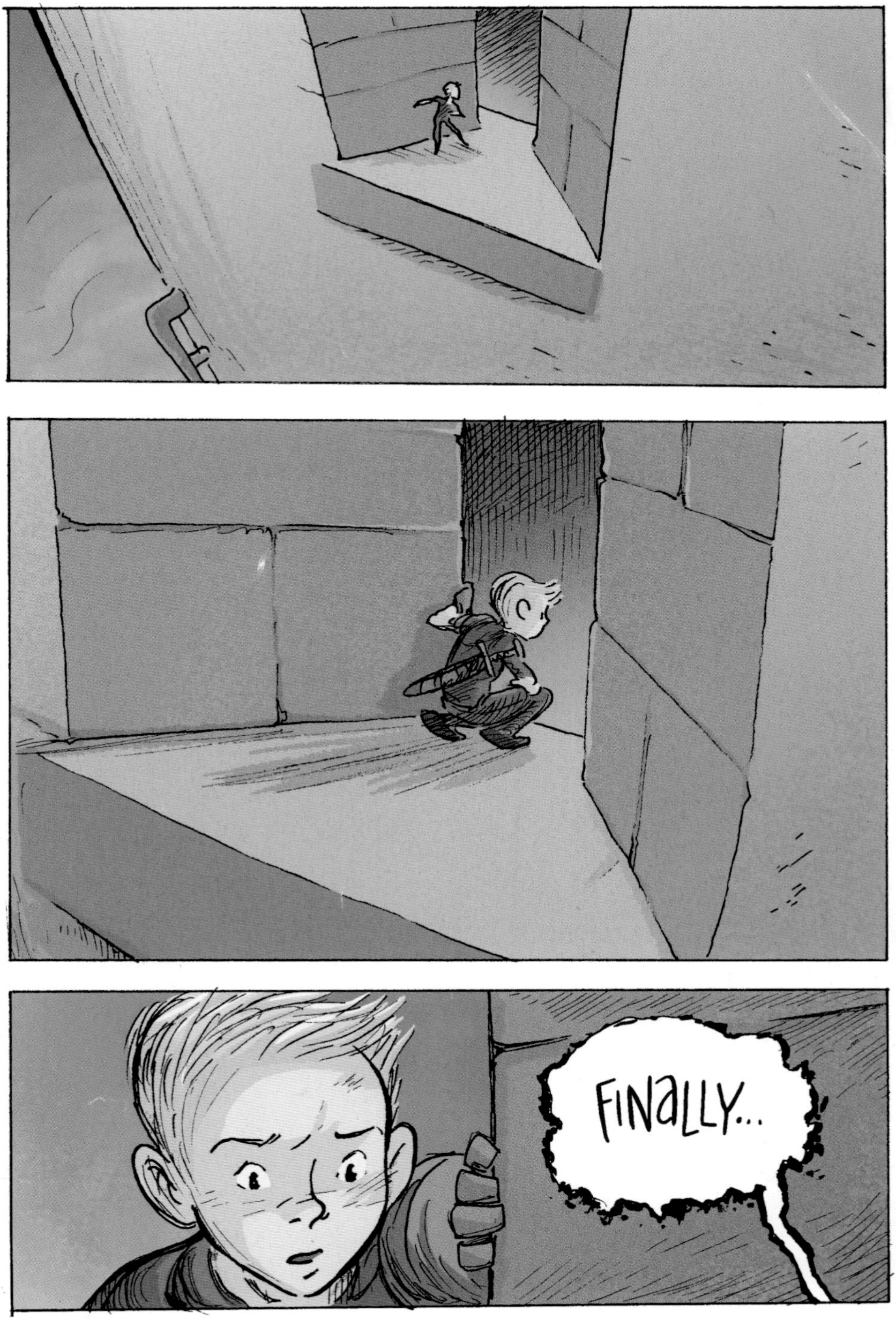
FINALLY...

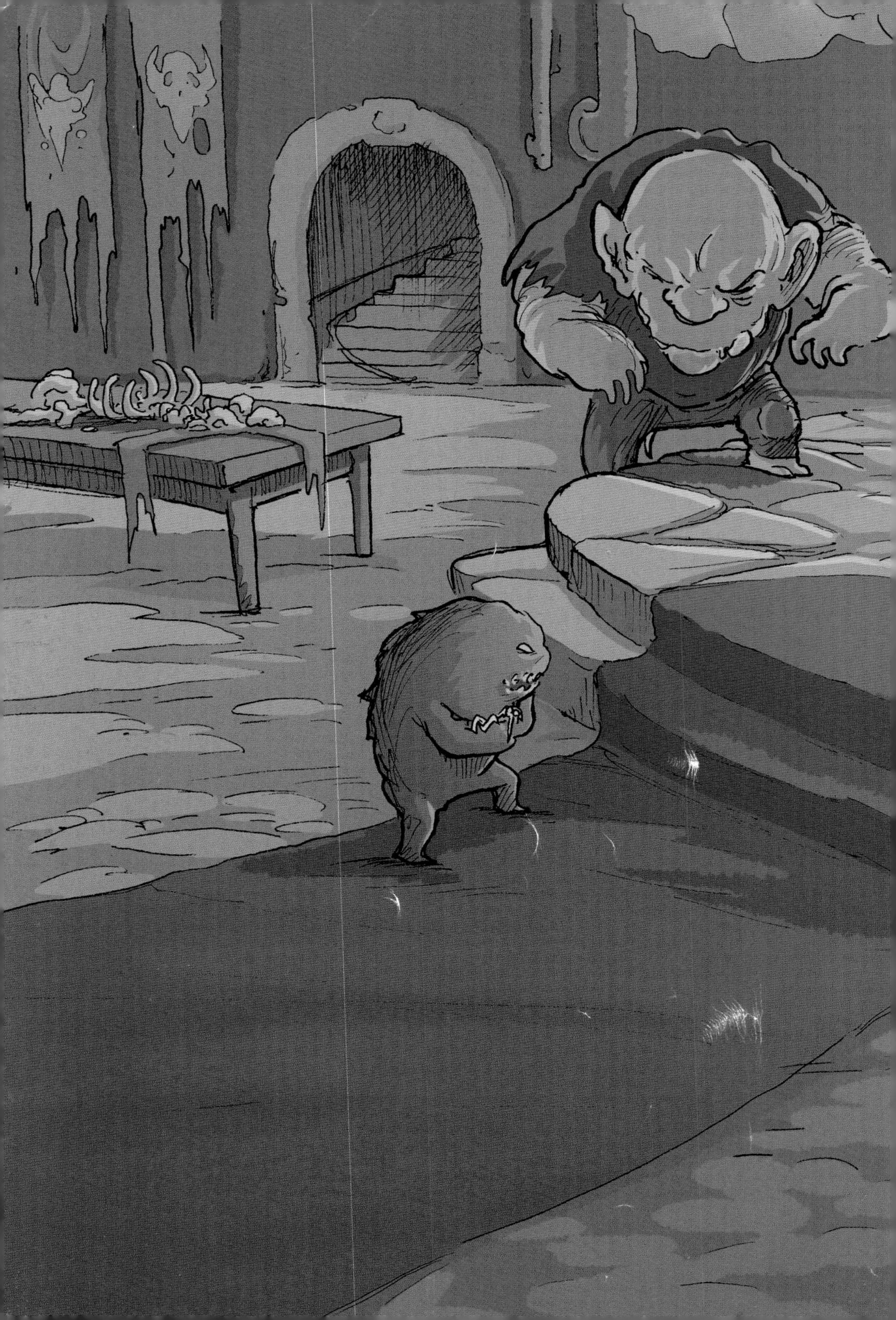

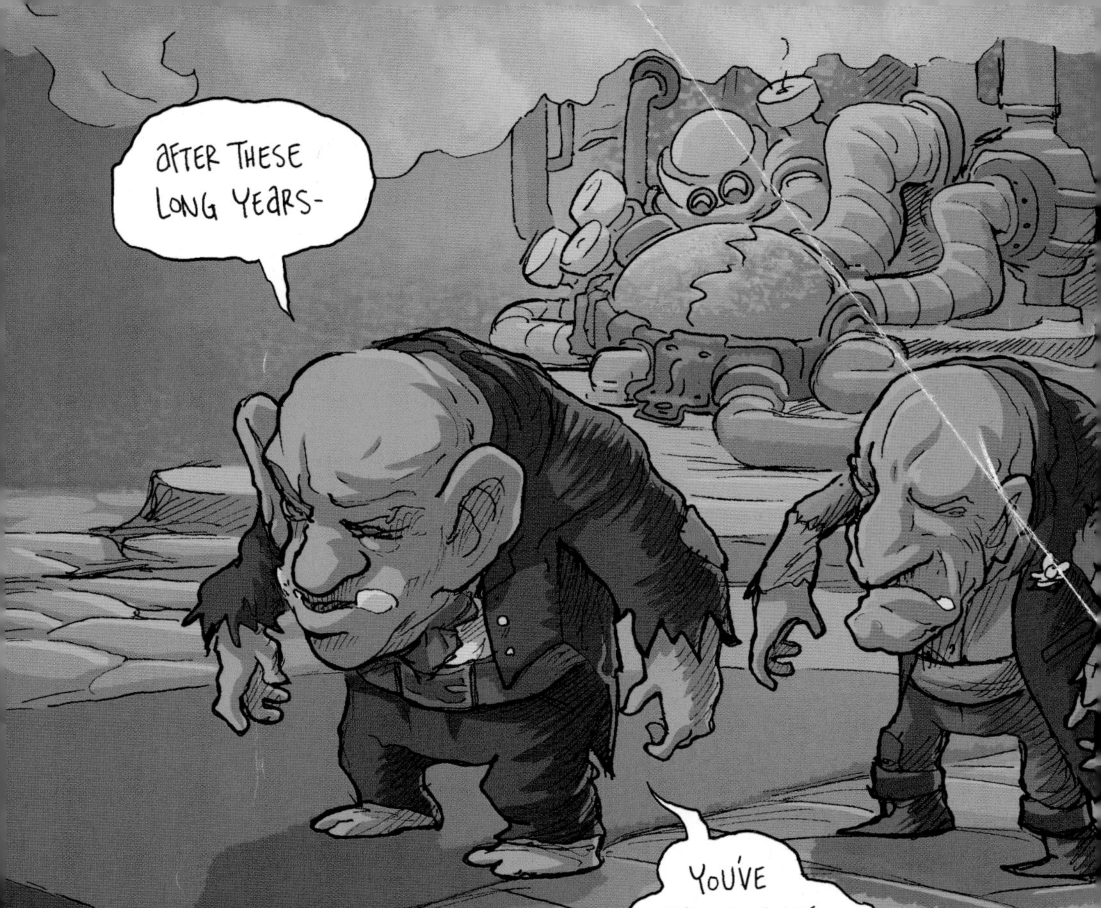
AFTER THESE LONG YEARS-
YOU'VE BROUGHT US SOMETHING OF VALUE.

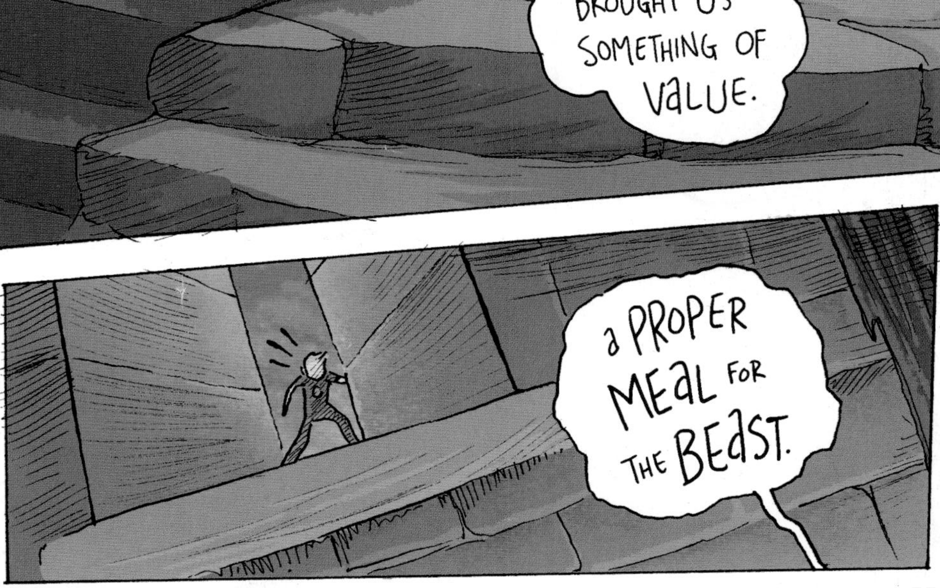
A PROPER MEAL FOR THE BEAST.

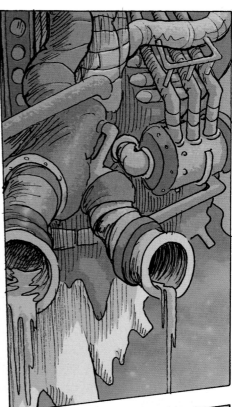

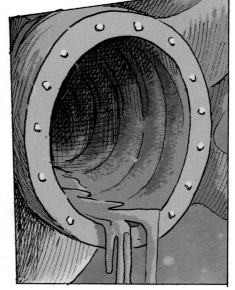

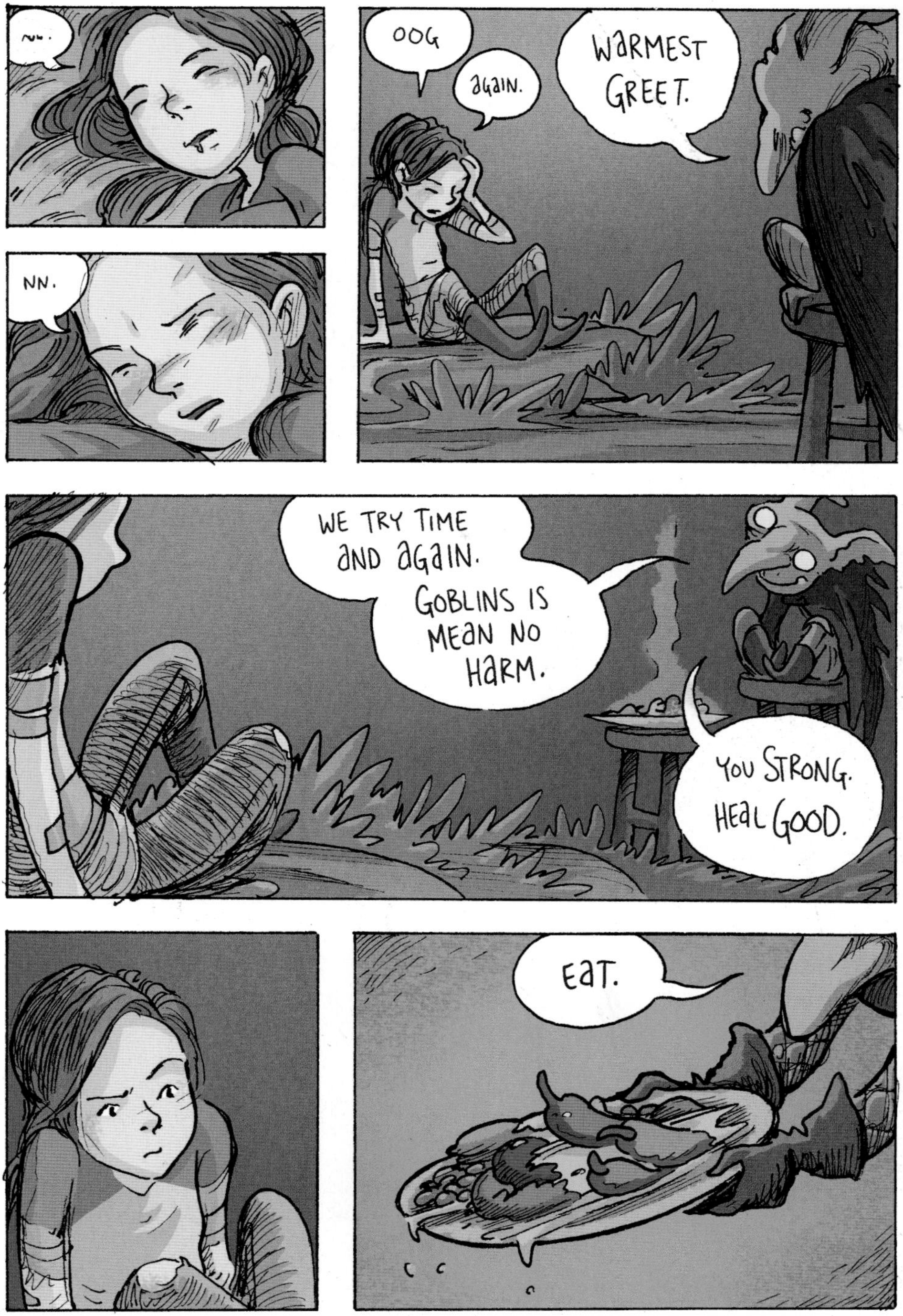
NN.
OOG
again.
WARMEST GREET.
WE TRY TIME AND AGAIN.
GOBLINS IS MEAN NO HARM.
YOU STRONG. HEAL GOOD.
EAT.

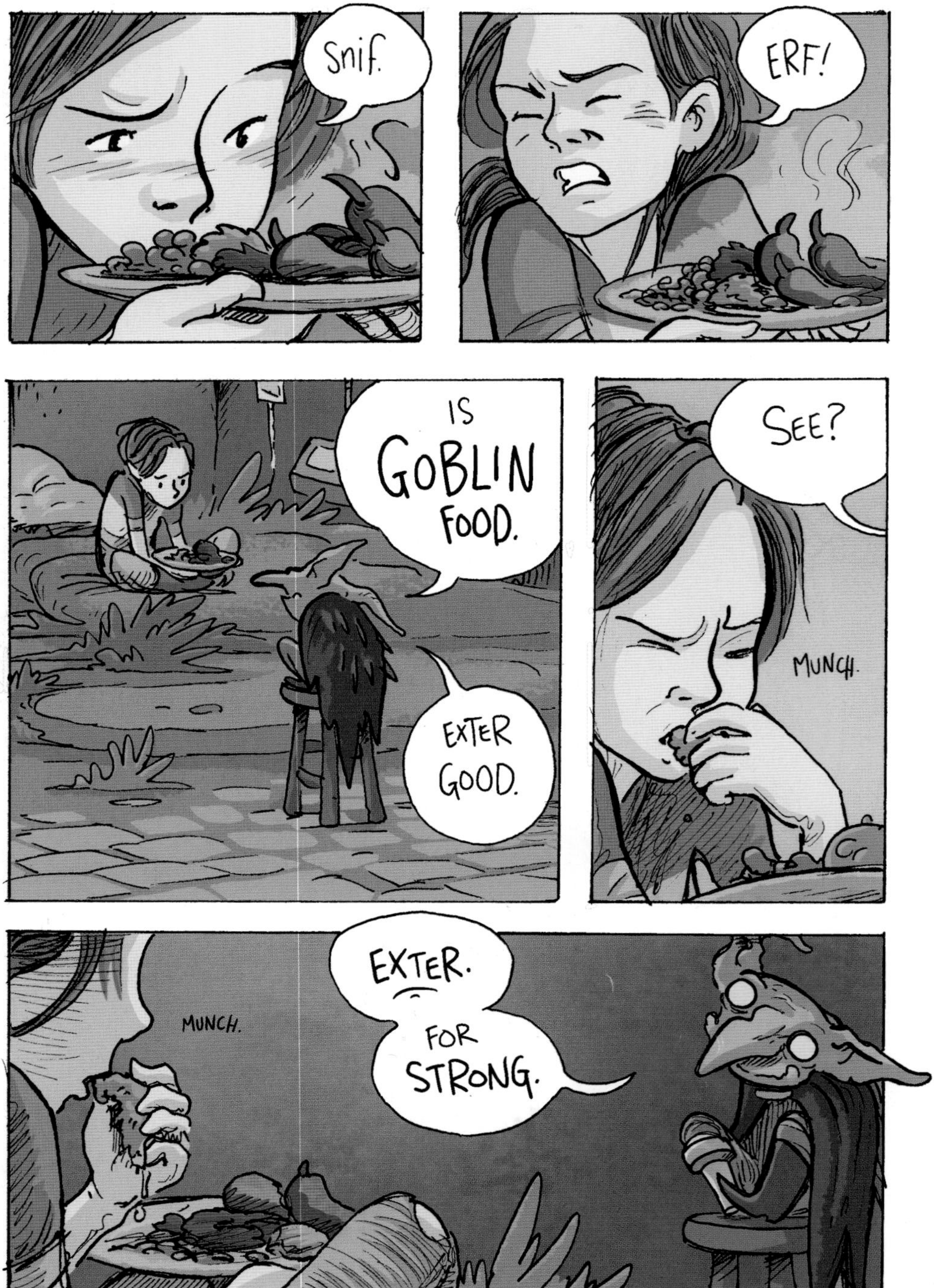
Snif.
ERF!
IS GOBLIN FOOD.
EXTER GOOD.
SEE?
MUNCH.
MUNCH.
EXTER.
FOR STRONG.

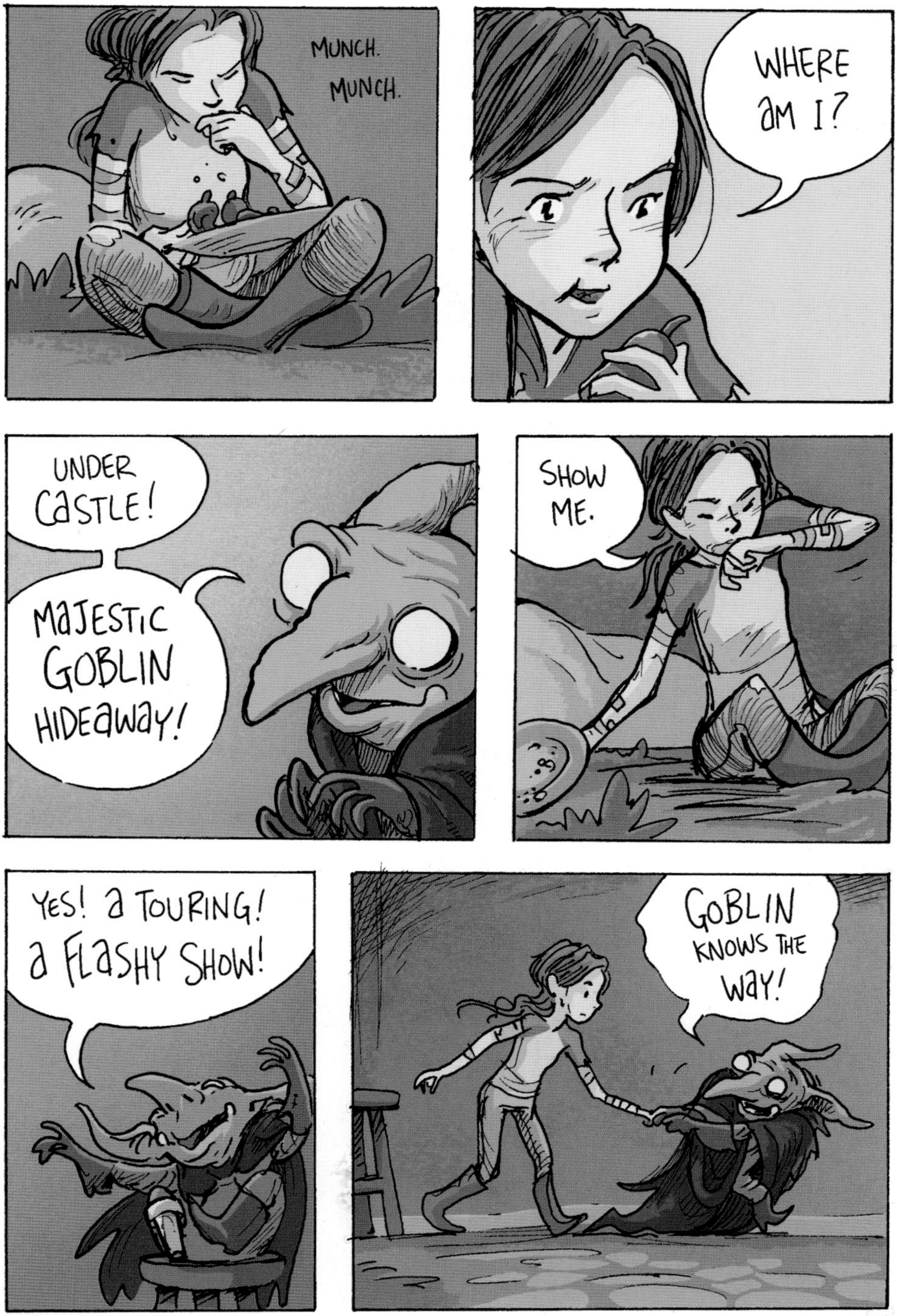
MUNCH.
MUNCH.
WHERE am I?
UNDER CASTLE!
MaJESTIC GOBLIN HIDEaway!
SHOW ME.
YES! a TOURING! a FLASHY SHOW!
GOBLIN KNOWS THE Way!

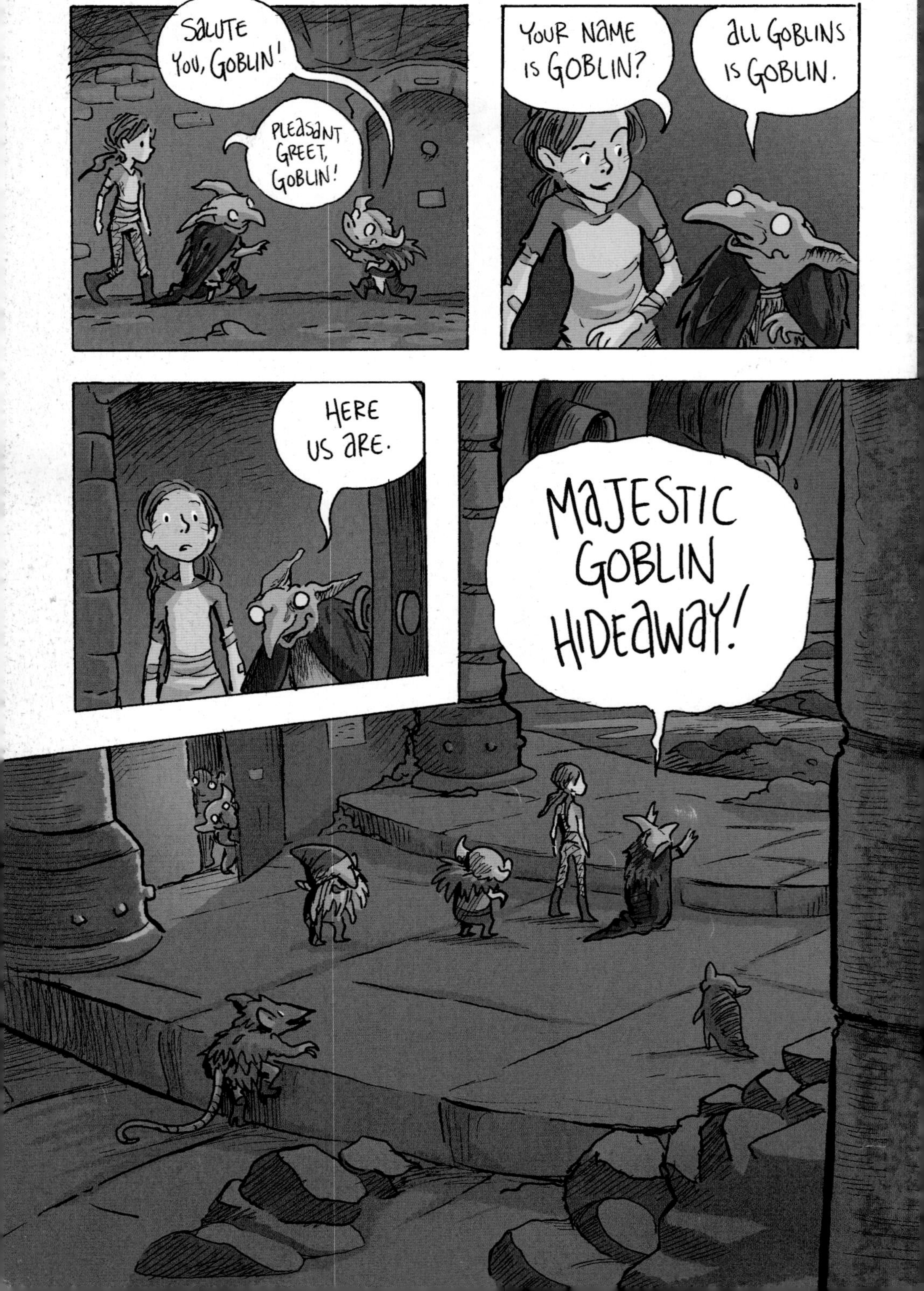
SALUTE YOU, GOBLIN!
PLEASANT GREET, GOBLIN!
YOUR NAME IS GOBLIN?
ALL GOBLINS IS GOBLIN.
HERE US ARE.
MAJESTIC GOBLIN HIDEAWAY!

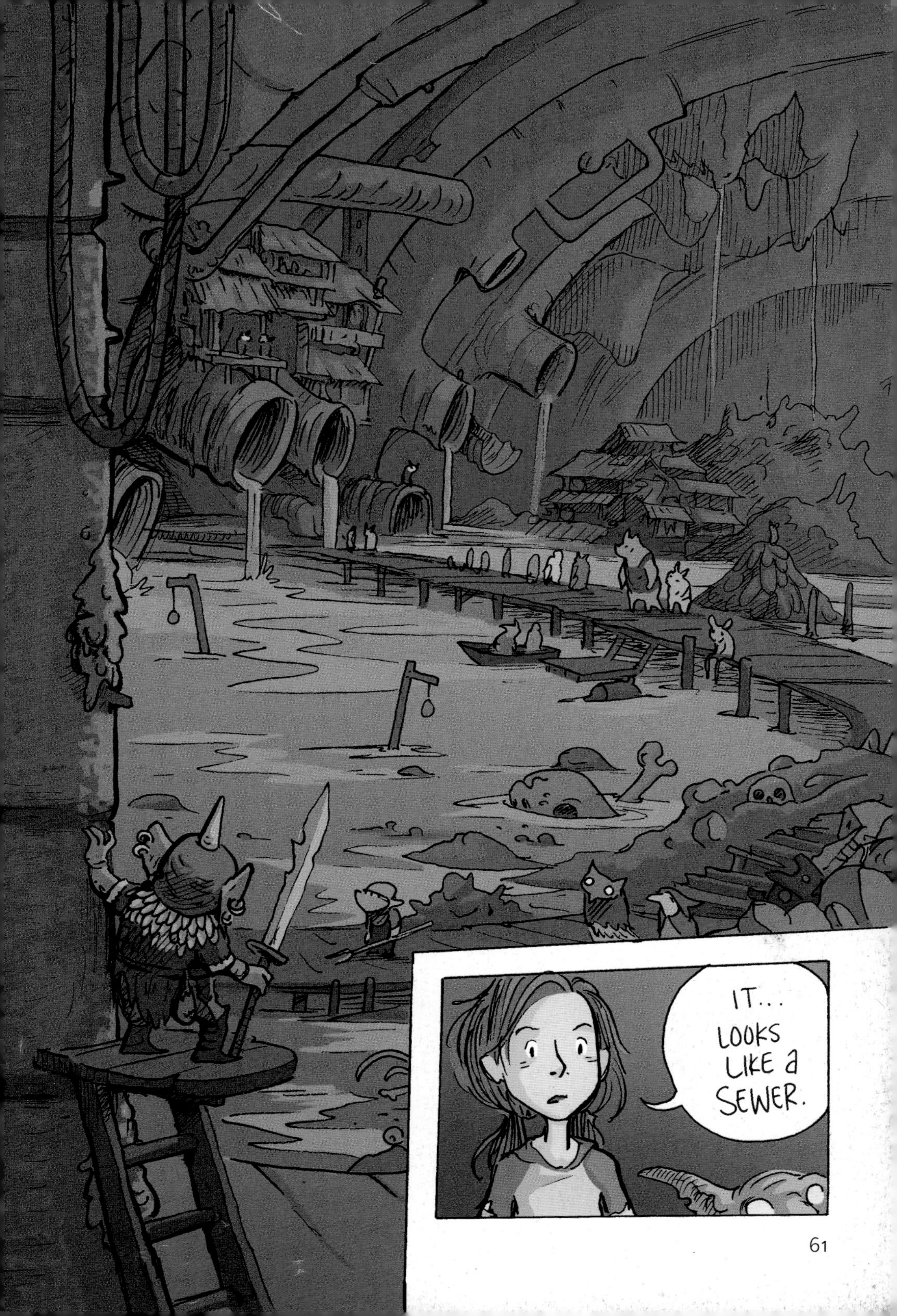
IT... LOOKS LIKE a SEWER.

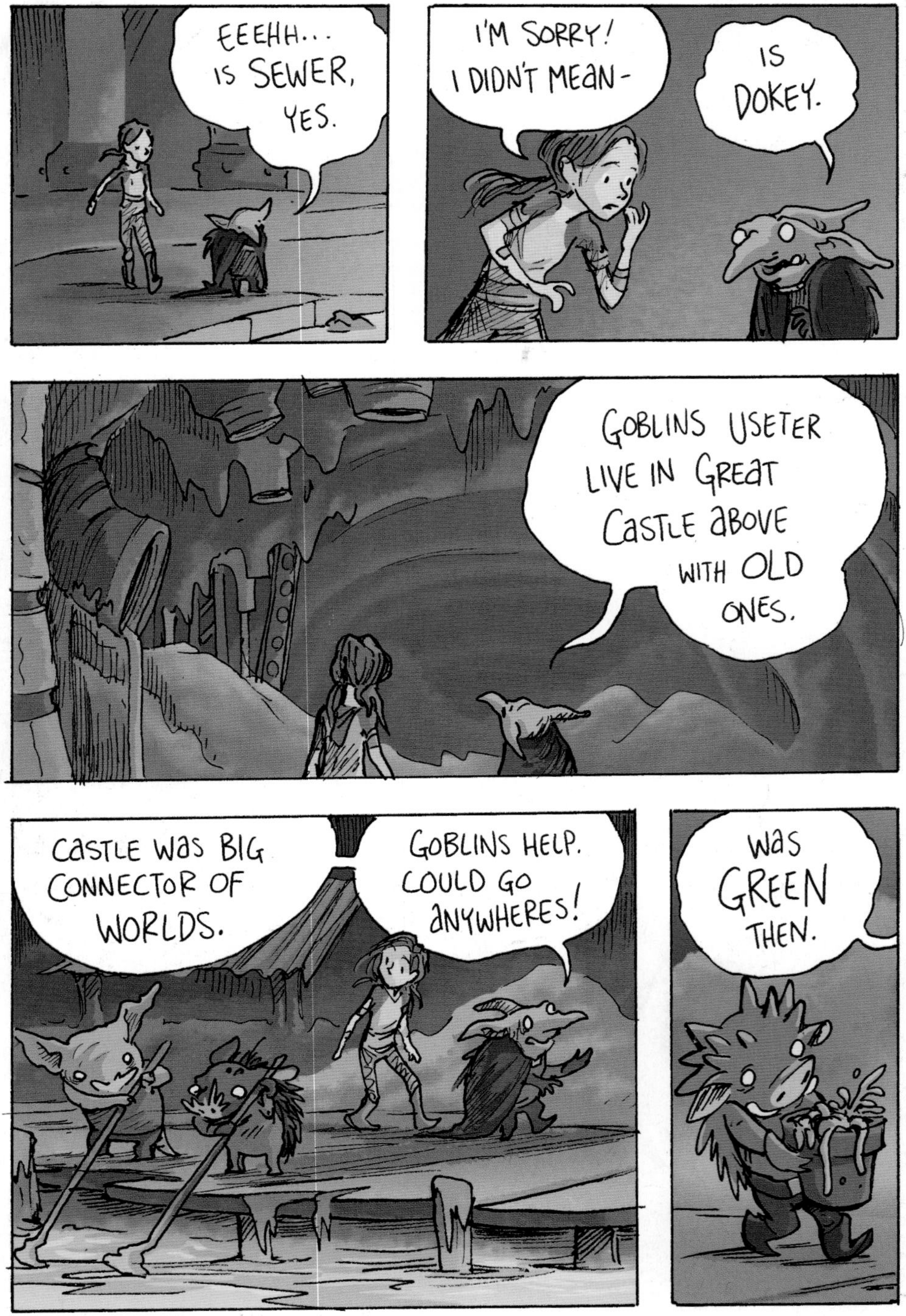
EEEHH... IS SEWER, YES.
I'M SORRY! I DIDN'T MEAN-
IS DOKEY.
GOBLINS USETER LIVE IN GREAT CASTLE ABOVE WITH OLD ONES.
CASTLE WAS BIG CONNECTOR OF WORLDS.
GOBLINS HELP. COULD GO ANYWHERES!
WAS GREEN THEN.

THEN GIANTS CAME.

NOW IS GRAY HERE, AND GREEN IS WEAK.

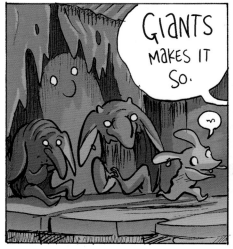

GIANTS MAKES IT SO.

OH —

GOBBLE. GORBLE GRBL.

HI THERE.

SLORP!

HA HA! OH NO!

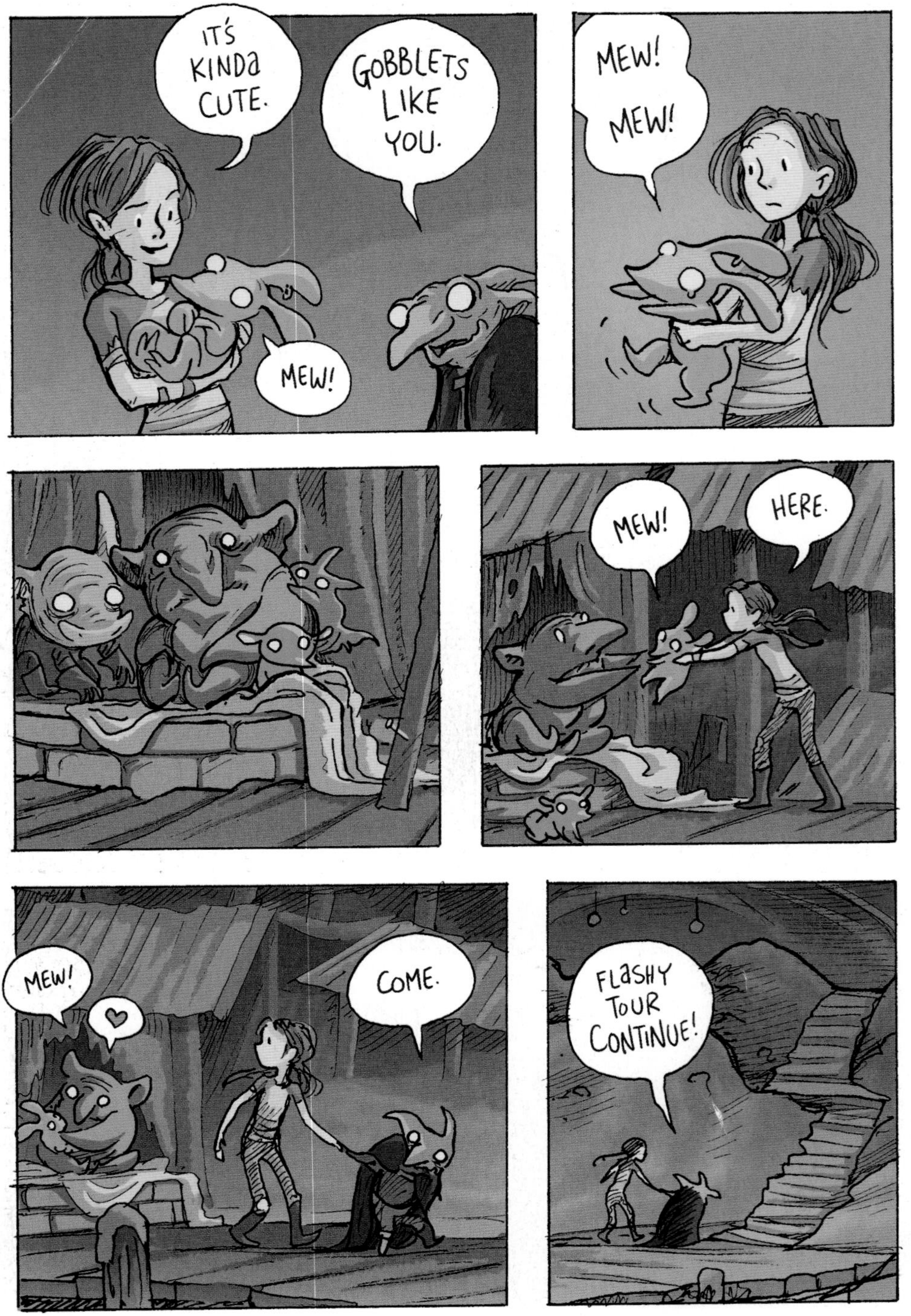
IT'S KINDA CUTE.
GOBBLETS LIKE YOU.
MEW!
MEW! MEW!
MEW!
HERE.
MEW!
COME.
FLASHY TOUR CONTINUE!

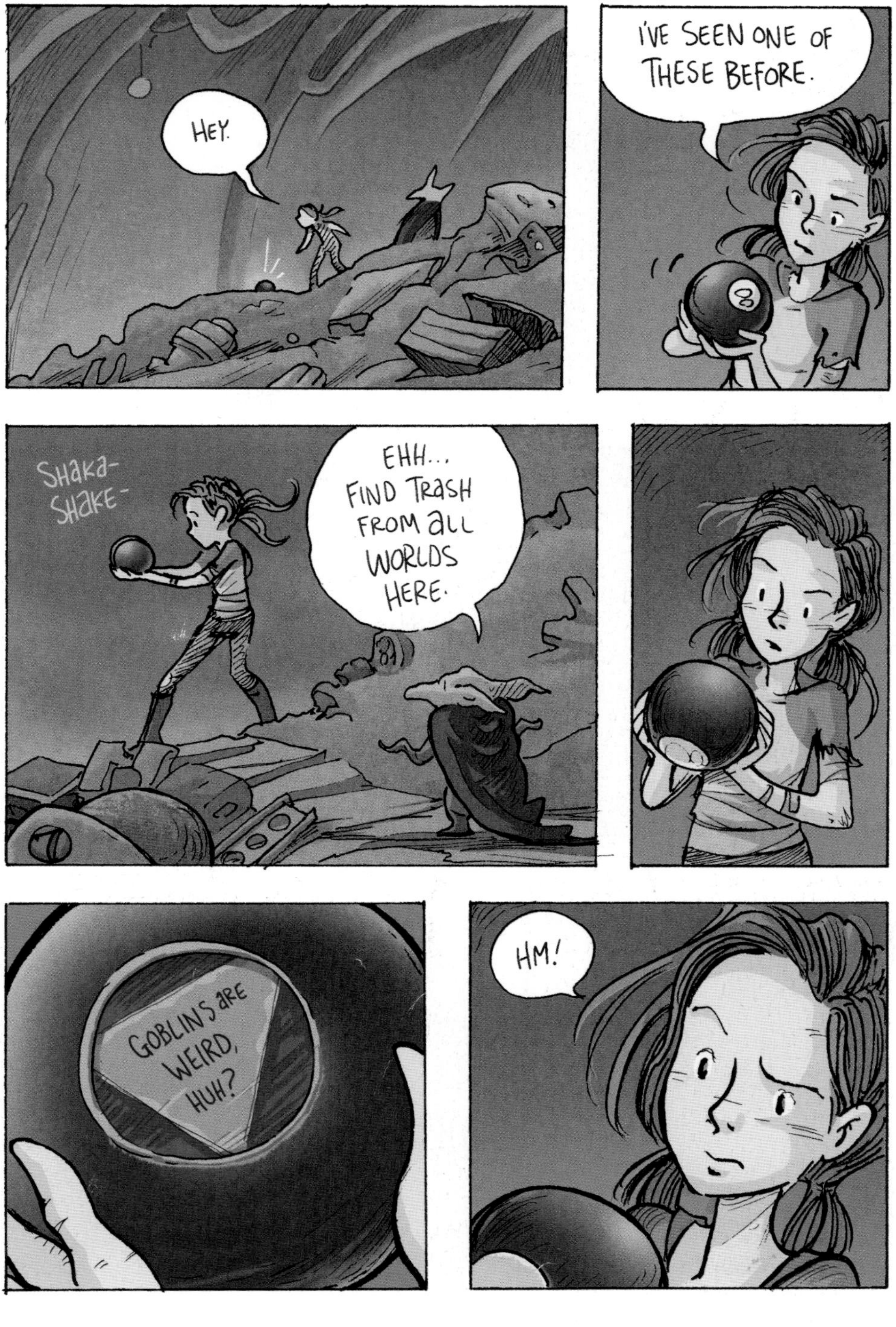
HEY.
I'VE SEEN ONE OF THESE BEFORE.
SHAKA-SHAKE-
EHH... FIND TRASH FROM ALL WORLDS HERE.
GOBLINS ARE WEIRD, HUH?
HM!

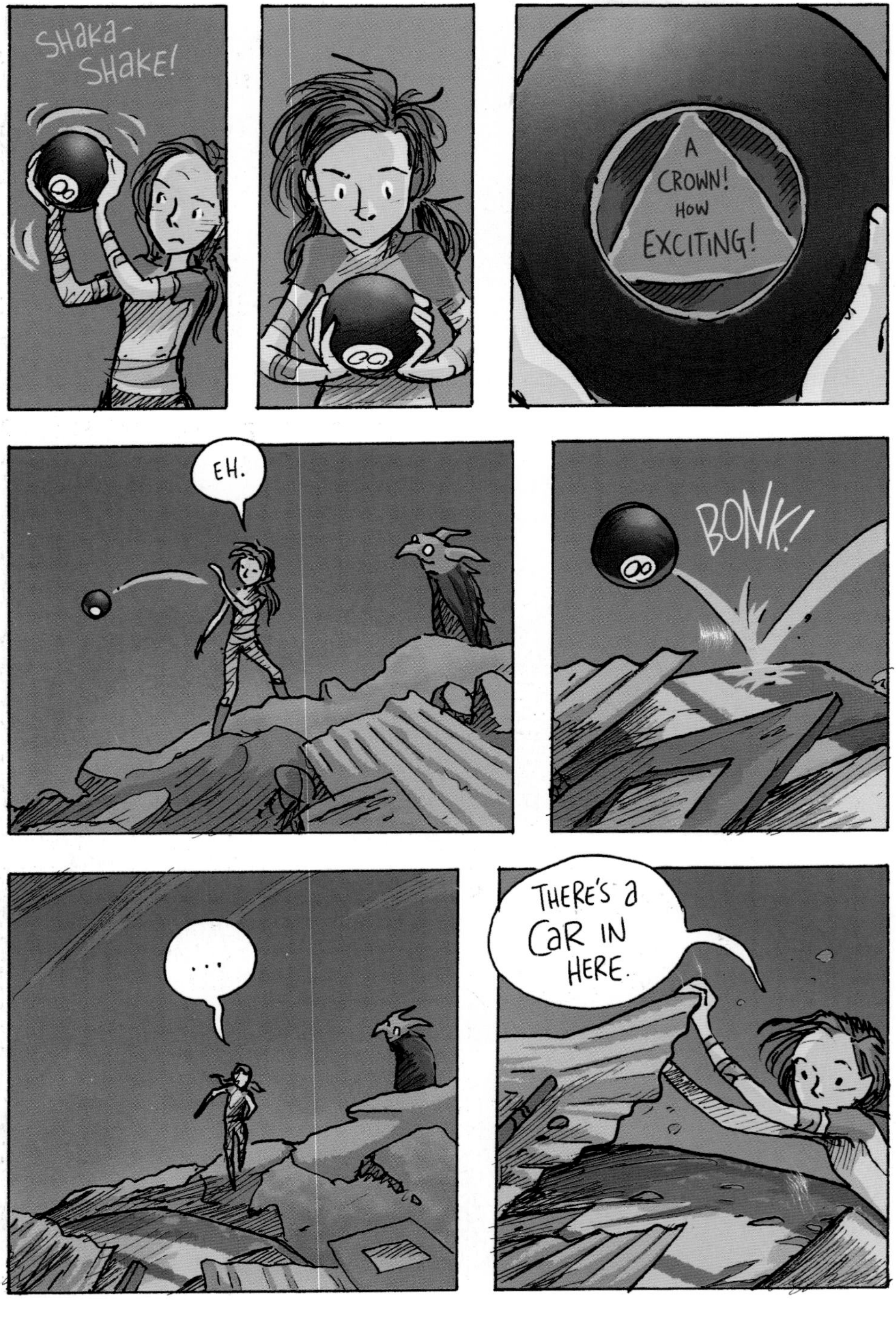
SHAKA-SHAKE!
A CROWN! HOW EXCITING!
EH.
BONK!
...
THERE'S a CaR IN HERE.

EHH. TRASH FROM ALL WORLDS.

THIS IS AN OLD SHELBY MUSTANG.

IT'S NOT TRASH.

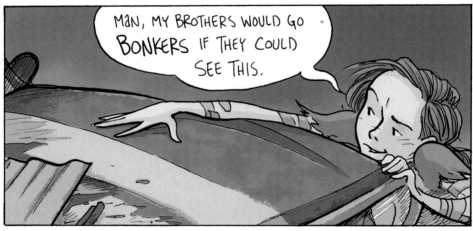

MAN, MY BROTHERS WOULD GO **BONKERS** IF THEY COULD SEE THIS.

HEY, GOBLIN! YOU DON'T THINK WE COULD—

WHERE IS SHE?!?

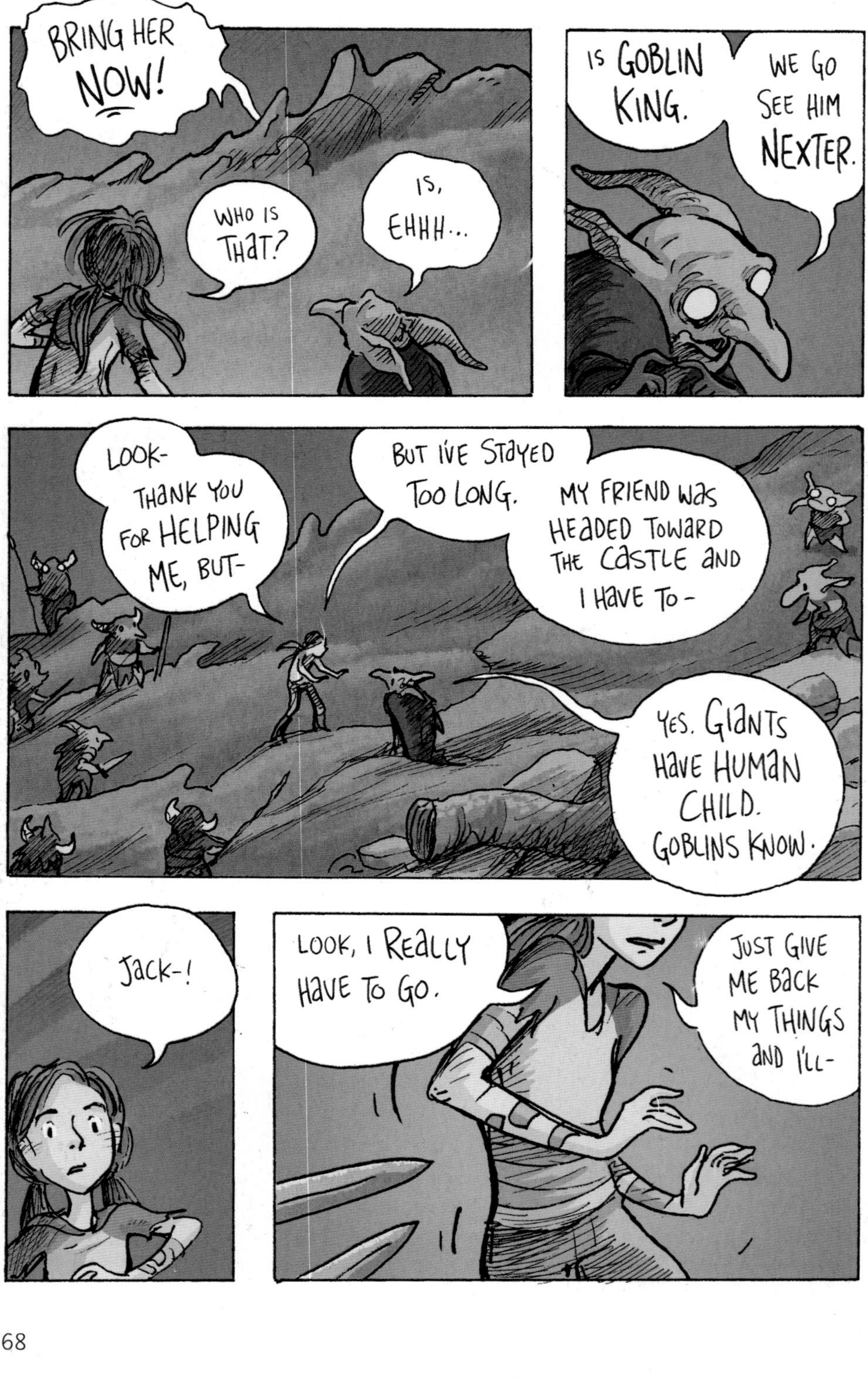
BRING HER NOW!
WHO IS THAT?
IS, EHHH...
IS GOBLIN KING.
WE GO SEE HIM NEXTER.
LOOK- THANK YOU FOR HELPING ME, BUT-
BUT I'VE STAYED TOO LONG.
MY FRIEND WAS HEADED TOWARD THE CASTLE AND I HAVE TO-
YES. GIANTS HAVE HUMAN CHILD. GOBLINS KNOW.
JACK-!
LOOK, I REALLY HAVE TO GO.
JUST GIVE ME BACK MY THINGS AND I'LL-

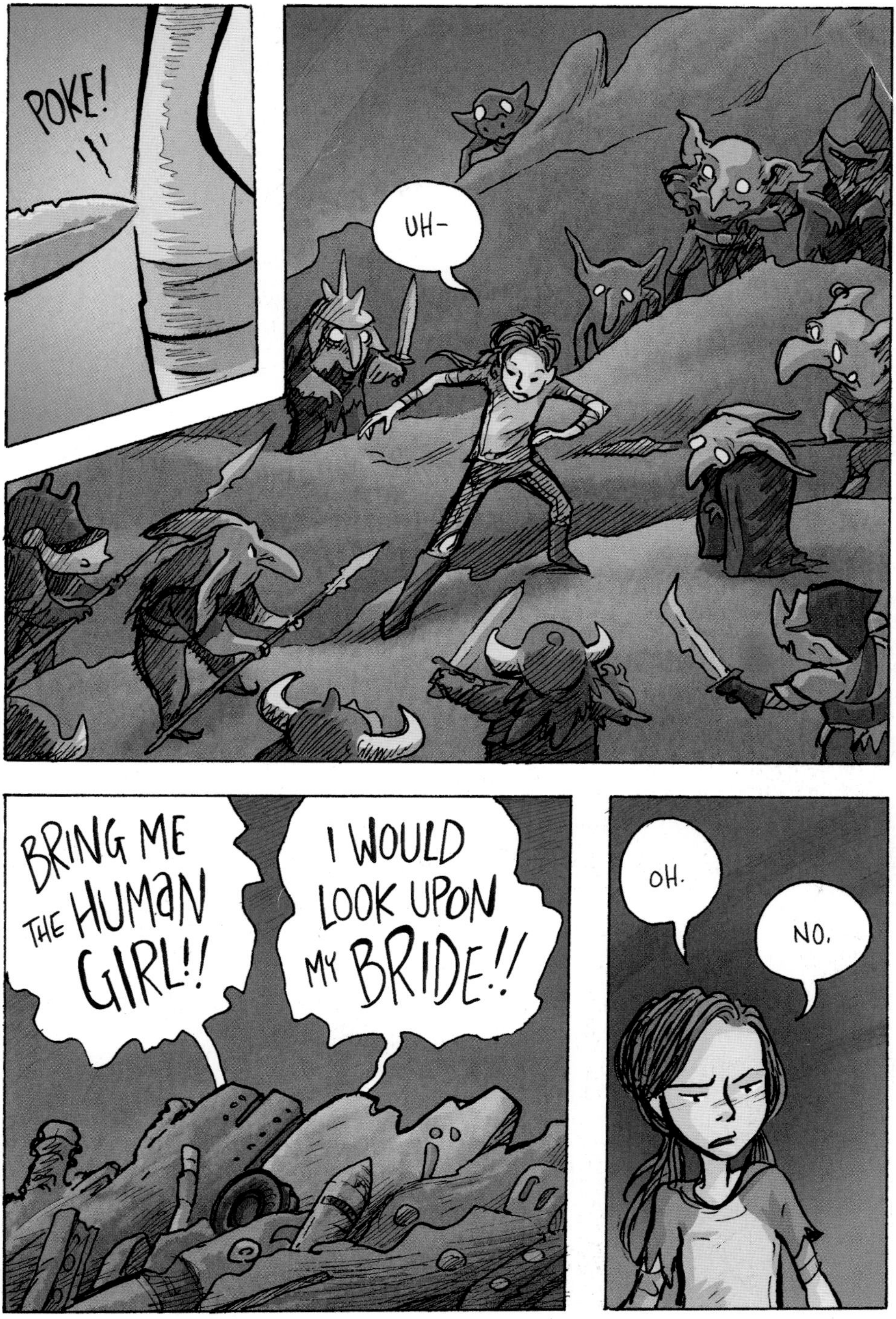
POKE!
UH-
BRING ME THE HUMAN GIRL!!
I WOULD LOOK UPON MY BRIDE!!
OH.
NO.

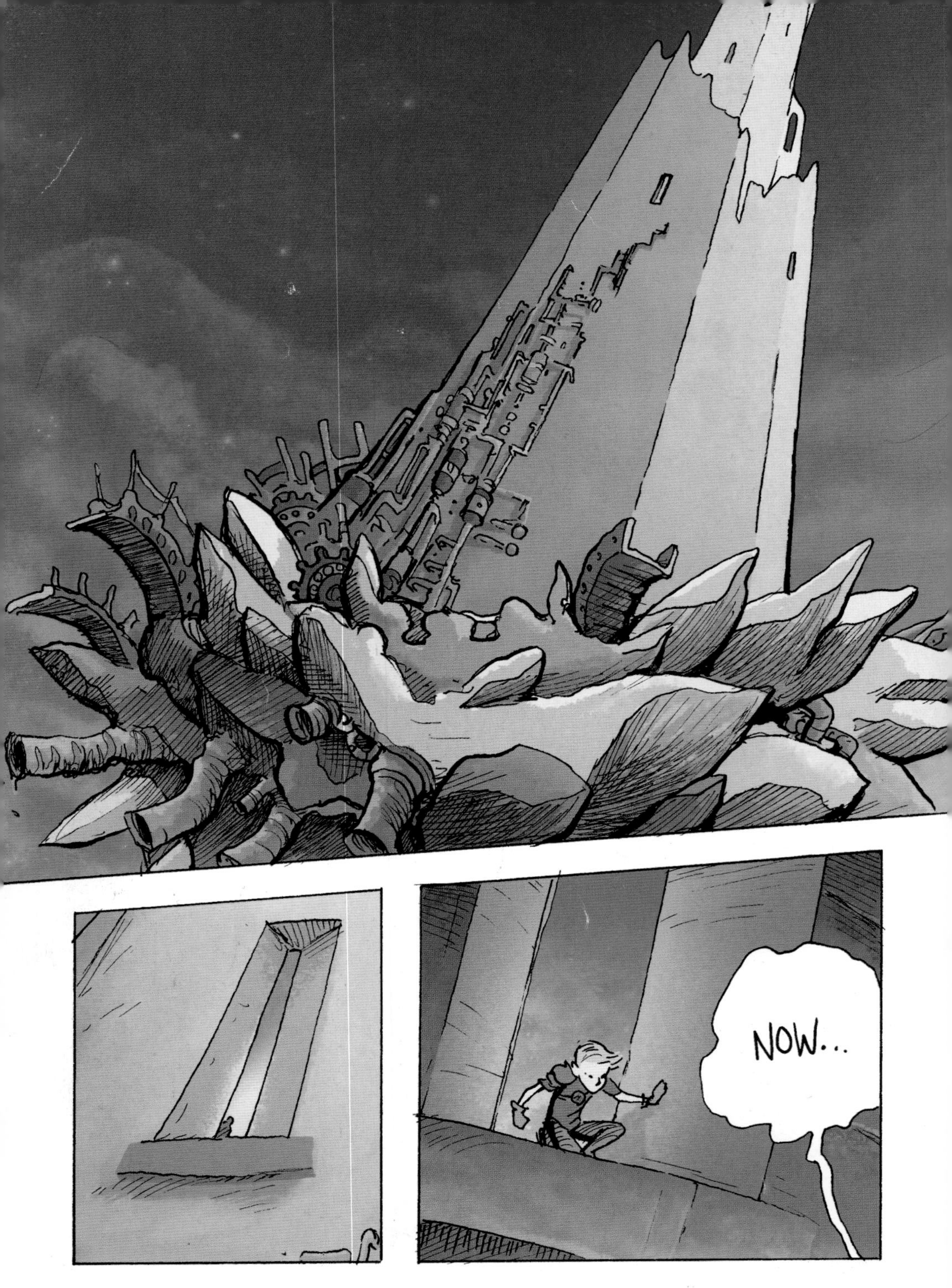
NOW...

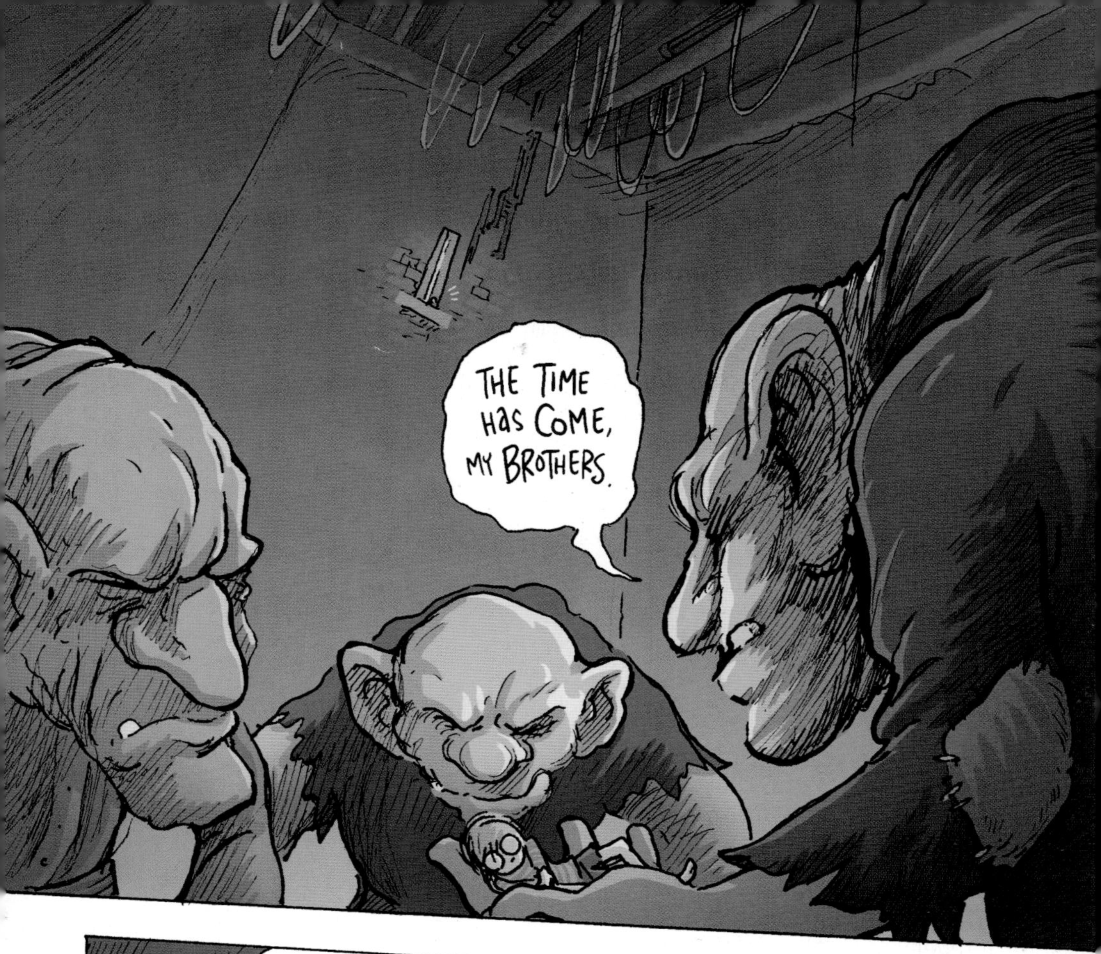
THE TIME HAS COME, MY BROTHERS.

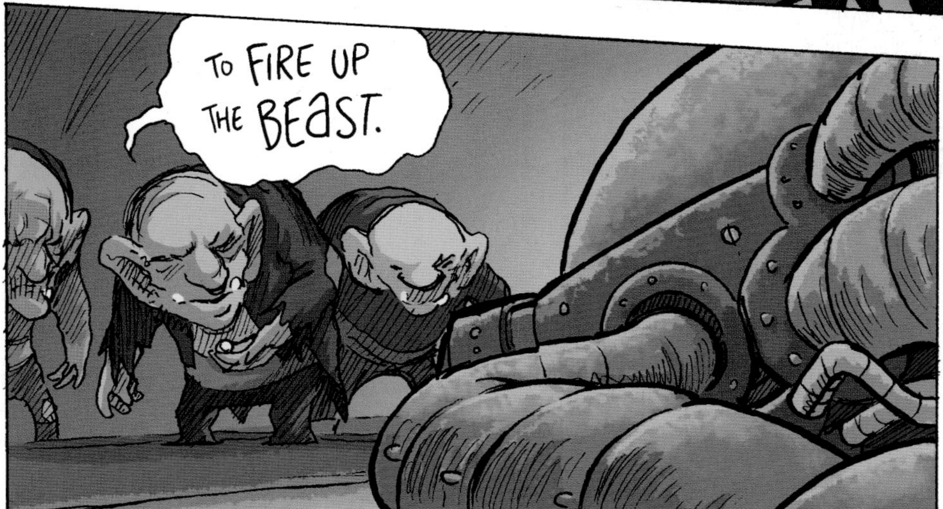
TO FIRE UP THE BEAST.

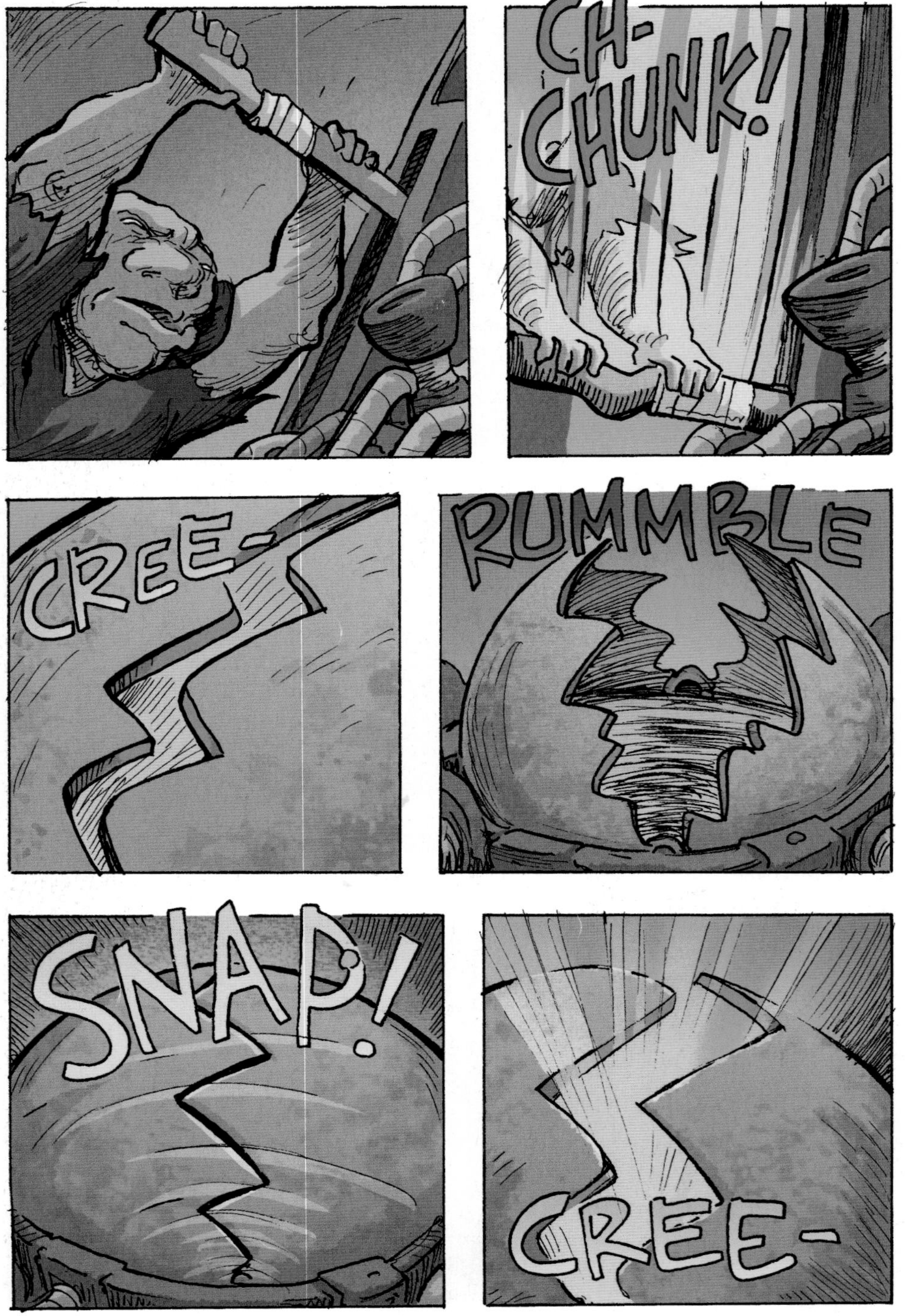
CH-CHUNK!
CREE-
RUMMBLE
SNAP!
CREE-

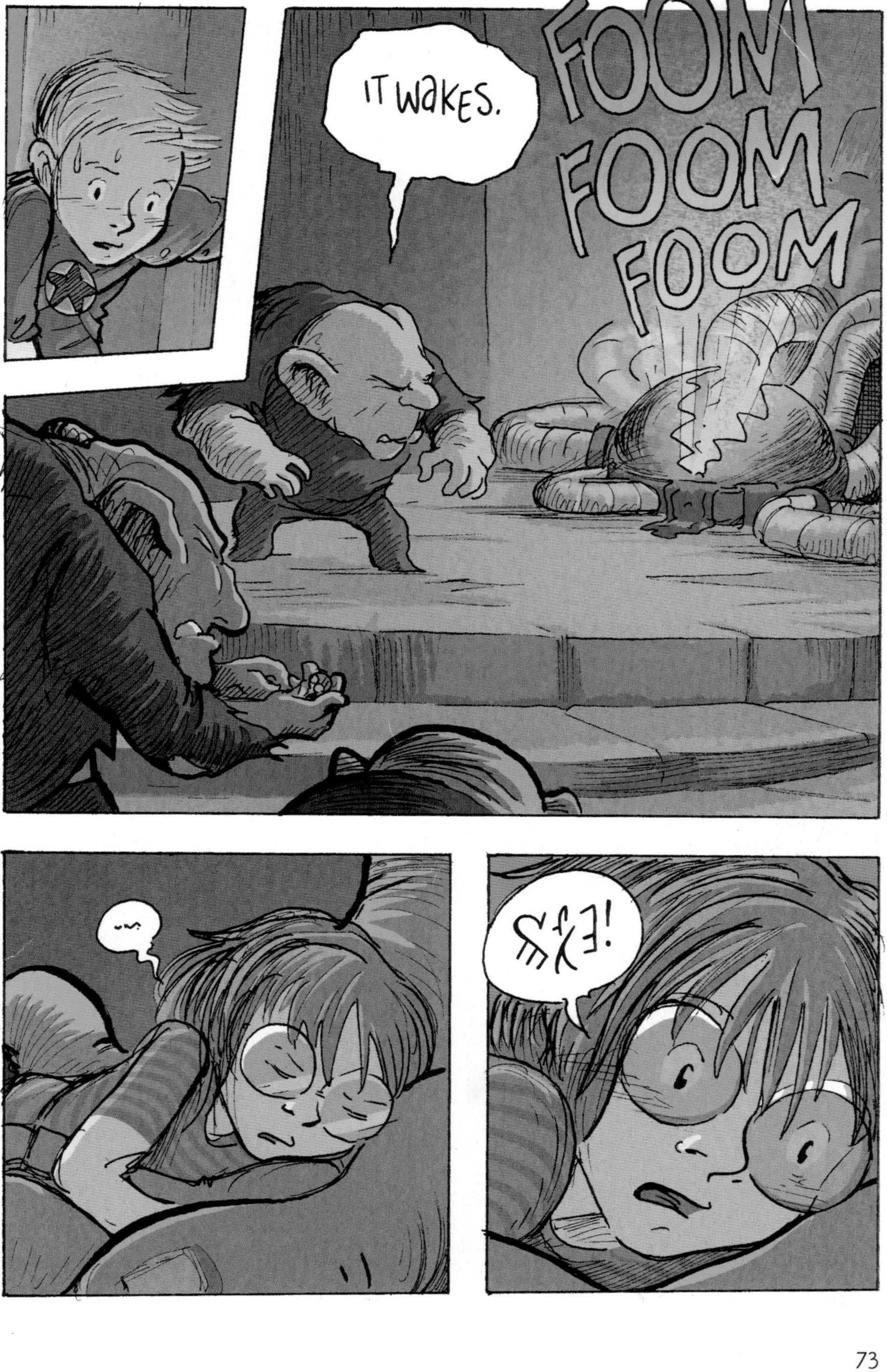
IT WAKES.
FOOM
FOOM
FOOM

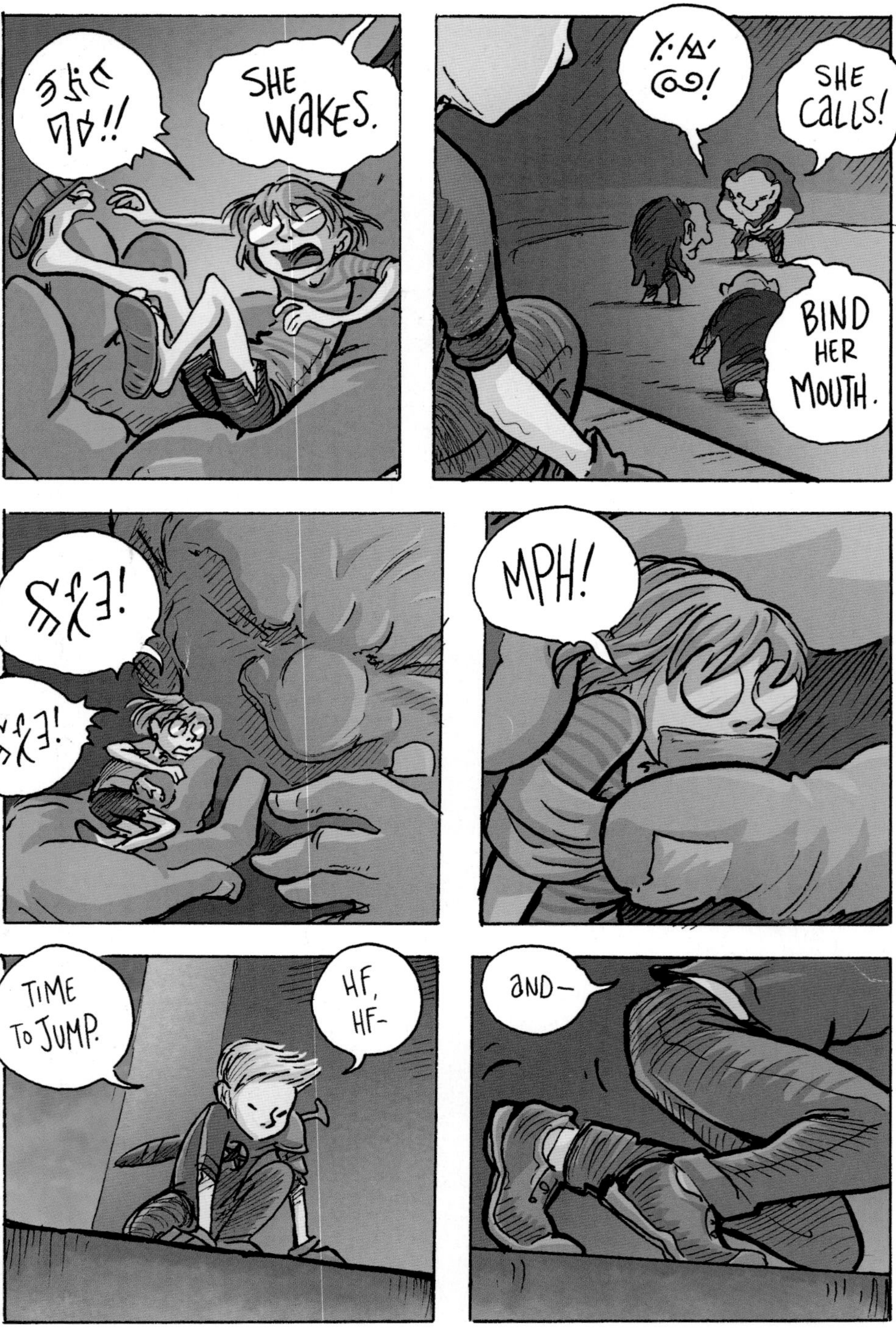
SHE WAKES.
SHE CALLS!
BIND HER MOUTH.
MPH!
TIME TO JUMP.
HF, HF-
and-

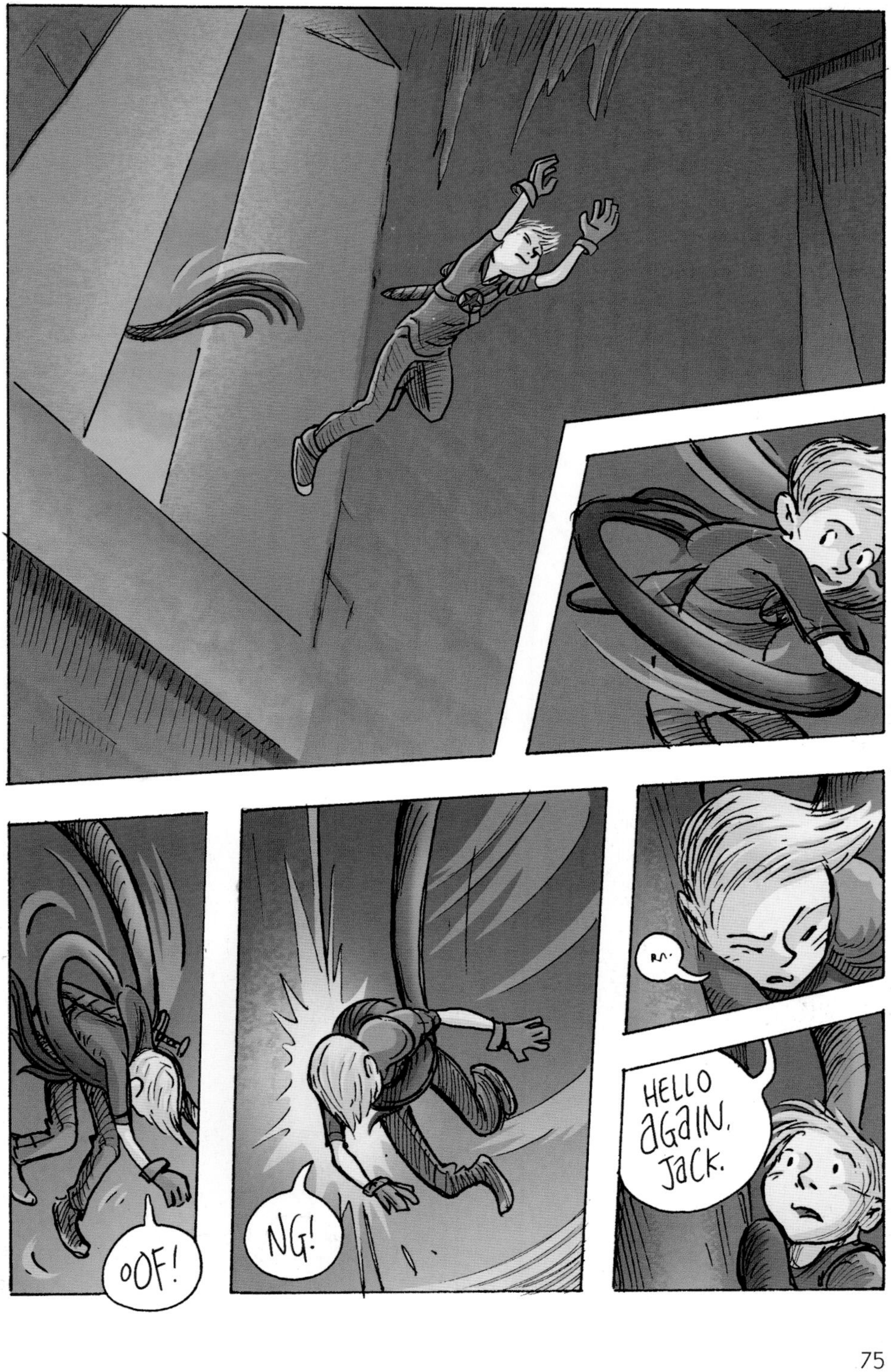
OOF!
NG!
HELLO again, Jack.

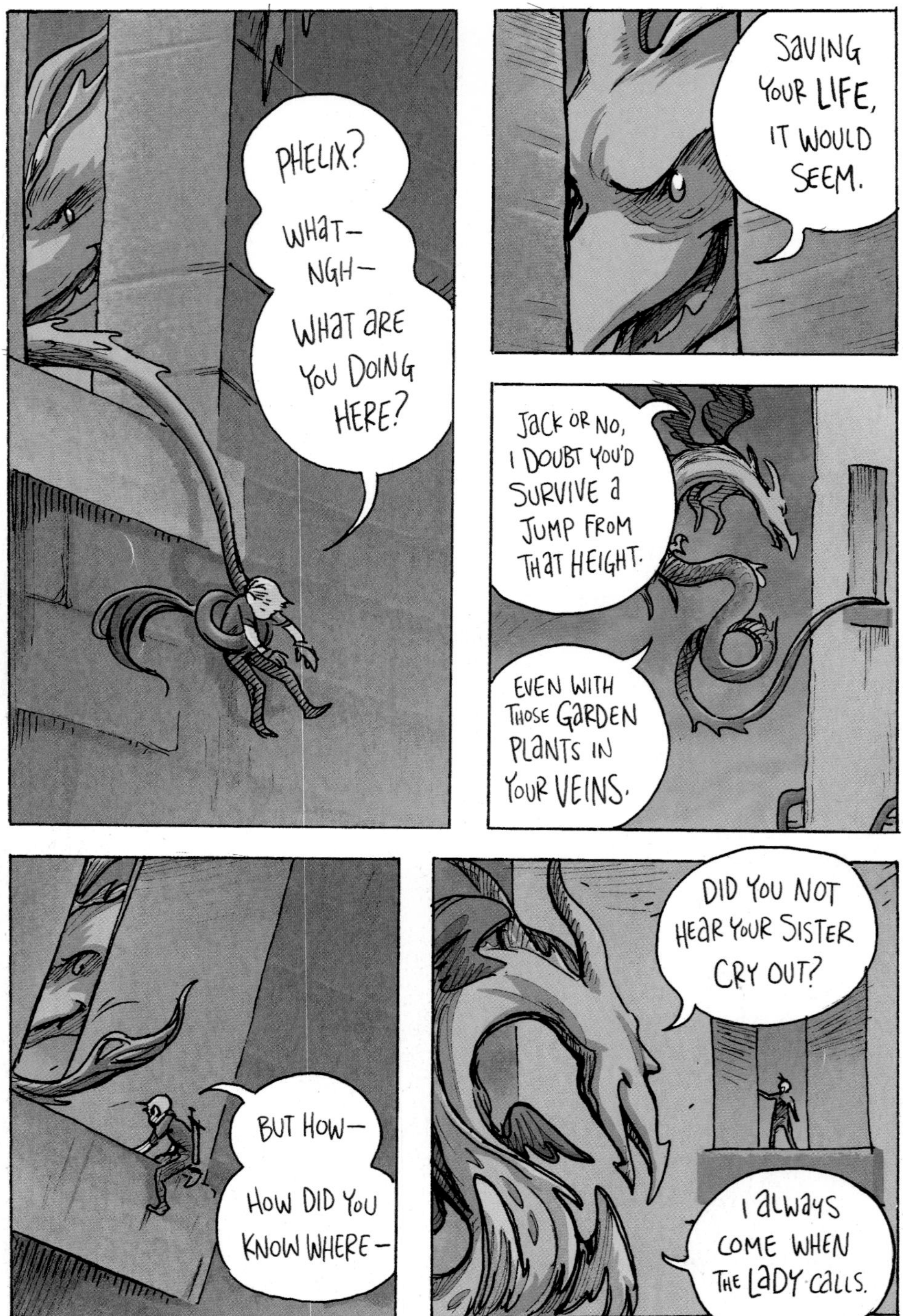
PHELIX?
WHAT—
NGH—
WHAT ARE YOU DOING HERE?
SAVING YOUR LIFE, IT WOULD SEEM.
JACK OR NO, I DOUBT YOU'D SURVIVE A JUMP FROM THAT HEIGHT.
EVEN WITH THOSE GARDEN PLANTS IN YOUR VEINS.
BUT HOW—
HOW DID YOU KNOW WHERE—
DID YOU NOT HEAR YOUR SISTER CRY OUT?
I ALWAYS COME WHEN THE LADY CALLS.

WE HAVE TO SAVE MADDY!

JACK...

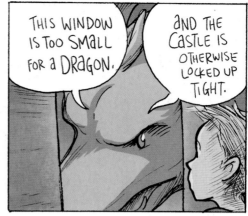

THIS WINDOW IS TOO SMALL FOR A DRAGON.

AND THE CASTLE IS OTHERWISE LOCKED UP TIGHT.

YOU'RE ON YOUR OWN.

BUT—!

TAKE HEART. THE LADY IS NOT IN IMMEDIATE DANGER.

OBSERVE.

THEIR MACHINE TAKES TIME TO HEAT UP.

THE GIANTS MUST FEED IT A LIVING HUMAN CHILD.

THEY WILL KEEP YOUR SISTER SAFE UNTIL THEIR BEAST IS READY.

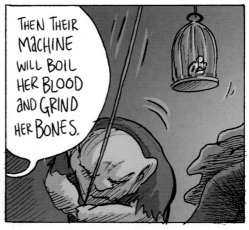

THEN THEIR MACHINE WILL BOIL HER BLOOD AND GRIND HER BONES.

BUT WHY? WHY ARE THEY DOING THIS?

THE FLESH AND BLOOD OF YOUR KIND HAS...

PROPERTIES.

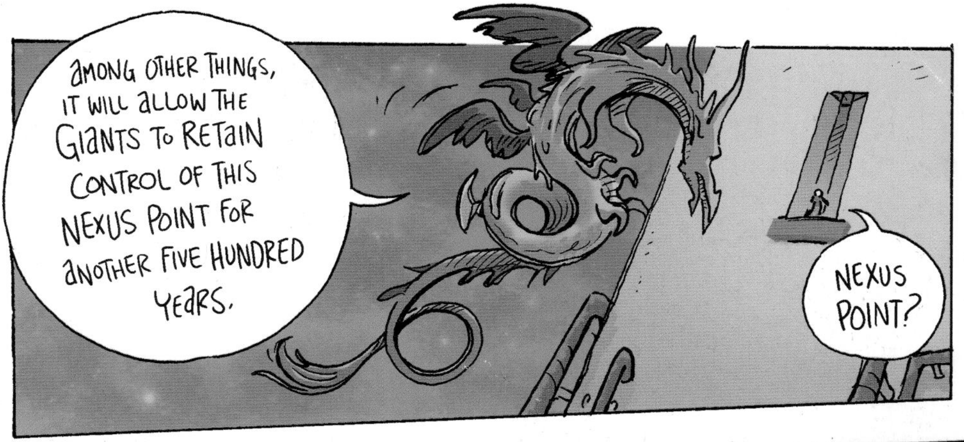
AMONG OTHER THINGS, IT WILL ALLOW THE GIANTS TO RETAIN CONTROL OF THIS NEXUS POINT FOR ANOTHER FIVE HUNDRED YEARS.
NEXUS POINT?

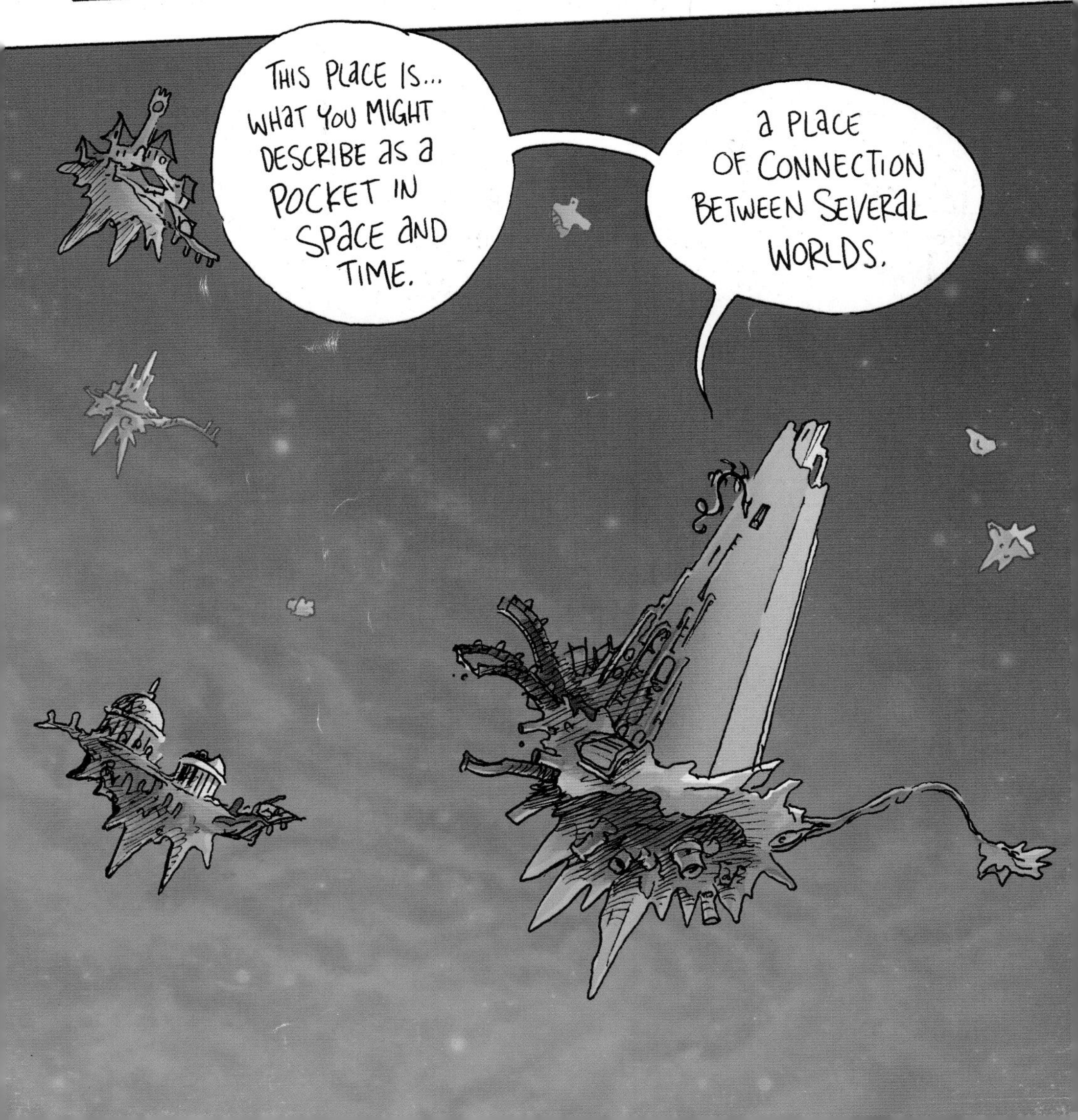
THIS PLACE IS... WHAT YOU MIGHT DESCRIBE AS A POCKET IN SPACE AND TIME.
A PLACE OF CONNECTION BETWEEN SEVERAL WORLDS.

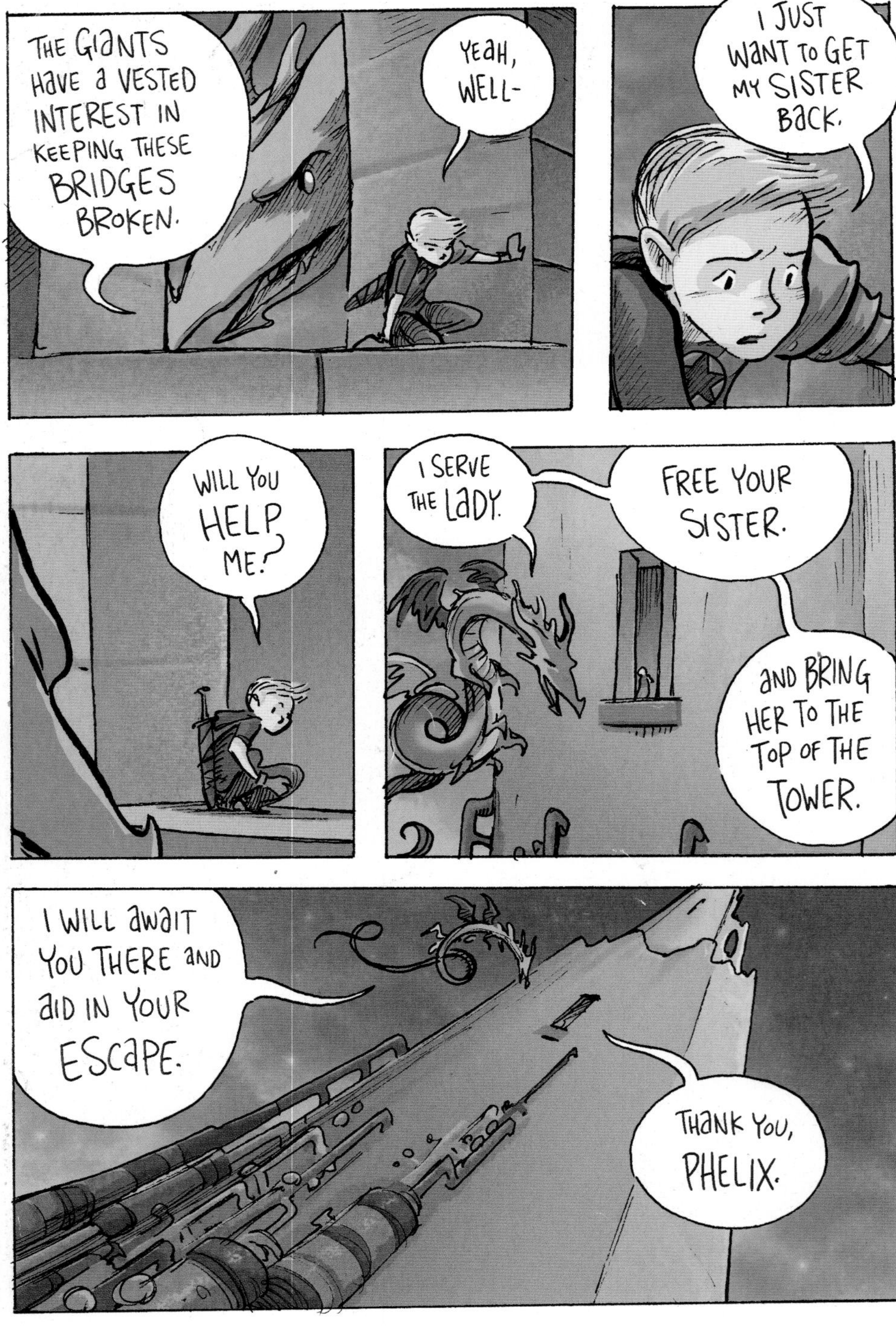
THE GIANTS HAVE A VESTED INTEREST IN KEEPING THESE BRIDGES BROKEN.
YEAH, WELL-
I JUST WANT TO GET MY SISTER BACK.
WILL YOU HELP ME?
I SERVE THE LADY.
FREE YOUR SISTER.
AND BRING HER TO THE TOP OF THE TOWER.
I WILL AWAIT YOU THERE AND AID IN YOUR ESCAPE.
THANK YOU, PHELIX.

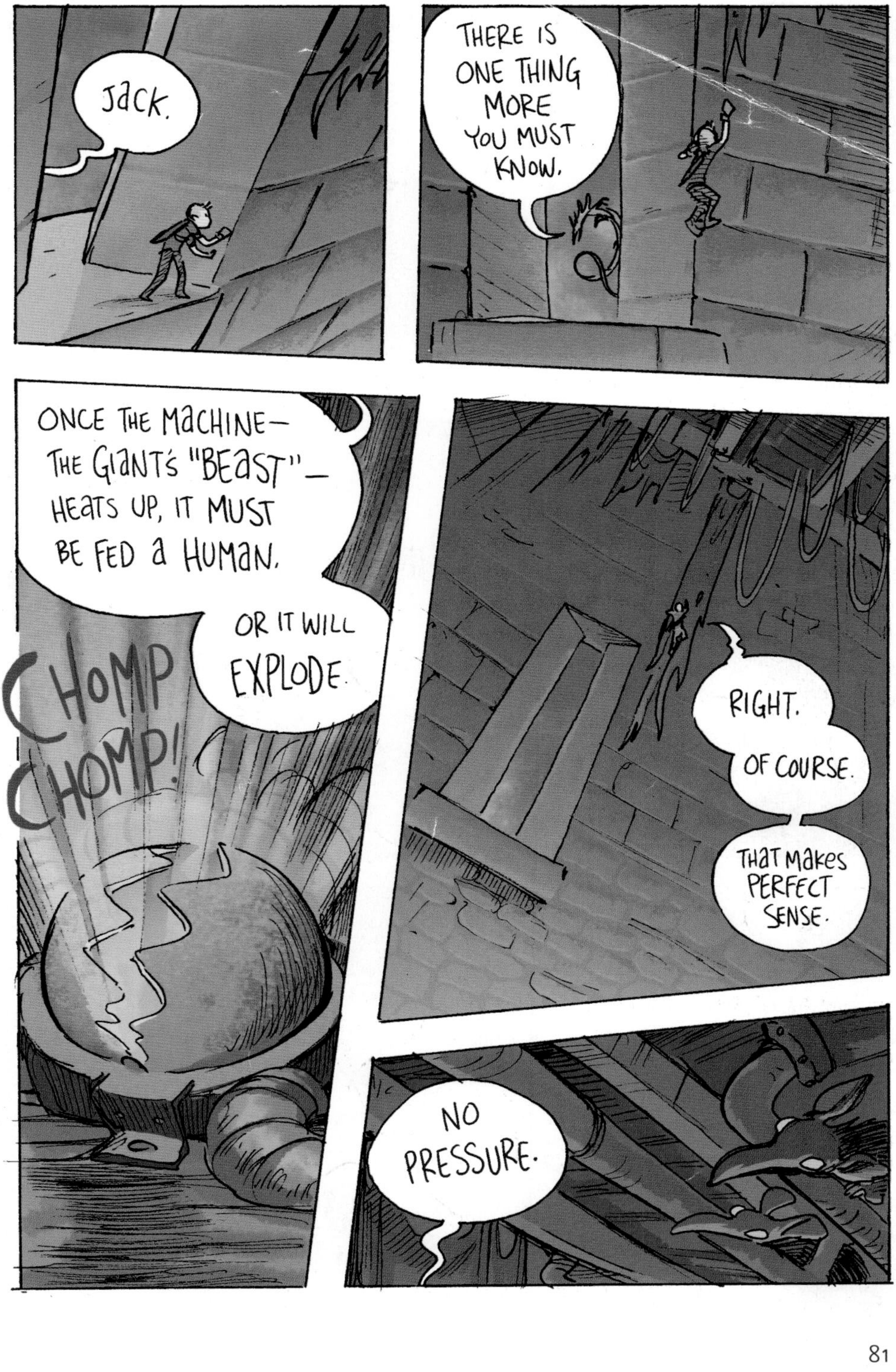
JACK.
THERE IS ONE THING MORE YOU MUST KNOW.
ONCE THE MACHINE— THE GIANT'S "BEAST"— HEATS UP, IT MUST BE FED A HUMAN.
OR IT WILL EXPLODE.
CHOMP CHOMP!
RIGHT.
OF COURSE.
THAT MAKES PERFECT SENSE.
NO PRESSURE.

OW! im GOING!

SORRY.

WE SORRY.

SORRY.

WELL, IF YOU DON'T WANT TO POKE ME WITH YOUR SWORDS, THEN DON'T—

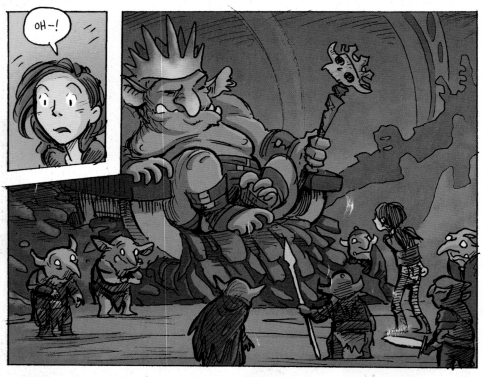

OH—!

HMMM...

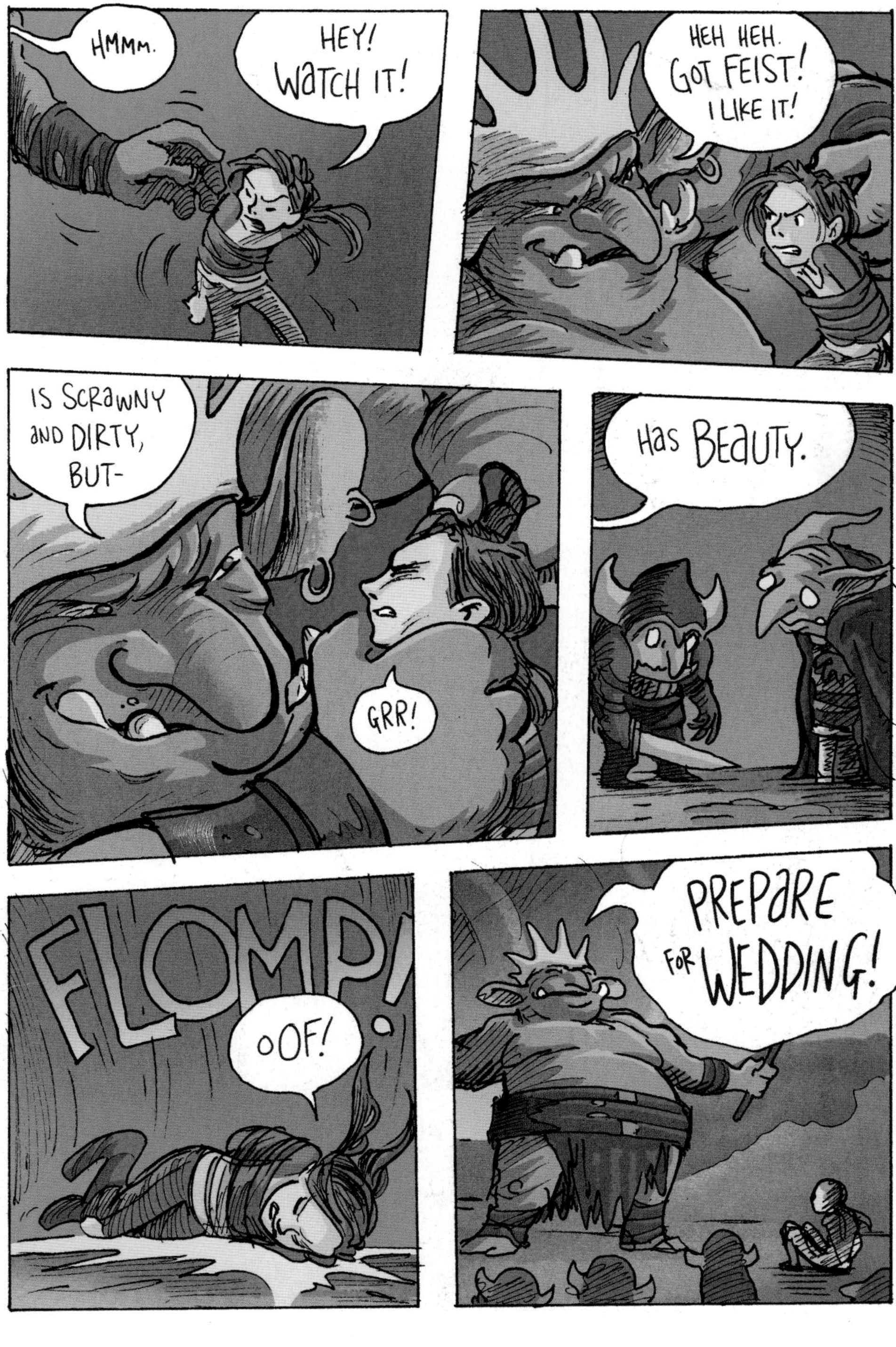

HMMM.
HEY! WATCH IT!
HEH HEH. GOT FEIST! I LIKE IT!
IS SCRAWNY AND DIRTY, BUT-
GRR!
HAS BEAUTY.
FLOMP!
OOF!
PREPARE FOR WEDDING!

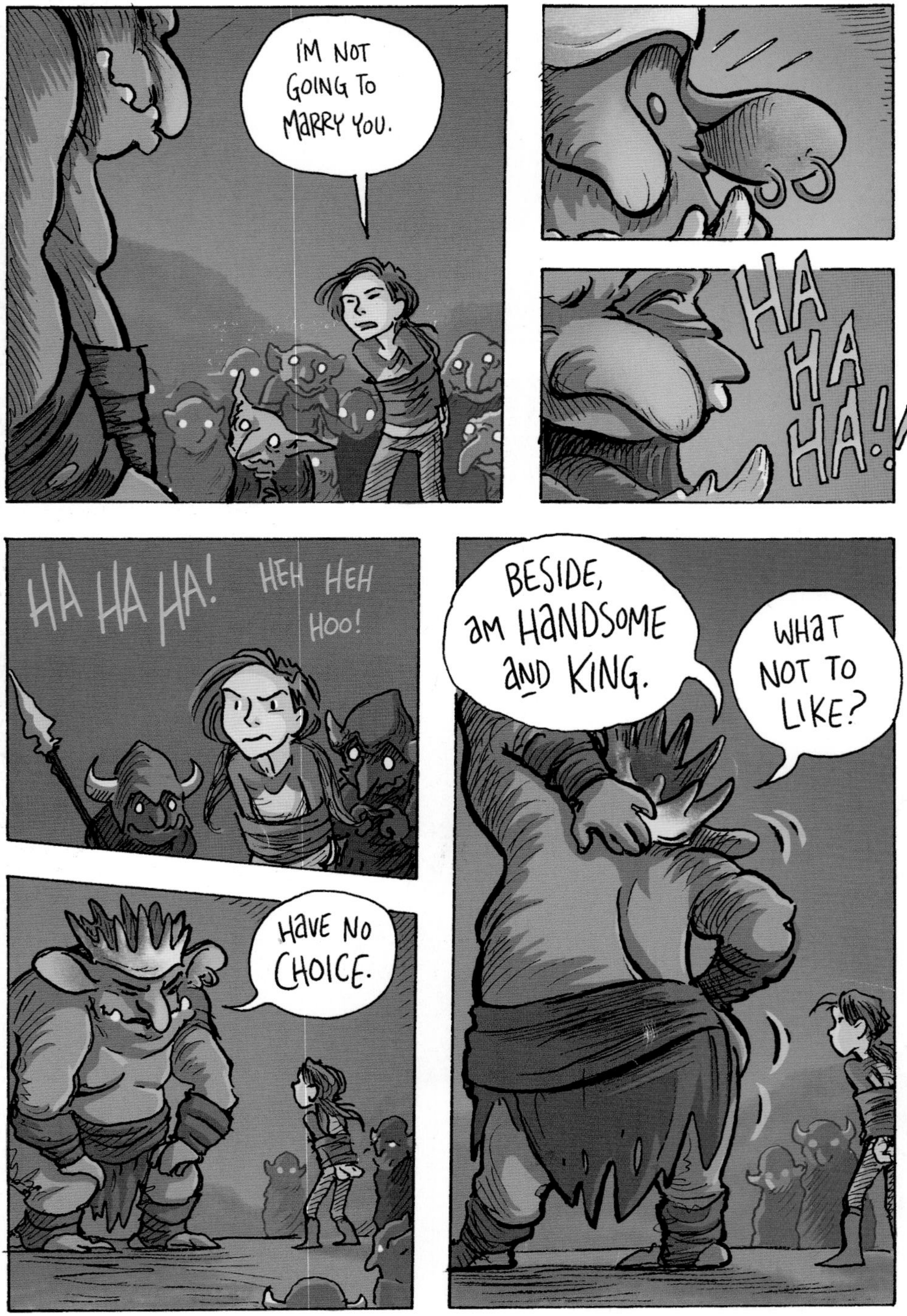

I'M NOT GOING TO MARRY YOU.
HA HA HA!!!
HA HA HA!
HEH HEH HOO!
HAVE NO CHOICE.
BESIDE, AM HANDSOME AND KING.
WHAT NOT TO LIKE?

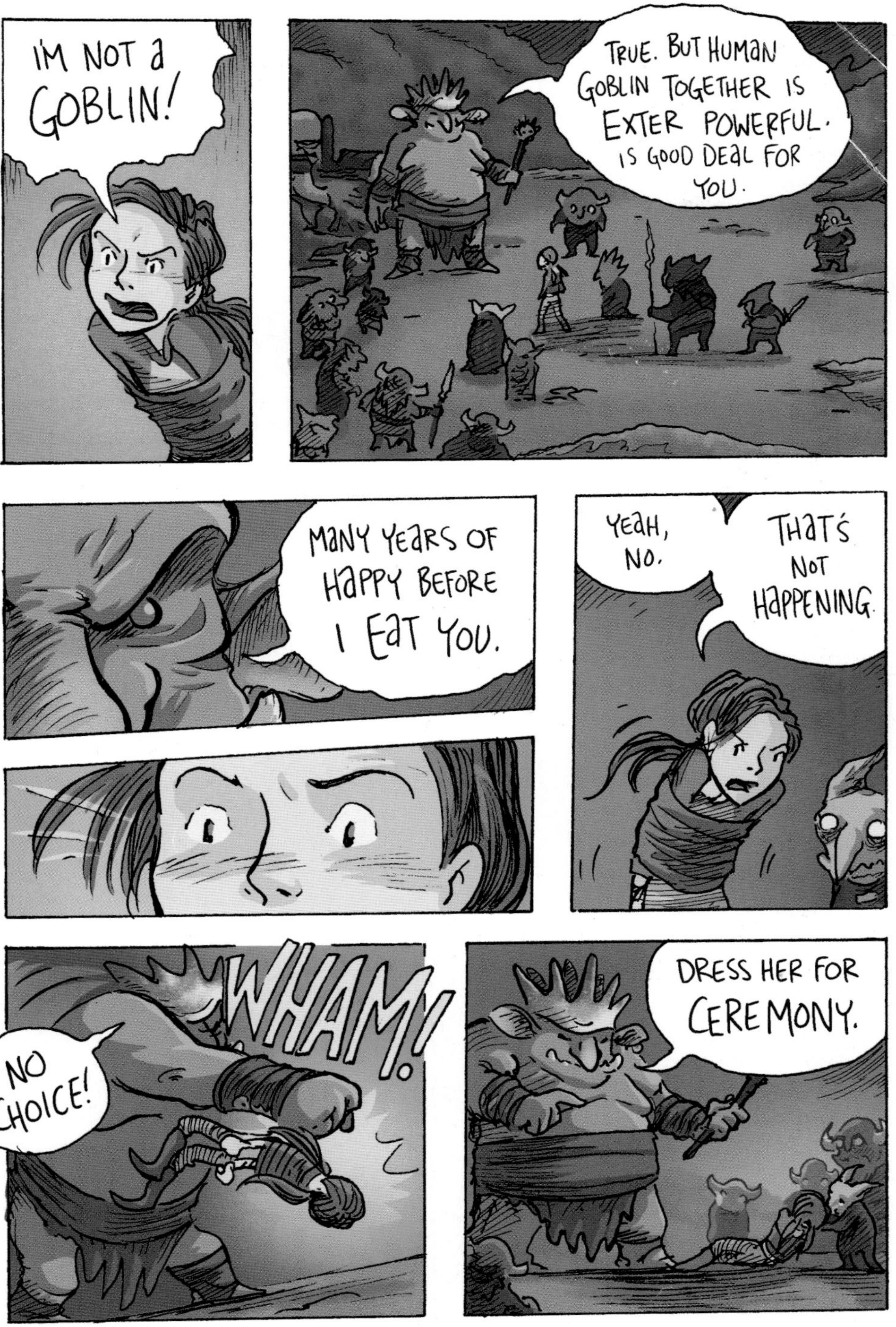
I'M NOT a GOBLIN!
TRUE. BUT HUMAN GOBLIN TOGETHER IS EXTER POWERFUL. IS GOOD DEAL FOR YOU.
MANY YEARS OF HAPPY BEFORE I EAT YOU.
YEAH, NO.
THAT'S NOT HAPPENING.
WHAM!
NO CHOICE!
DRESS HER FOR CEREMONY.

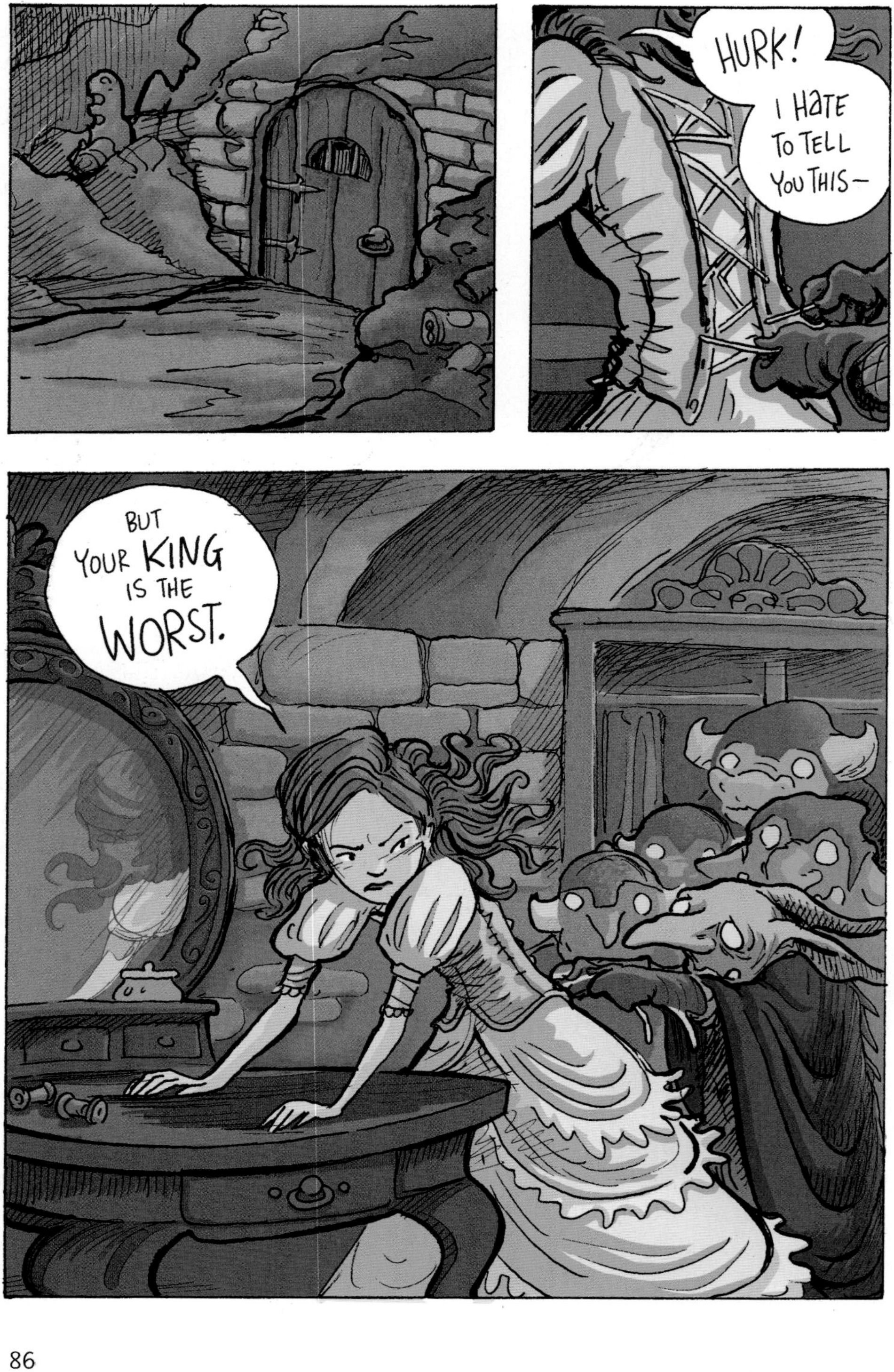
HURK!
I HATE TO TELL YOU THIS—
BUT YOUR KING IS THE WORST.

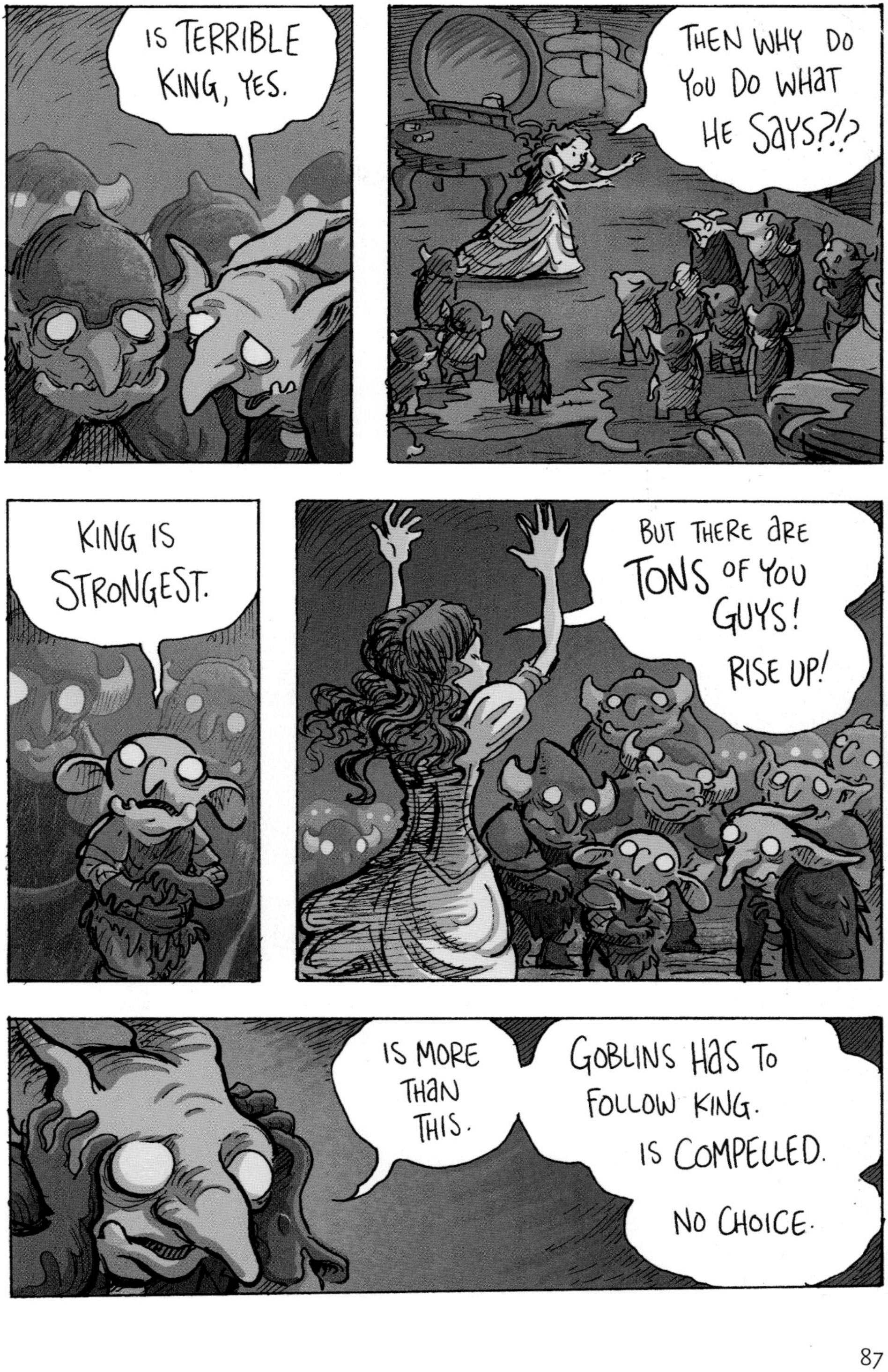
IS TERRIBLE KING, YES.
THEN WHY DO YOU DO WHAT HE SAYS?!?
KING IS STRONGEST.
BUT THERE ARE TONS OF YOU GUYS! RISE UP!
GOBLINS HAS TO FOLLOW KING. IS COMPELLED. NO CHOICE.
IS MORE THAN THIS.

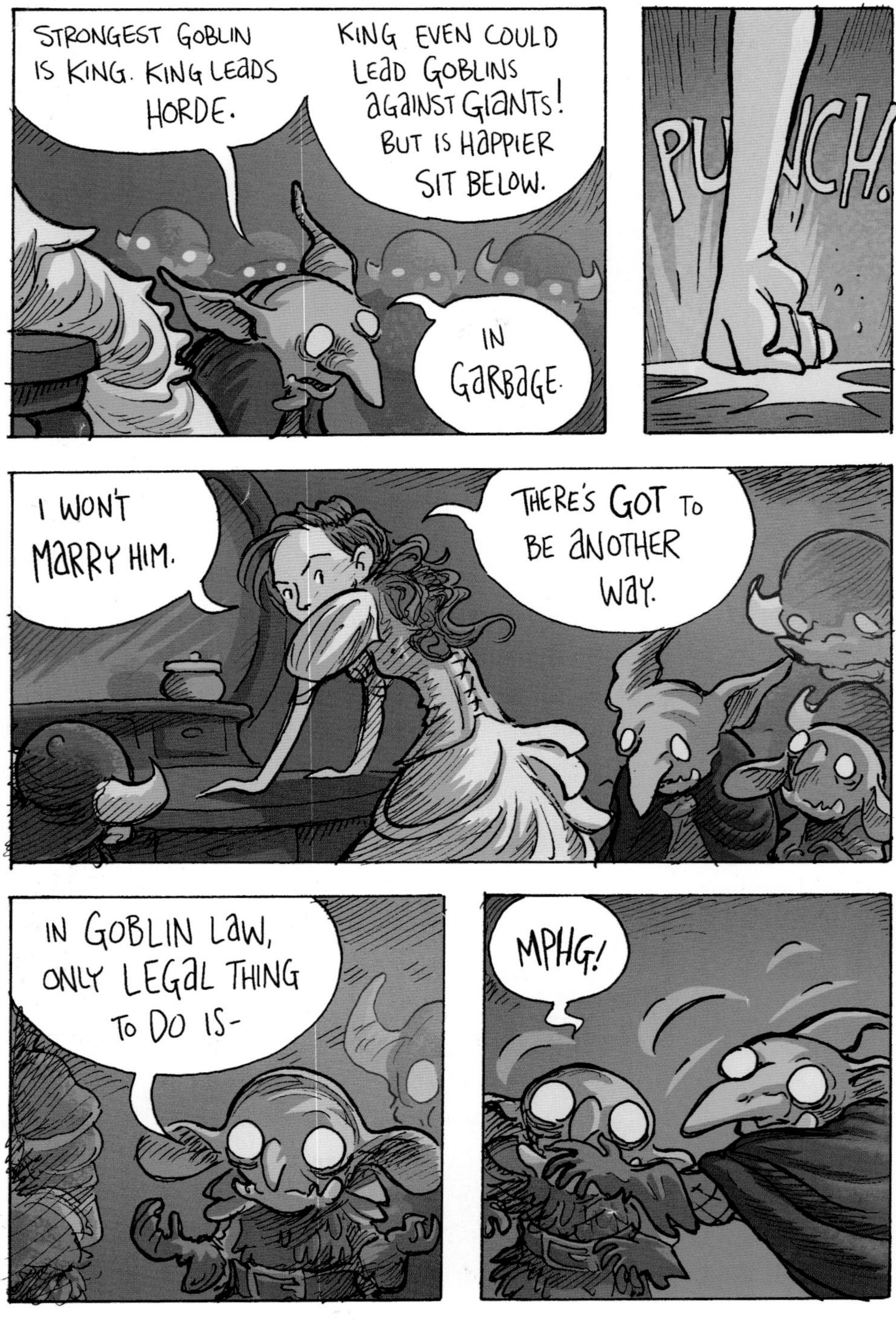
STRONGEST GOBLIN IS KING. KING LEADS HORDE.
KING EVEN COULD LEAD GOBLINS AGAINST GIANTS! BUT IS HAPPIER SIT BELOW.
IN GARBAGE.
PUNCH!
I WON'T MARRY HIM.
THERE'S GOT TO BE ANOTHER WAY.
IN GOBLIN LAW, ONLY LEGAL THING TO DO IS-
MPHG!

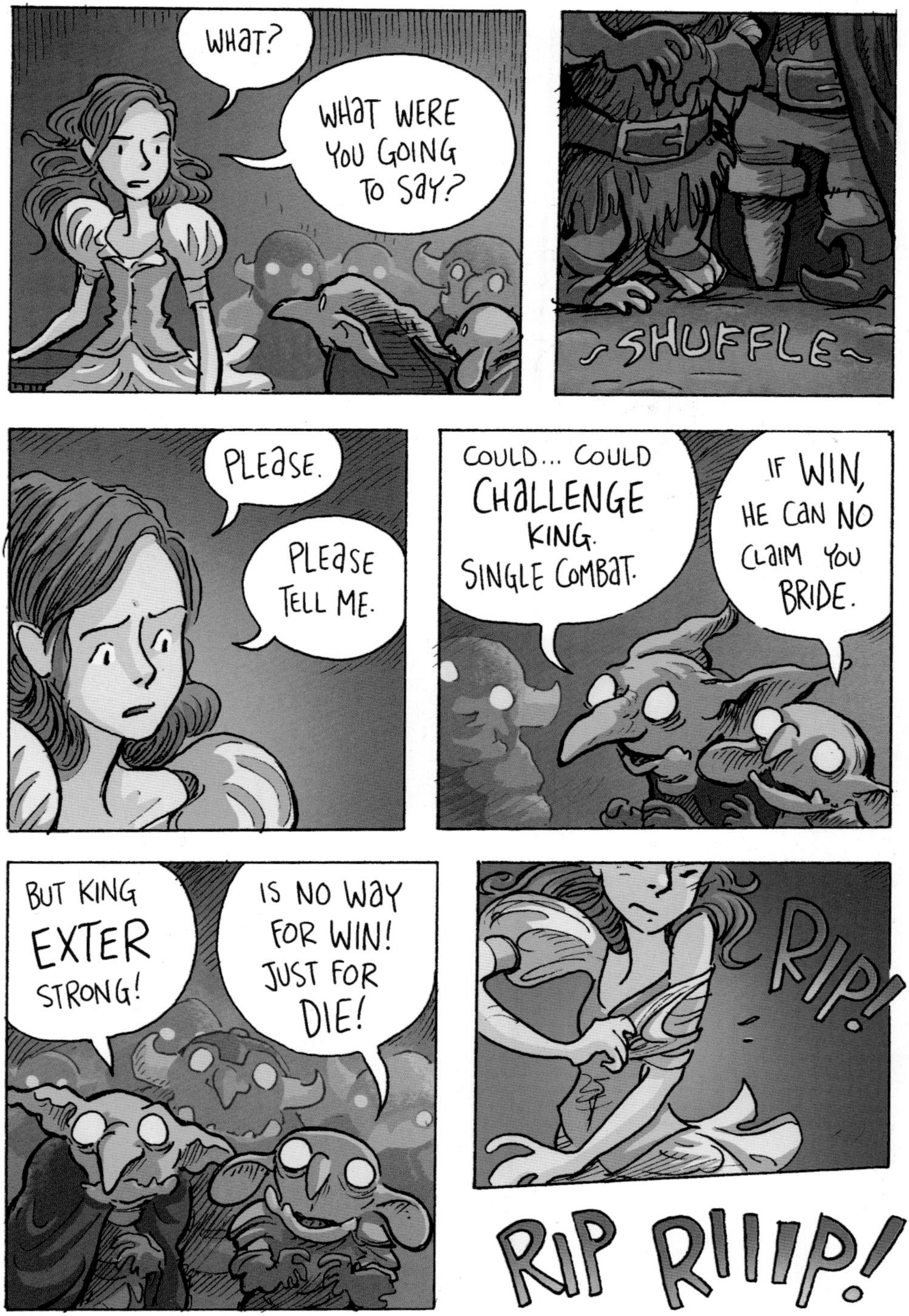
WHAT?
WHAT WERE YOU GOING TO SAY?
~SHUFFLE~
PLEASE.
PLEASE TELL ME.
COULD... COULD CHALLENGE KING. SINGLE COMBAT.
IF WIN, HE CAN NO CLAIM YOU BRIDE.
BUT KING EXTER STRONG!
IS NO WAY FOR WIN! JUST FOR DIE!
RIP!
RIP RIIIP!

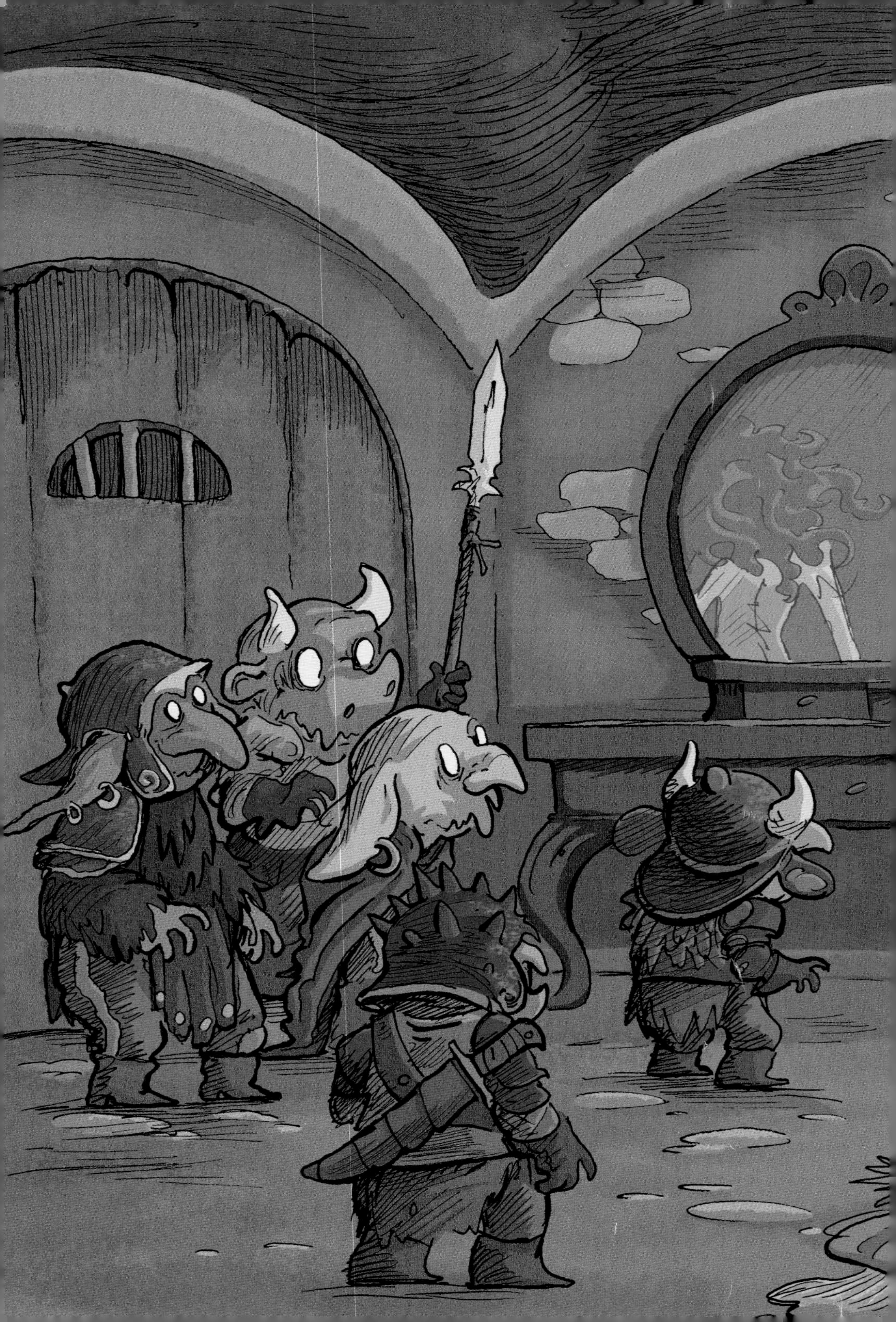

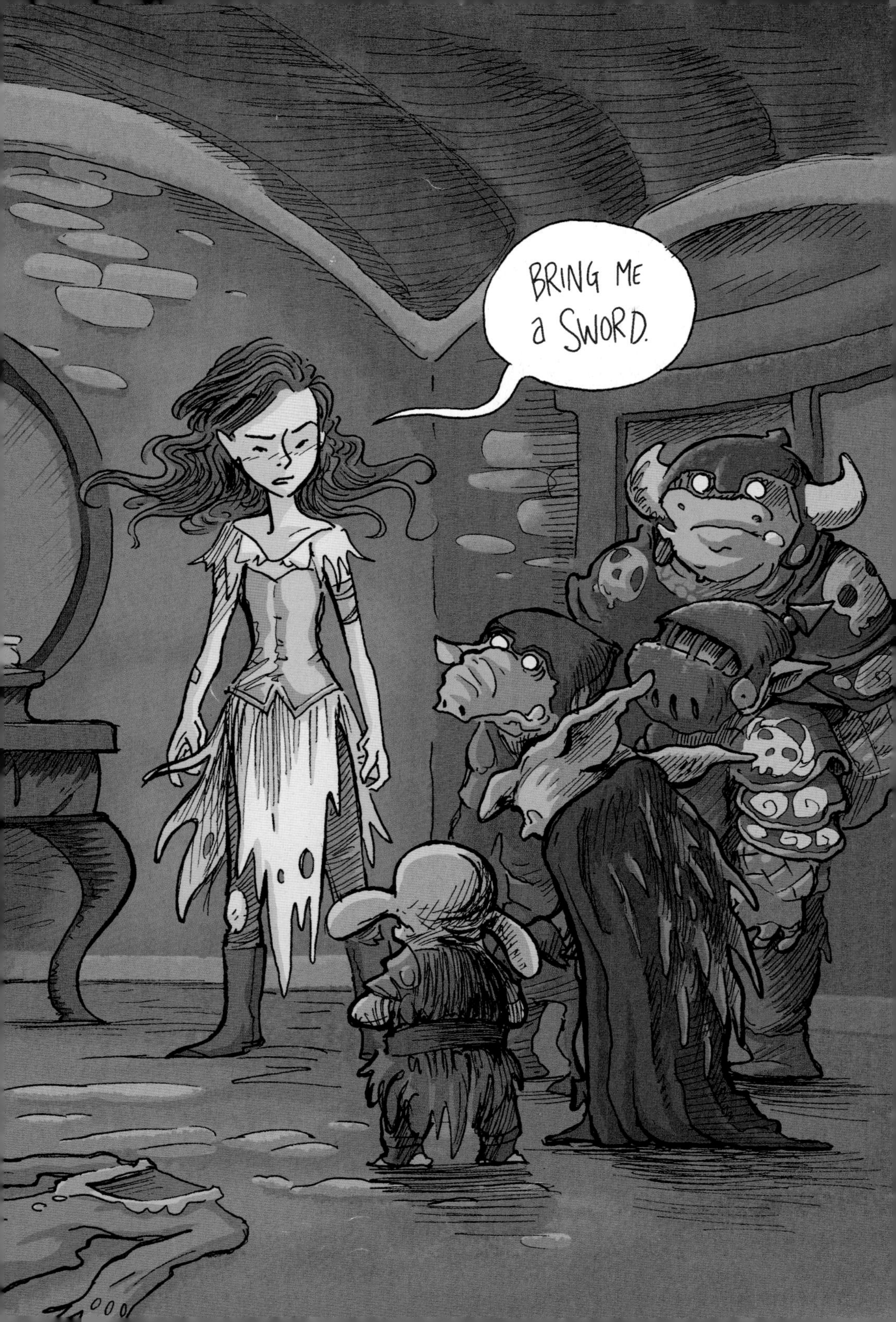
BRING ME a SWORD.

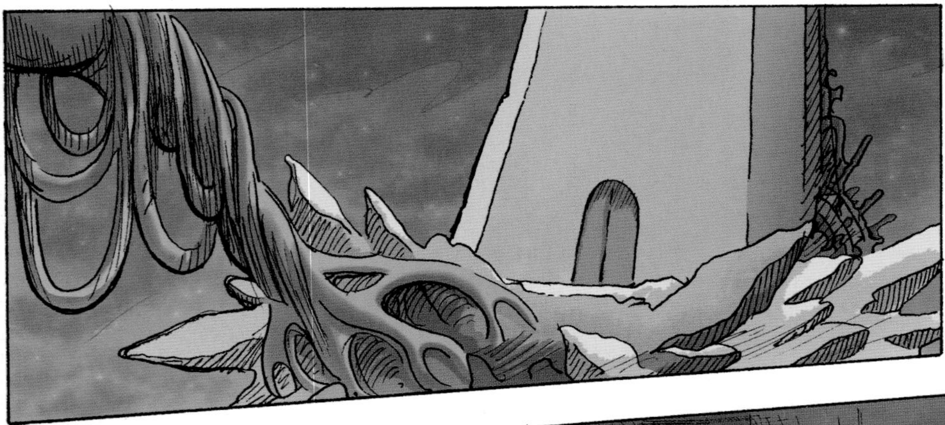

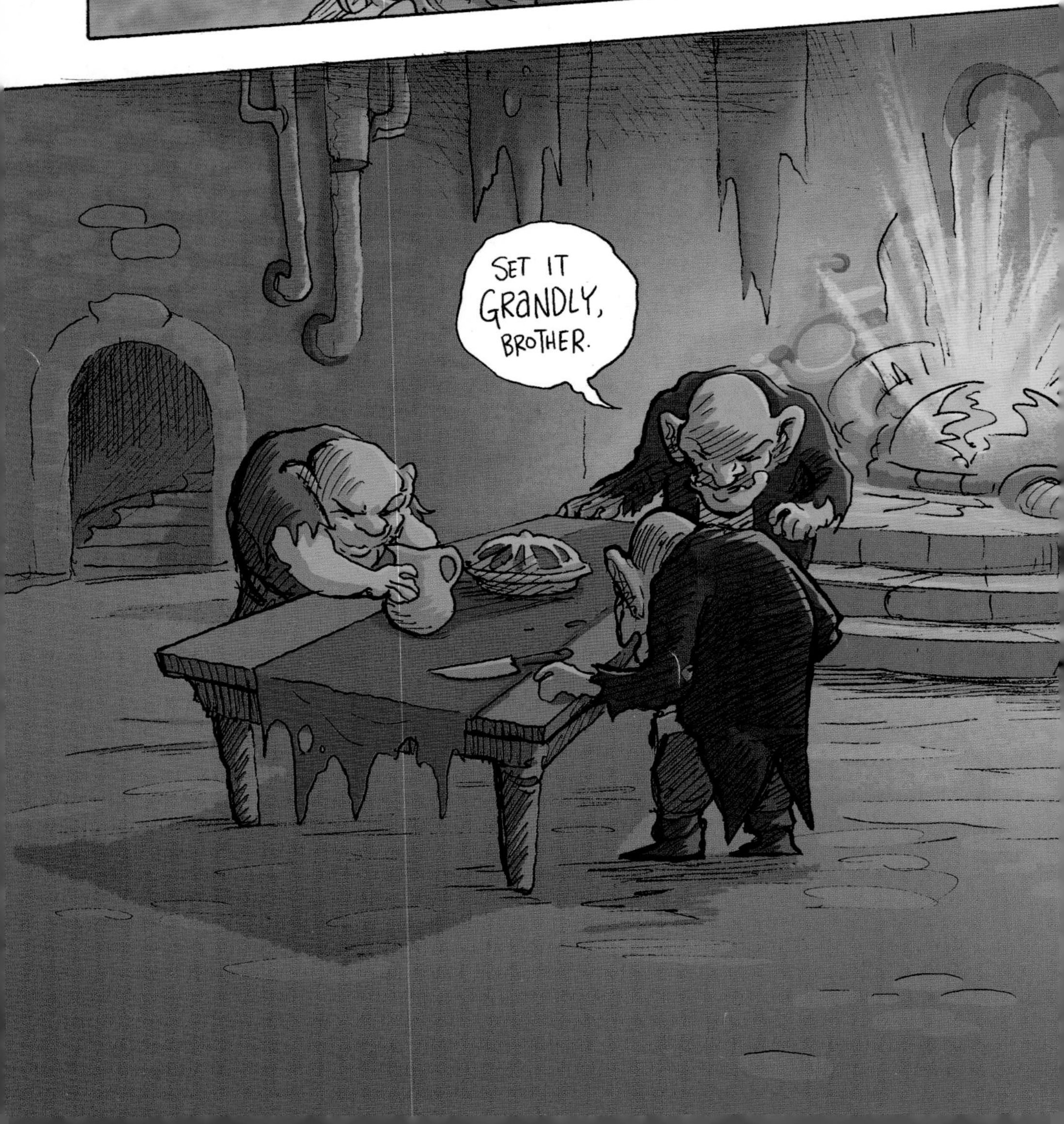
SET IT GRANDLY, BROTHER.

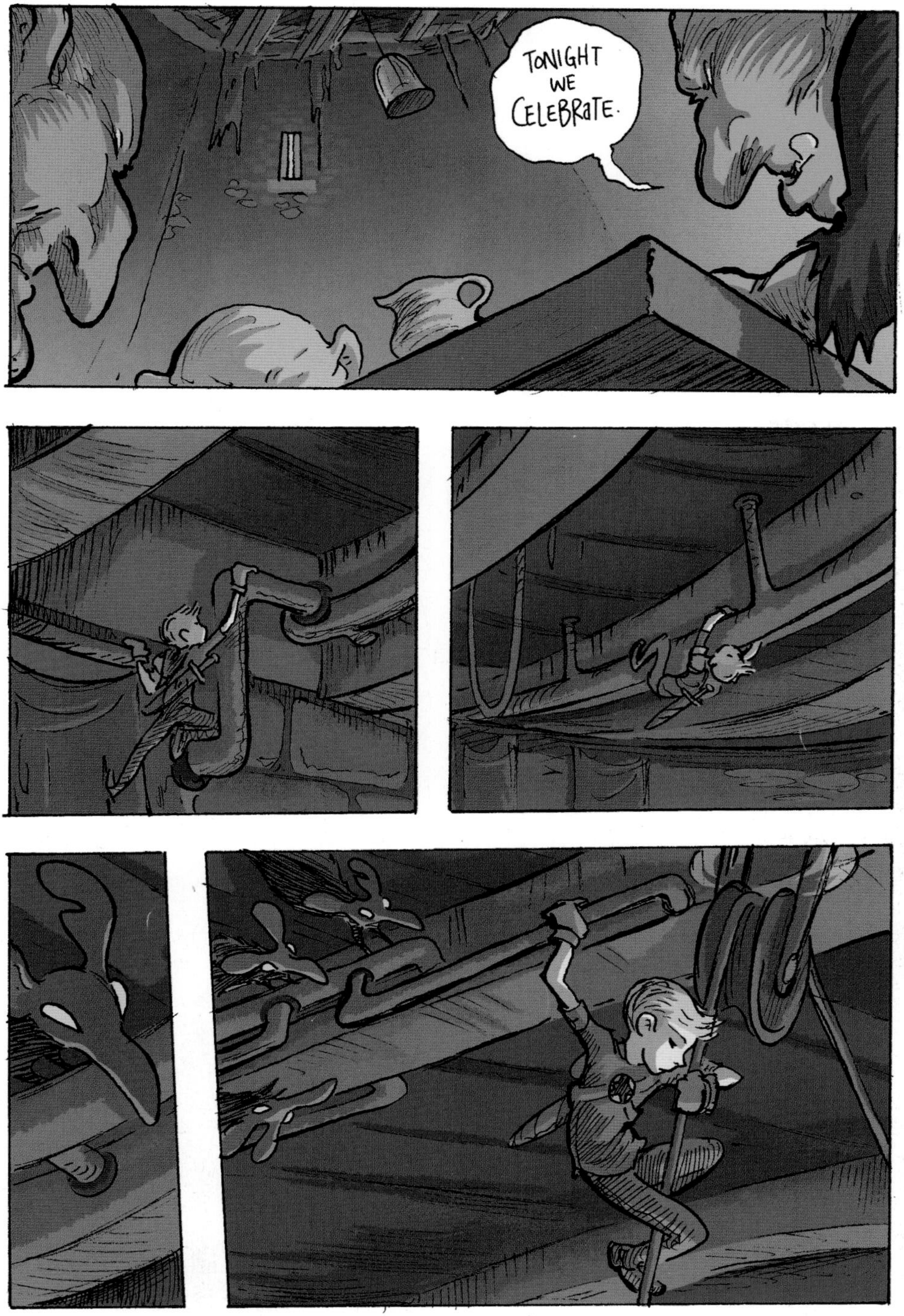
TONIGHT WE CELEBRATE.

PSST! MADDY!

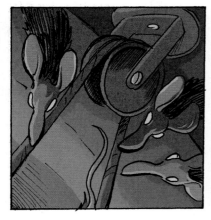

MADDY! UP HERE!

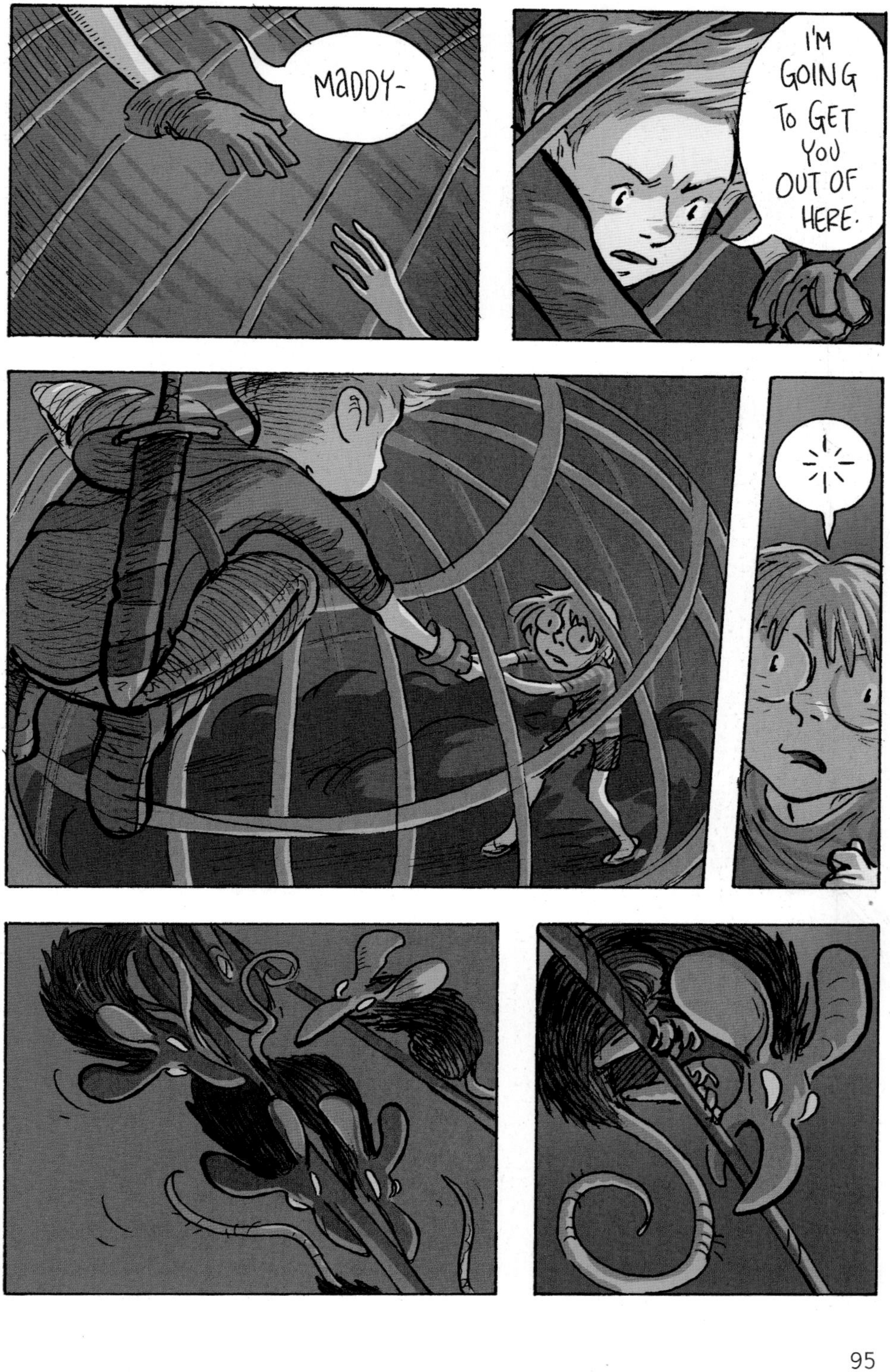
MADDY-
I'M GOING TO GET YOU OUT OF HERE.

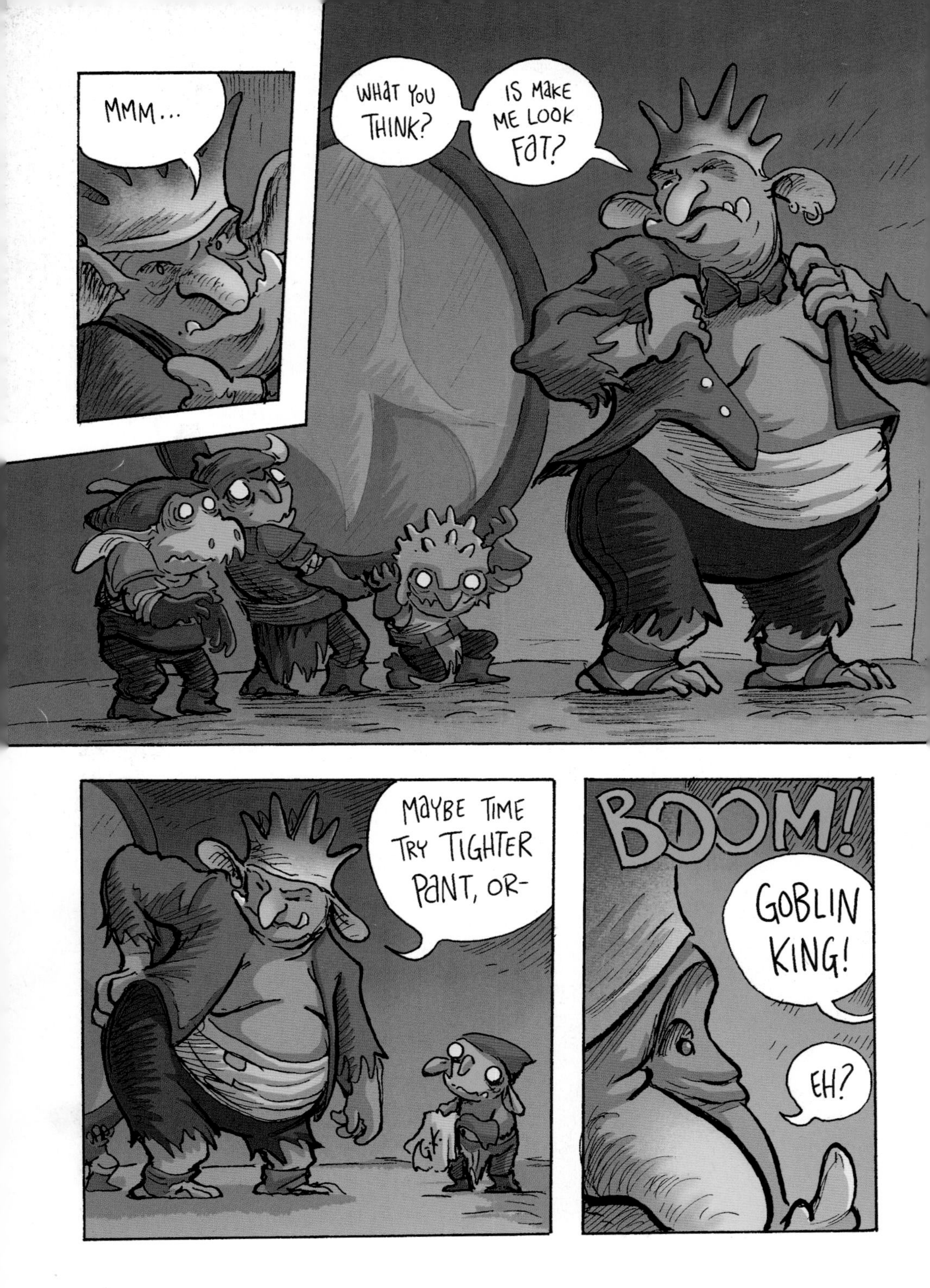
MMM...
WHAT YOU THINK?
IS MAKE ME LOOK FAT?
MAYBE TIME TRY TIGHTER PANT, OR-
BOOM!
GOBLIN KING!
EH?

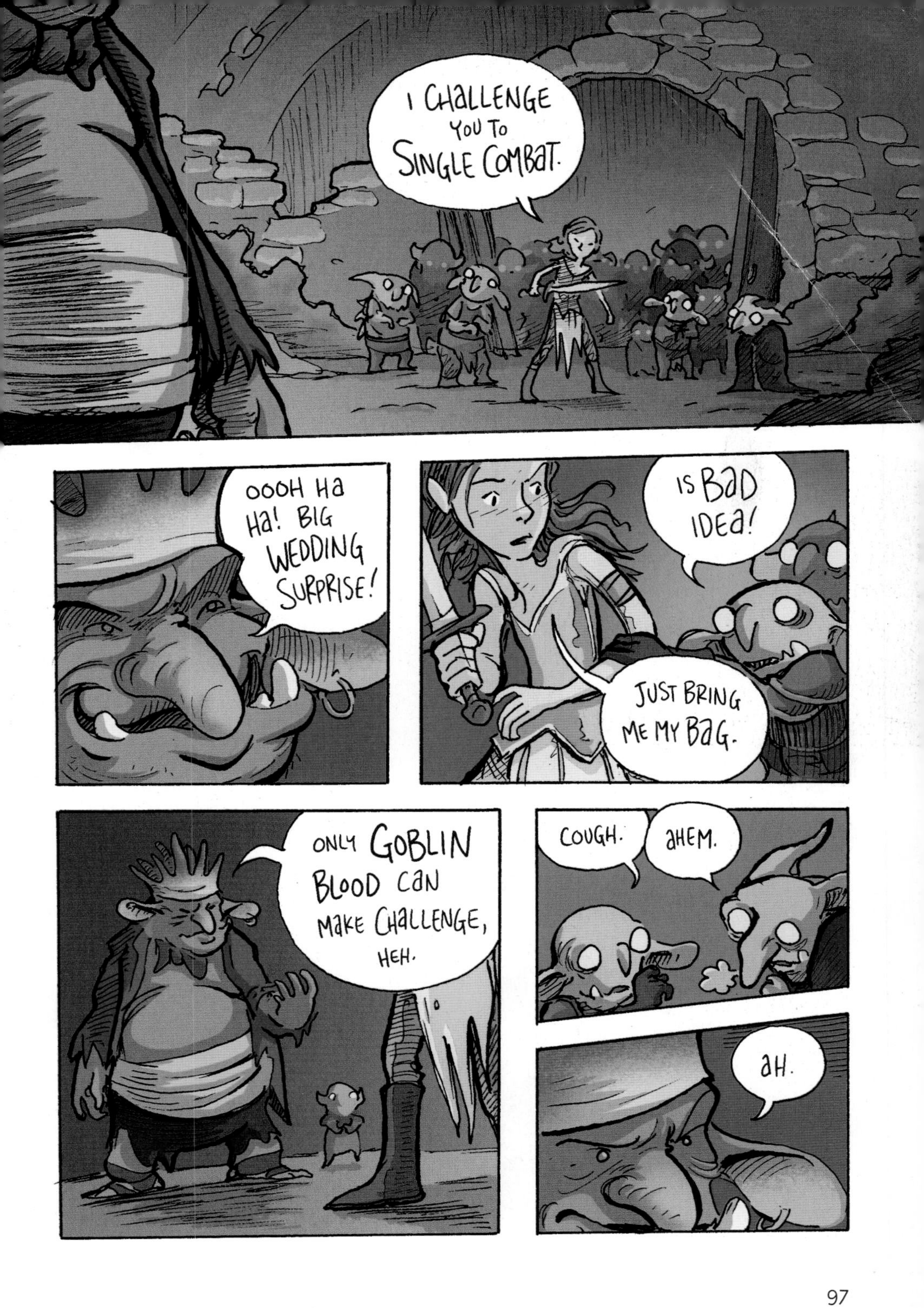
I CHALLENGE YOU TO SINGLE COMBAT.
OOOH HA HA! BIG WEDDING SURPRISE!
IS BAD IDEA!
JUST BRING ME MY BAG.
ONLY GOBLIN BLOOD CAN MAKE CHALLENGE, HEH.
COUGH.
AHEM.
AH.

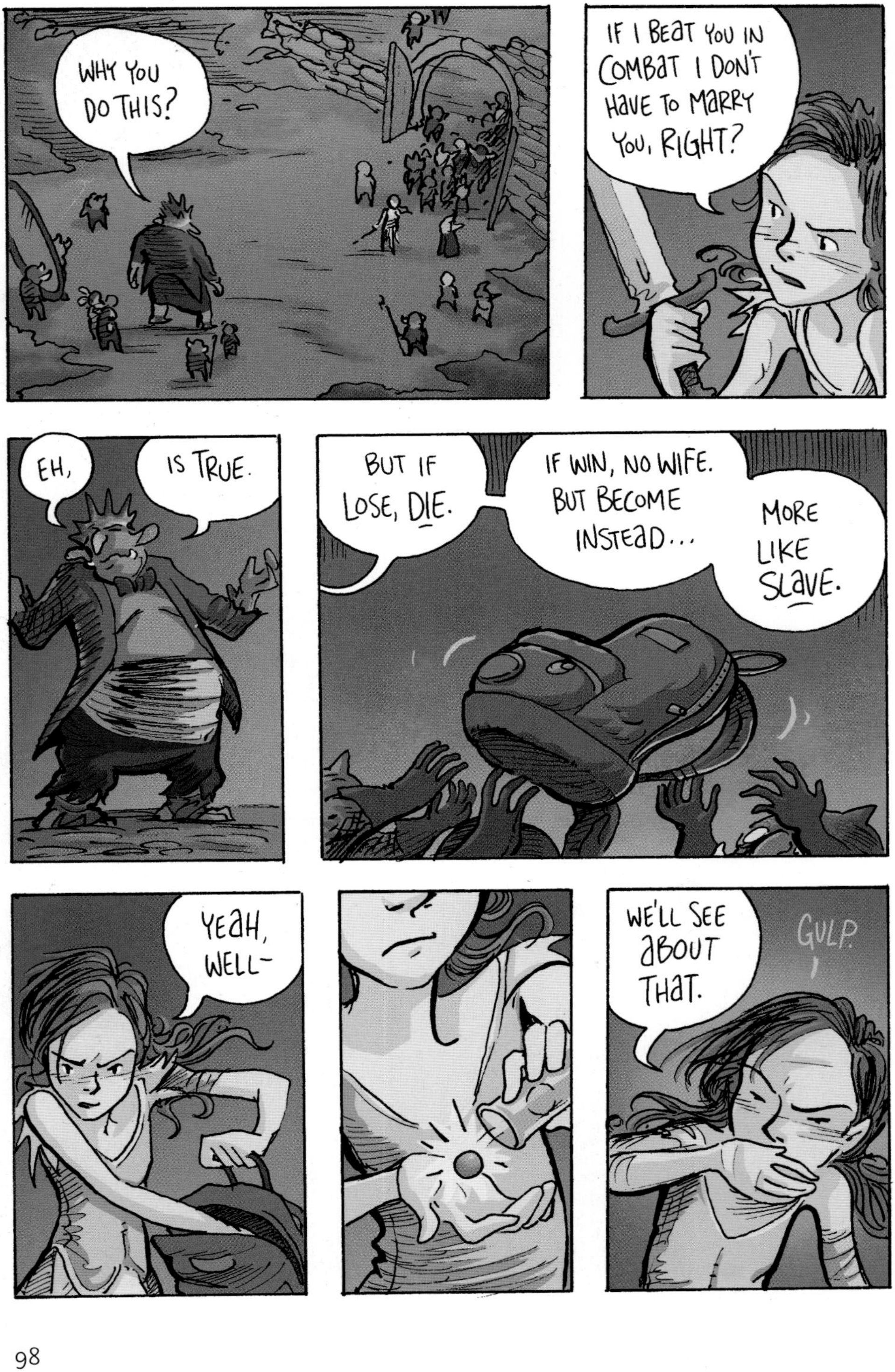
WHY YOU DO THIS?
IF I BEAT YOU IN COMBAT I DON'T HAVE TO MARRY YOU, RIGHT?
EH,
IS TRUE.
BUT IF LOSE, DIE.
IF WIN, NO WIFE. BUT BECOME INSTEAD...
MORE LIKE SLAVE.
YEAH, WELL-
WE'LL SEE ABOUT THAT.
GULP.

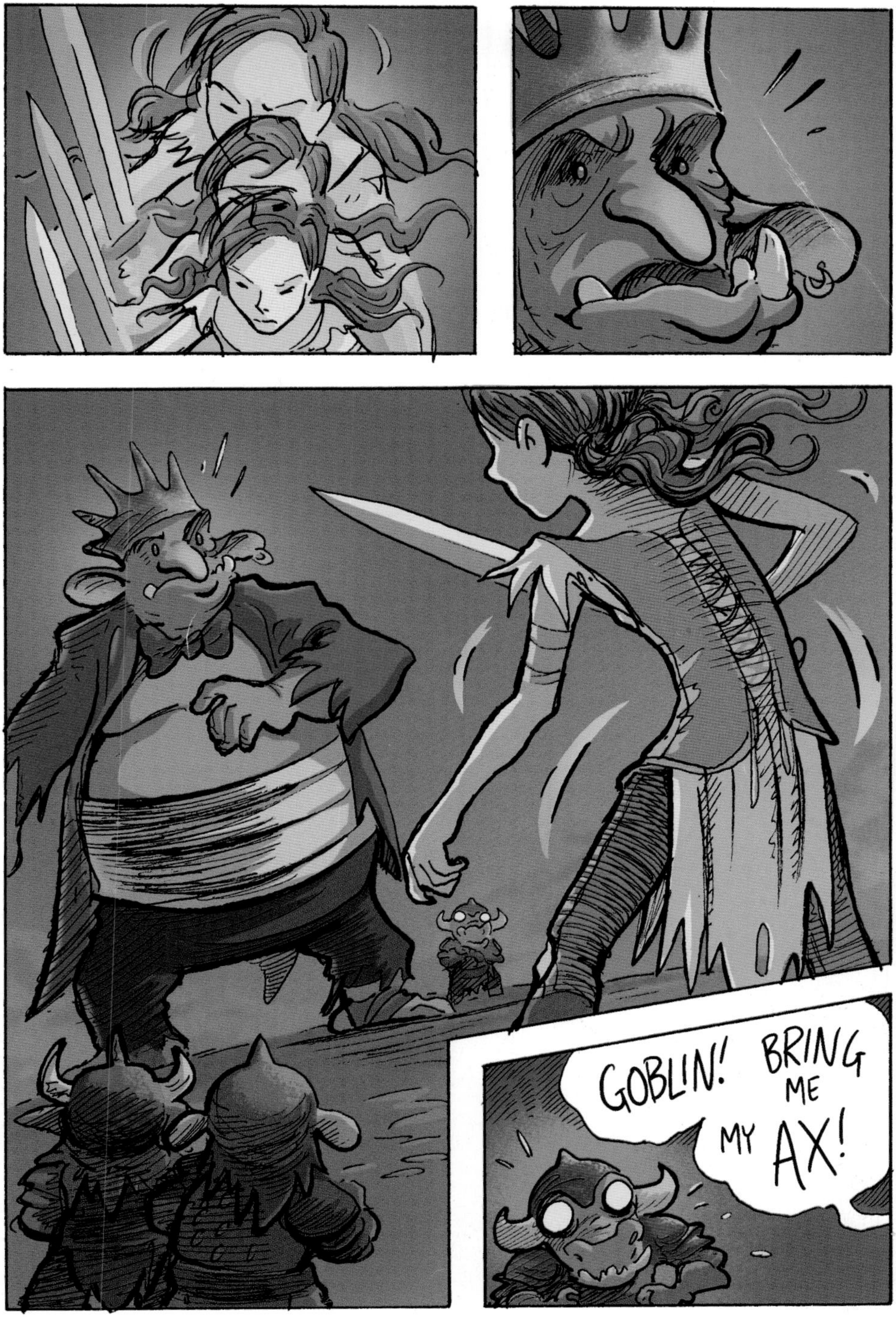
GOBLIN! BRING ME MY AX!

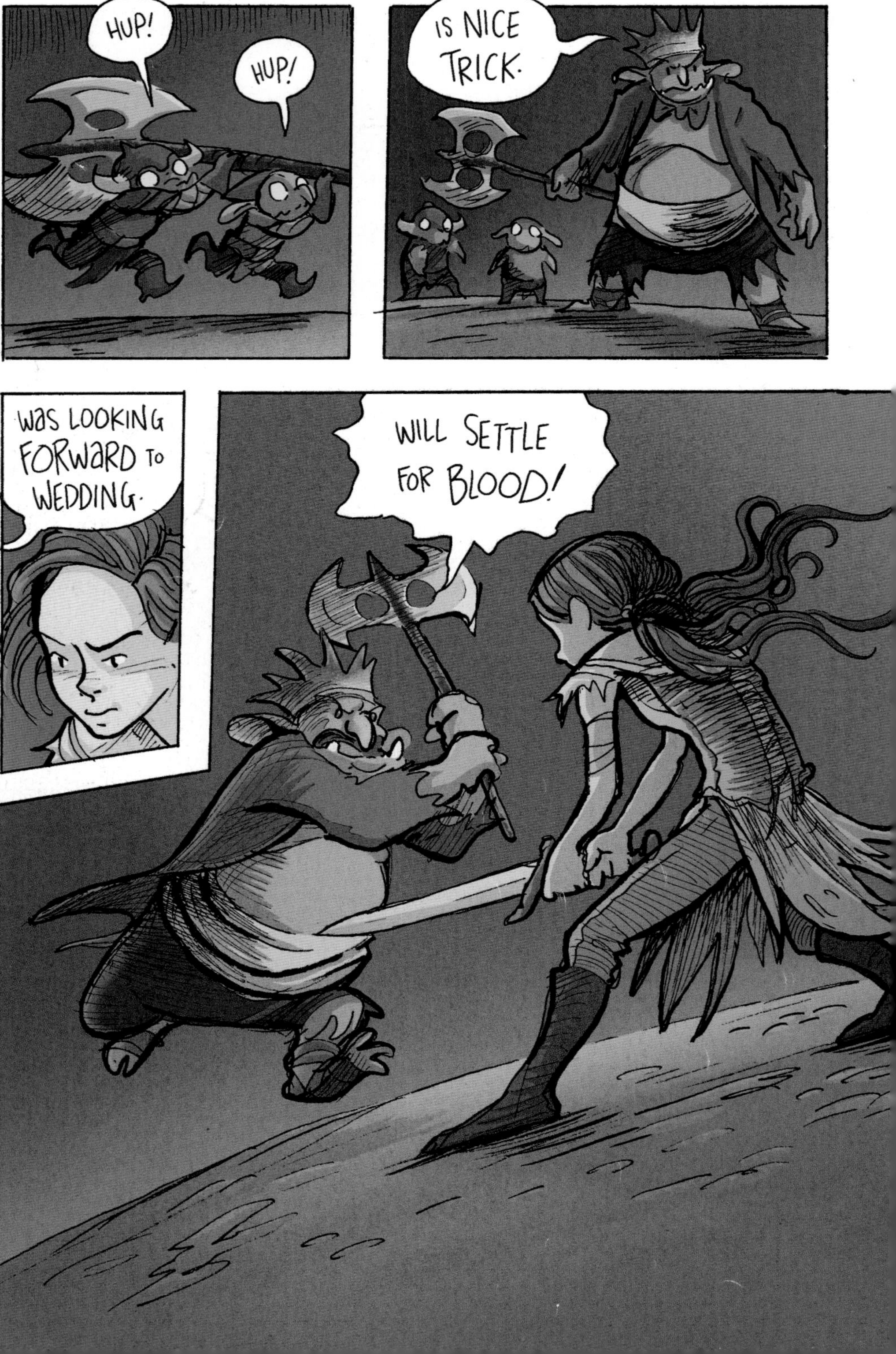
HUP!
HUP!
IS NICE TRICK.
WAS LOOKING FORWARD TO WEDDING.
WILL SETTLE FOR BLOOD!

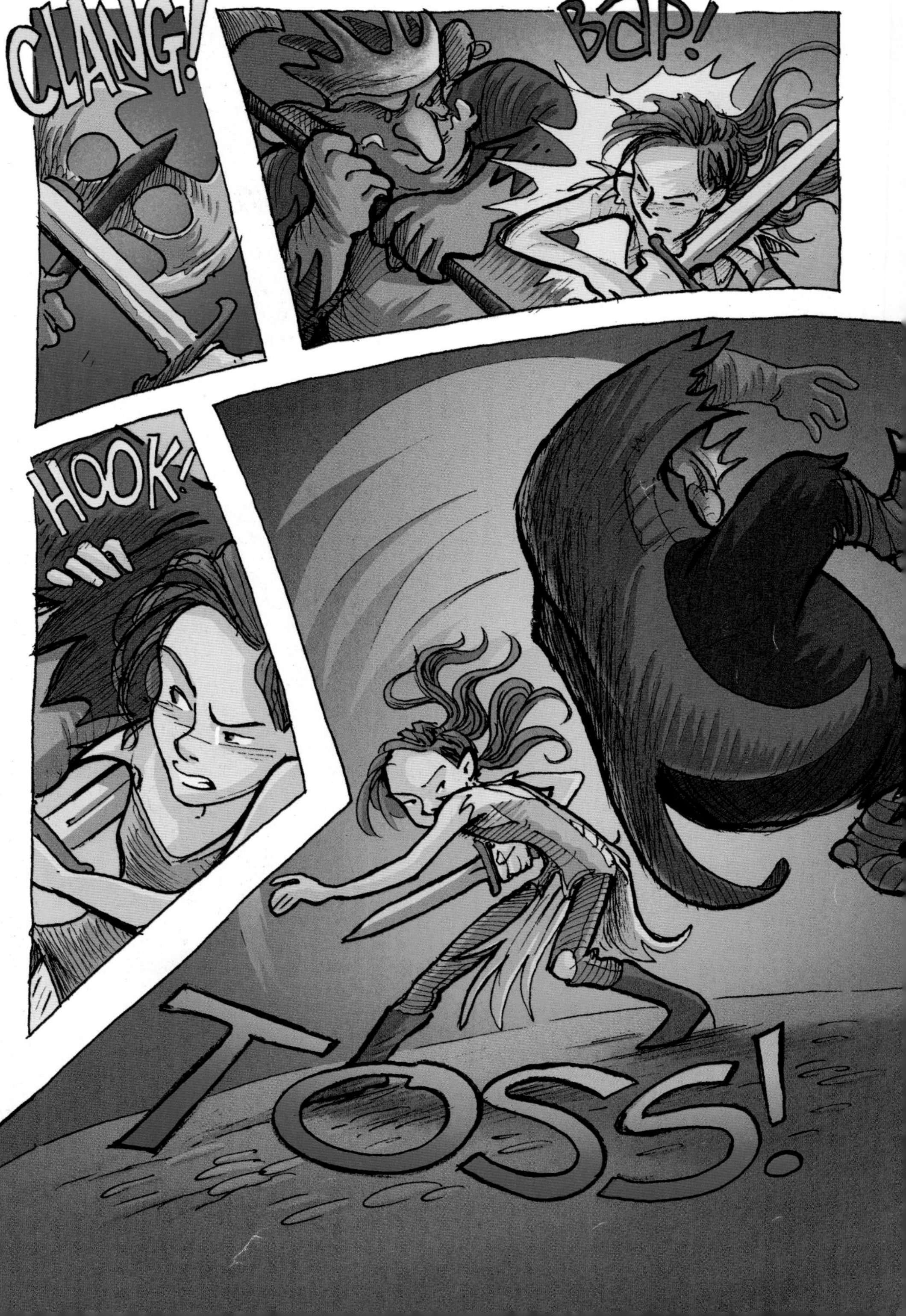
CLANG!
BAP!
HOOK!
TOSS!

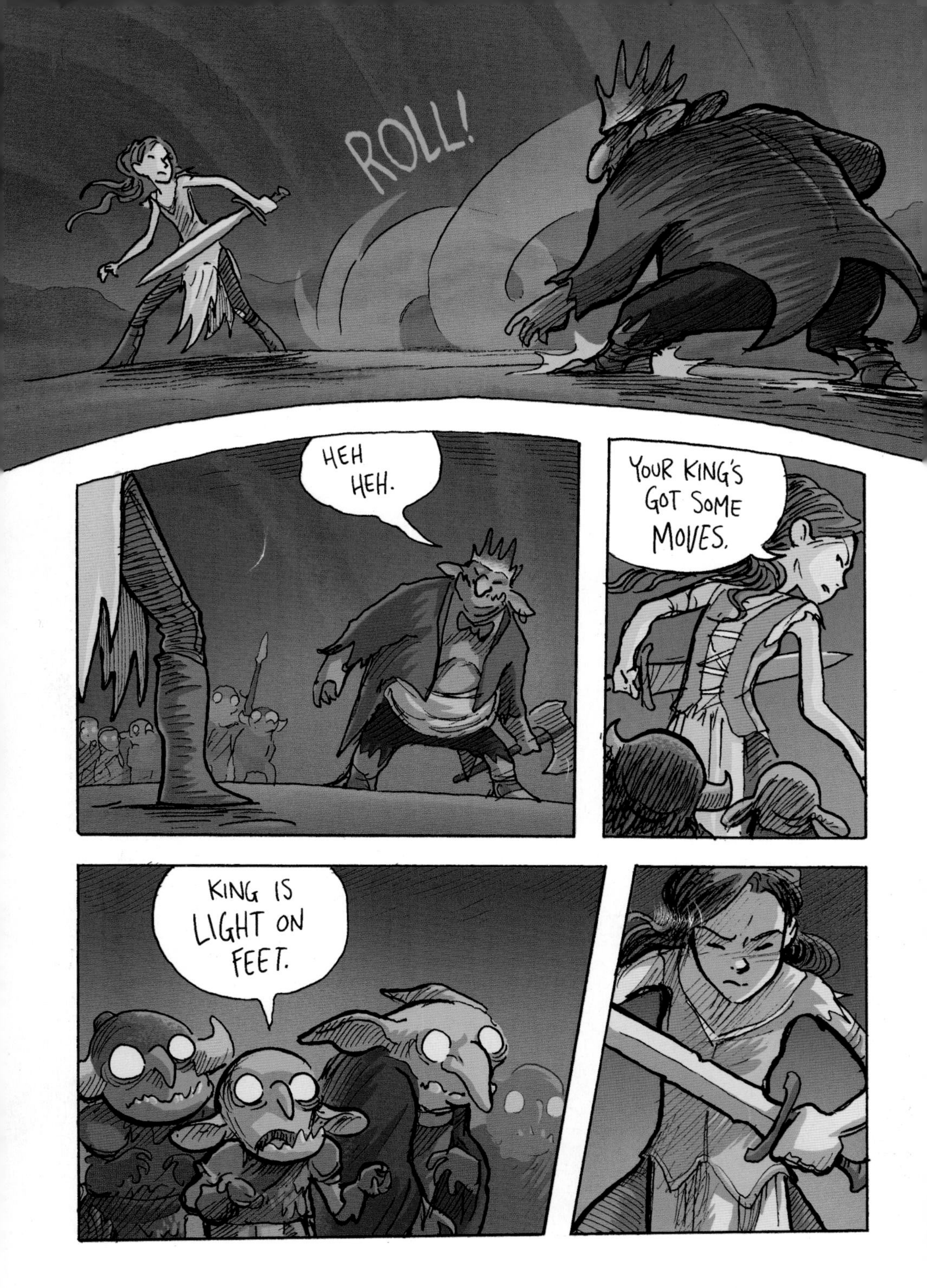
ROLL!
HEH HEH.
YOUR KING'S GOT SOME MOVES.
KING IS LIGHT ON FEET.

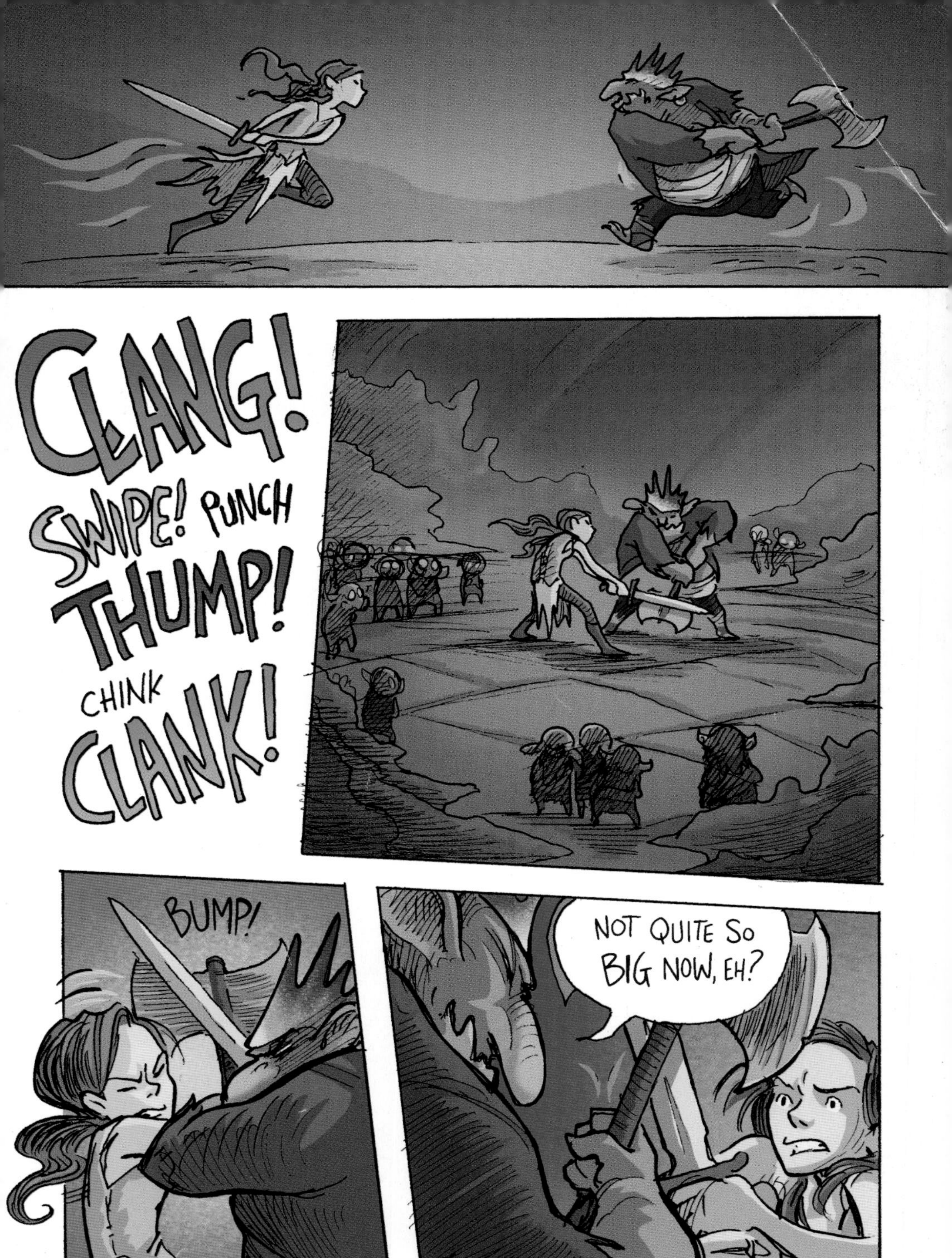
CLANG!
SWIPE! PUNCH
THUMP!
CHINK
CLANK!
BUMP!
NOT QUITE SO BIG NOW, EH?

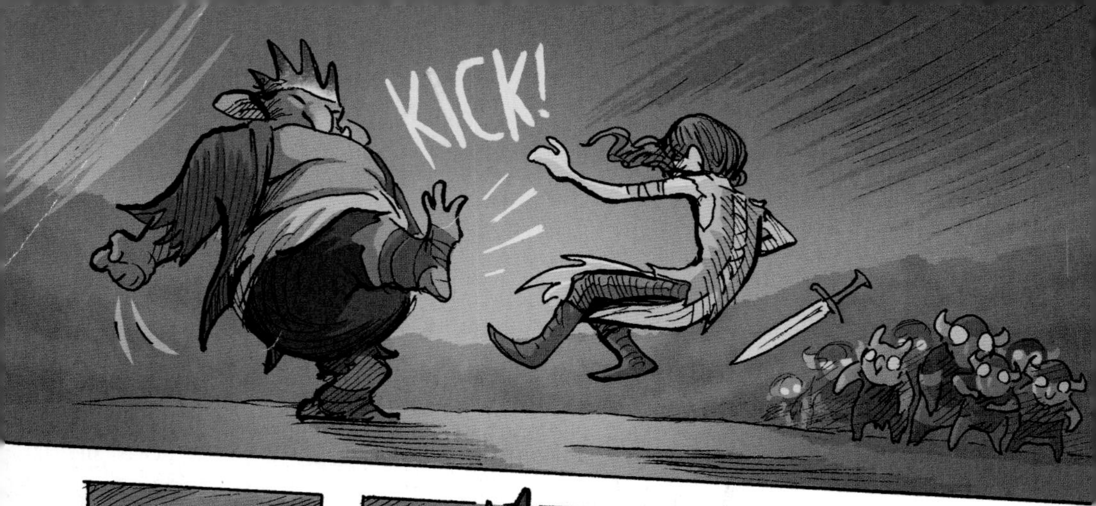
KICK!

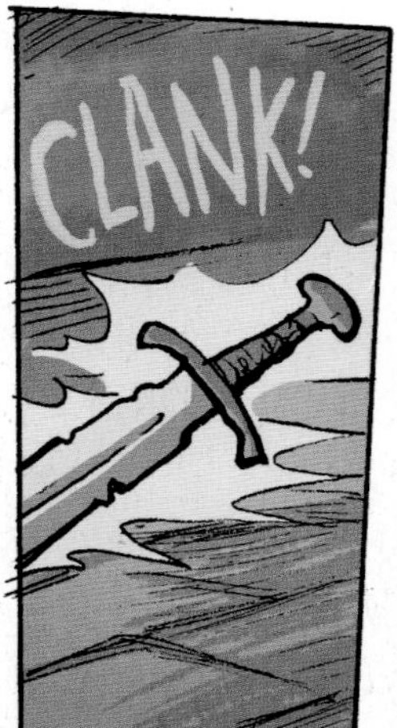
CLANK!

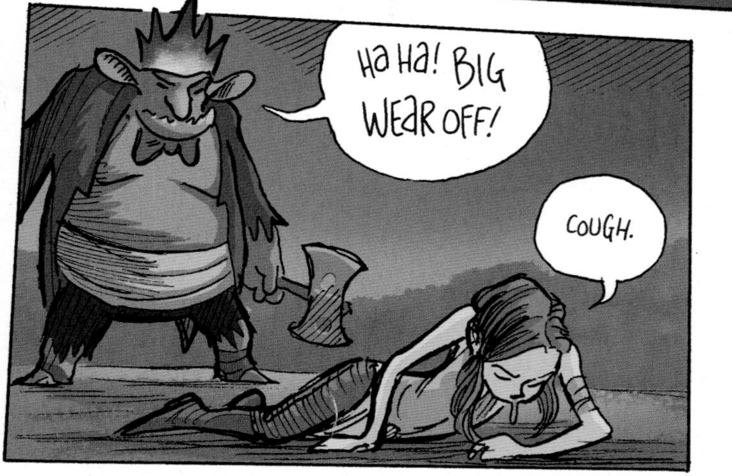
HA HA! BIG WEAR OFF!
COUGH.

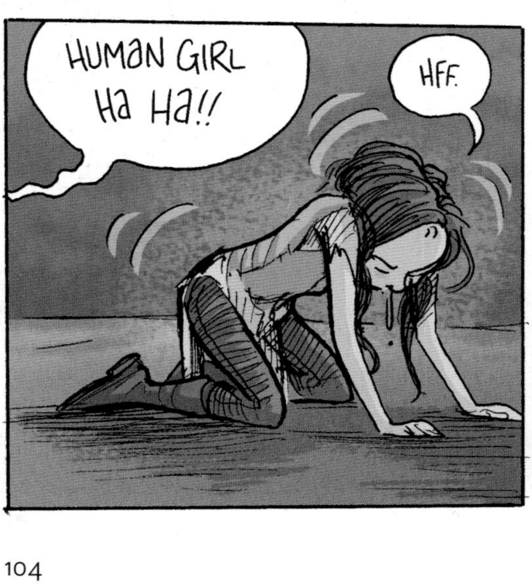
HUMAN GIRL HA HA!!
HFF.

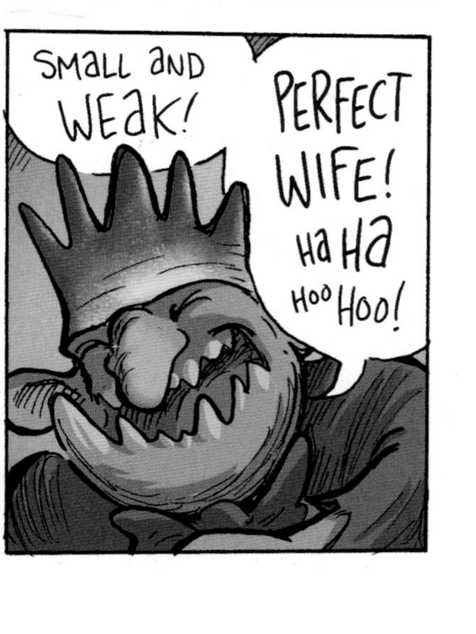
SMALL AND WEAK!
PERFECT WIFE! HA HA HOO HOO!

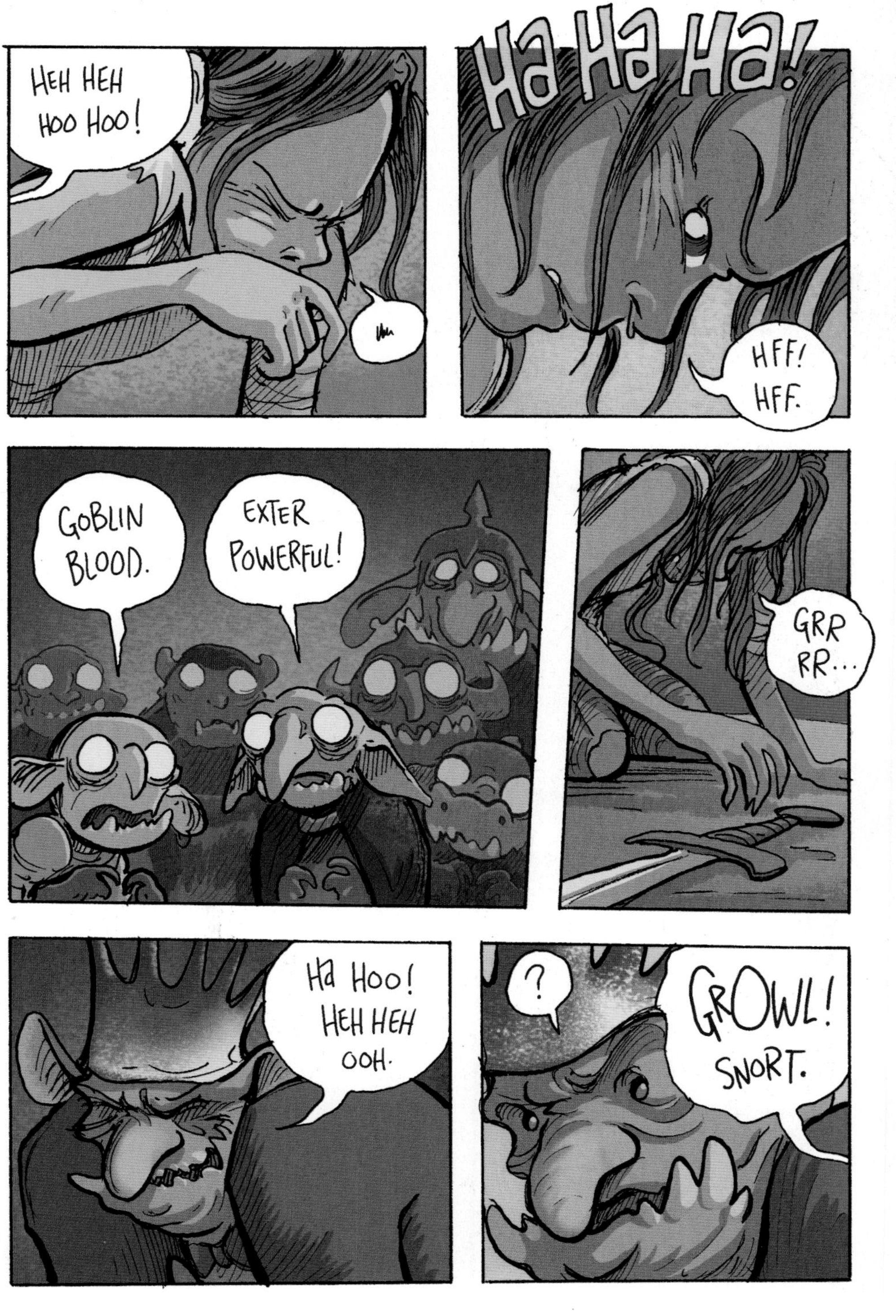
HEH HEH HOO HOO!
HA HA HA HA!
HFF! HFF.
GOBLIN BLOOD.
EXTER POWERFUL!
GRR RR...
HA HOO! HEH HEH OOH.
?
GROWL! SNORT.

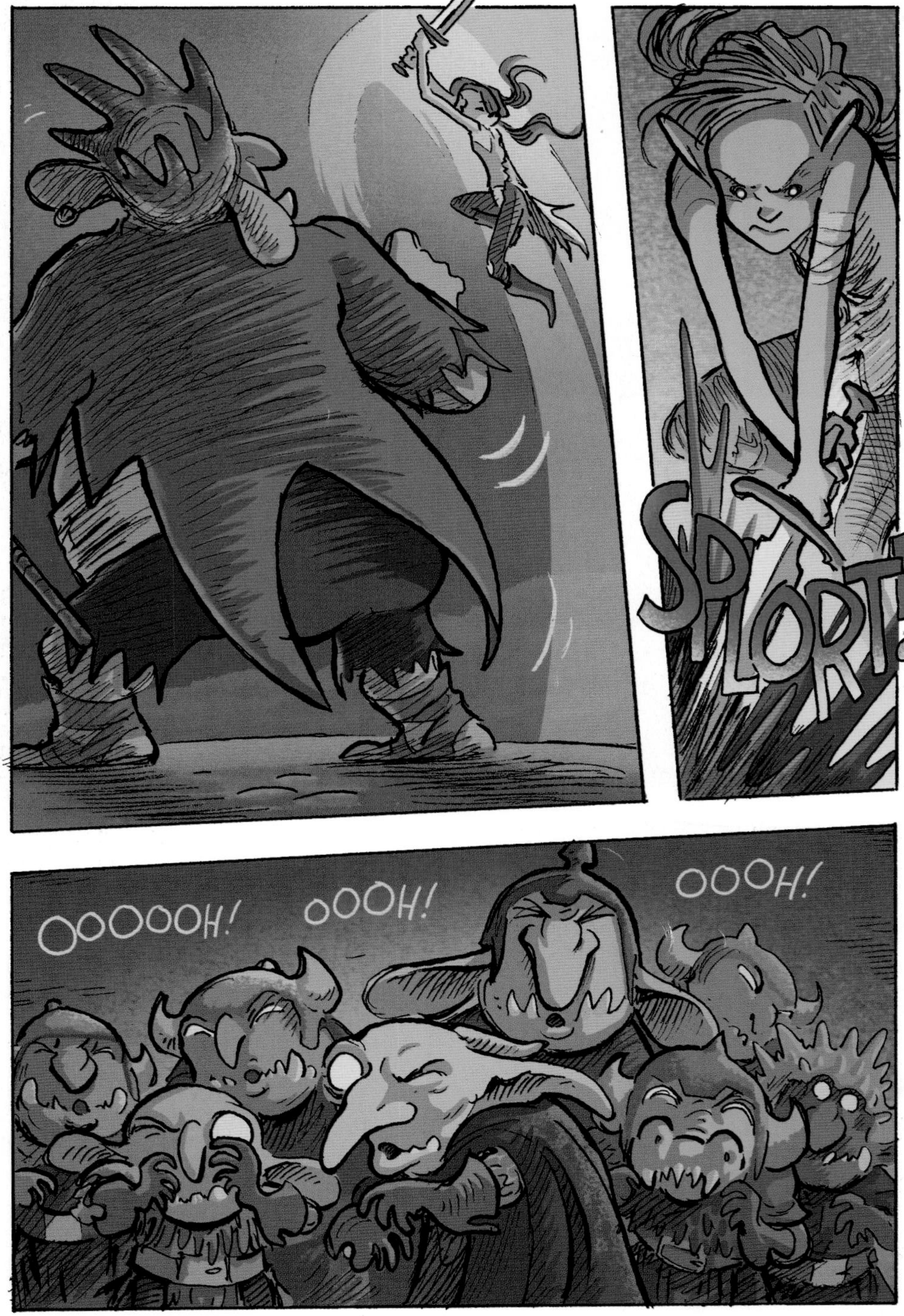
SPLORT!
OOOOOH!
OOOH!
OOOH!

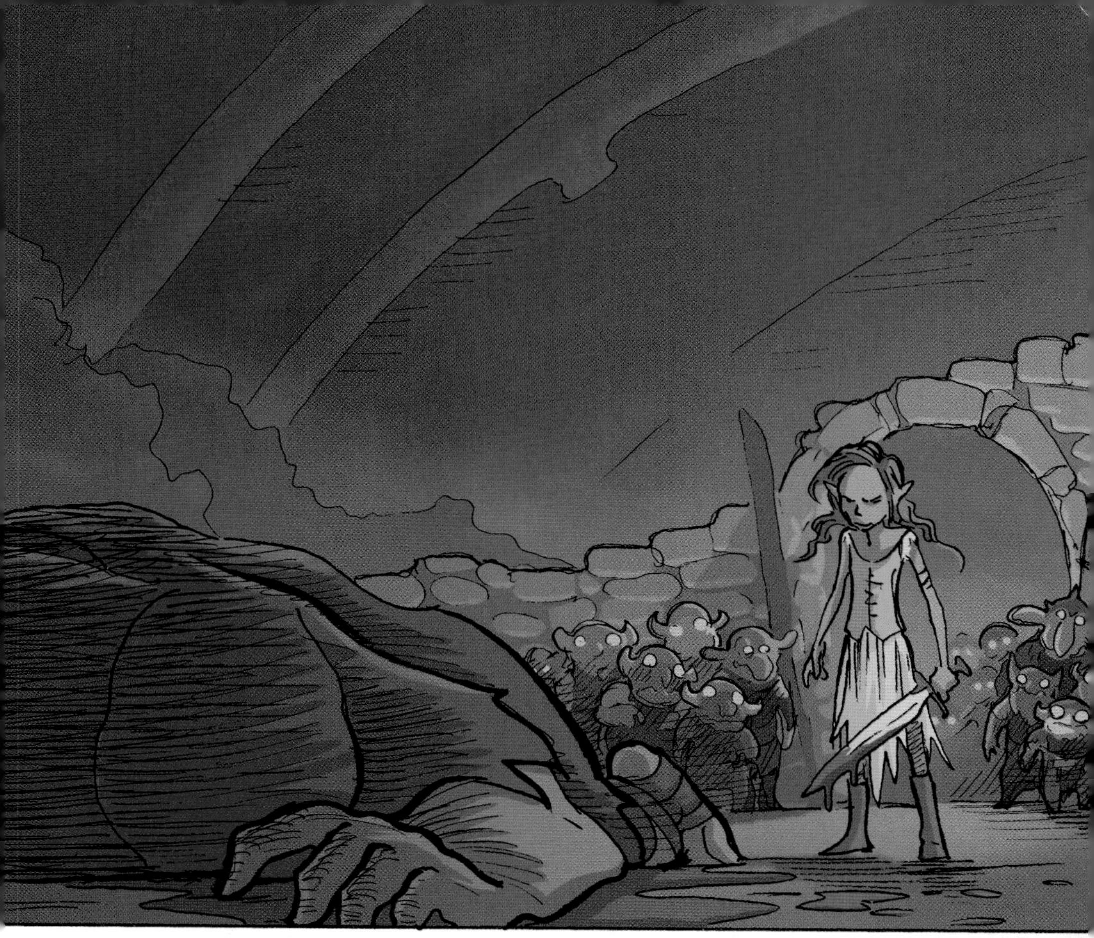

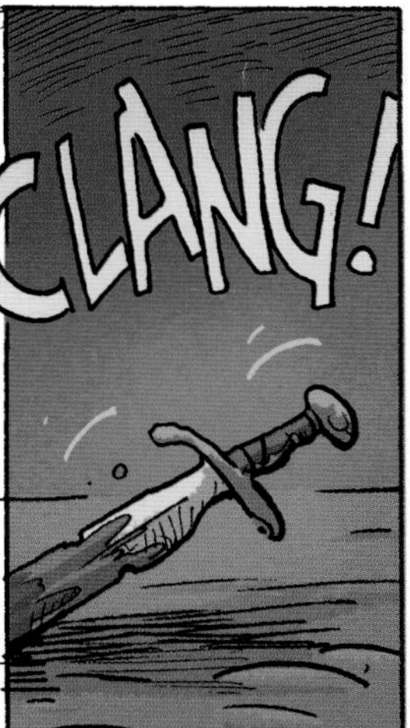
CLANG!

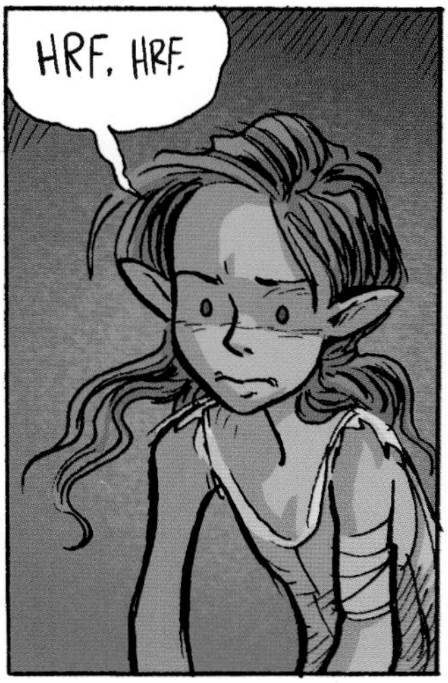
HRF. HRF.

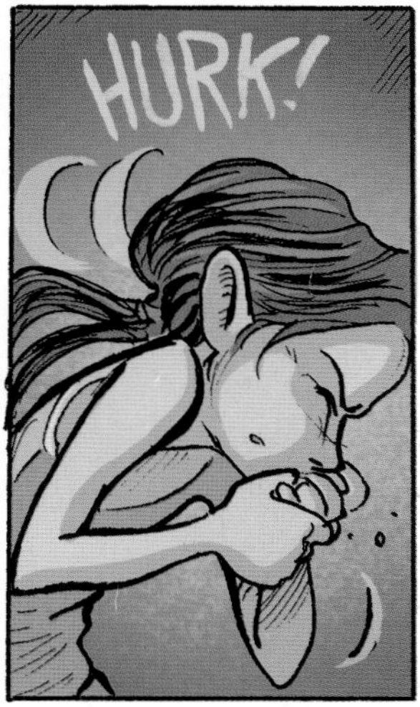
HURK!

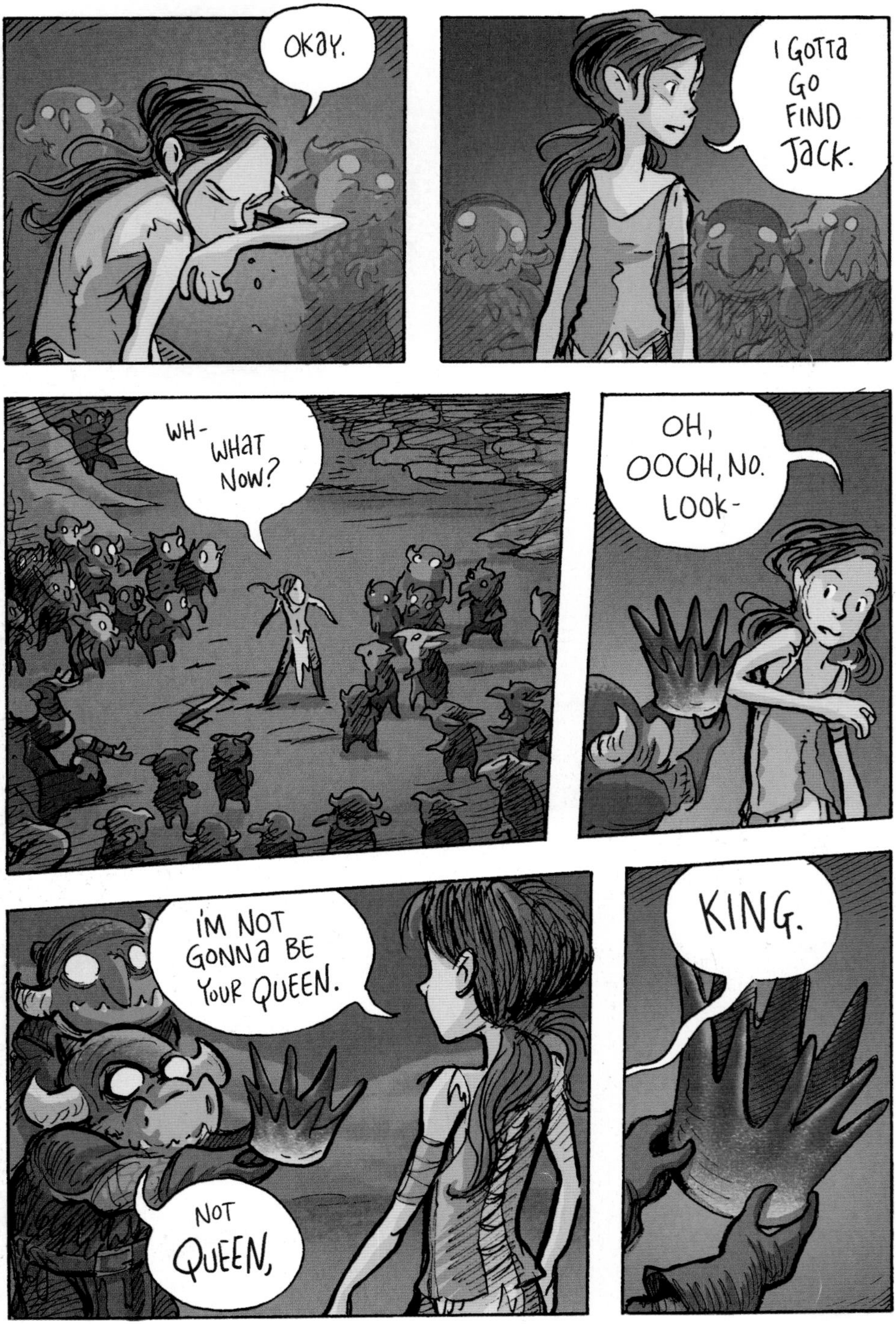
OKAY.
I GOTTA GO FIND JACK.
WH- WHAT NOW?
OH, OOOH, NO. LOOK-
I'M NOT GONNA BE YOUR QUEEN.
NOT QUEEN,
KING.

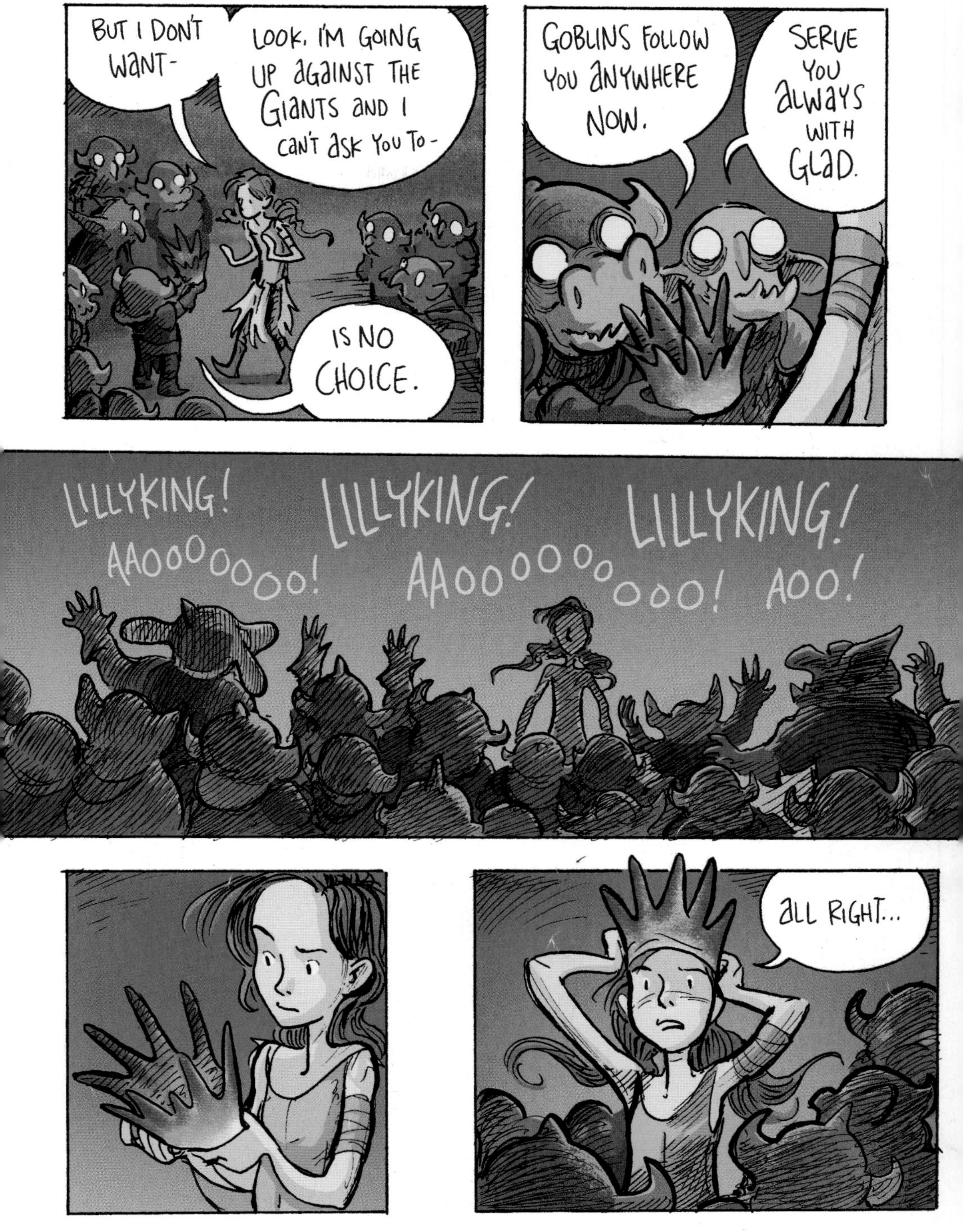
BUT I DON'T WANT-
LOOK. I'M GOING UP AGAINST THE GIANTS AND I CAN'T ASK YOU TO-
IS NO CHOICE.
GOBLINS FOLLOW YOU ANYWHERE NOW.
SERVE YOU ALWAYS WITH GLAD.
LILLYKING! AAOOOOOOO! LILLYKING! AAOOOOOOOOO! LILLYKING! AOO!
ALL RIGHT...

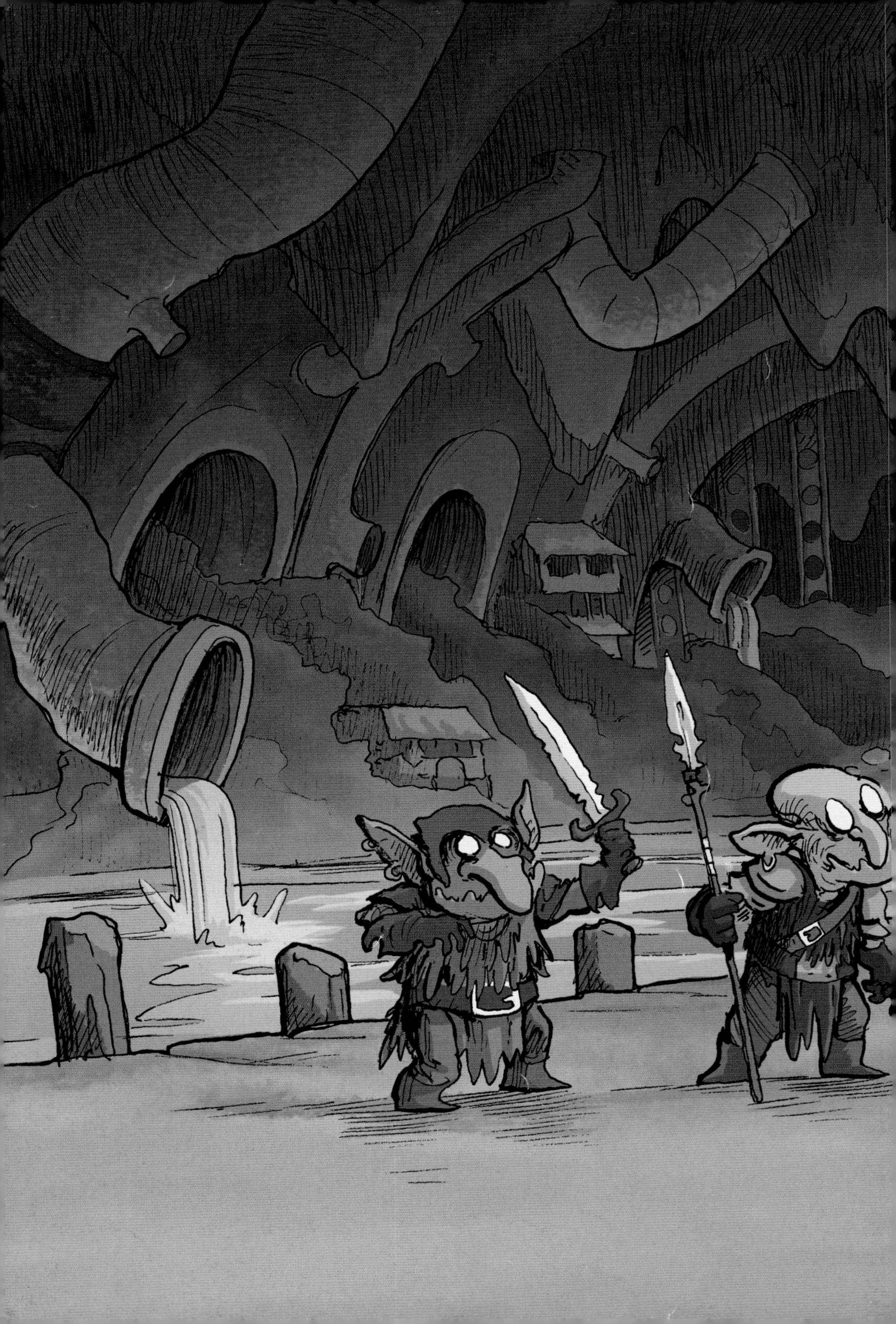

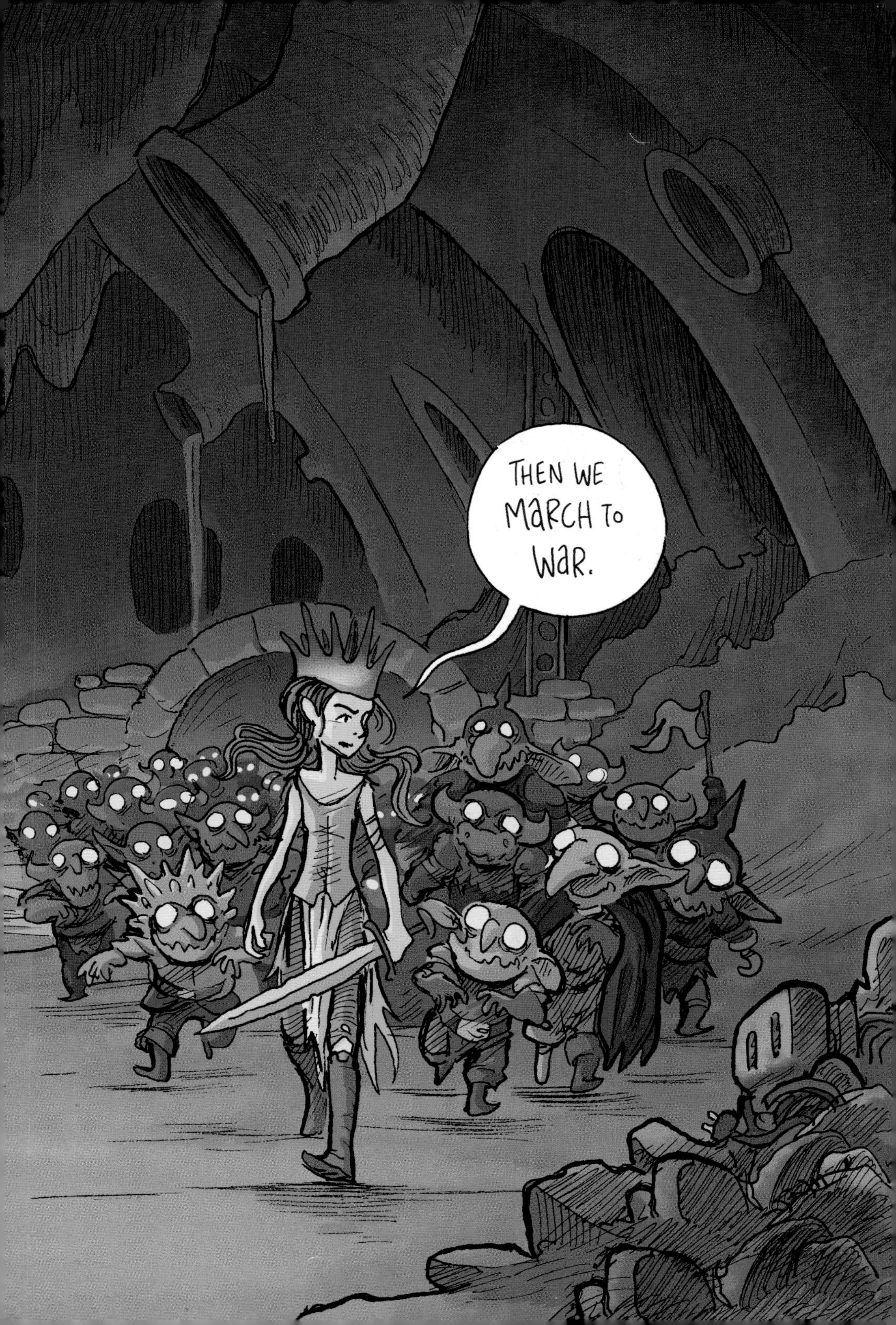
THEN WE MARCH TO WAR.

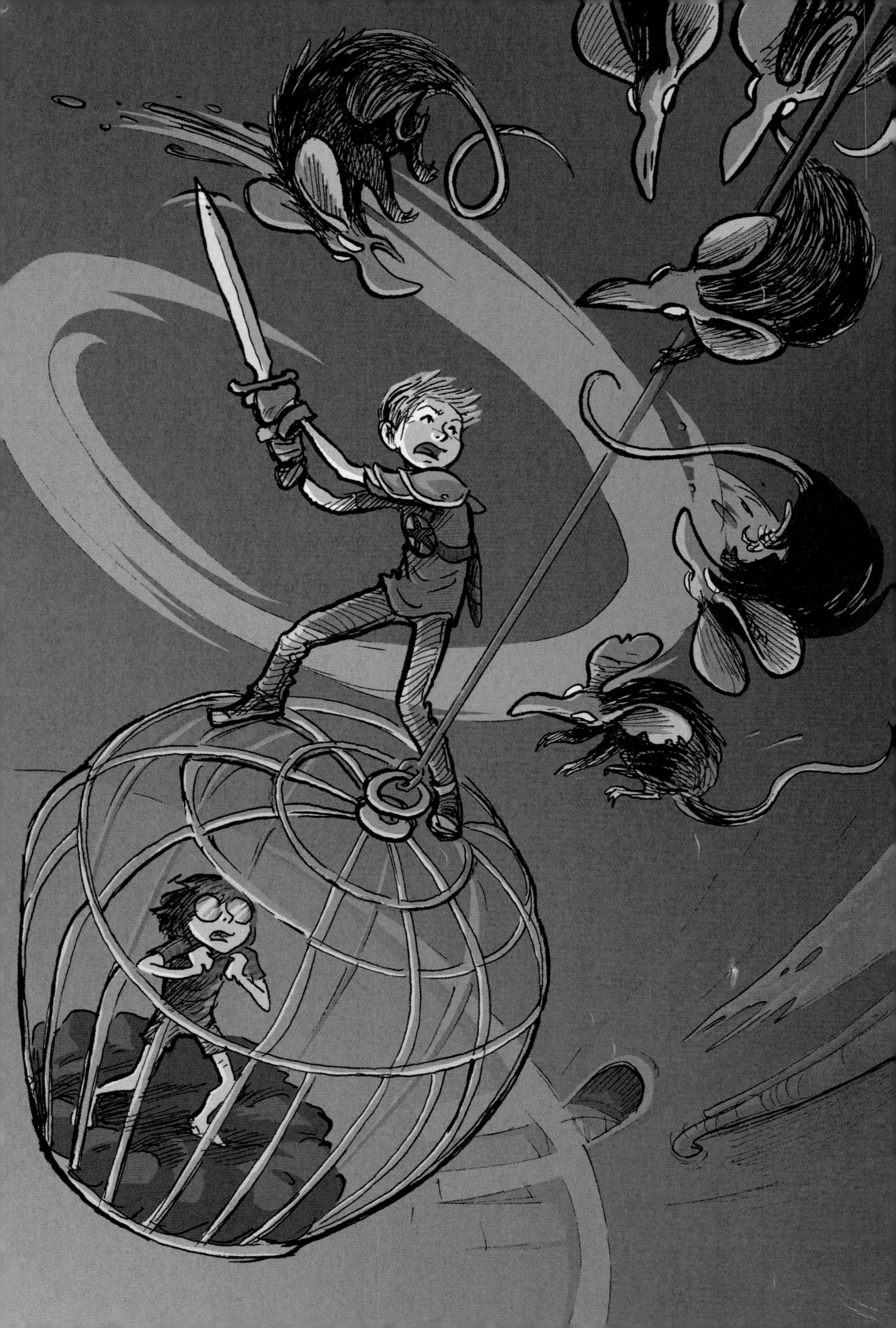

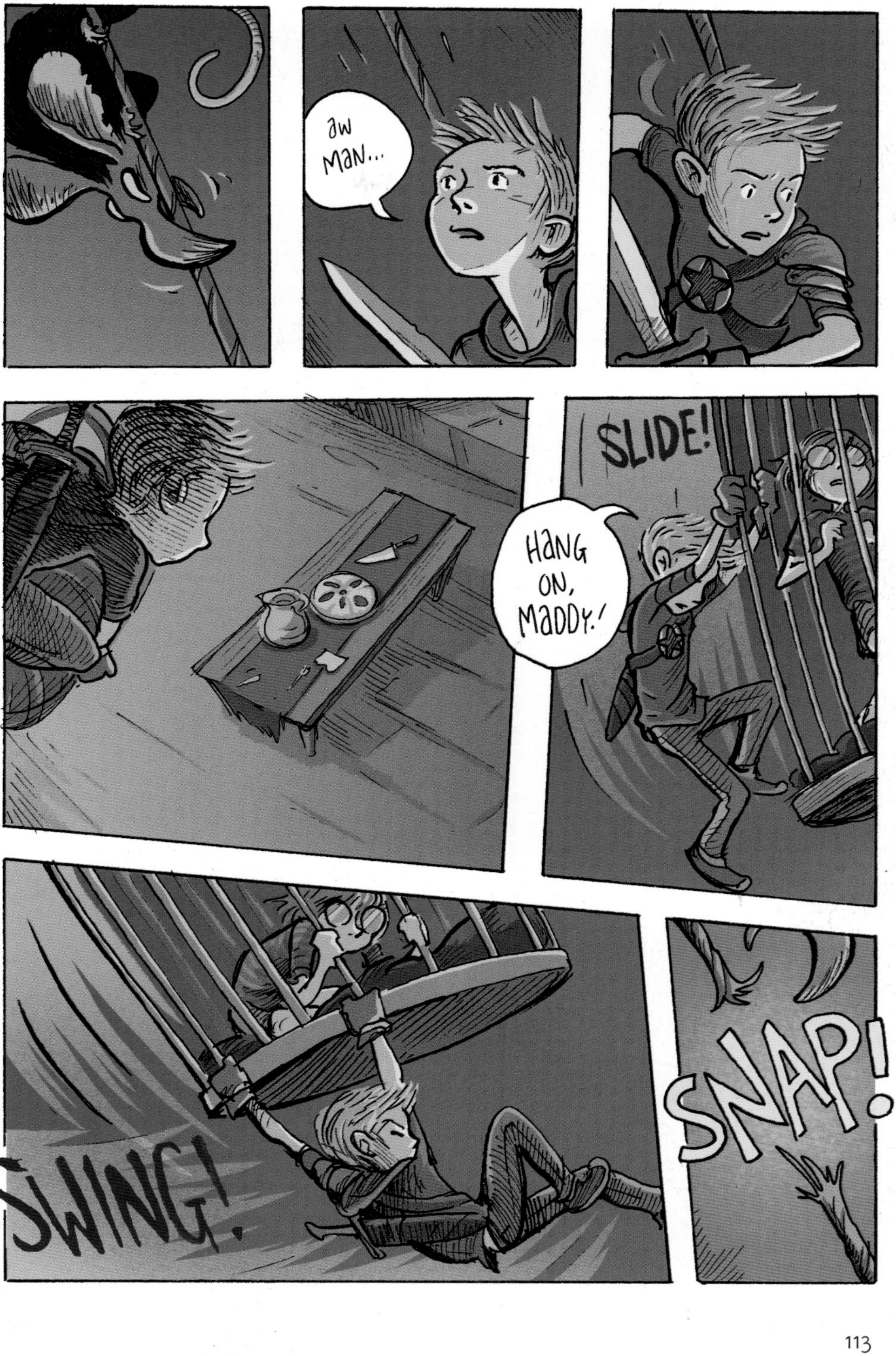
aw man...
SLIDE!
HANG ON, MADDY!
SWING!
SNAP!

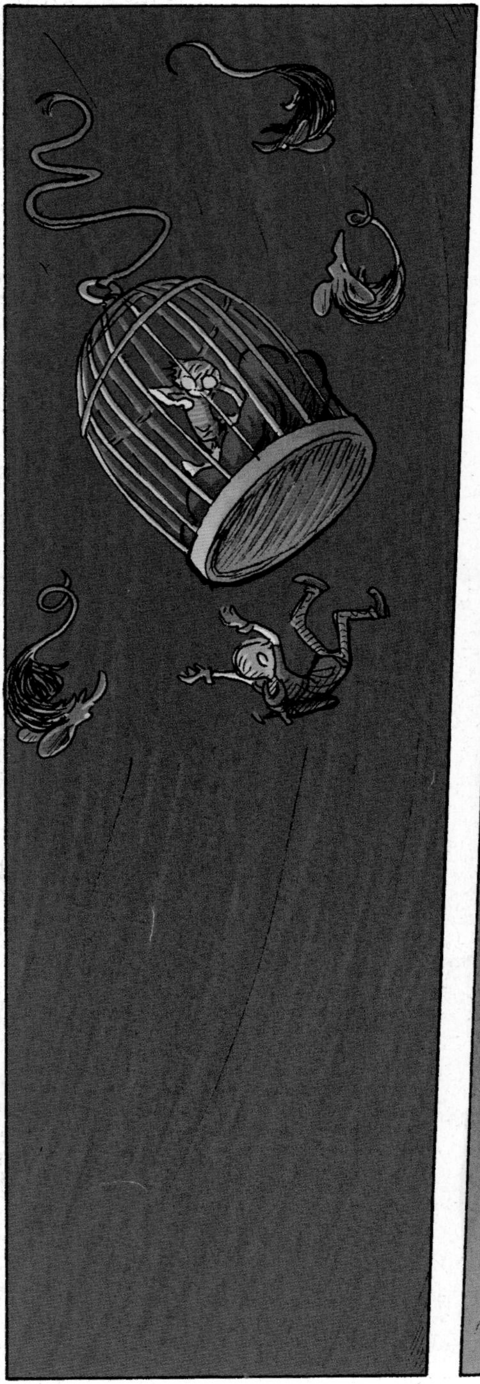

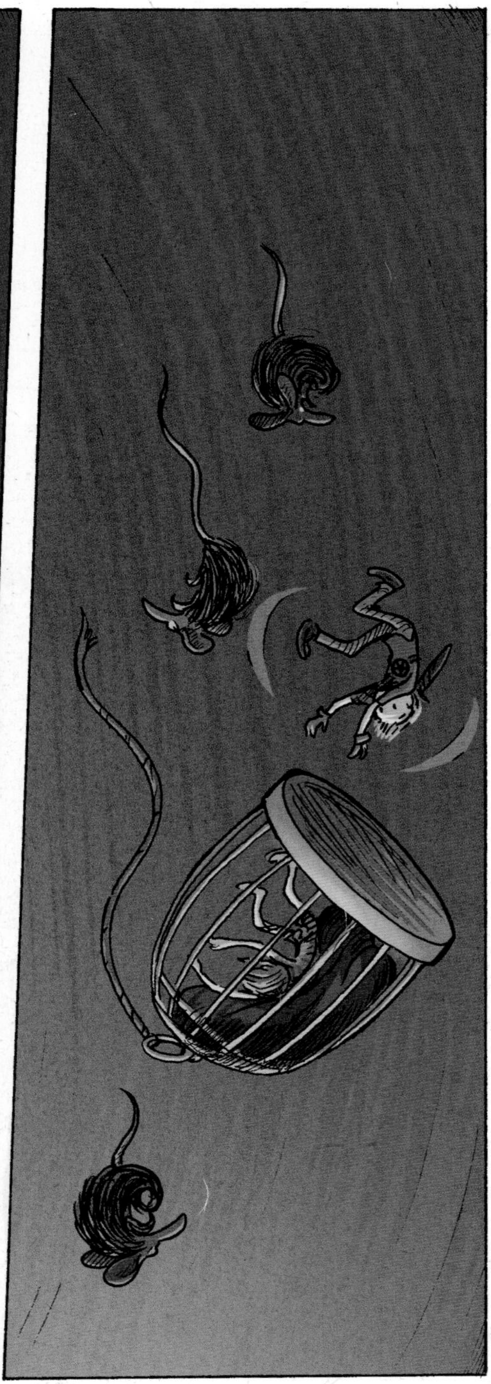

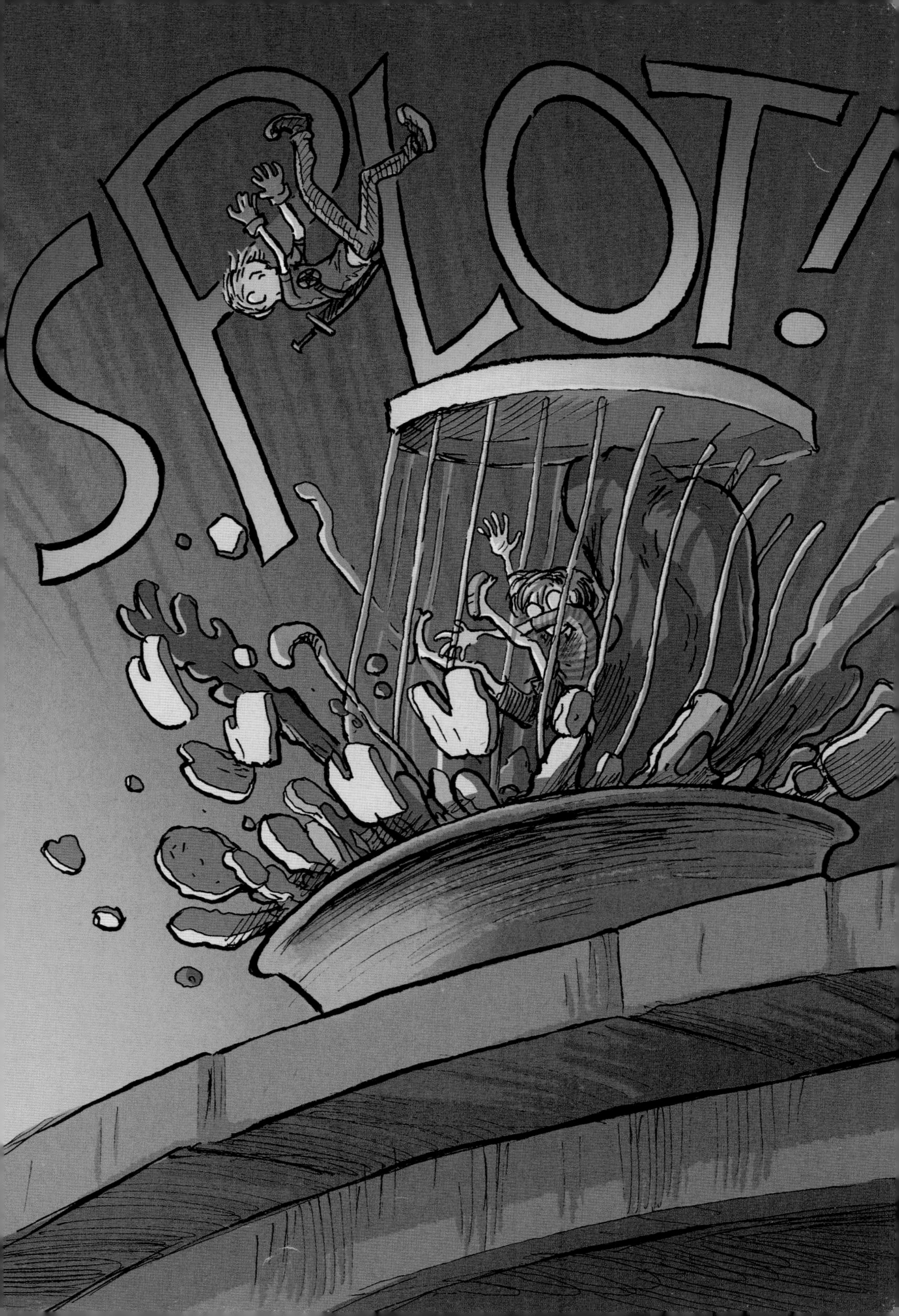
SPLOT!

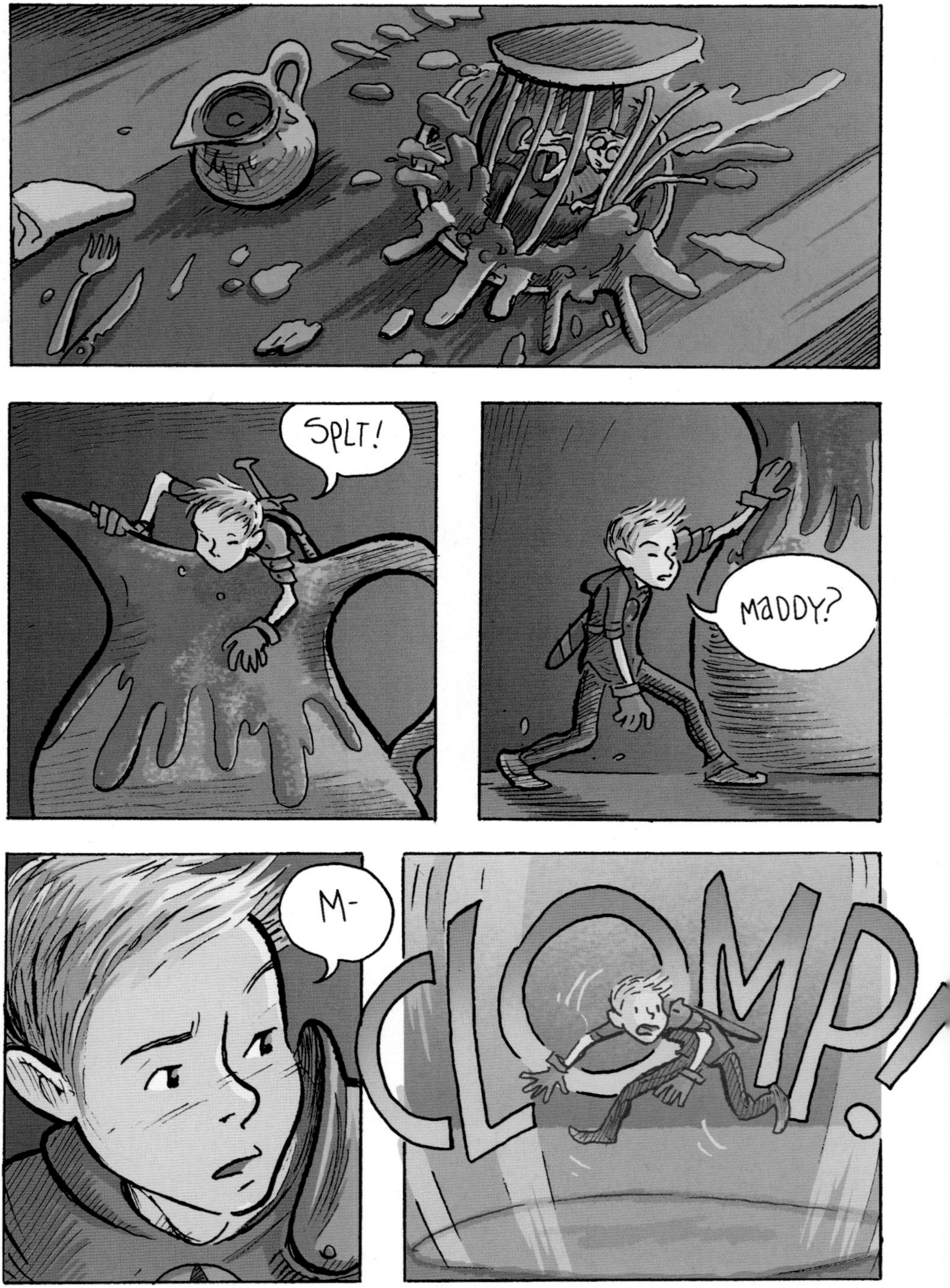
SPLT!
MADDY?
M-
CLOMP!

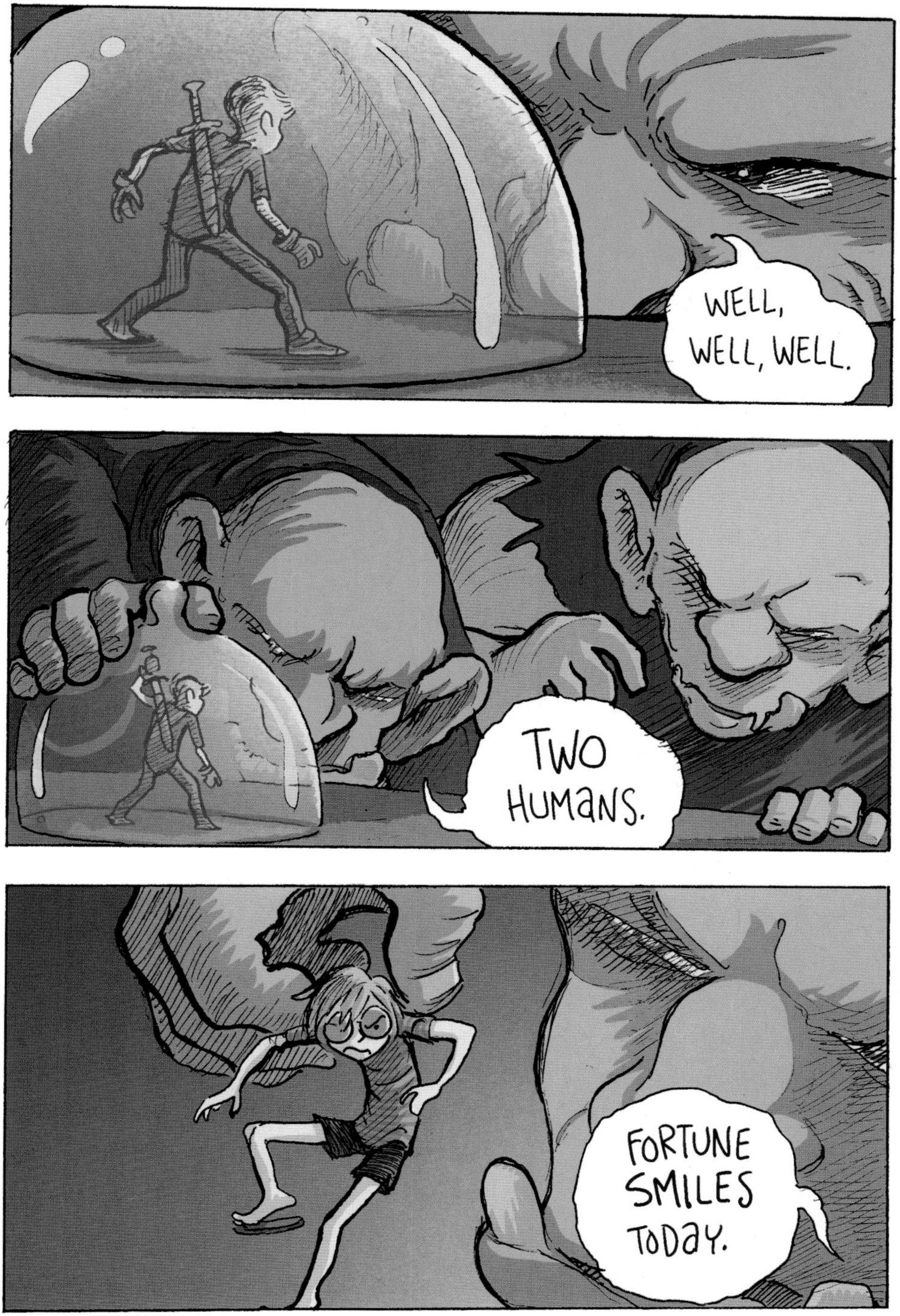
WELL,
WELL, WELL.
TWO
HUMANS.
FORTUNE
SMILES
TODAY.

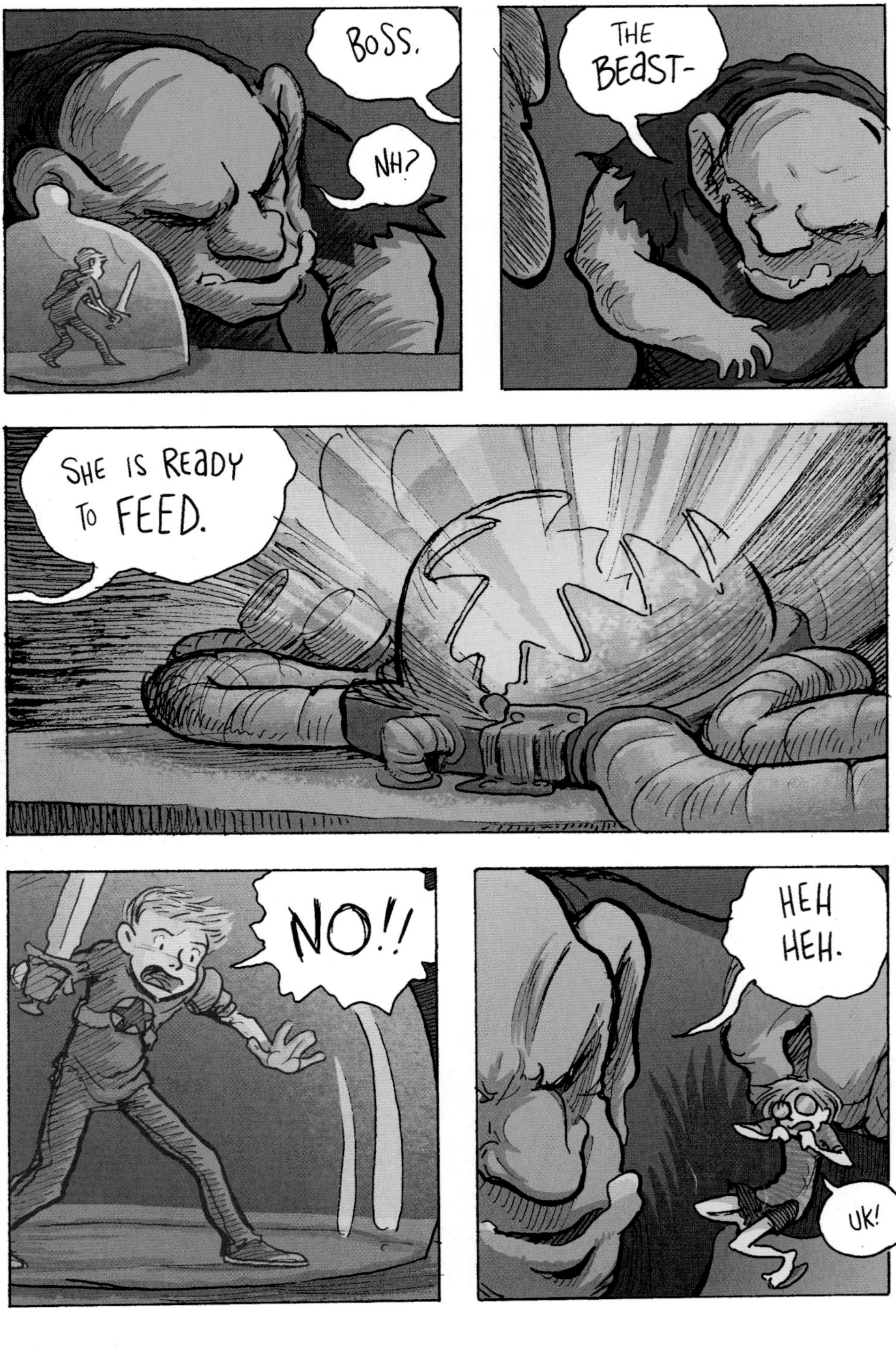
BOSS.
NH?
THE BEAST-
SHE IS READY TO FEED.
NO!!
HEH HEH.
UK!

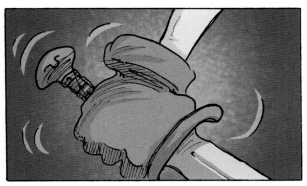

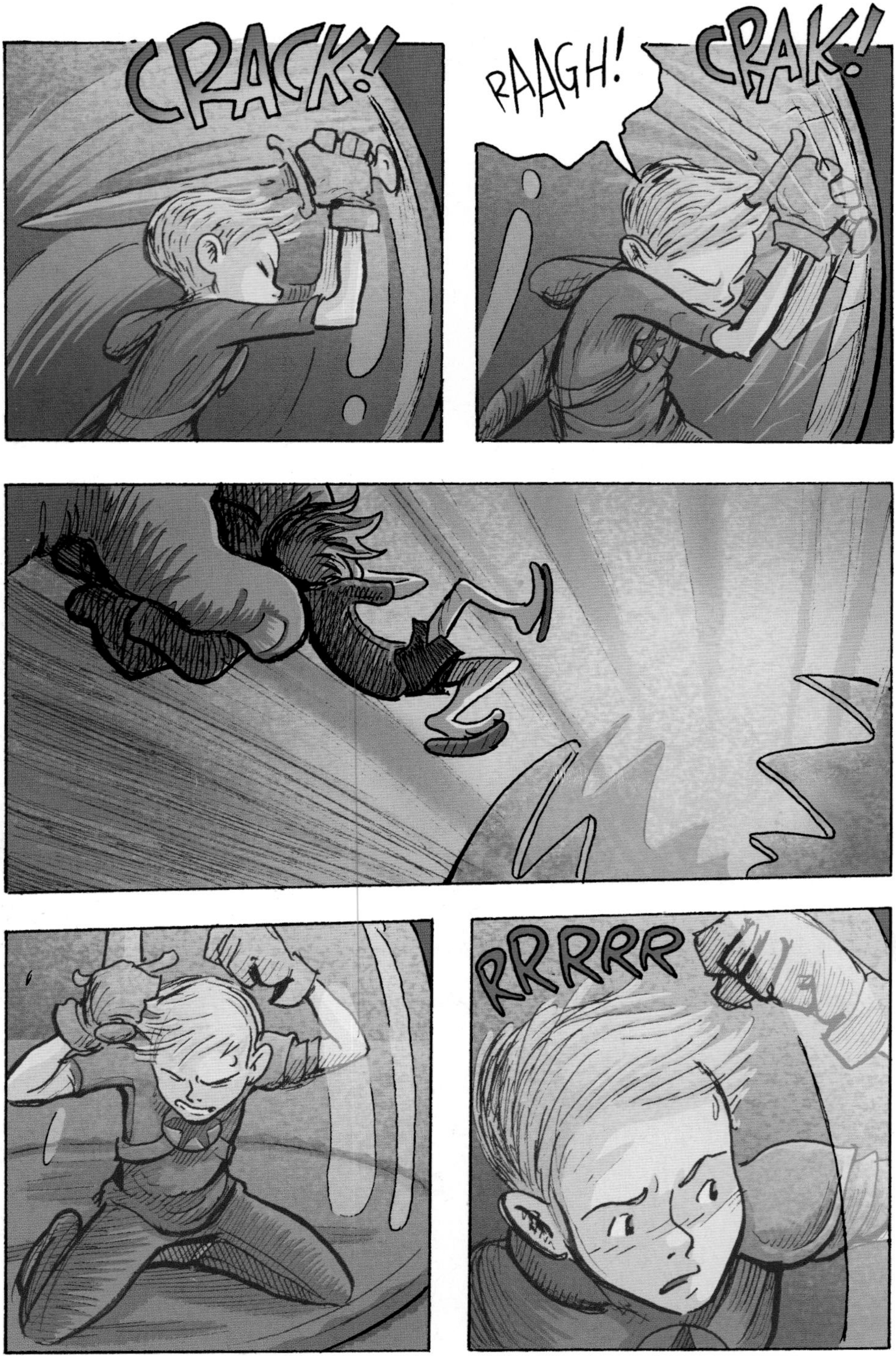
CRACK!
RAAGH!
CRAK!
RRRRR

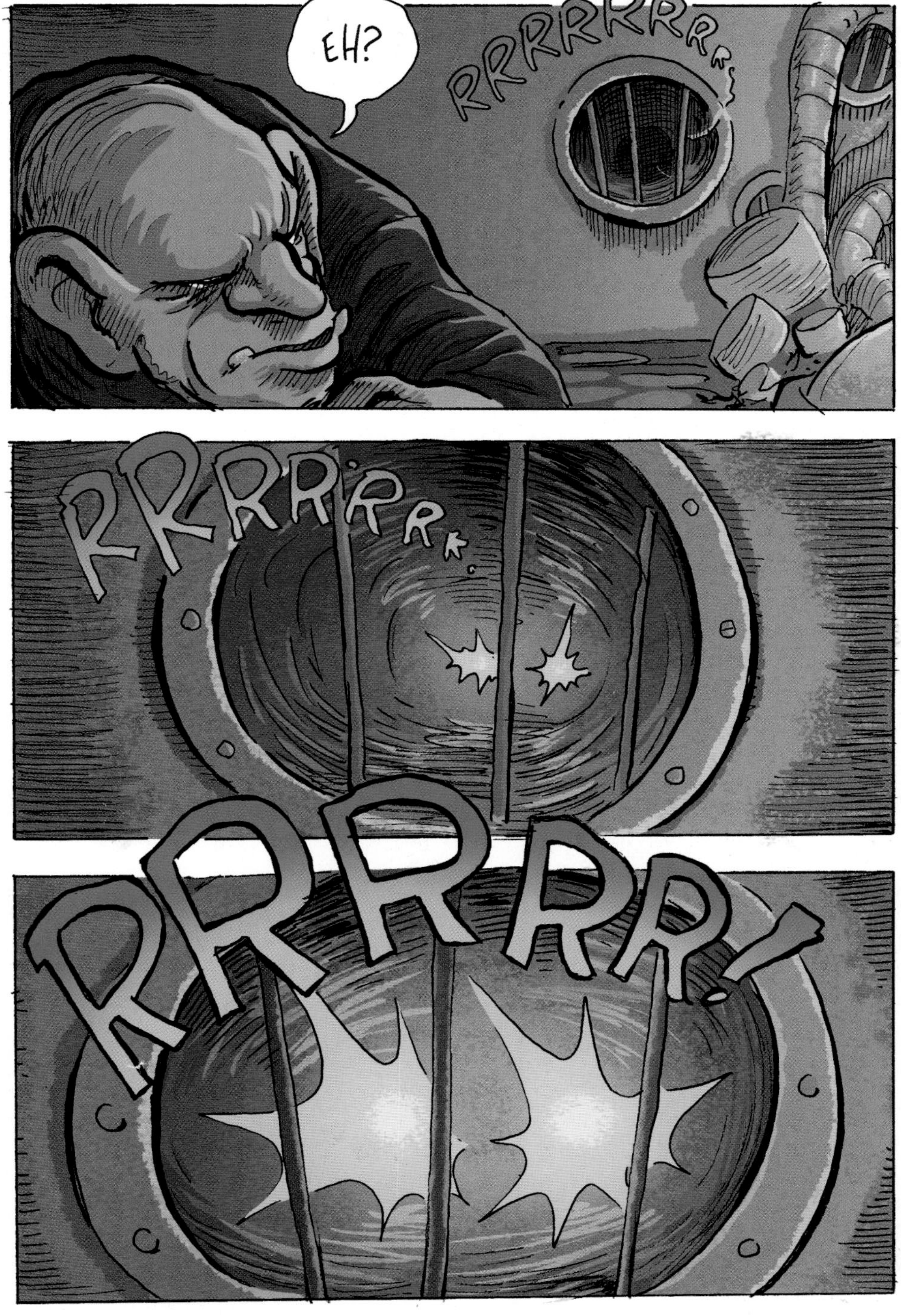
EH?
RRRRRRRR
RRRRRRR
RRRRRR!

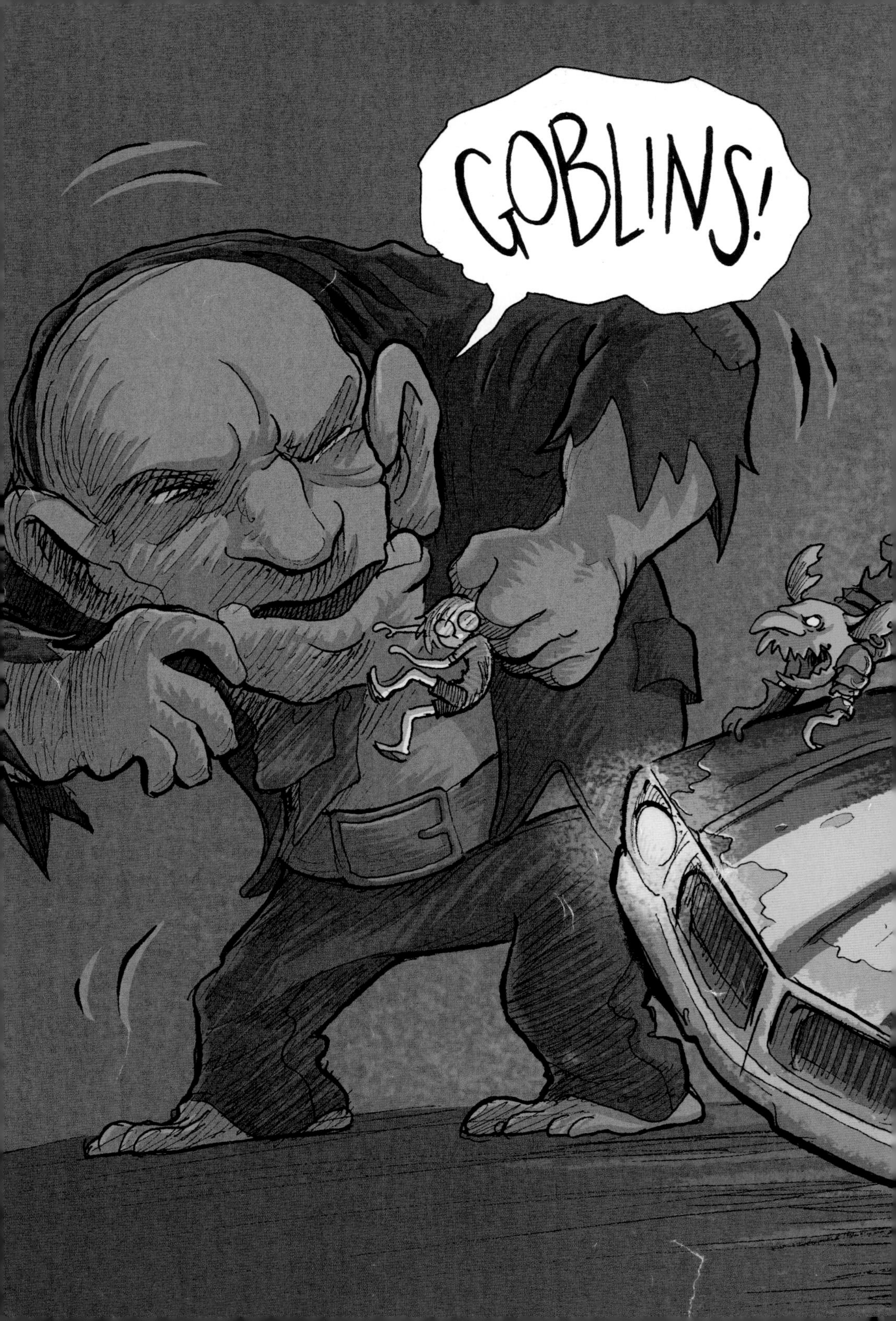
GOBLINS!

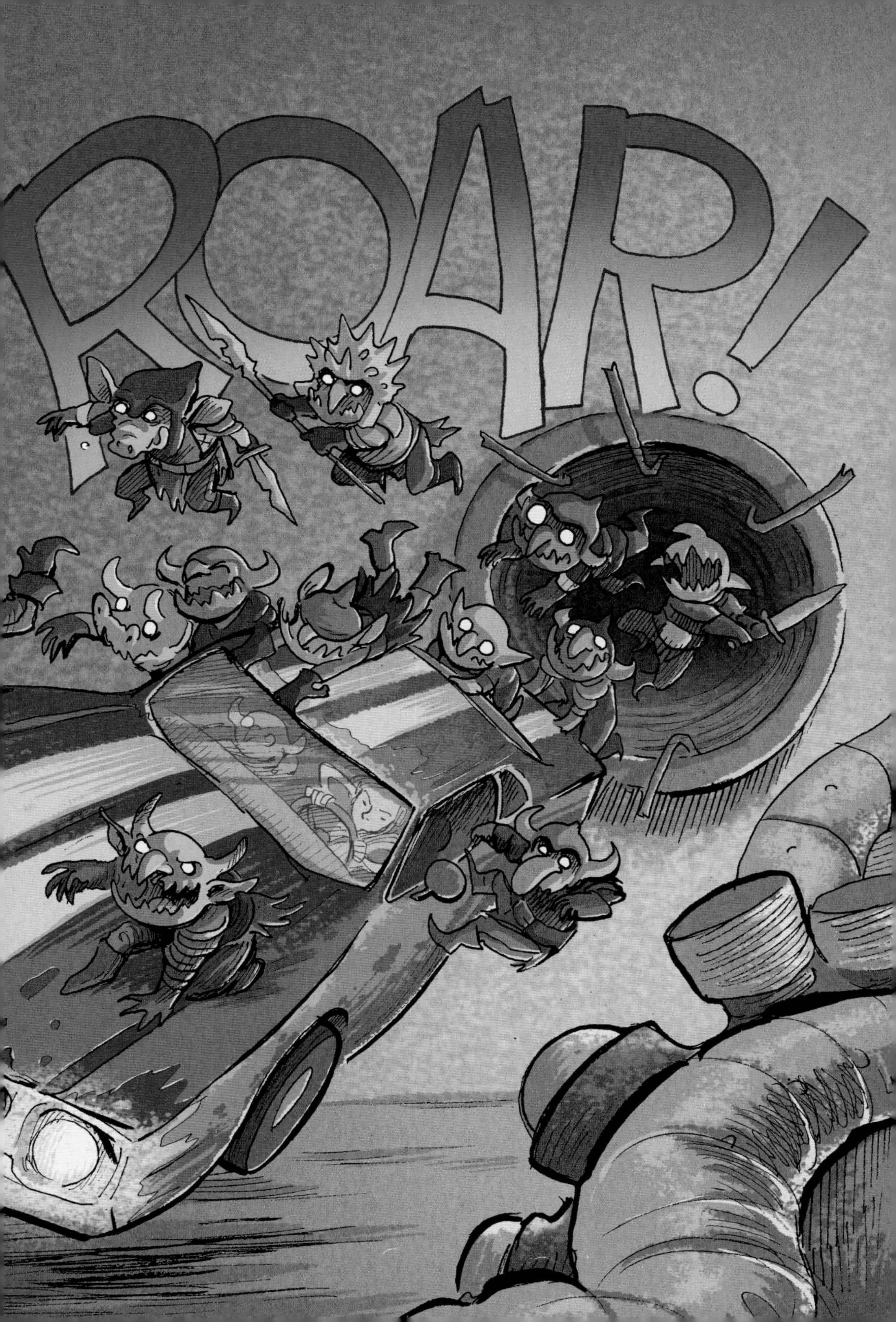
ROAR!

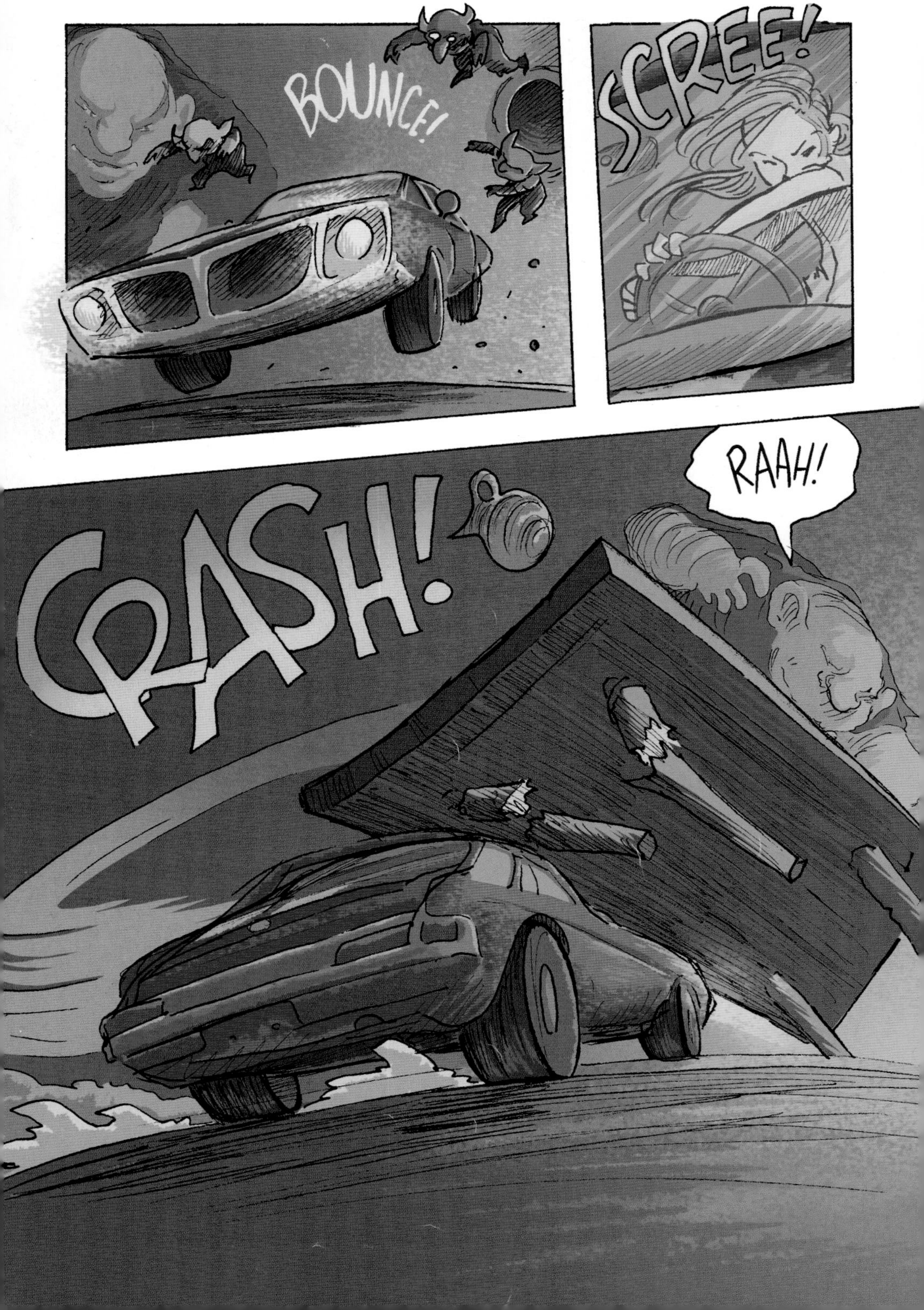
BOUNCE!
SCREE!
CRASH!
RAAH!

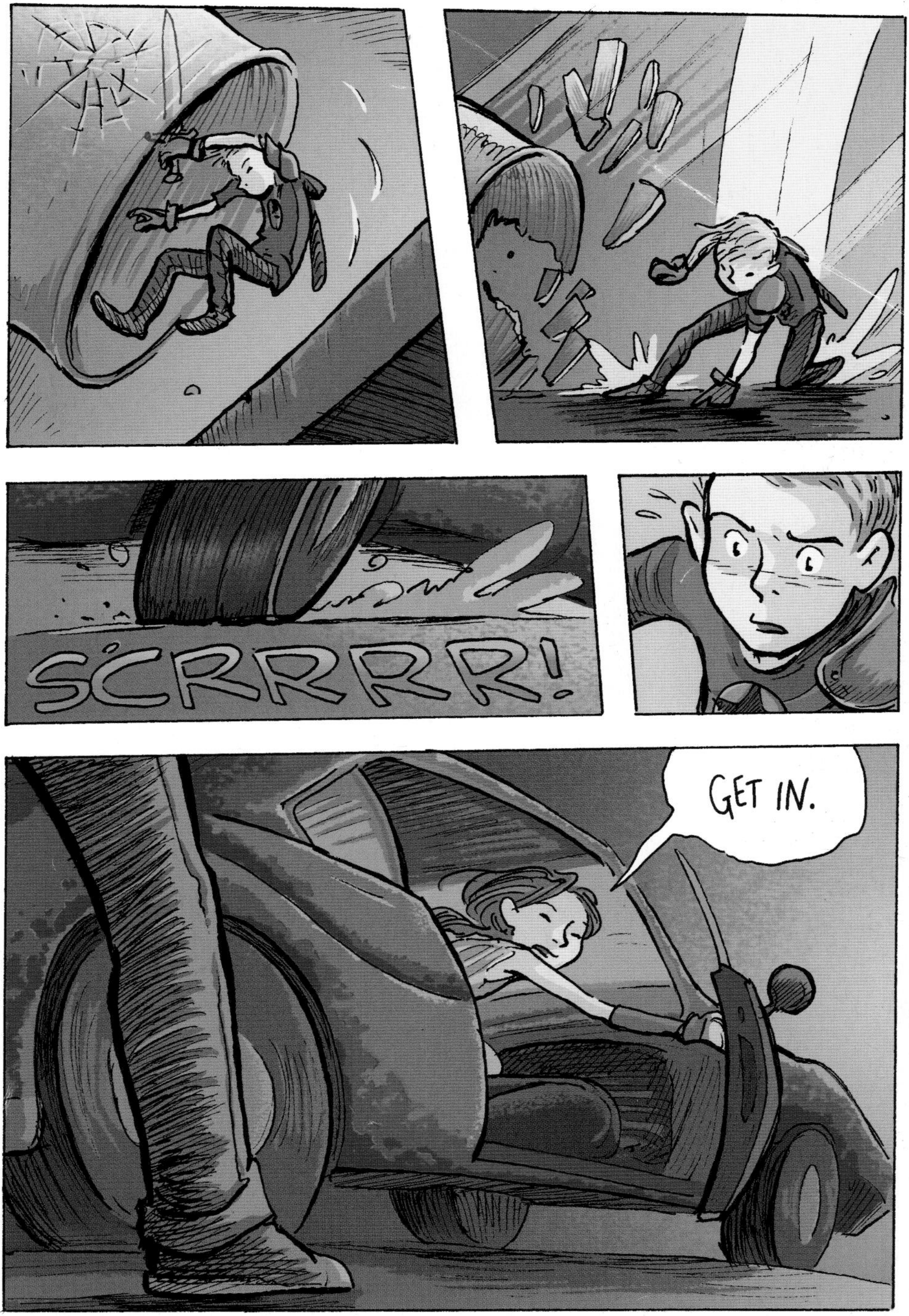
SCRRRR!
GET IN.

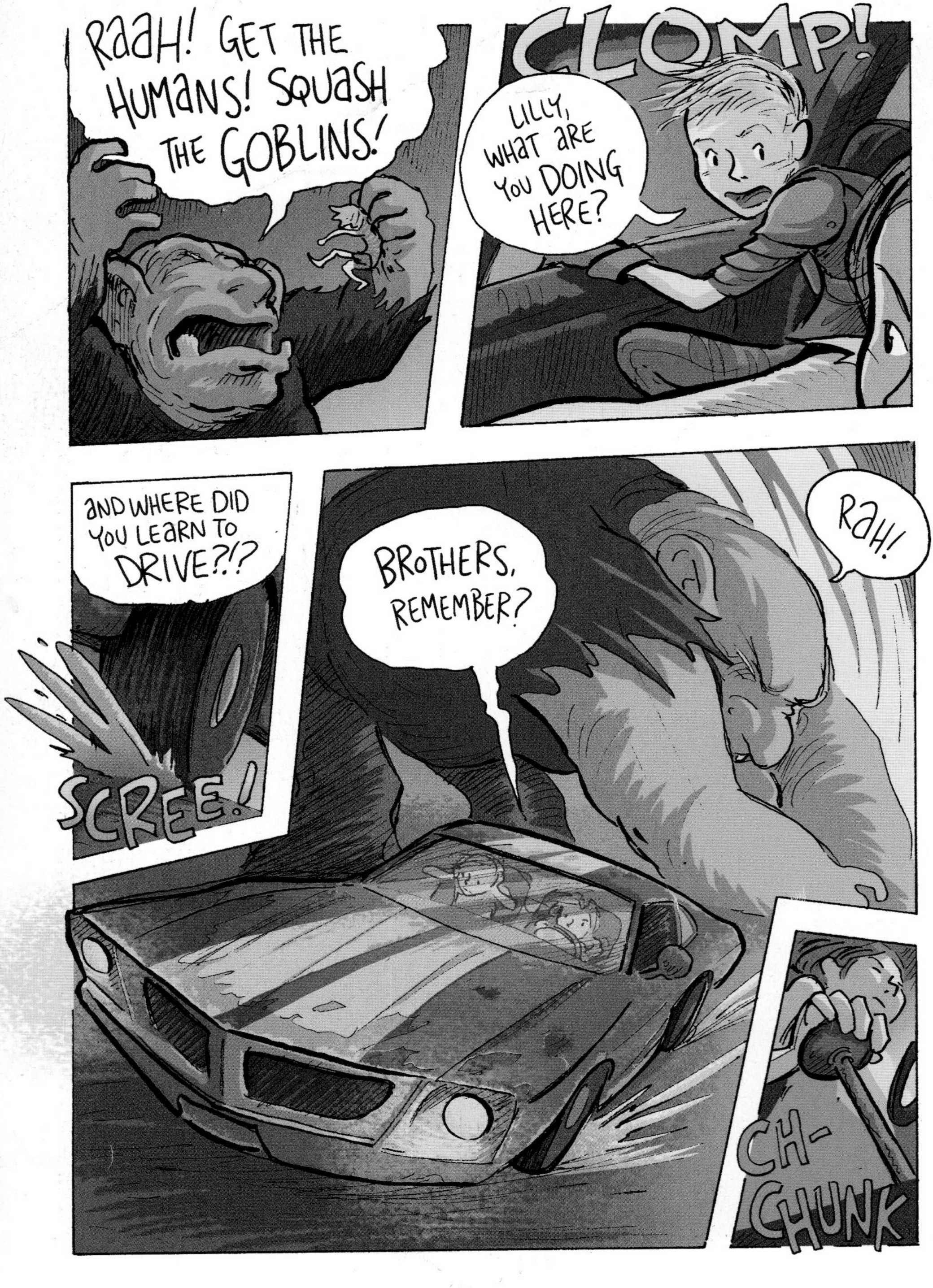

RAAH! GET THE HUMANS! SQUASH THE GOBLINS!
CLOMP!
LILLY, WHAT ARE YOU DOING HERE?
AND WHERE DID YOU LEARN TO DRIVE?!?
SCREE!
BROTHERS, REMEMBER?
RAH!
CH-CHUNK

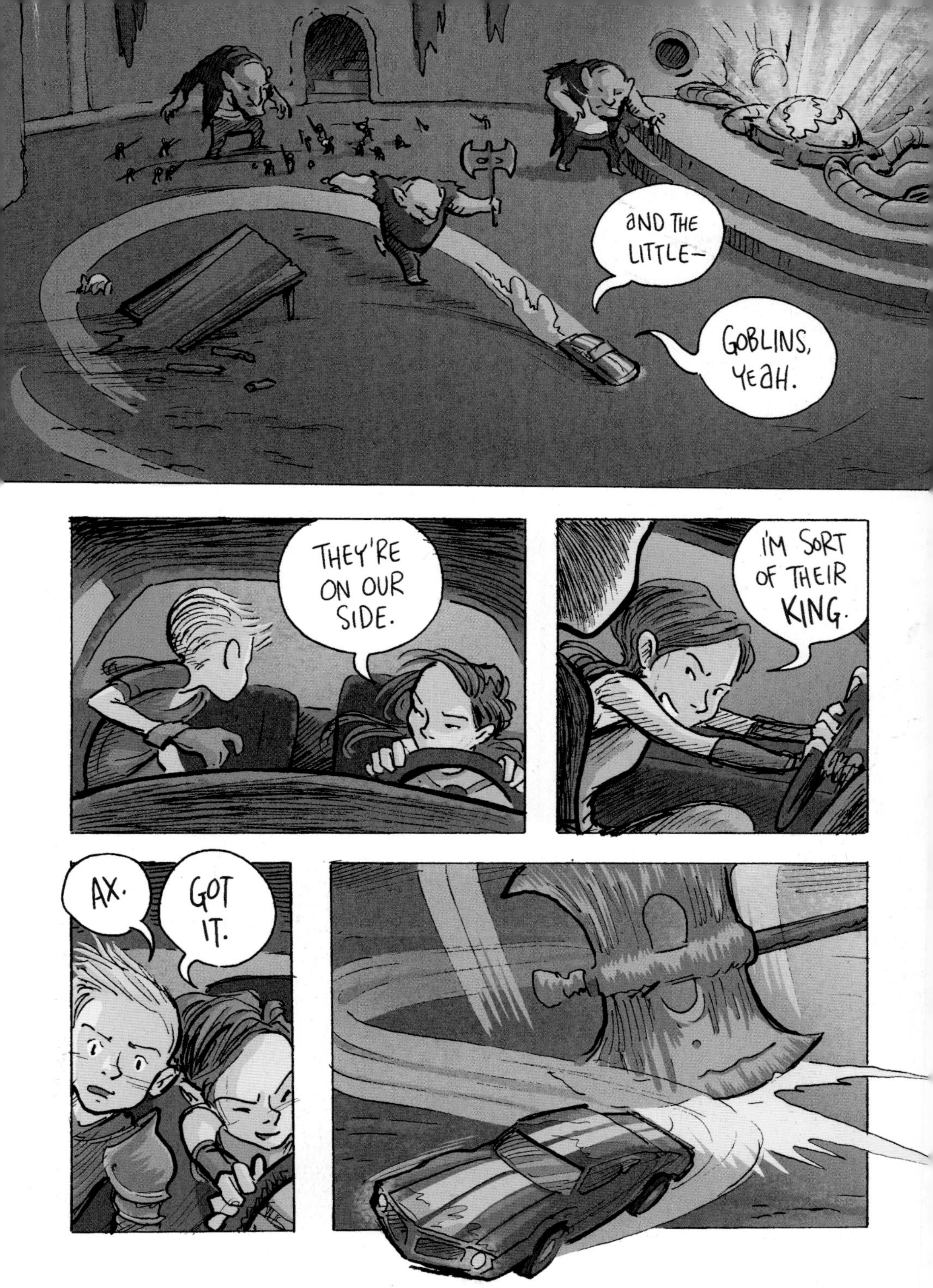
AND THE LITTLE–
GOBLINS, YEAH.
THEY'RE ON OUR SIDE.
I'M SORT OF THEIR KING.
AX.
GOT IT.

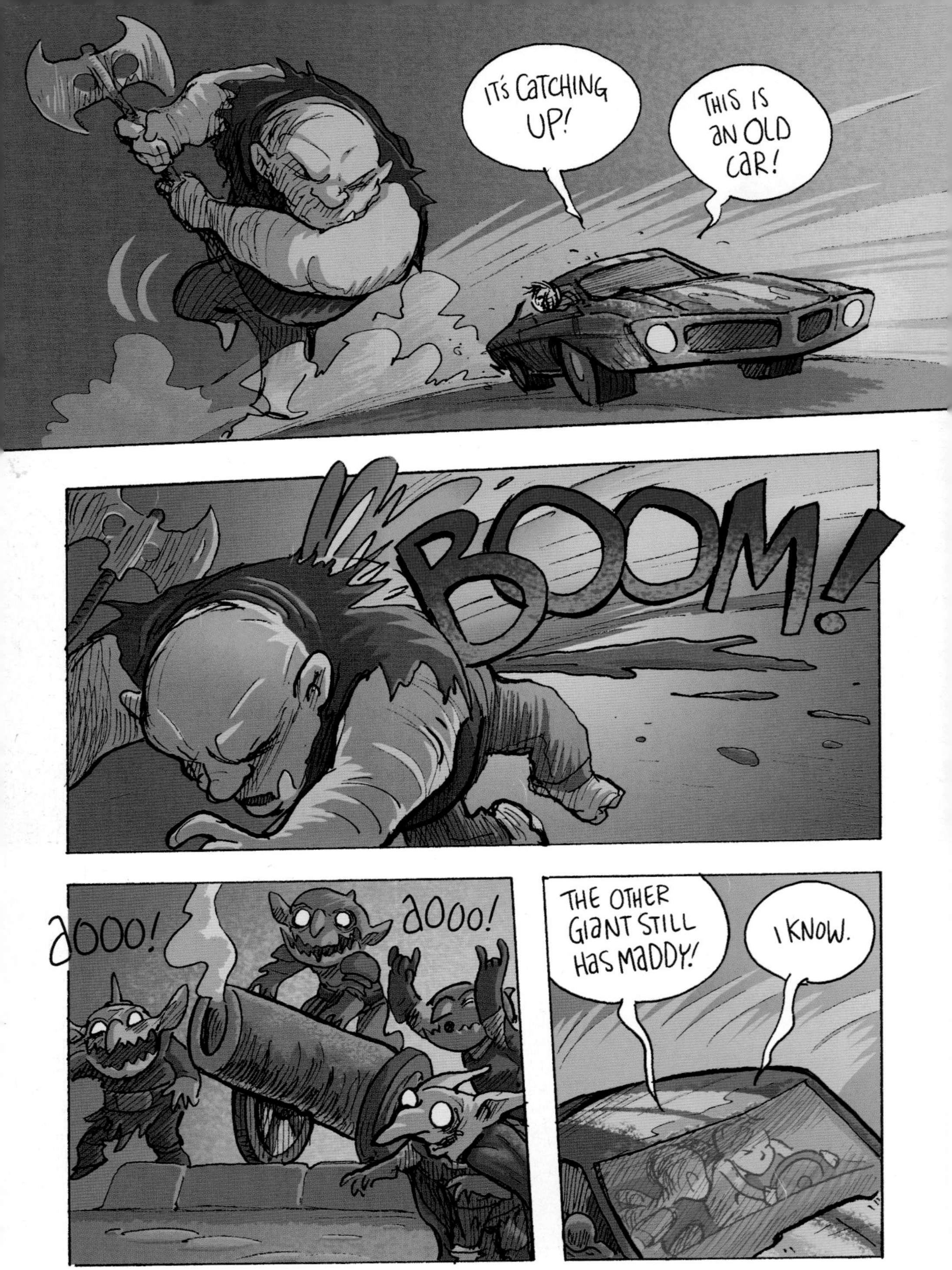
IT'S CATCHING UP!
THIS IS AN OLD CAR!
BOOM!
AOOO!
AOOO!
THE OTHER GIANT STILL HAS MADDY!
I KNOW.

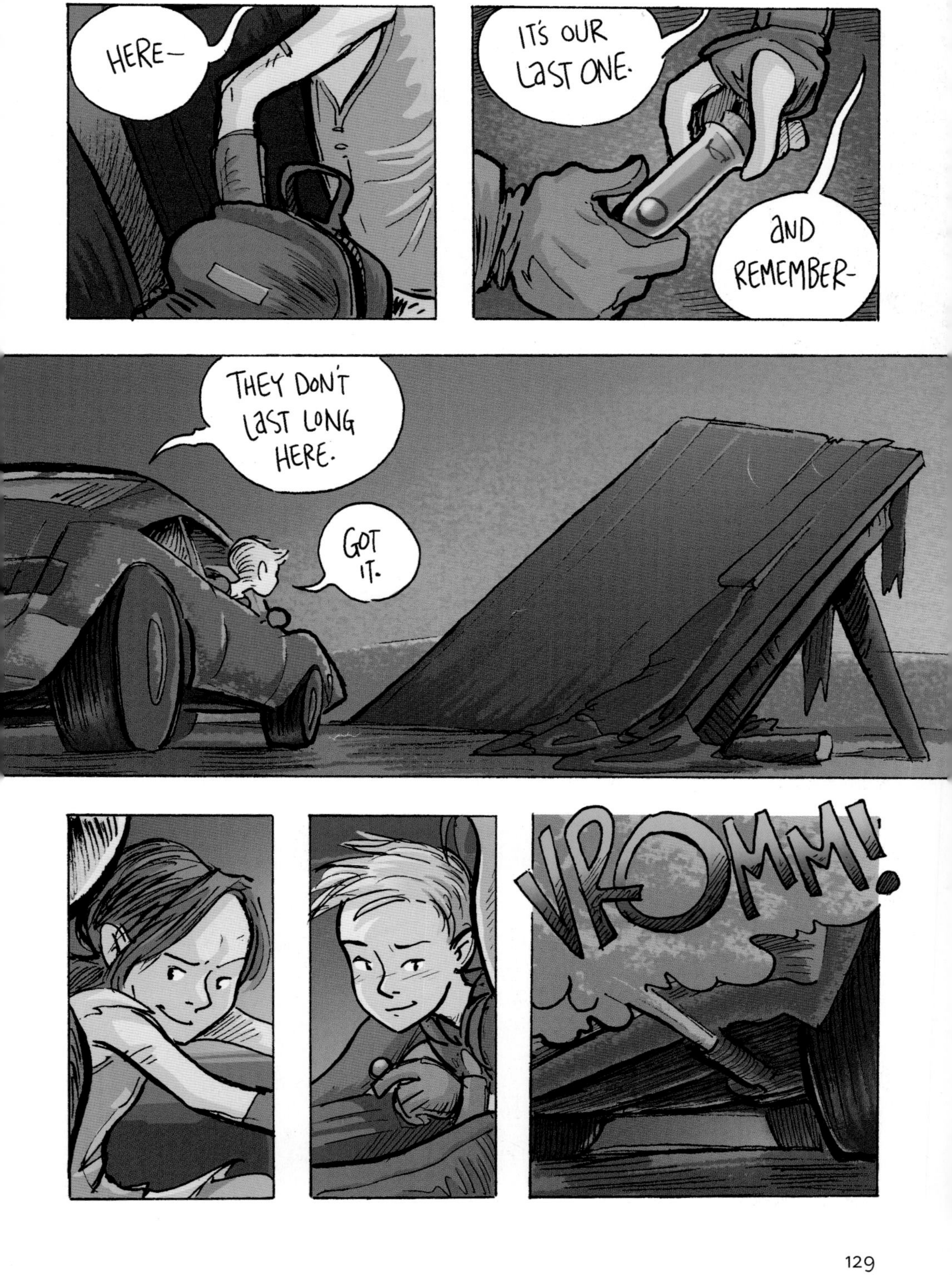
HERE—
IT'S OUR LAST ONE.
AND REMEMBER—
THEY DON'T LAST LONG HERE.
GOT IT.
VROMM!

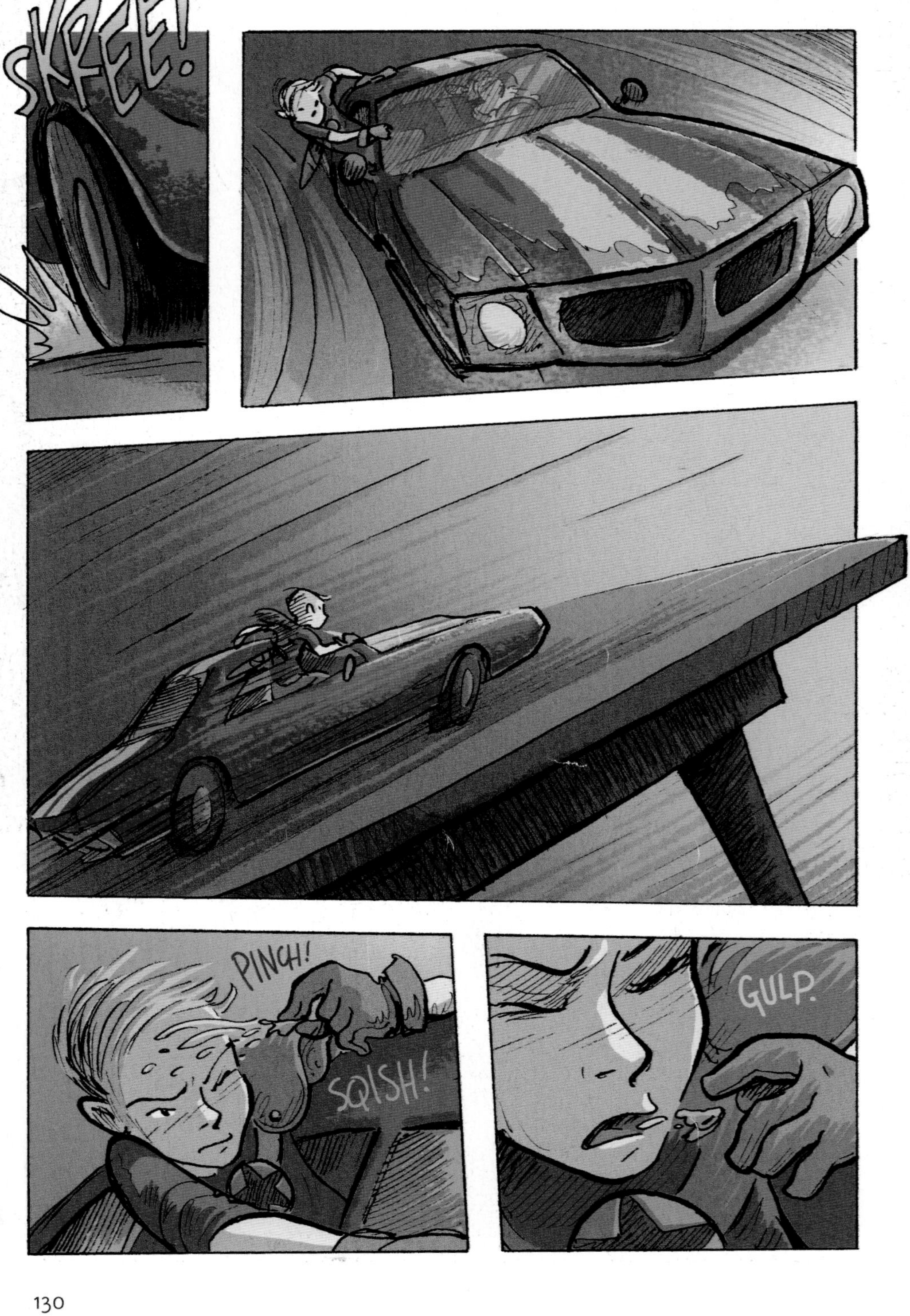
SKREE!
PINCH!
SQISH!
GULP.

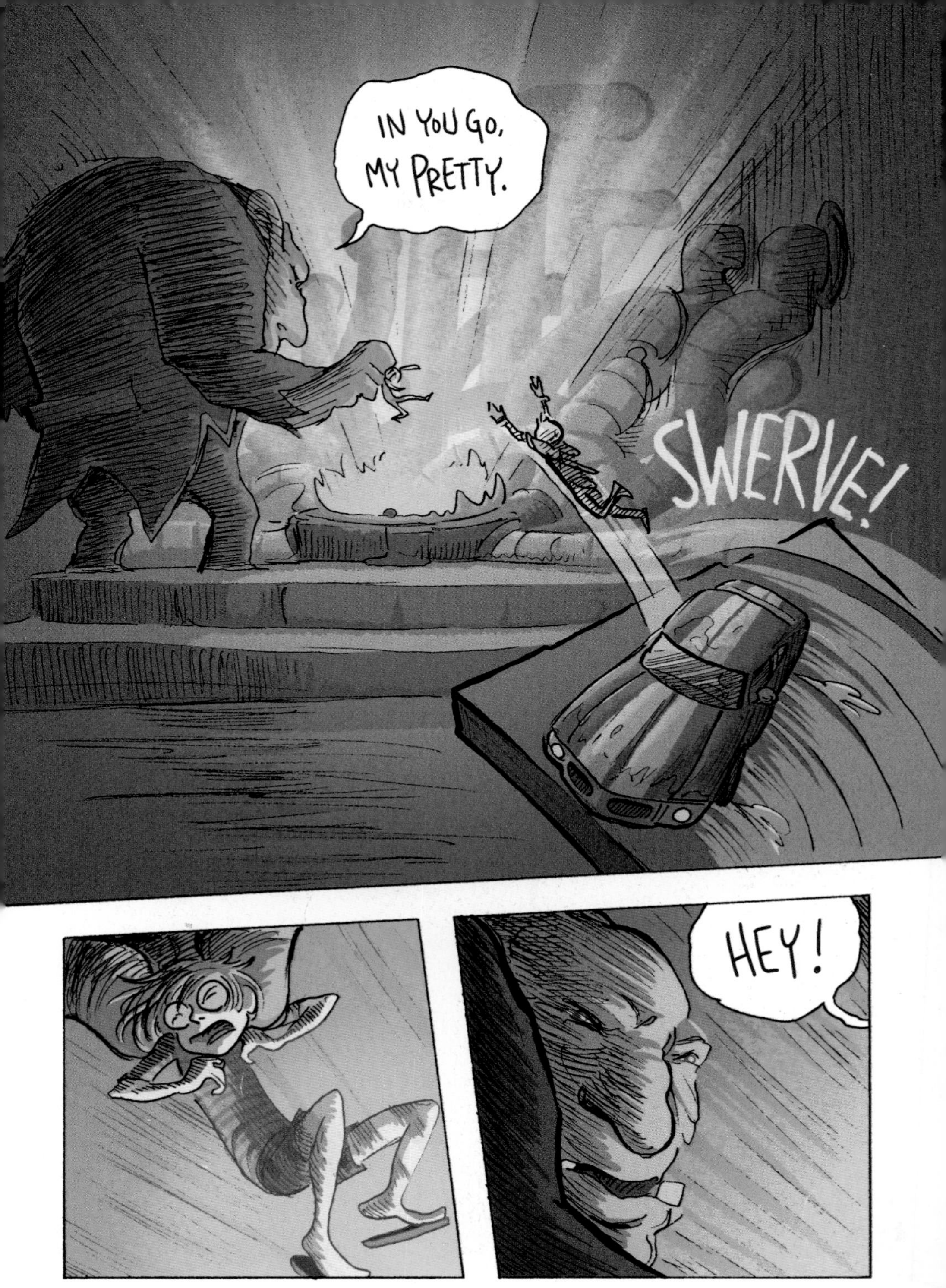
IN YOU GO,
MY PRETTY.
SWERVE!
HEY!

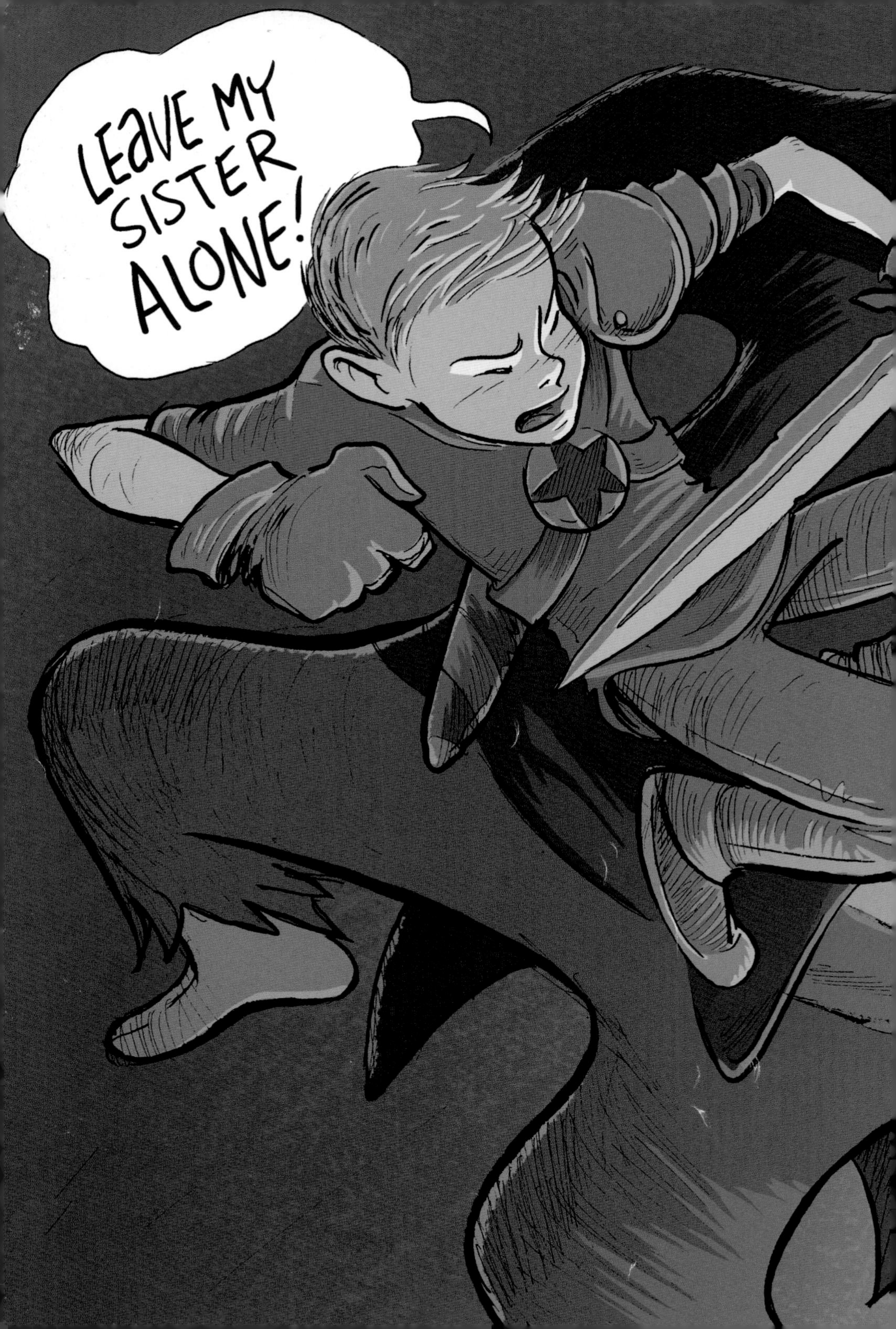
LEAVE MY SISTER ALONE!

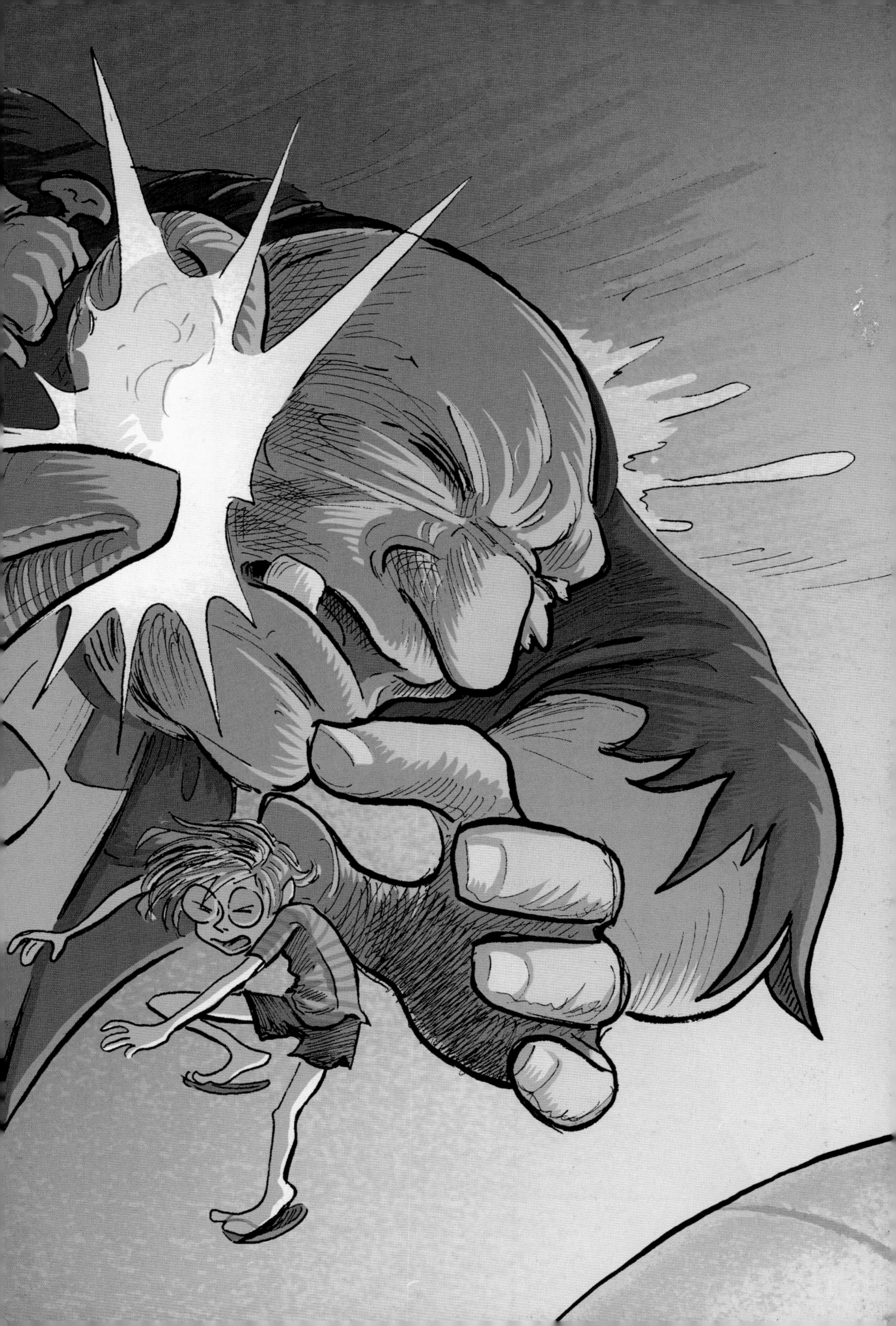

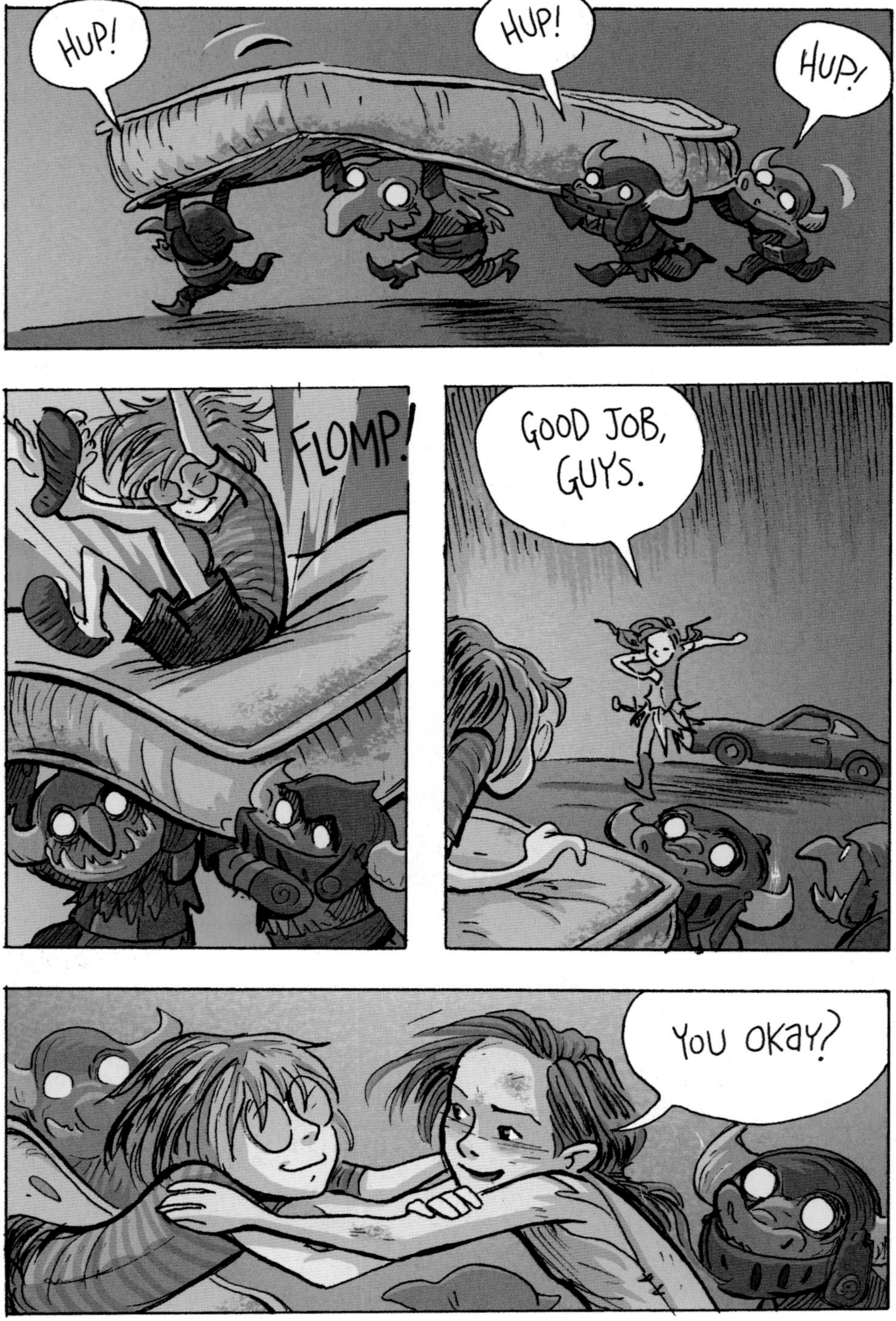
HUP!
HUP!
HUP!
FLOMP!
GOOD JOB, GUYS.
YOU OKAY?

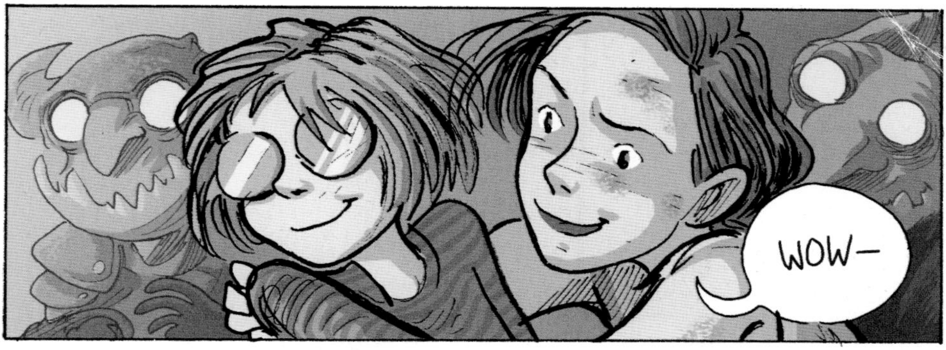
WOW–

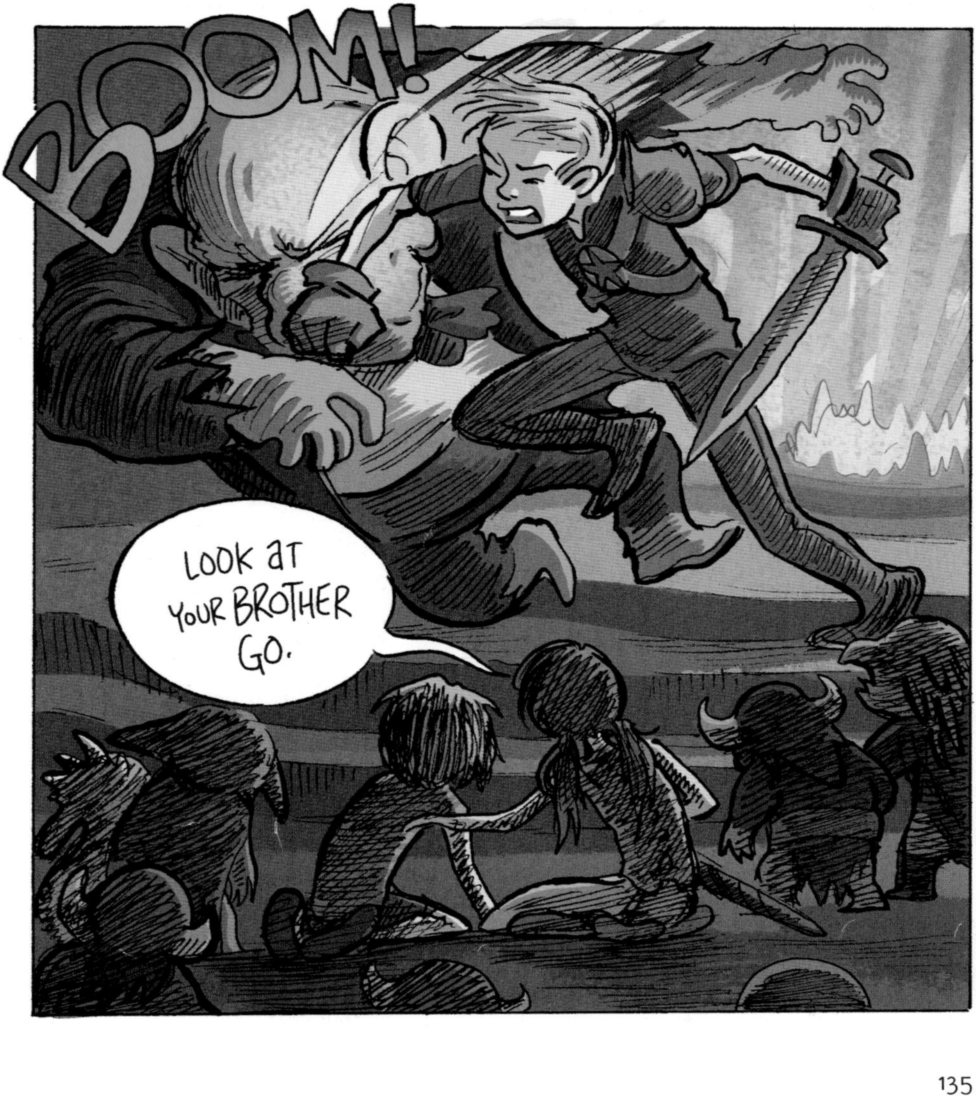
BOOM!
LOOK AT YOUR BROTHER GO.

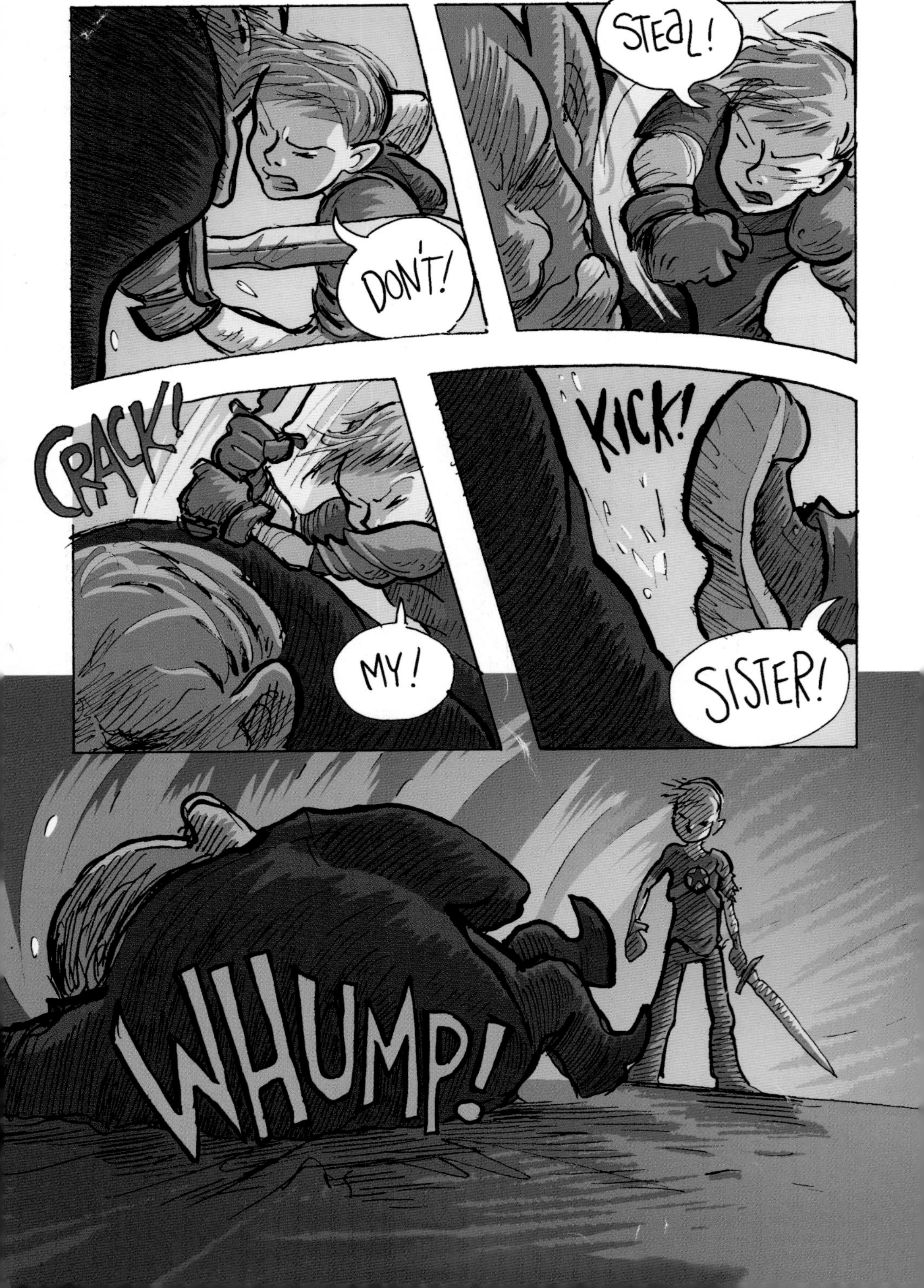
DON'T!
STEAL!
CRACK!
MY!
KICK!
SISTER!
WHUMP!

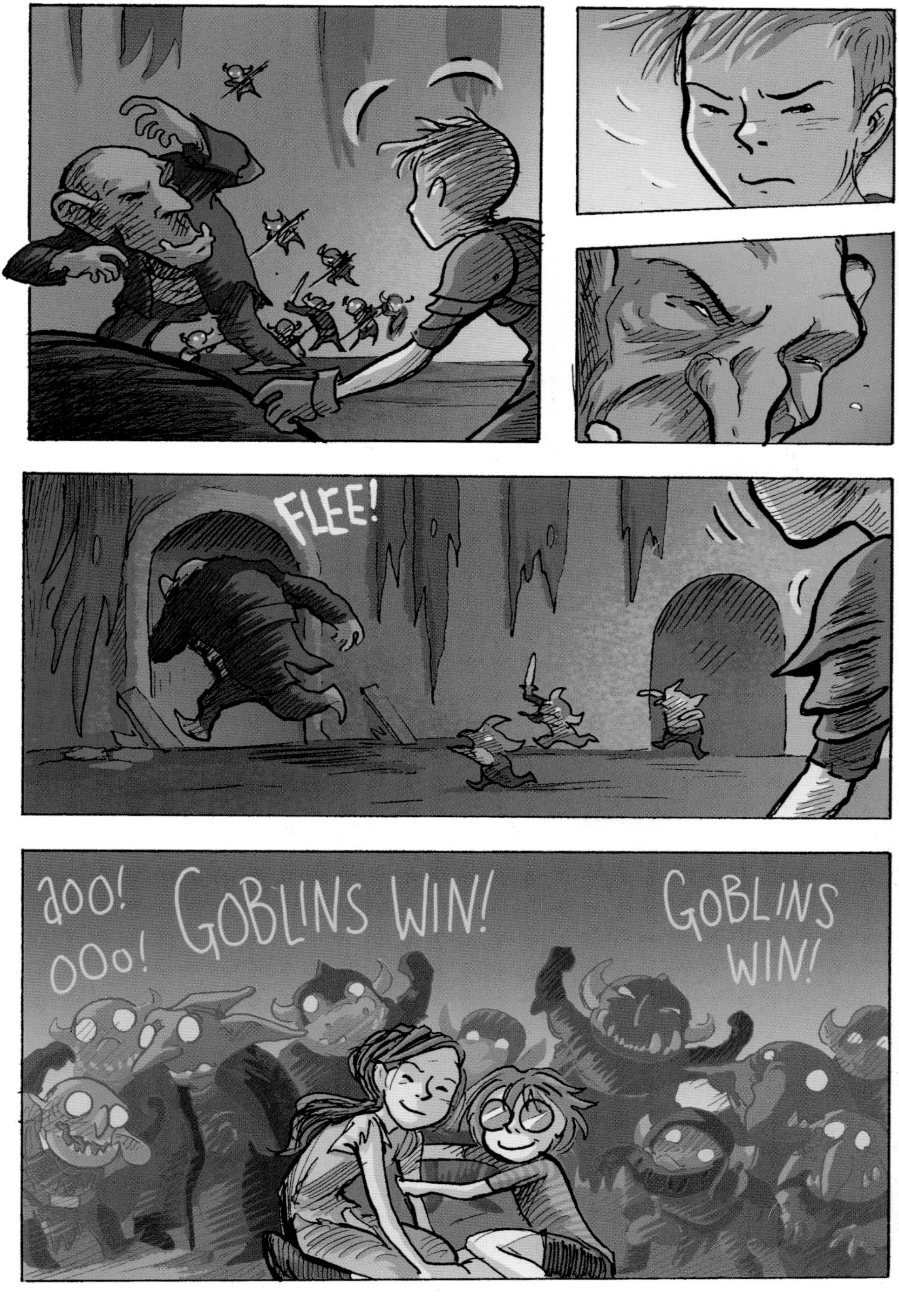
FLEE!
aoo! ooo!
GOBLINS WIN!
GOBLINS WIN!

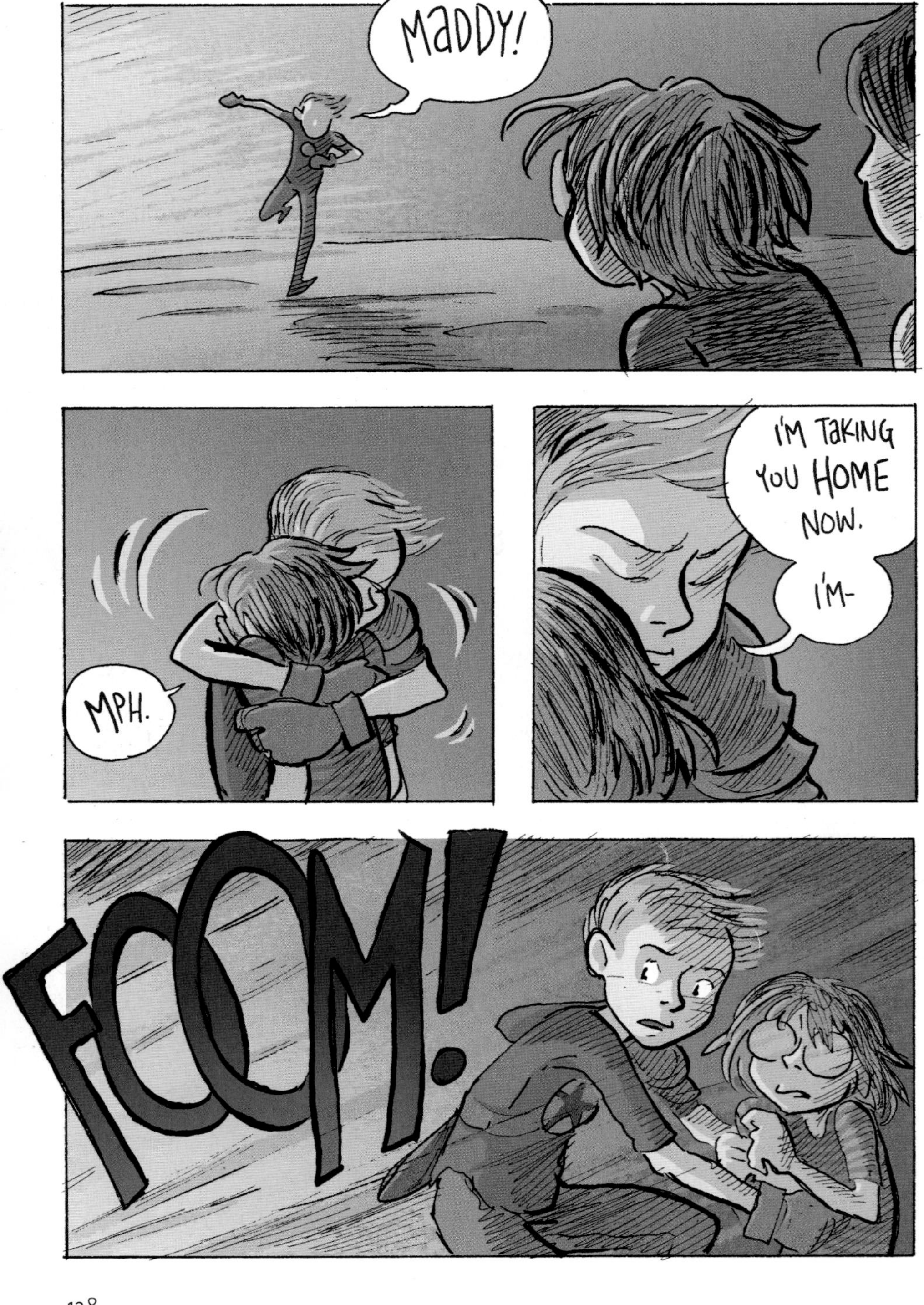
MADDY!
MPH.
I'M TAKING YOU HOME NOW.
I'M-
FOOM!

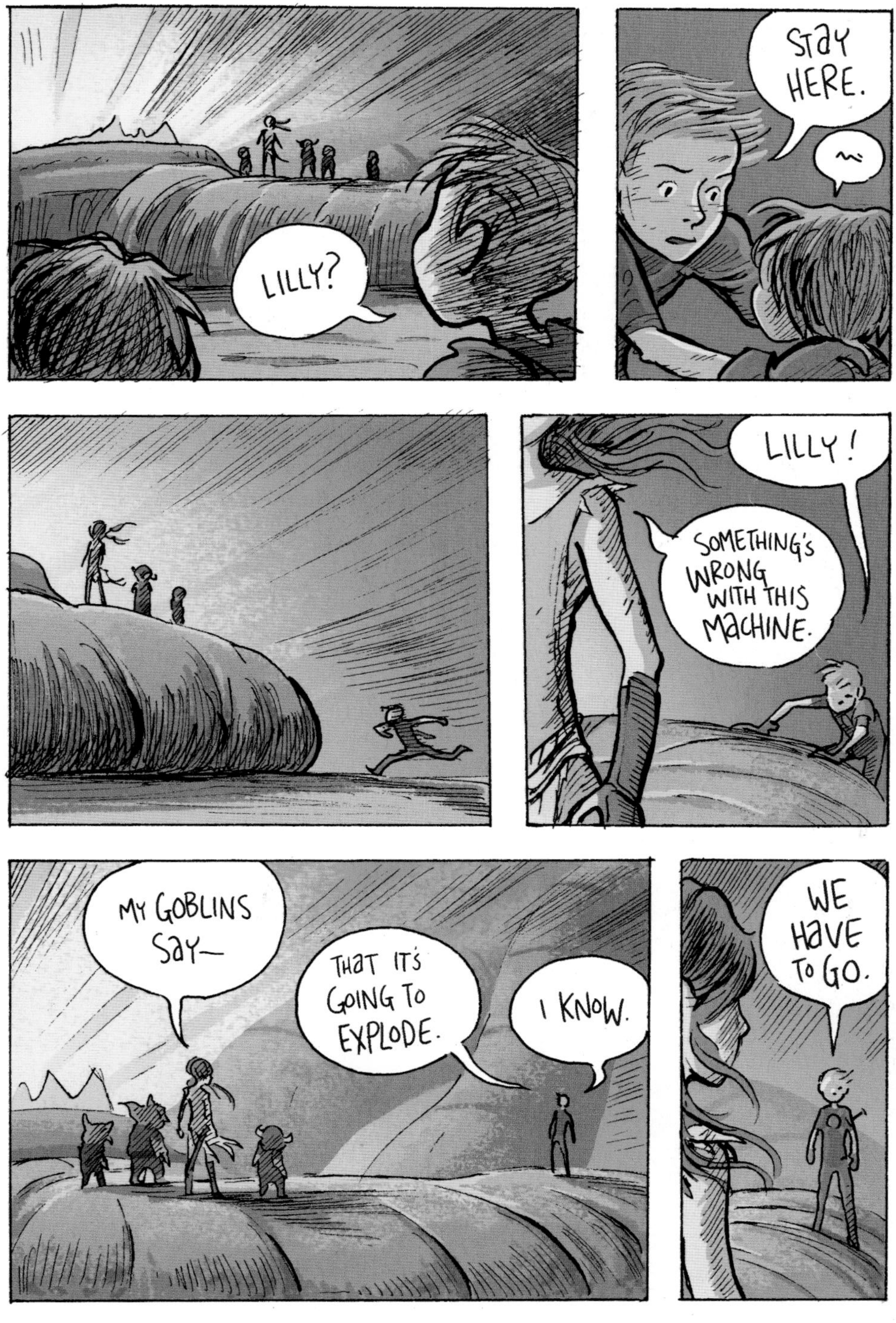

LILLY?
STAY HERE.
LILLY!
SOMETHING'S WRONG WITH THIS MACHINE.
MY GOBLINS SAY—
THAT IT'S GOING TO EXPLODE.
I KNOW.
WE HAVE TO GO.

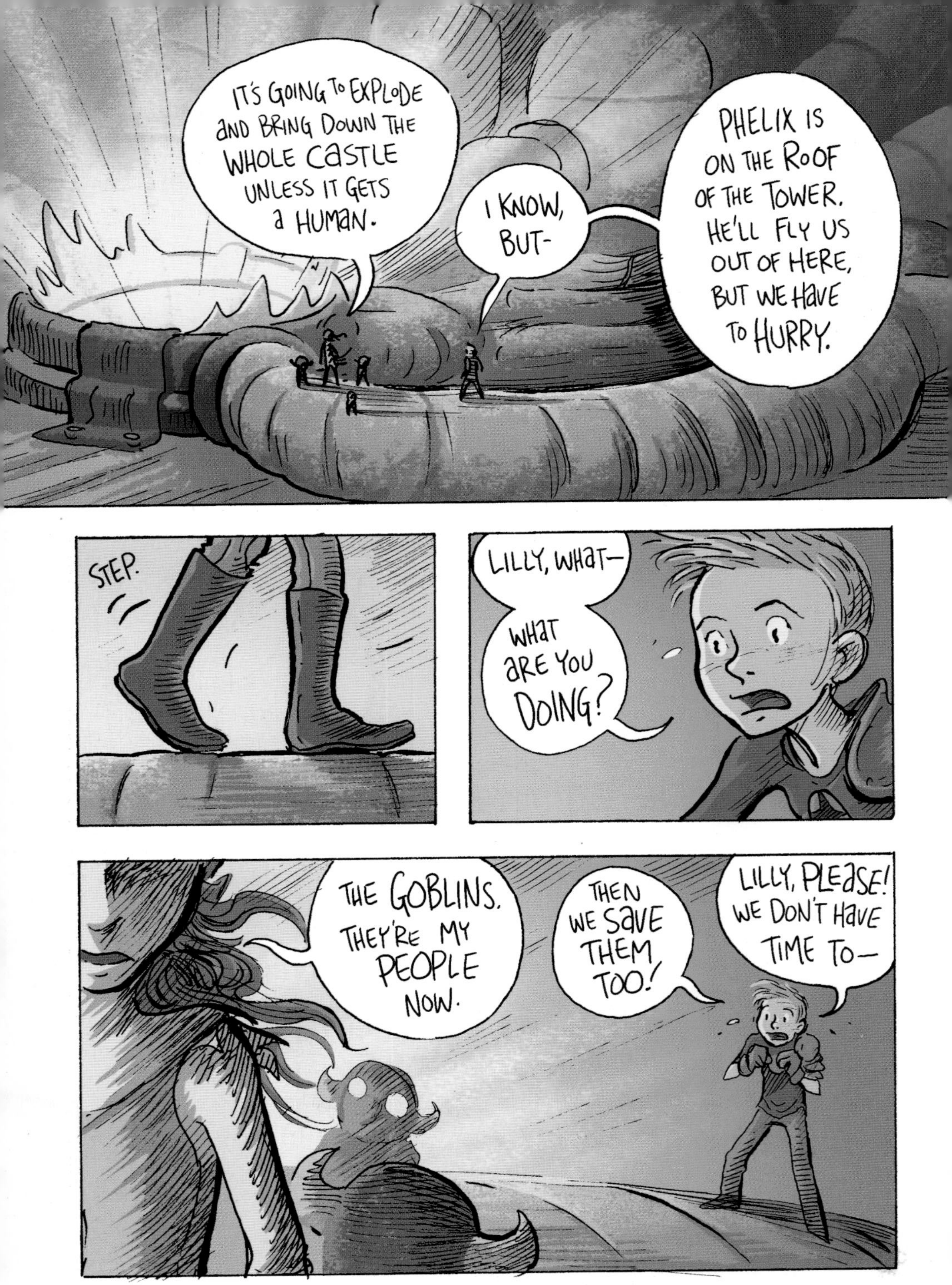
IT'S GOING TO EXPLODE AND BRING DOWN THE WHOLE CASTLE UNLESS IT GETS A HUMAN.
I KNOW, BUT-
PHELIX IS ON THE ROOF OF THE TOWER. HE'LL FLY US OUT OF HERE, BUT WE HAVE TO HURRY.
STEP.
LILLY, WHAT—
WHAT ARE YOU DOING?
THE GOBLINS. THEY'RE MY PEOPLE NOW.
THEN WE SAVE THEM TOO!
LILLY, PLEASE! WE DON'T HAVE TIME TO—

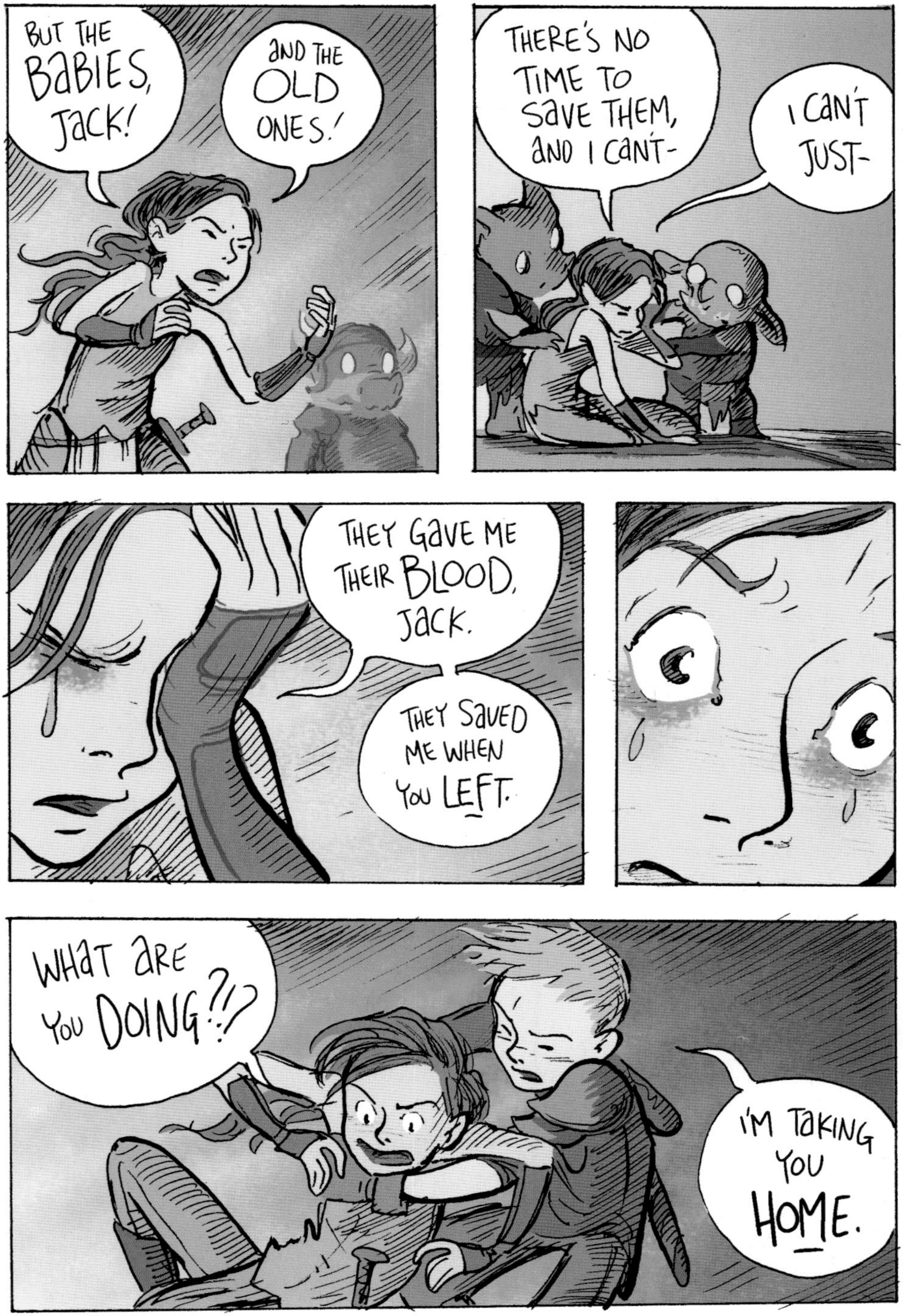
BUT THE BABIES, JACK!
AND THE OLD ONES!
THERE'S NO TIME TO SAVE THEM, AND I CAN'T-
I CAN'T JUST-
THEY GAVE ME THEIR BLOOD, JACK.
THEY SAVED ME WHEN YOU LEFT.
WHAT ARE YOU DOING?!?
I'M TAKING YOU HOME.

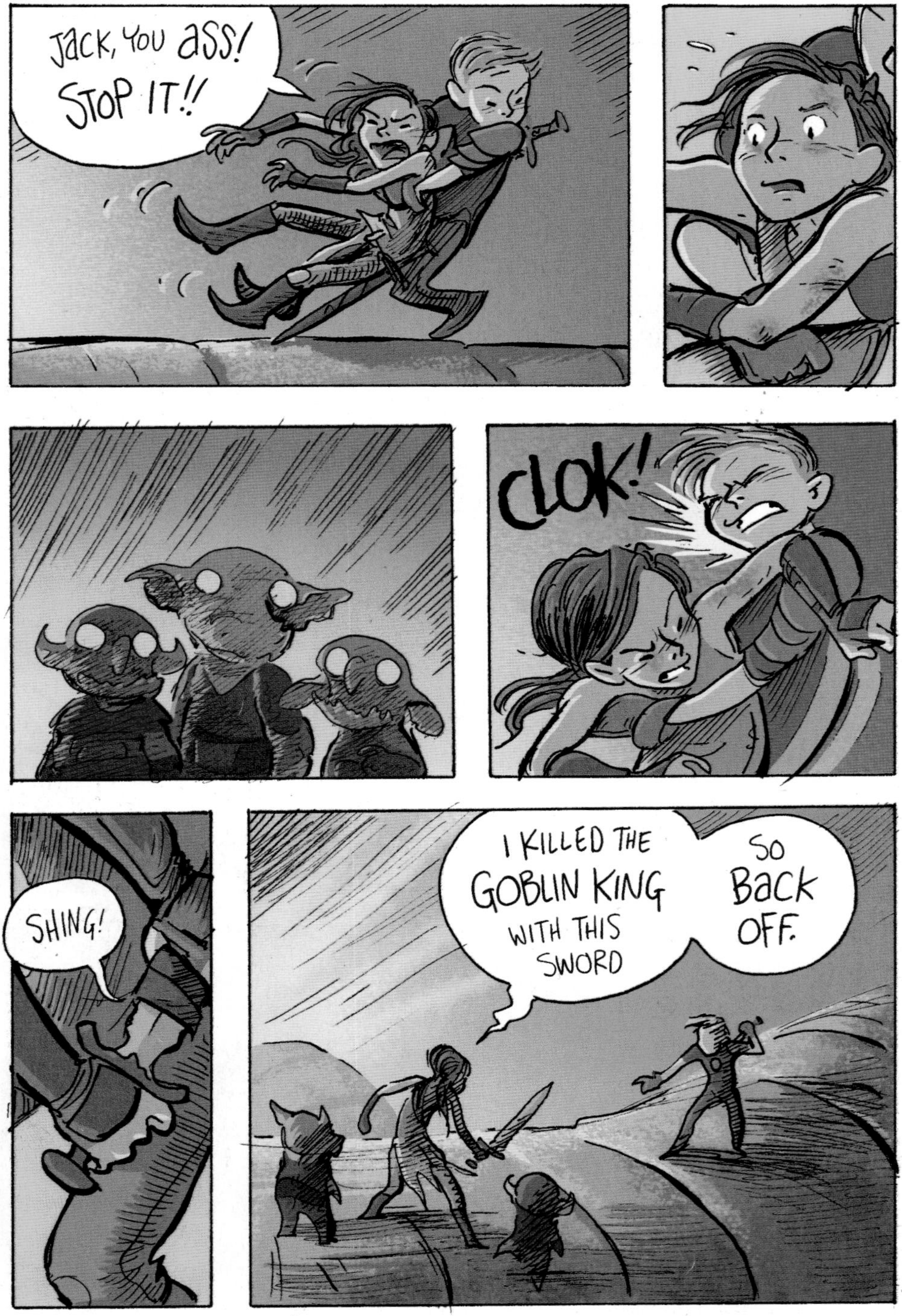
JACK, YOU ASS! STOP IT!!
CLOK!
SHING!
I KILLED THE GOBLIN KING WITH THIS SWORD
SO BACK OFF.

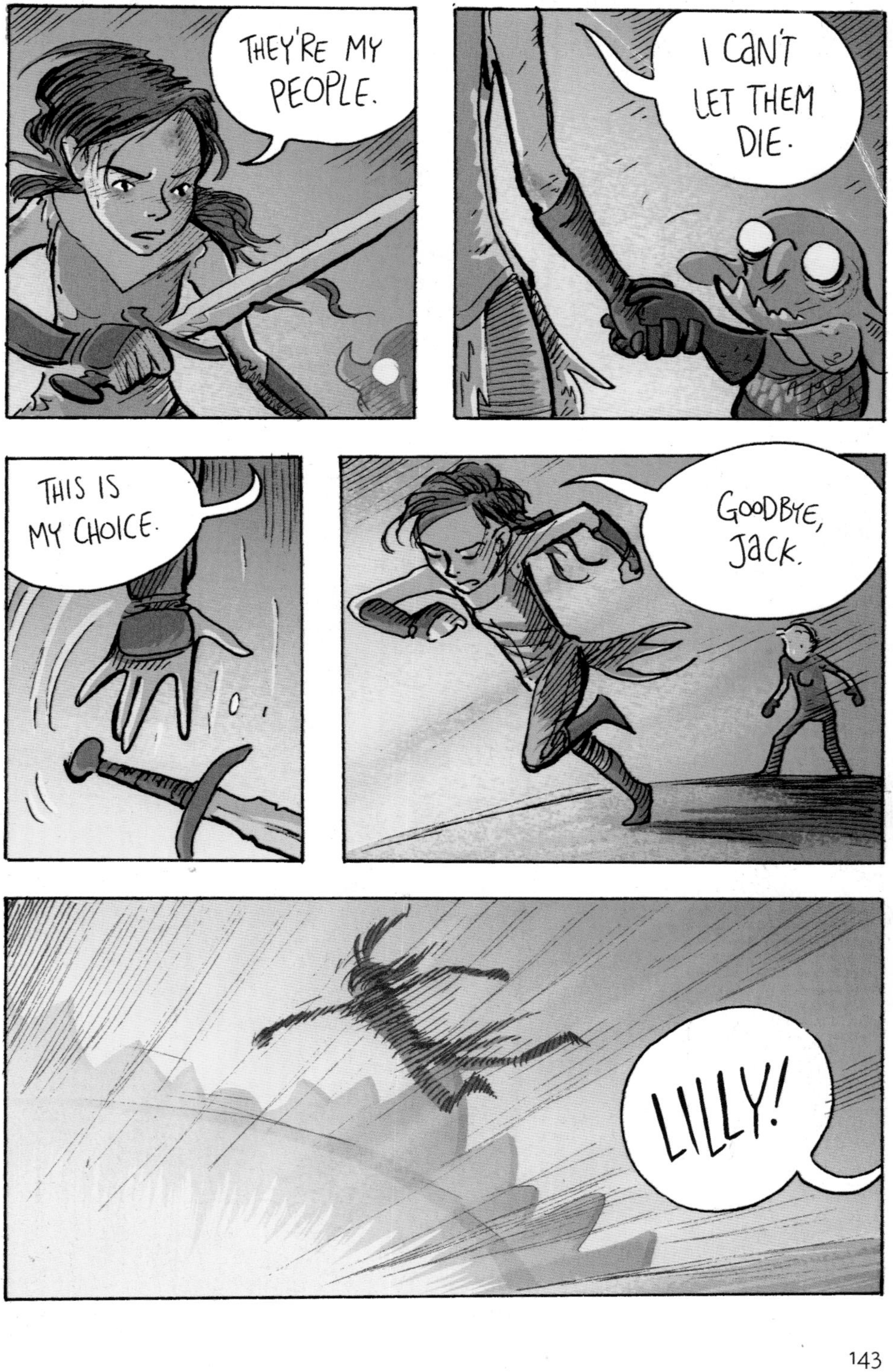
THEY'RE MY PEOPLE.
I CAN'T LET THEM DIE.
THIS IS MY CHOICE.
GOODBYE, JACK.
LILLY!

LILLY!!
SOB.
SHUDDER
KLNK!
CHK!
FOOOM!

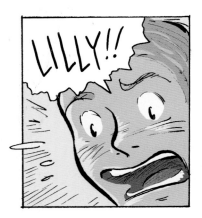

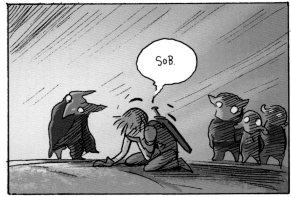

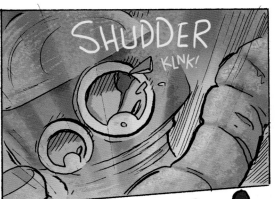

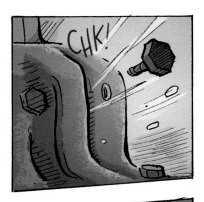

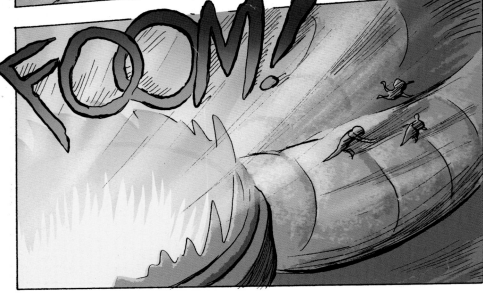

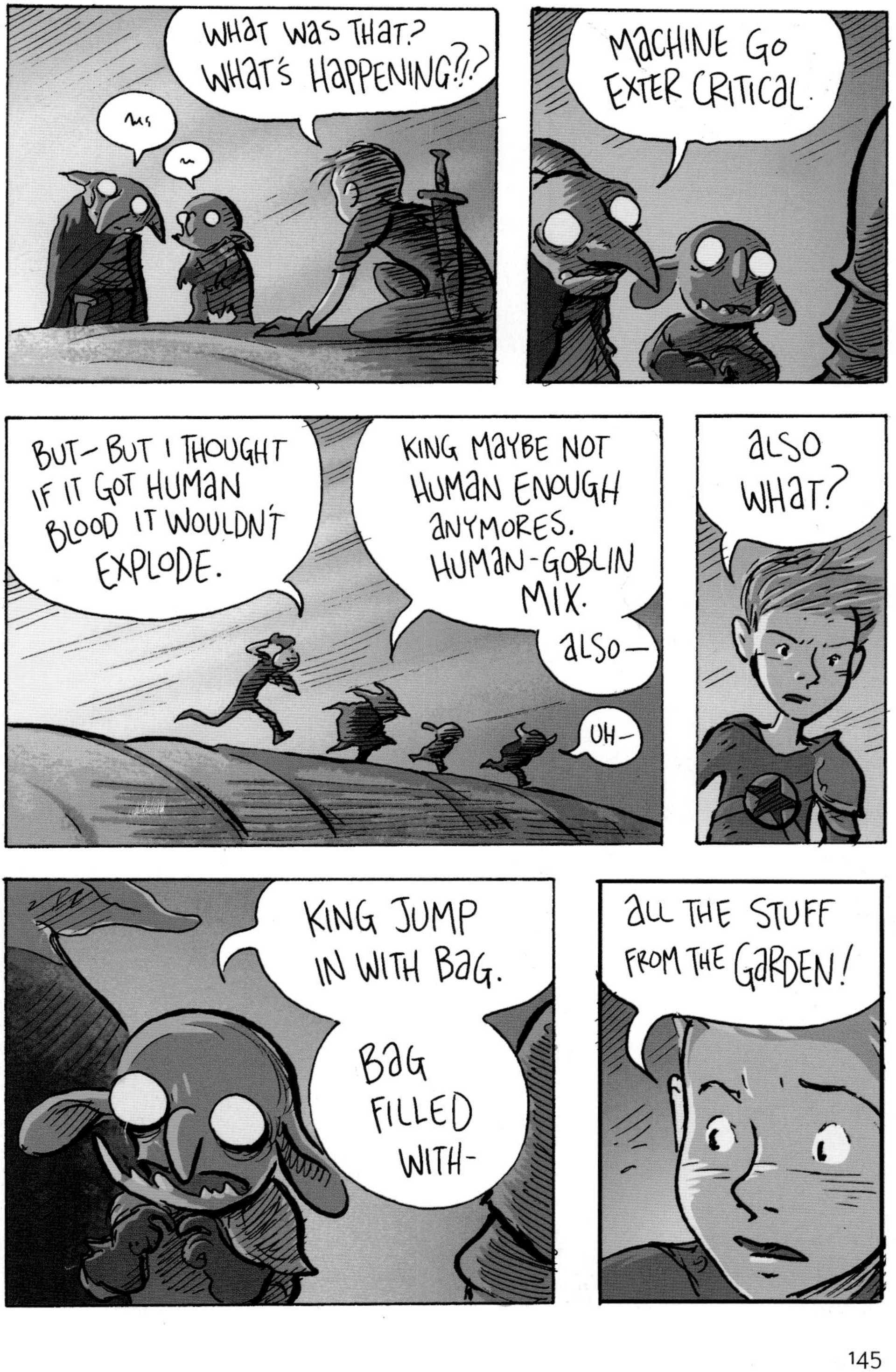
WHAT WAS THAT? WHAT'S HAPPENING?!?
MACHINE GO EXTER CRITICAL.
BUT— BUT I THOUGHT IF IT GOT HUMAN BLOOD IT WOULDN'T EXPLODE.
KING MAYBE NOT HUMAN ENOUGH ANYMORES. HUMAN-GOBLIN MIX.
ALSO—
UH—
ALSO WHAT?
KING JUMP IN WITH BAG.
BAG FILLED WITH-
ALL THE STUFF FROM THE GARDEN!

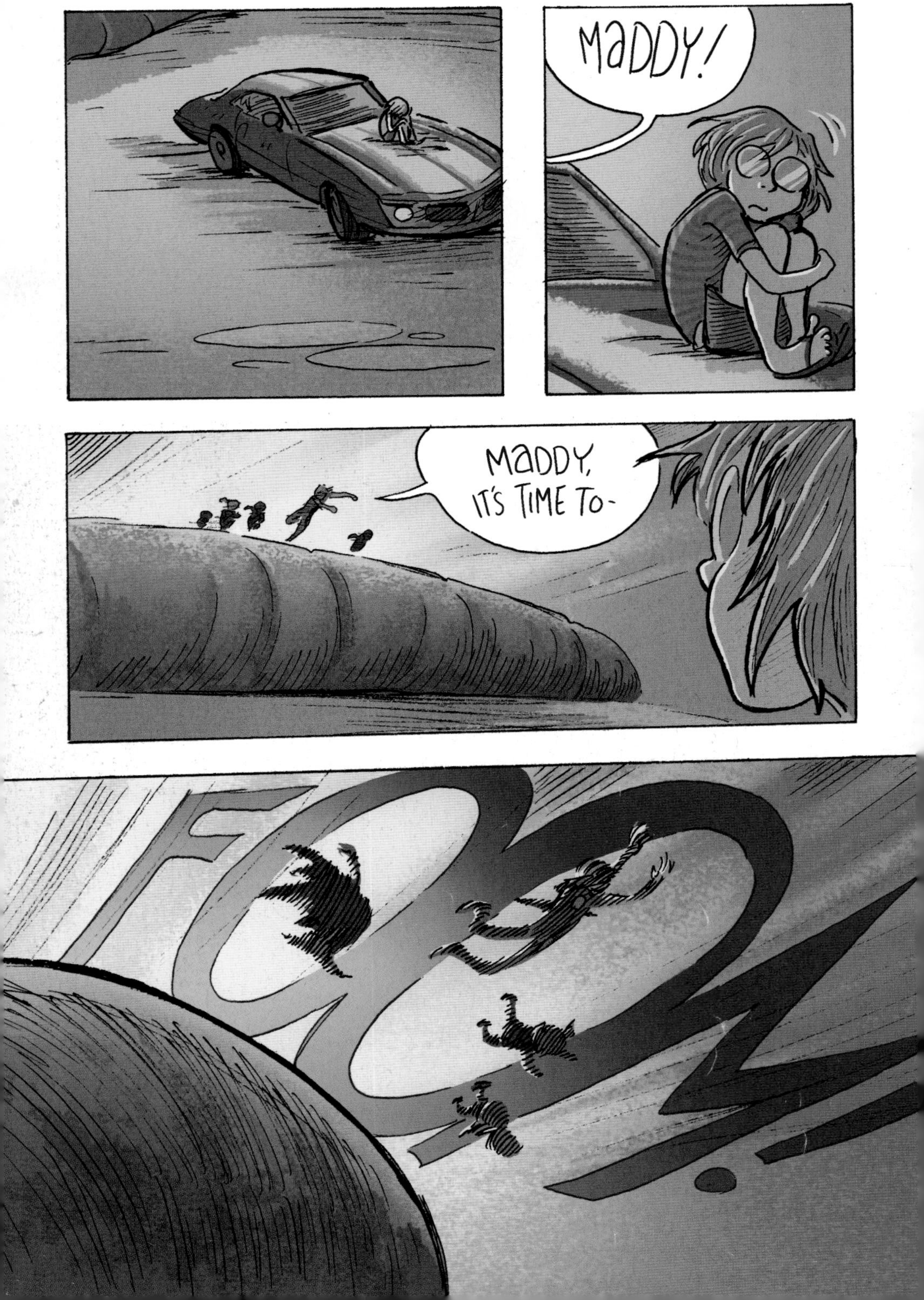
MADDY!
MADDY, IT'S TIME TO-
FOOM!

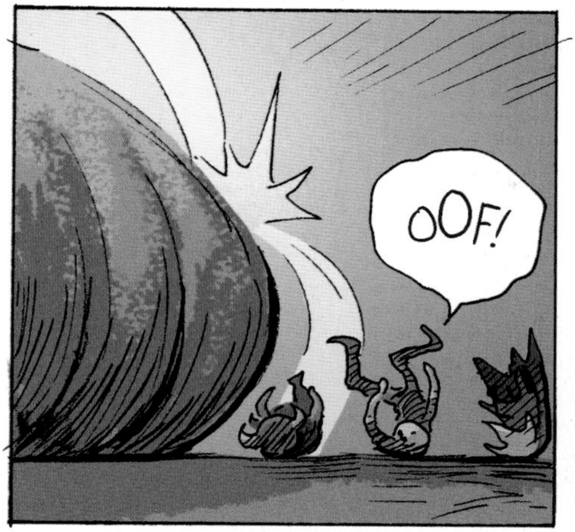
OOF!

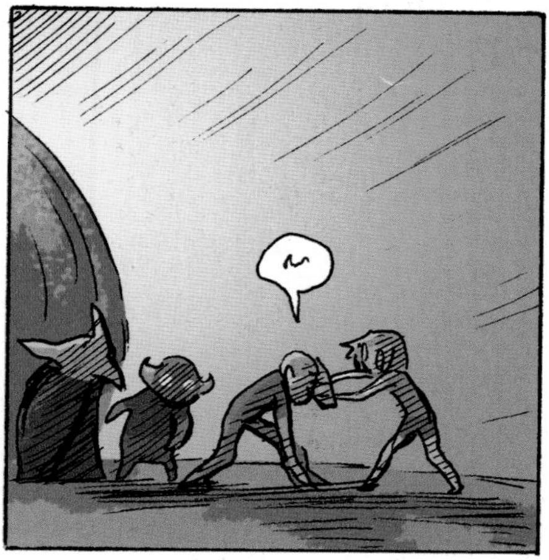
~

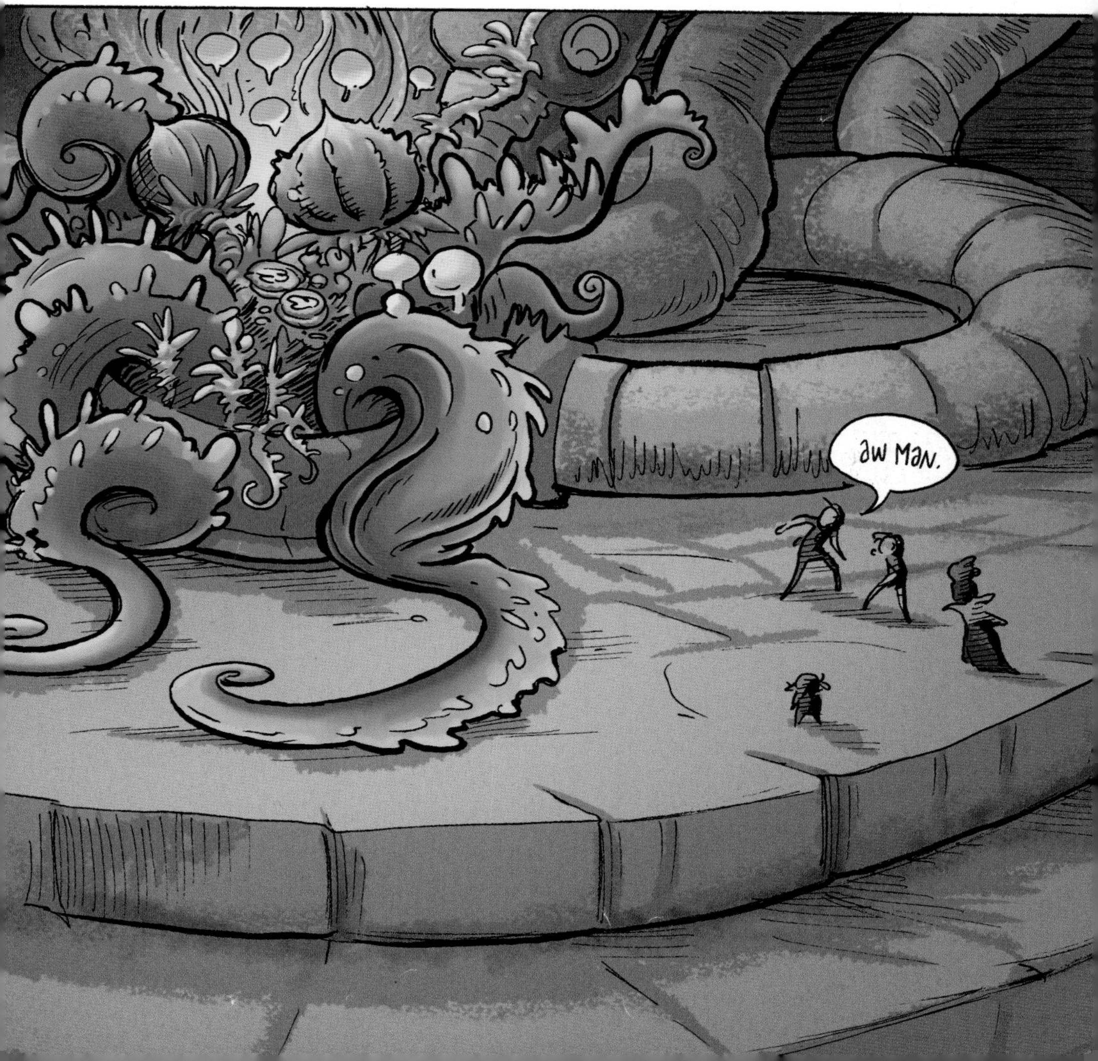
aw man.

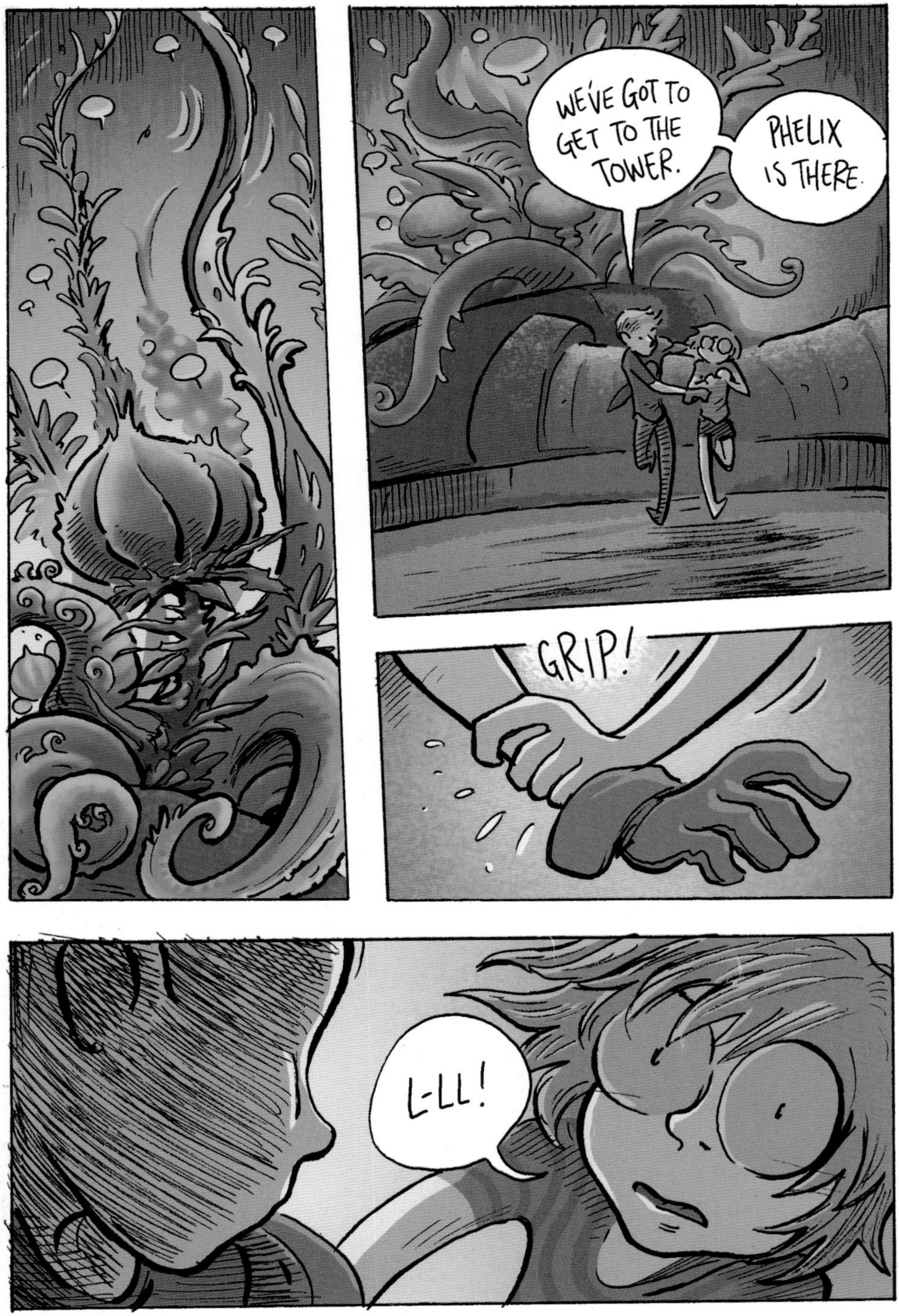
WE'VE GOT TO GET TO THE TOWER.
PHELIX IS THERE.
GRIP!
L-LL!

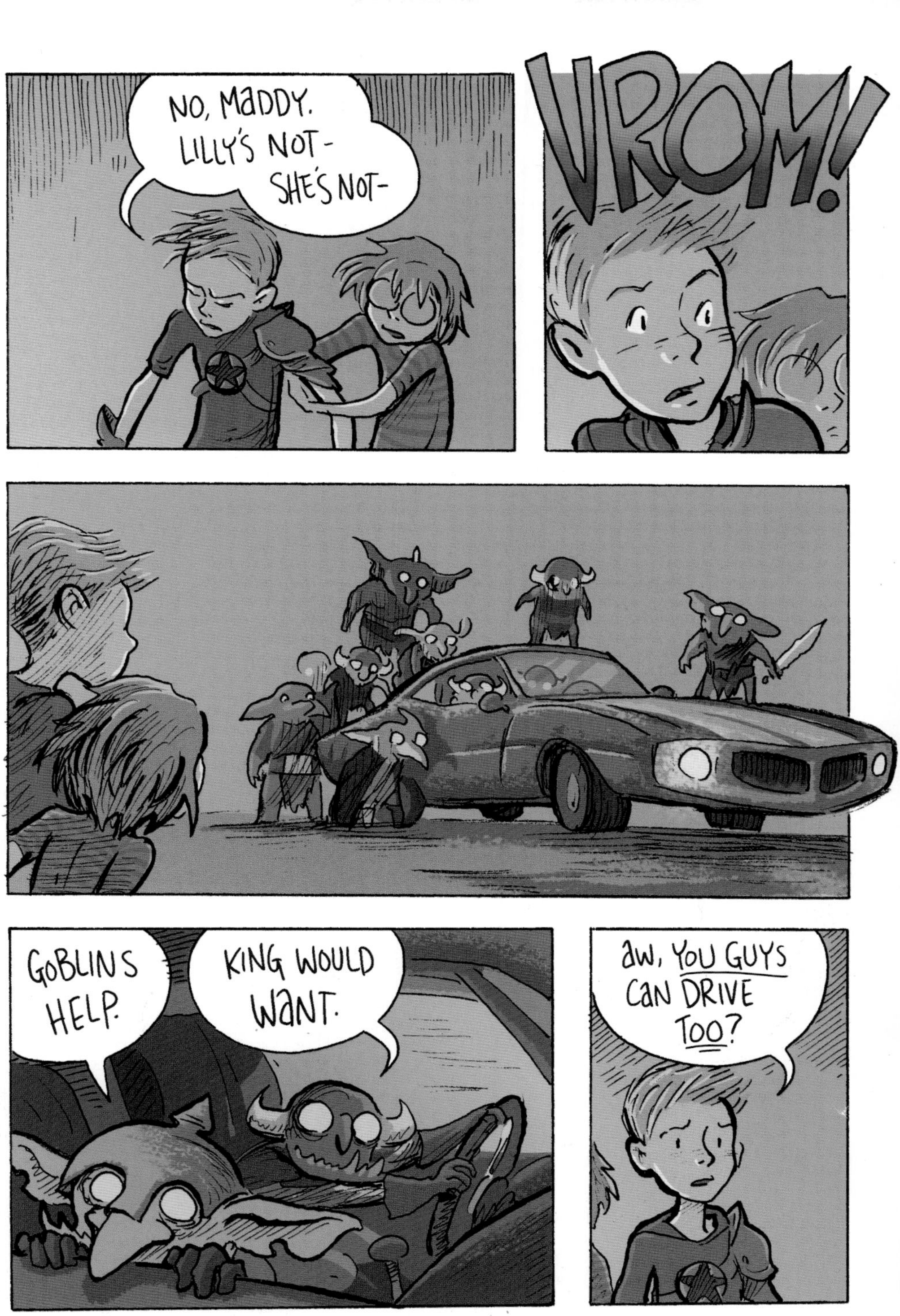
NO, MADDY. LILLY'S NOT- SHE'S NOT-
VROM!
GOBLINS HELP.
KING WOULD WANT.
AW, YOU GUYS CAN DRIVE TOO?

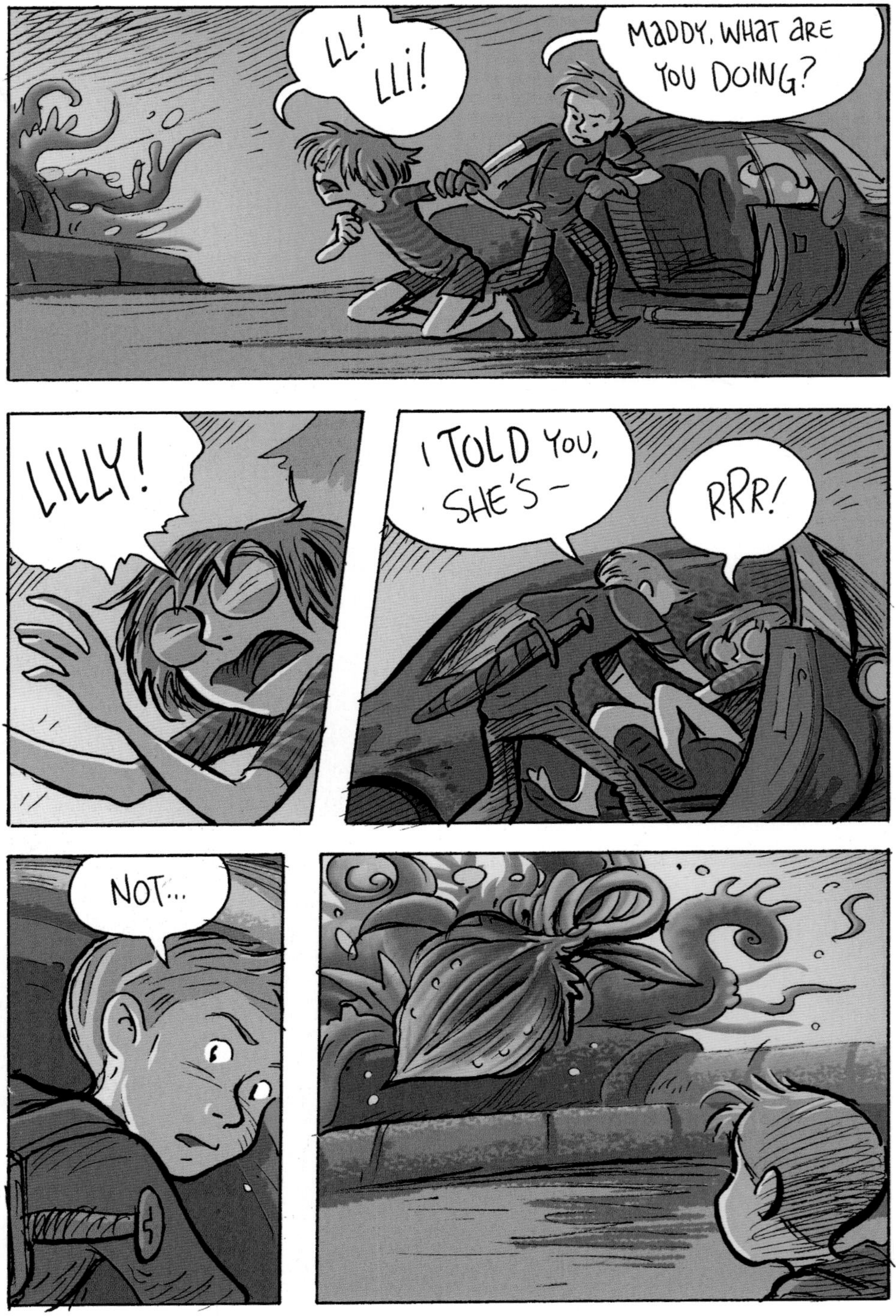
LL!
LLI!
MADDY, WHAT ARE YOU DOING?
LILLY!
I TOLD YOU, SHE'S –
RRR!
NOT...

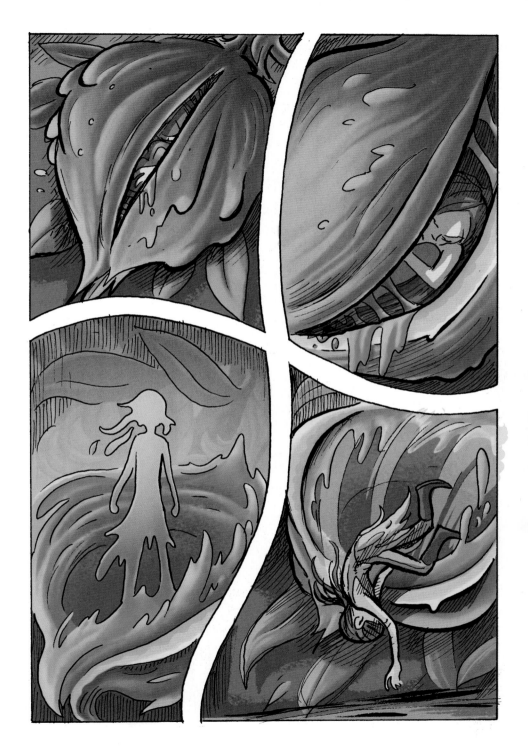

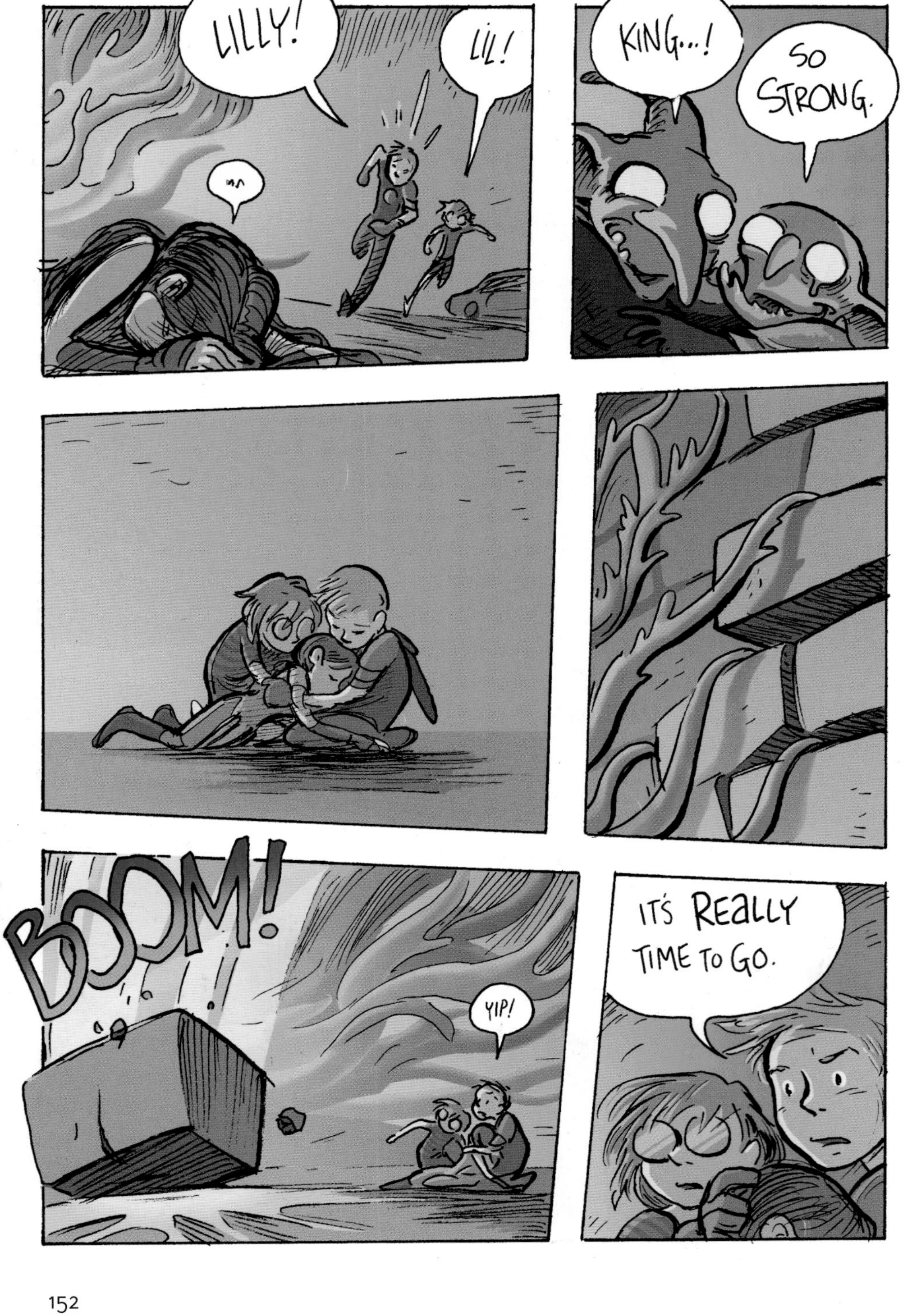

LILLY!
LIL!
KING...!
SO STRONG.
BOOM!
YIP!
IT'S REALLY TIME TO GO.

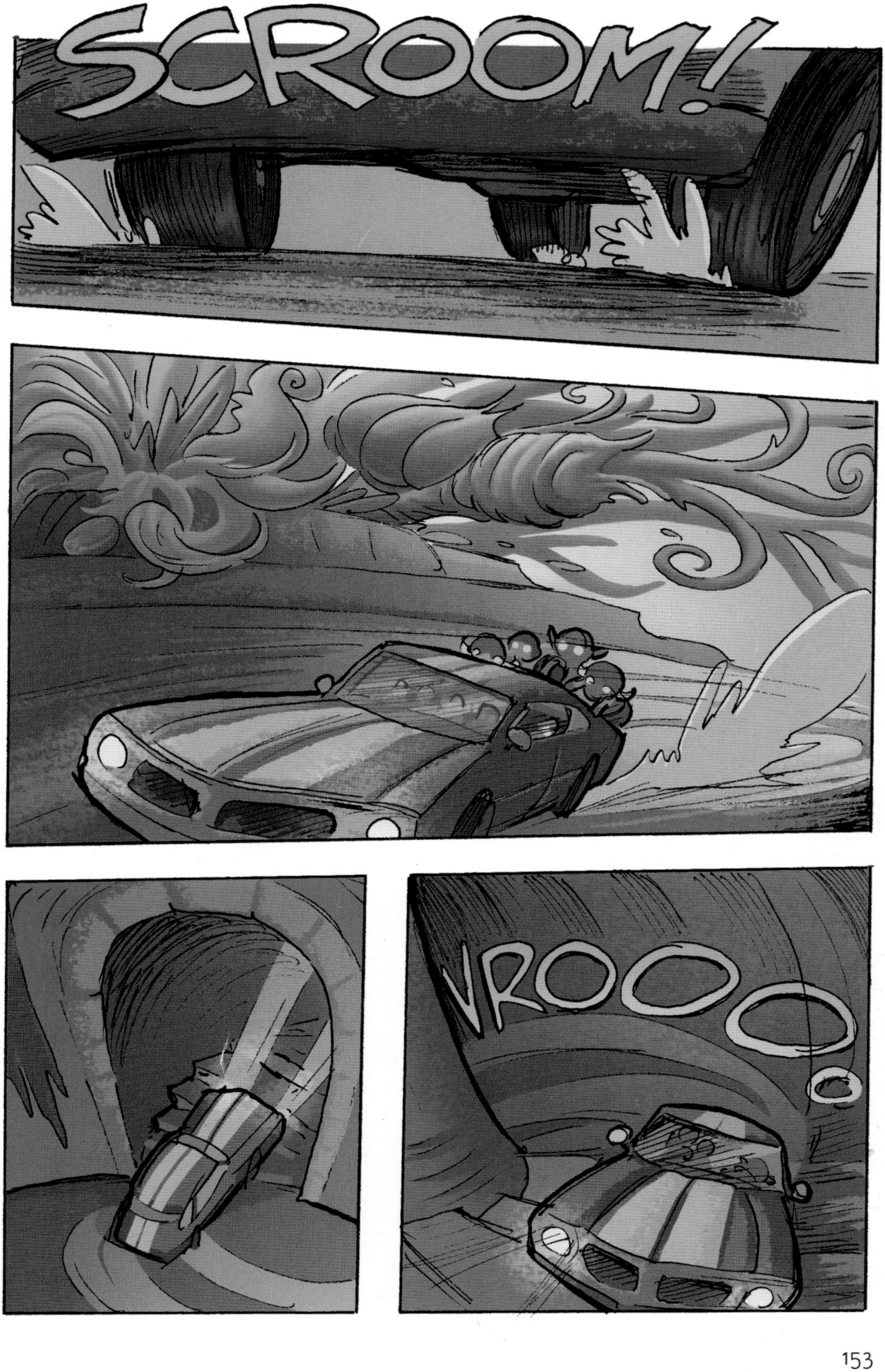
SCROOM!
VROOOO

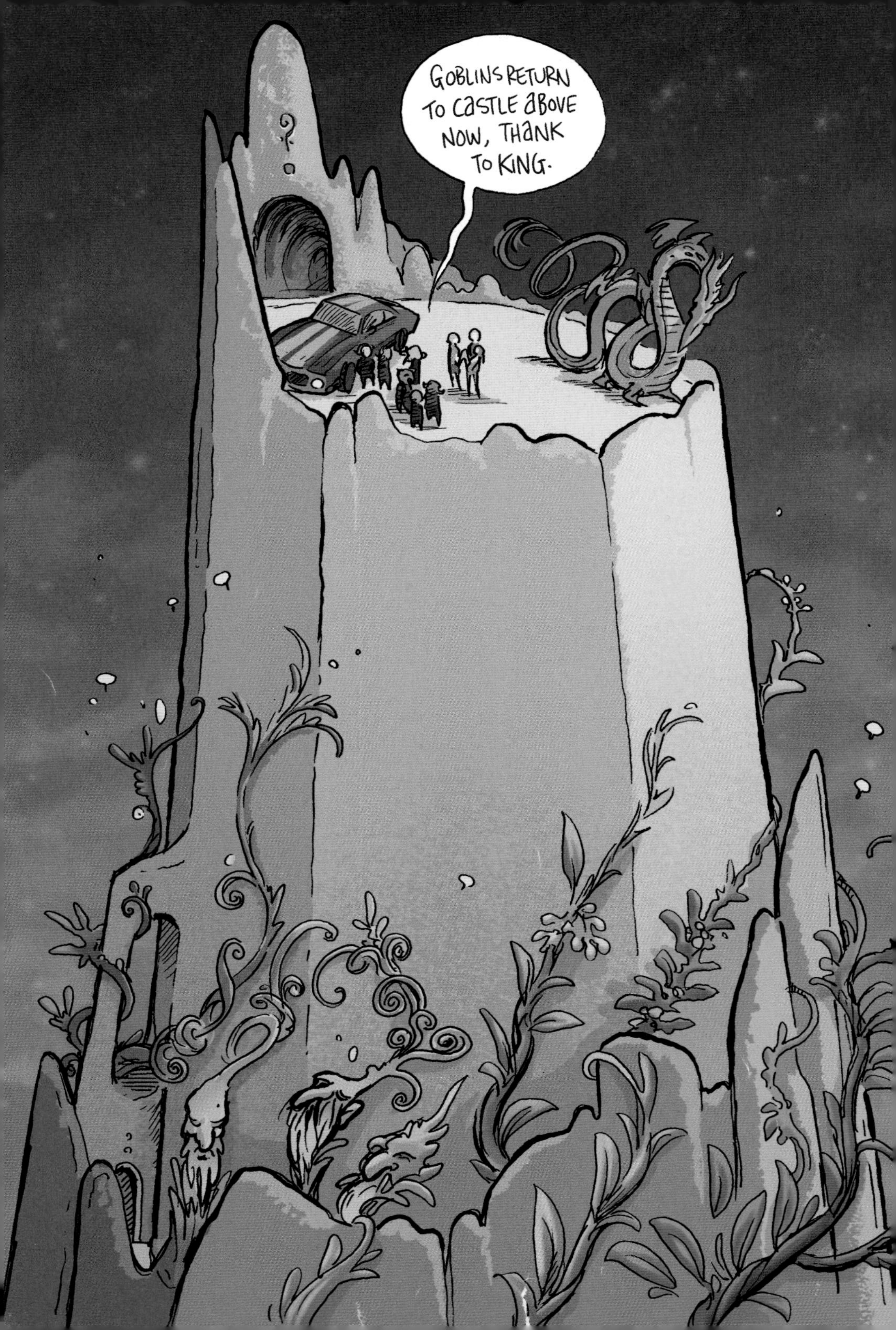
GOBLINS RETURN TO CASTLE ABOVE NOW, THANK TO KING.

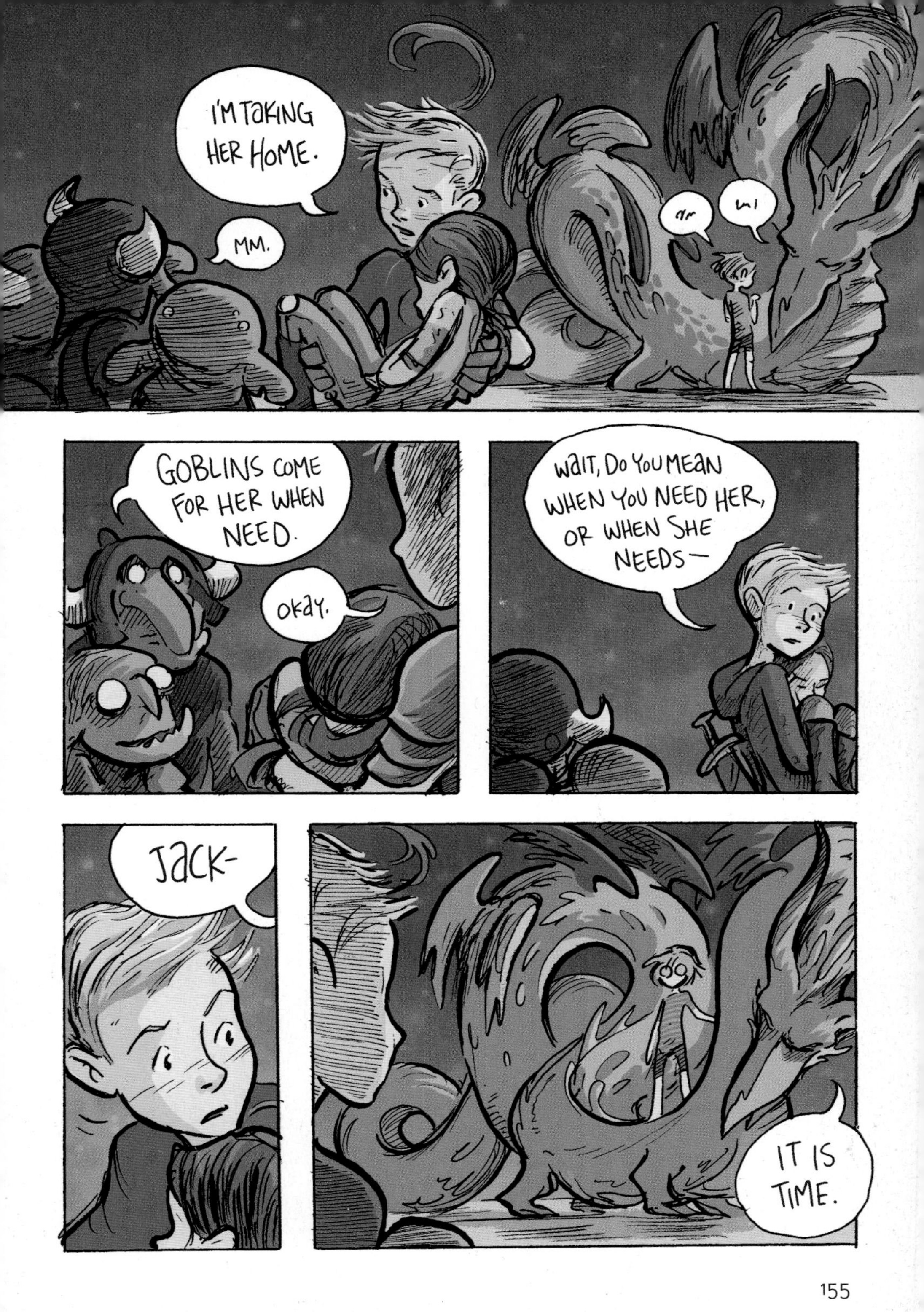

I'M TAKING HER HOME.
MM.
GOBLINS COME FOR HER WHEN NEED.
OKAY.
WAIT, DO YOU MEAN WHEN YOU NEED HER, OR WHEN SHE NEEDS—
JACK-
IT IS TIME.

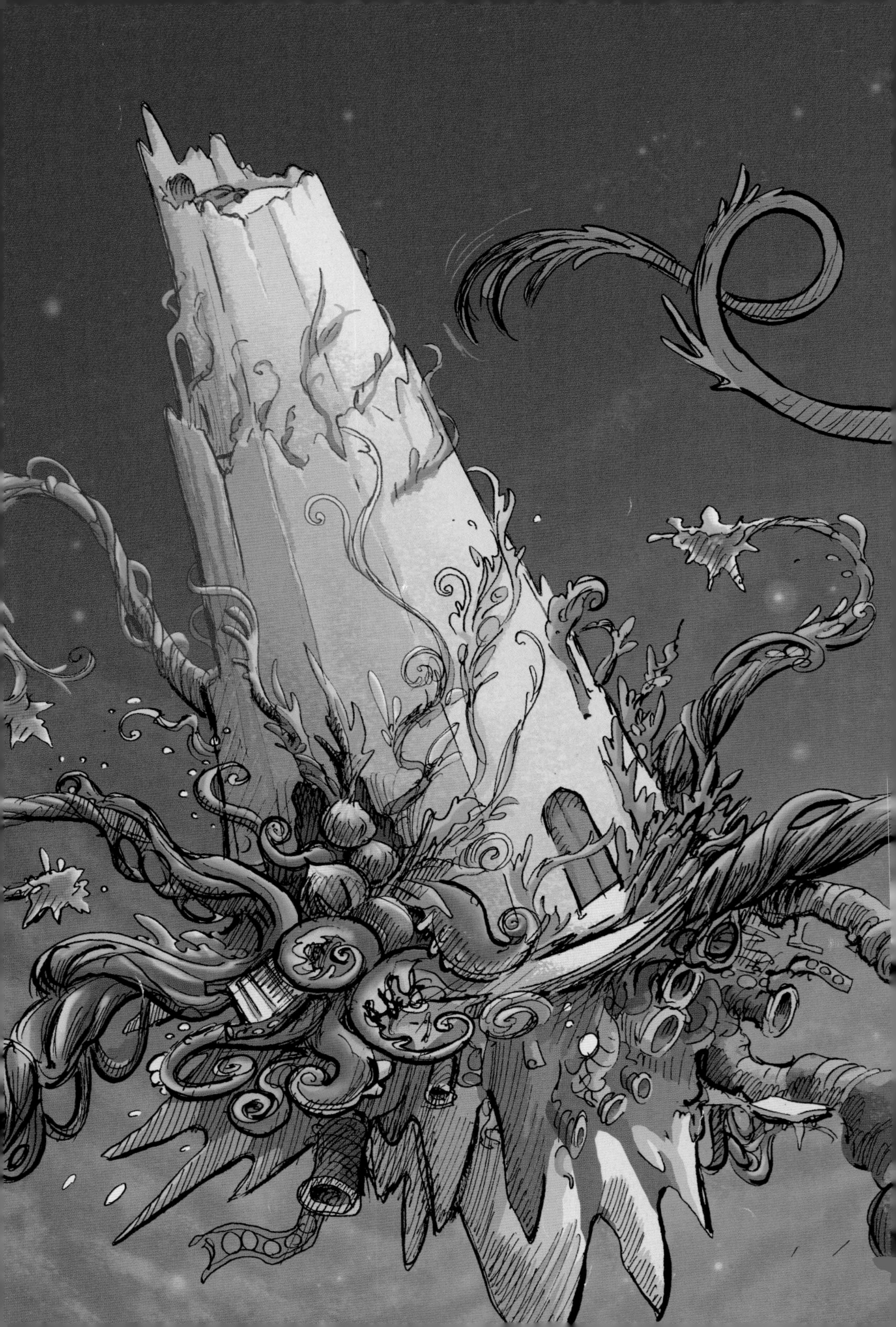

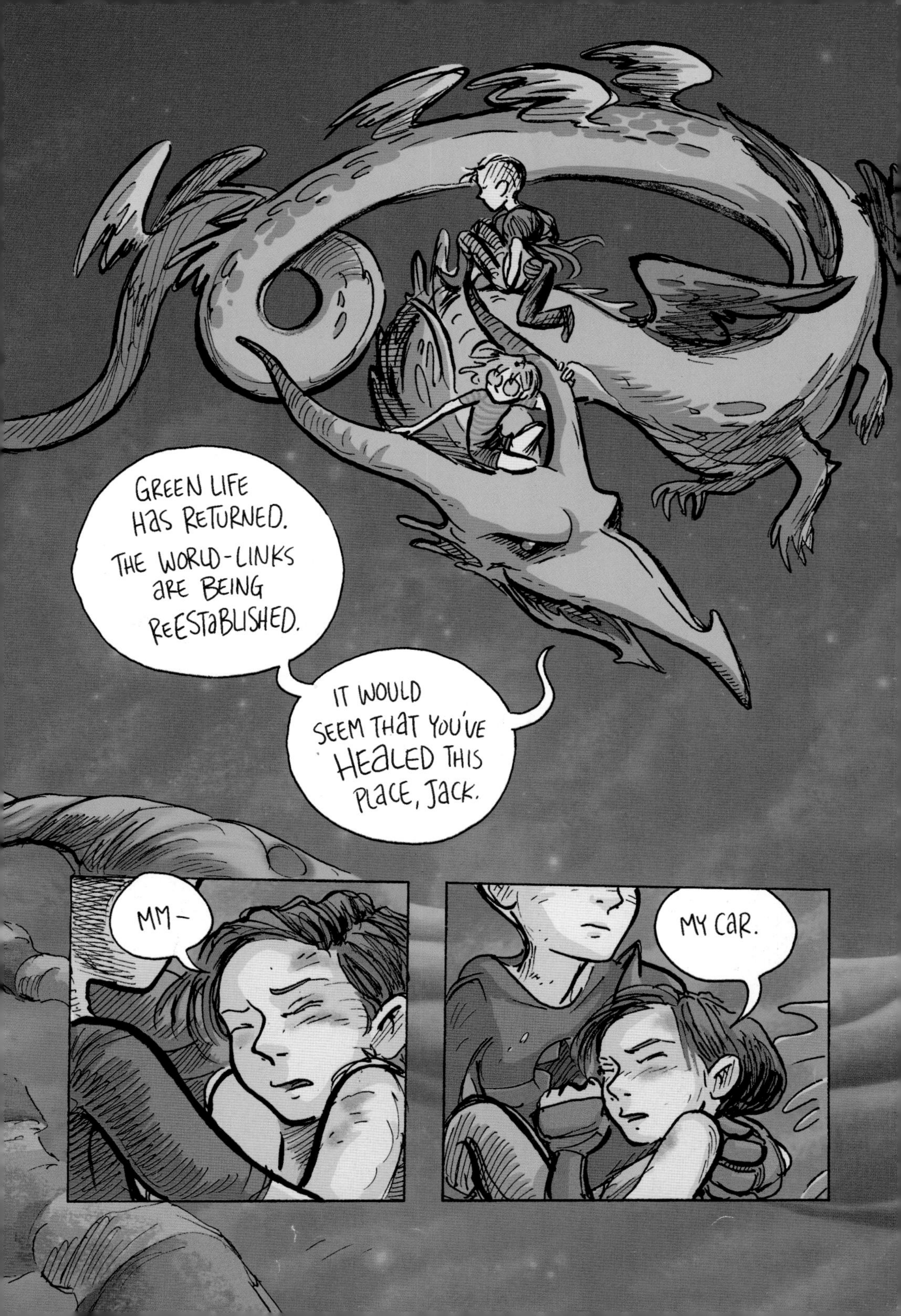
GREEN LIFE HAS RETURNED. THE WORLD-LINKS ARE BEING REESTABLISHED.
IT WOULD SEEM THAT YOU'VE HEALED THIS PLACE, JACK.
MM-
MY CAR.

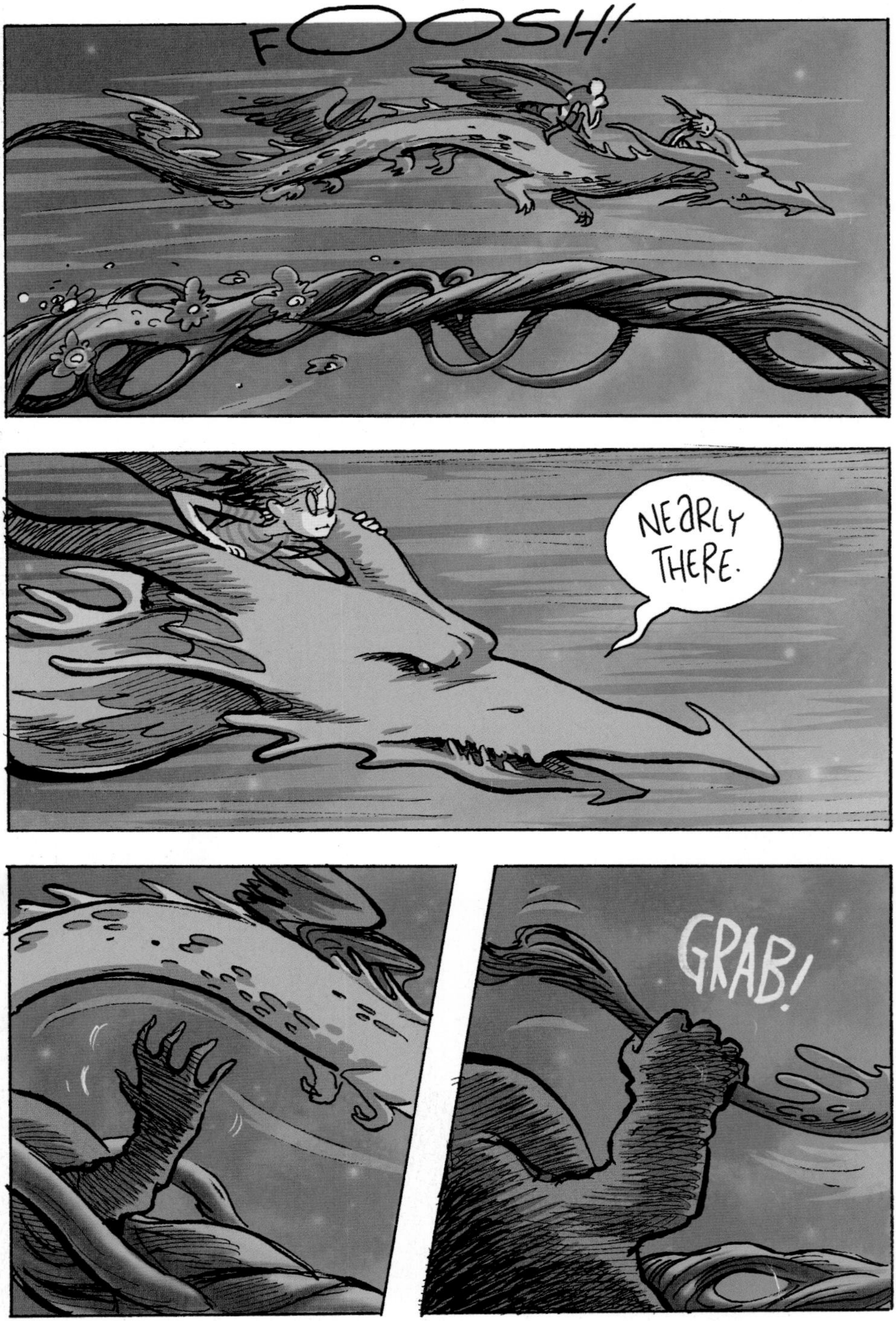
FOOOSH!
NEARLY THERE.
GRAB!

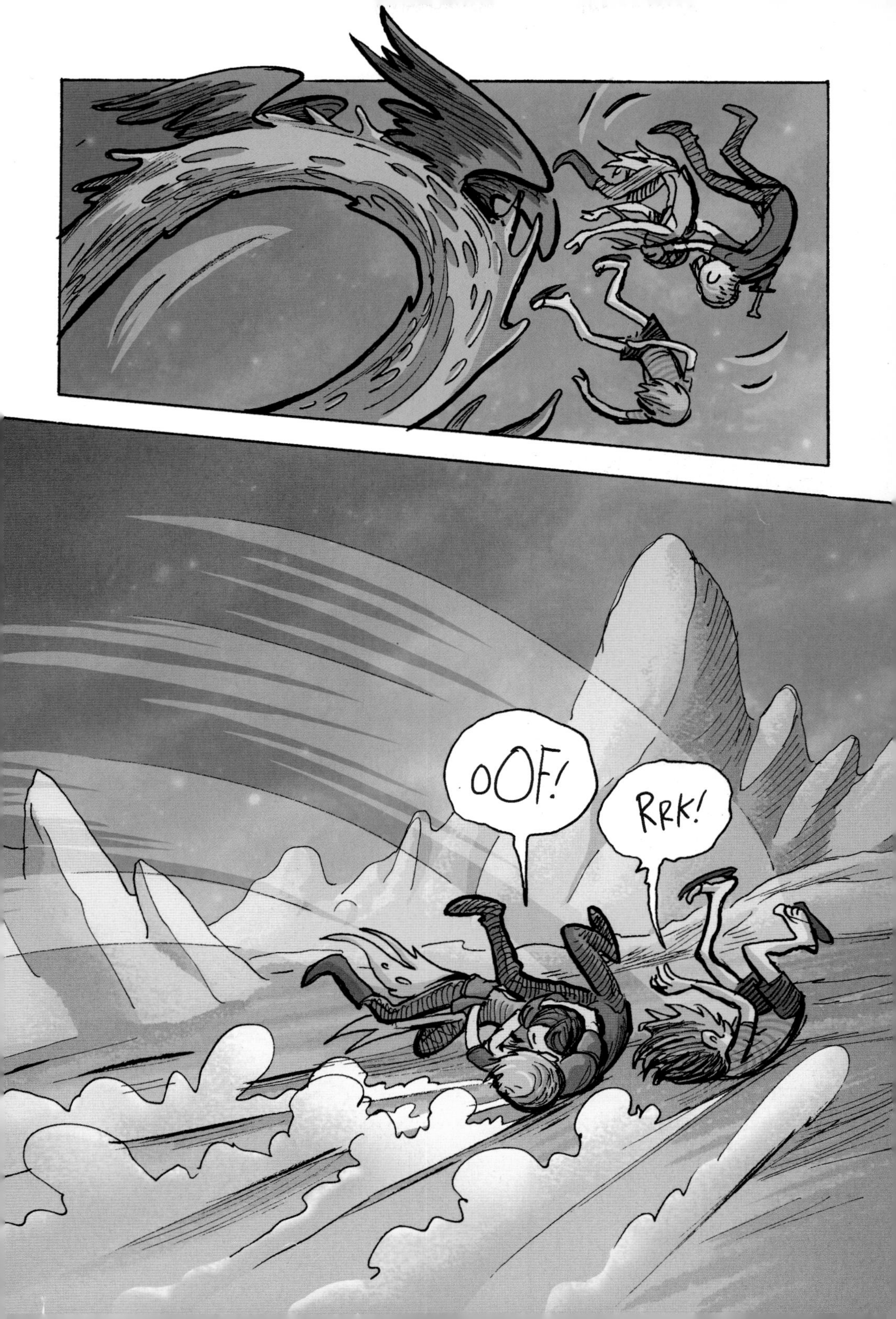
OOF!
RRK!

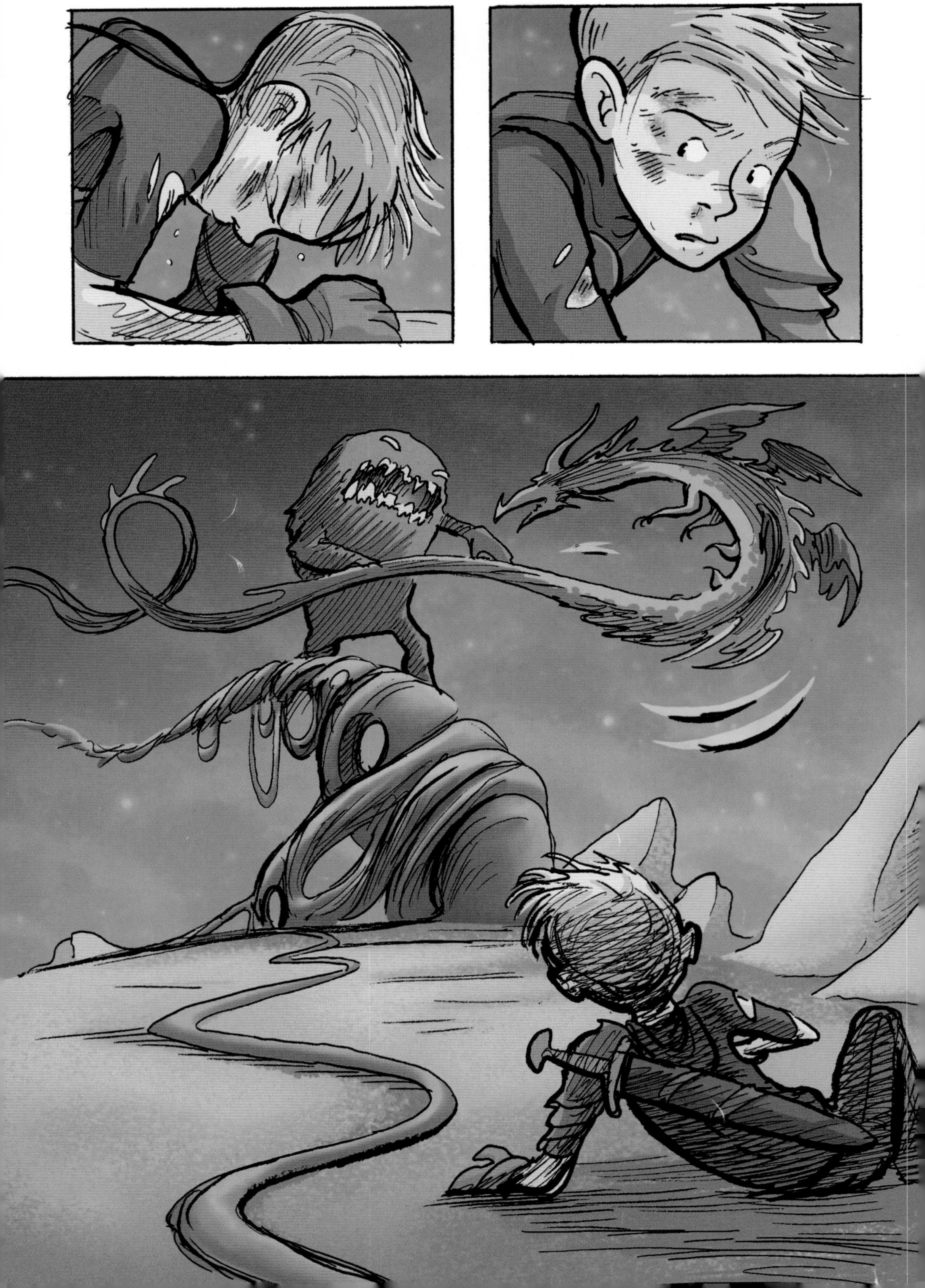

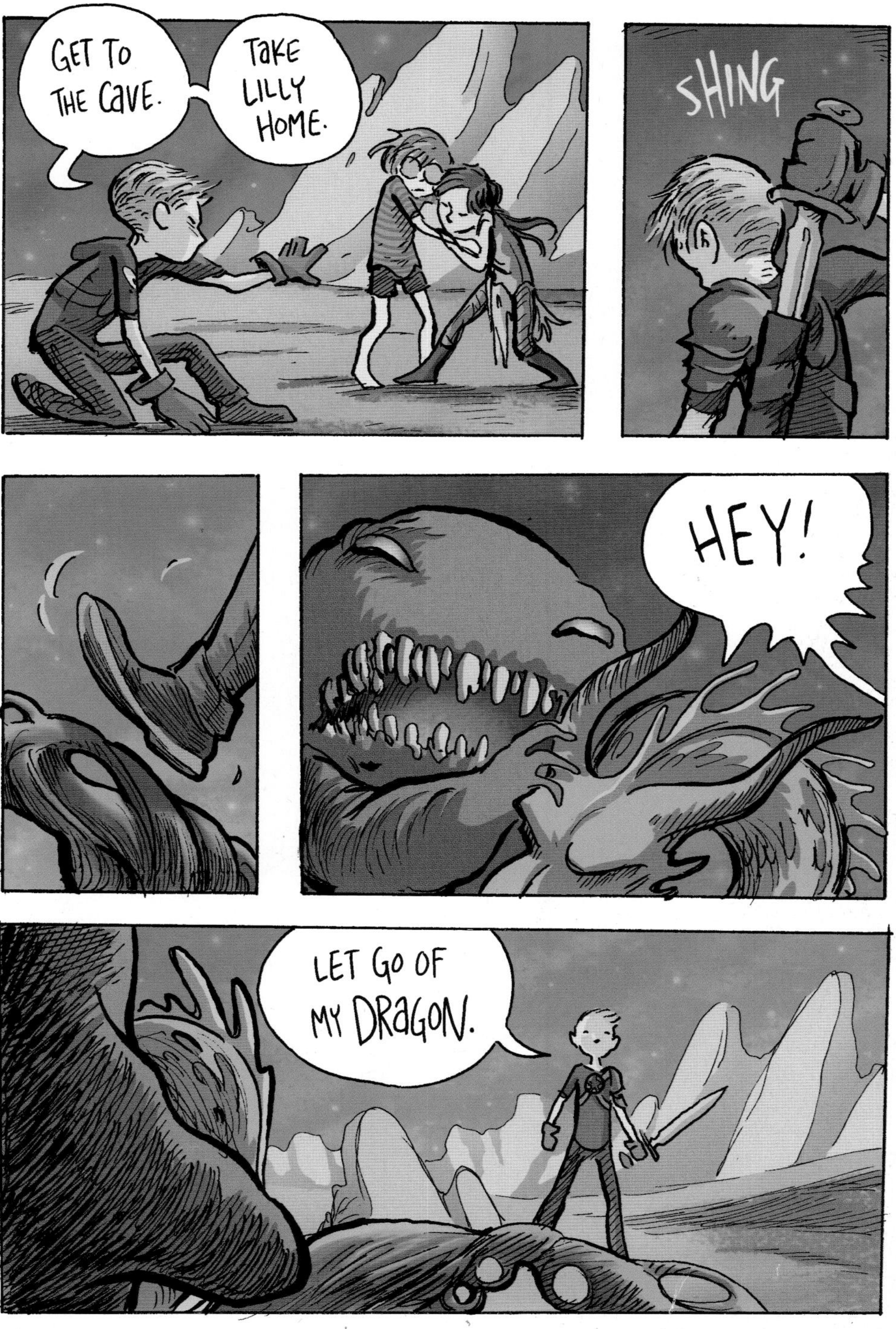
GET TO THE CAVE.
TAKE LILLY HOME.
SHING
HEY!
LET GO OF MY DRAGON.

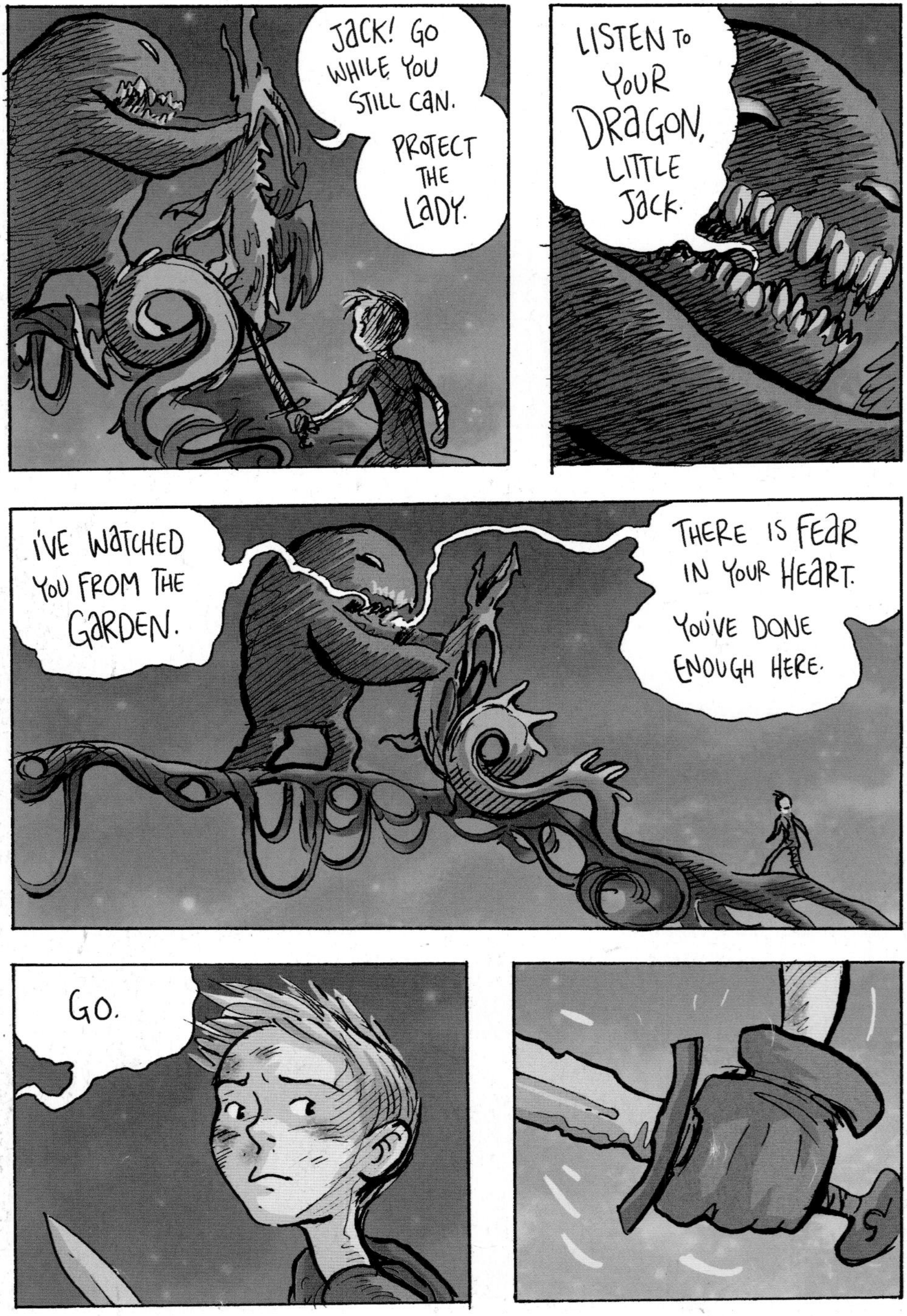
JACK! GO WHILE YOU STILL CAN.
PROTECT THE LADY.
LISTEN TO YOUR DRAGON, LITTLE JACK.
I'VE WATCHED YOU FROM THE GARDEN.
THERE IS FEAR IN YOUR HEART.
YOU'VE DONE ENOUGH HERE.
GO.

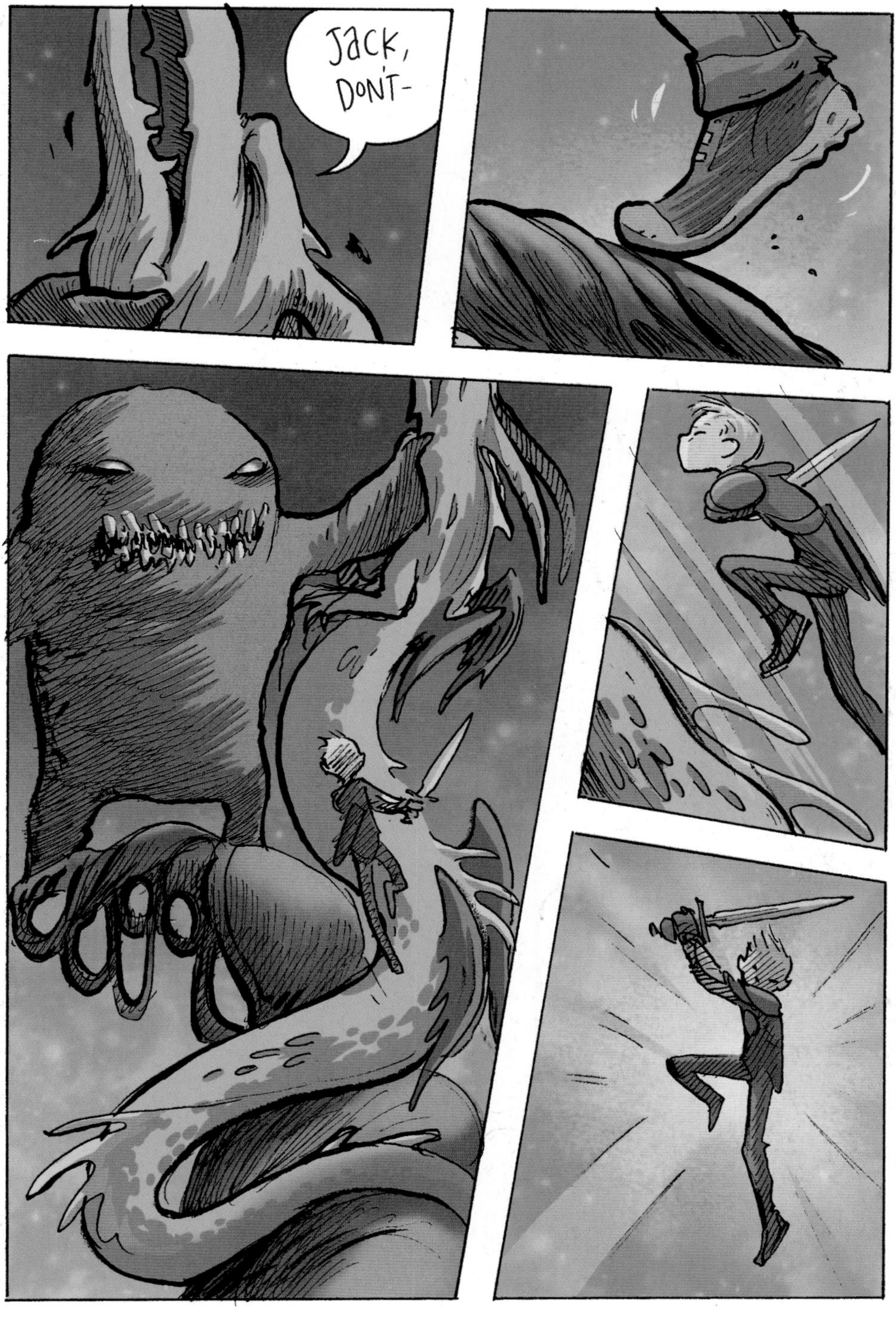
JACK, DON'T-

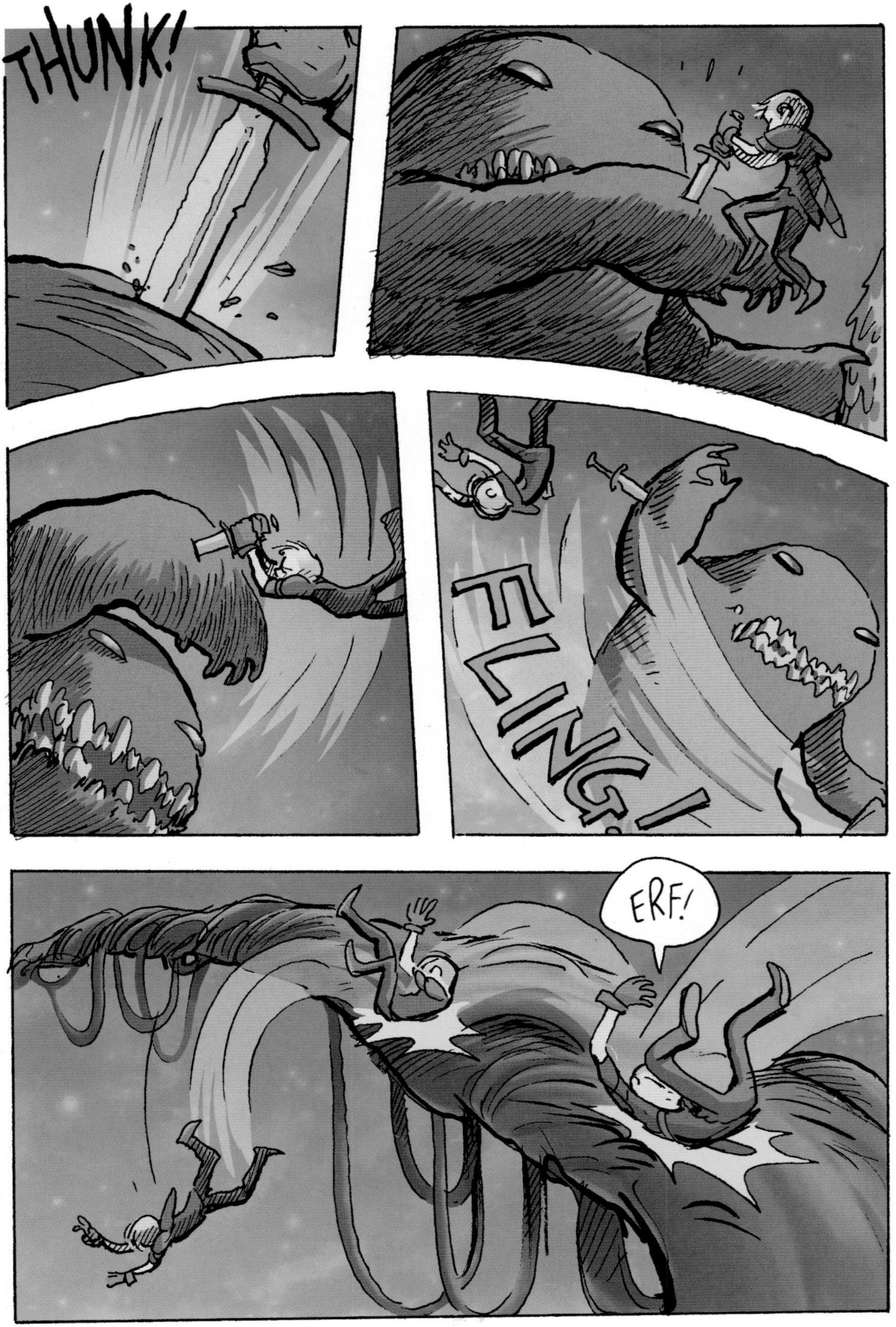
THUNK!
FLING!
ERF!

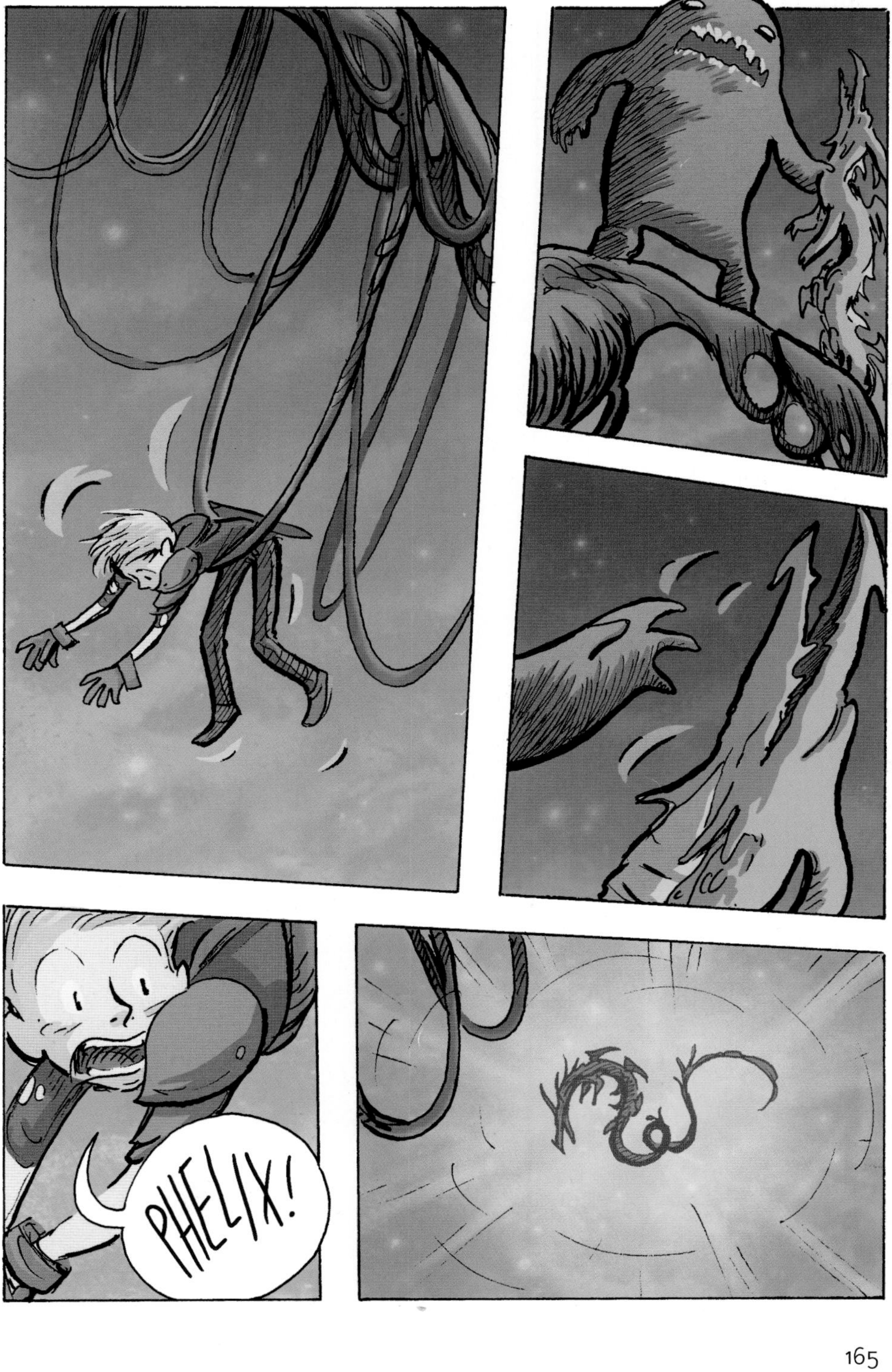
PHELIX!

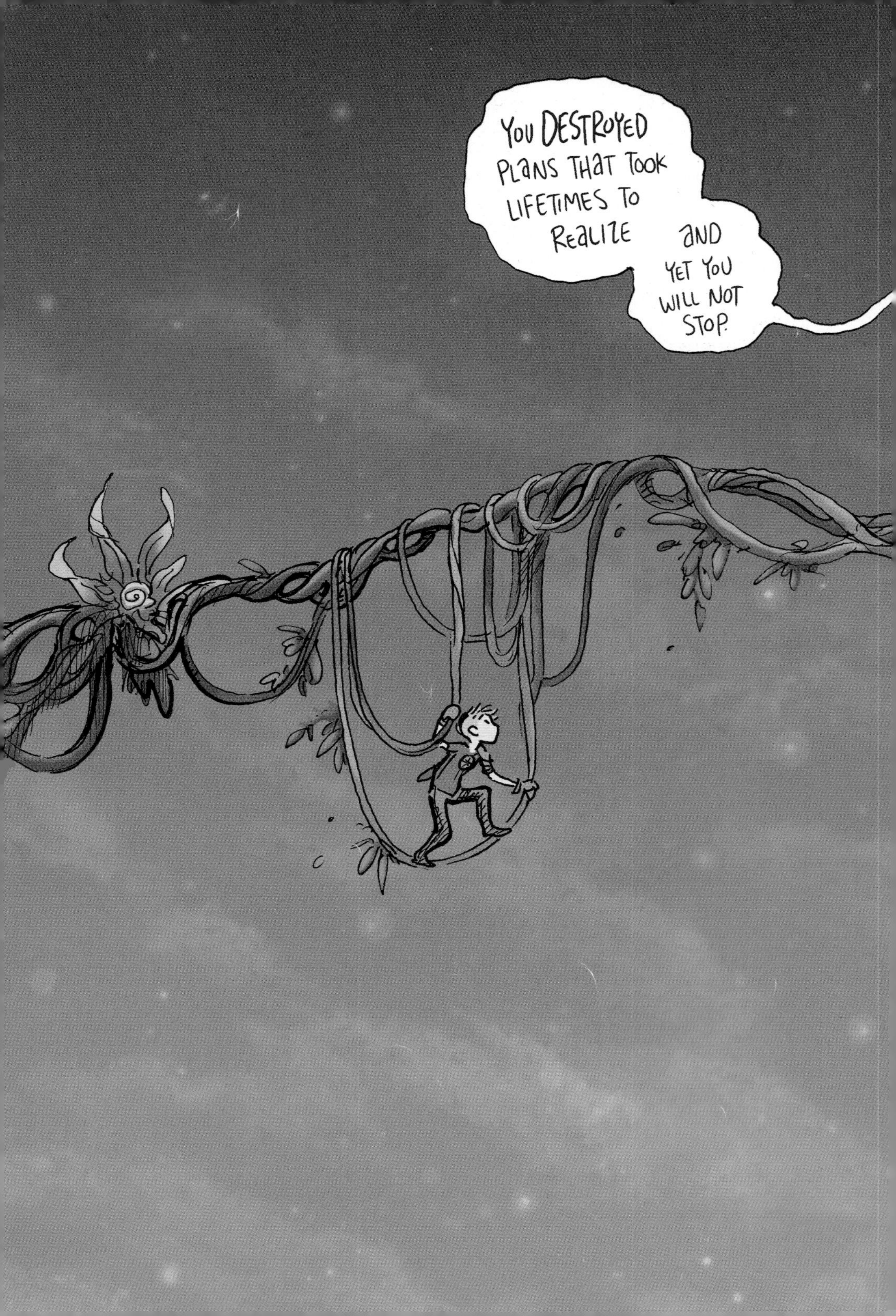
YOU DESTROYED PLANS THAT TOOK LIFETIMES TO REALIZE AND YET YOU WILL NOT STOP.

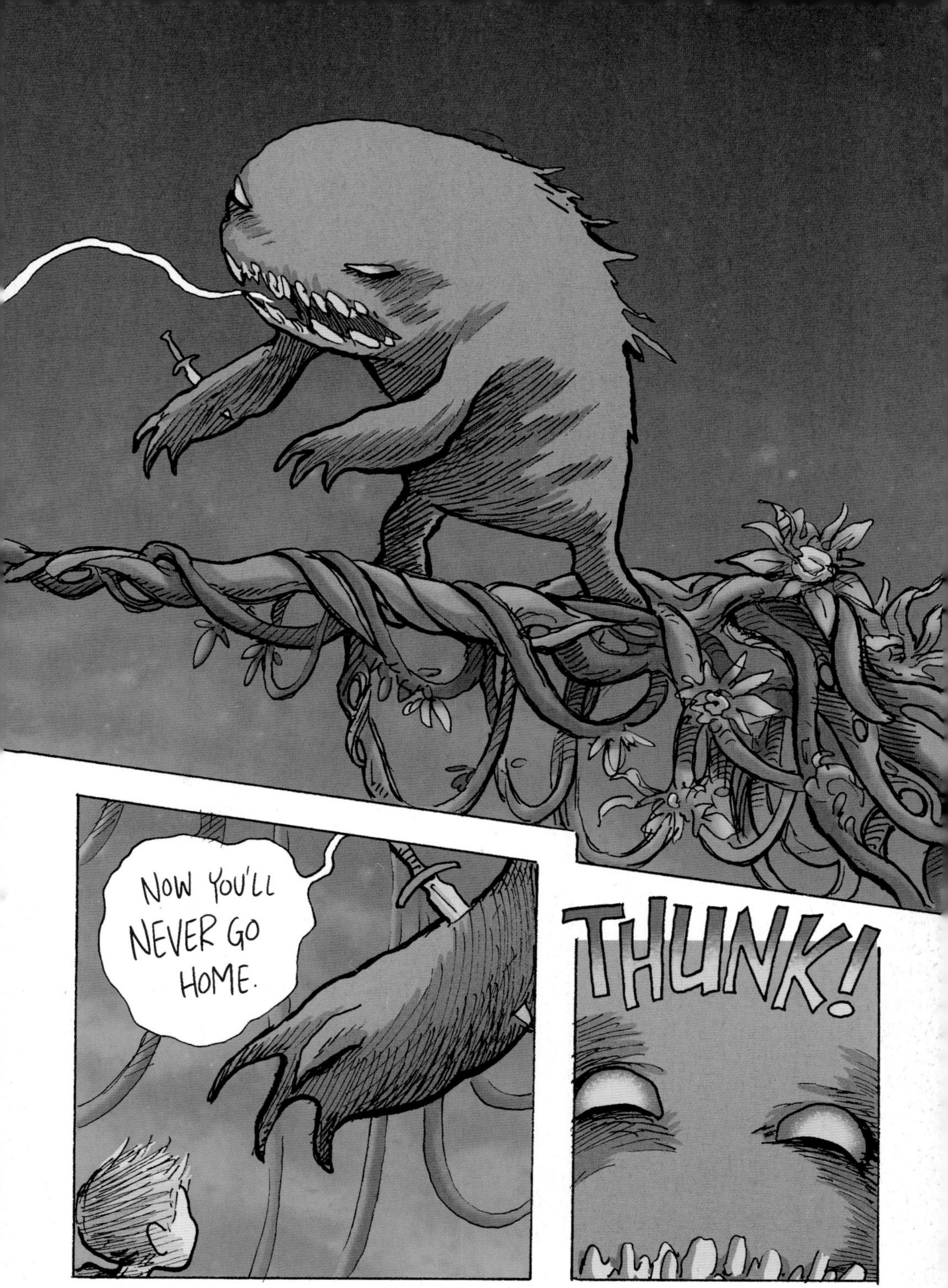
NOW YOU'LL NEVER GO HOME.
THUNK!

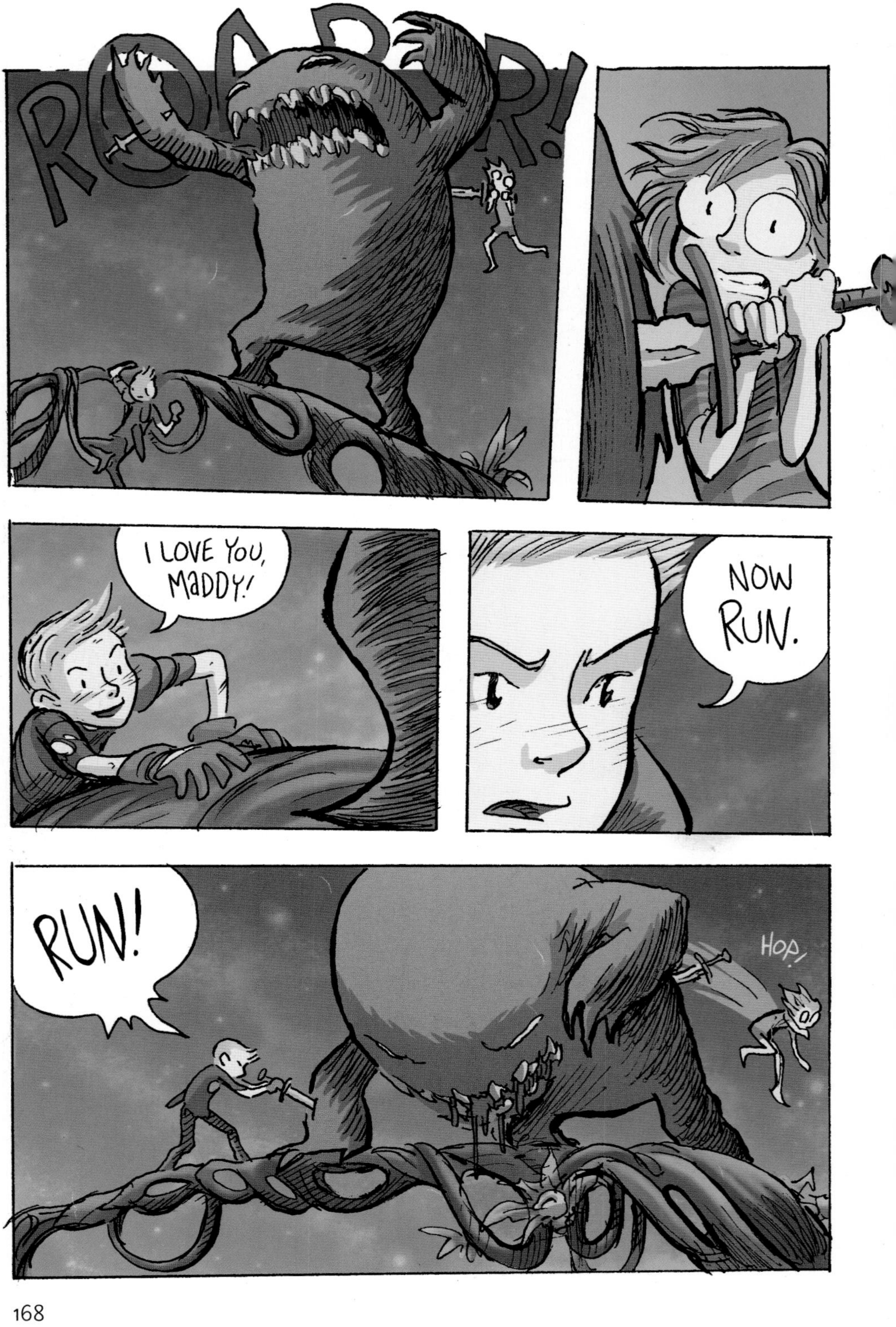
ROARR!
I LOVE YOU, MADDY!
NOW RUN.
RUN!
HOP!

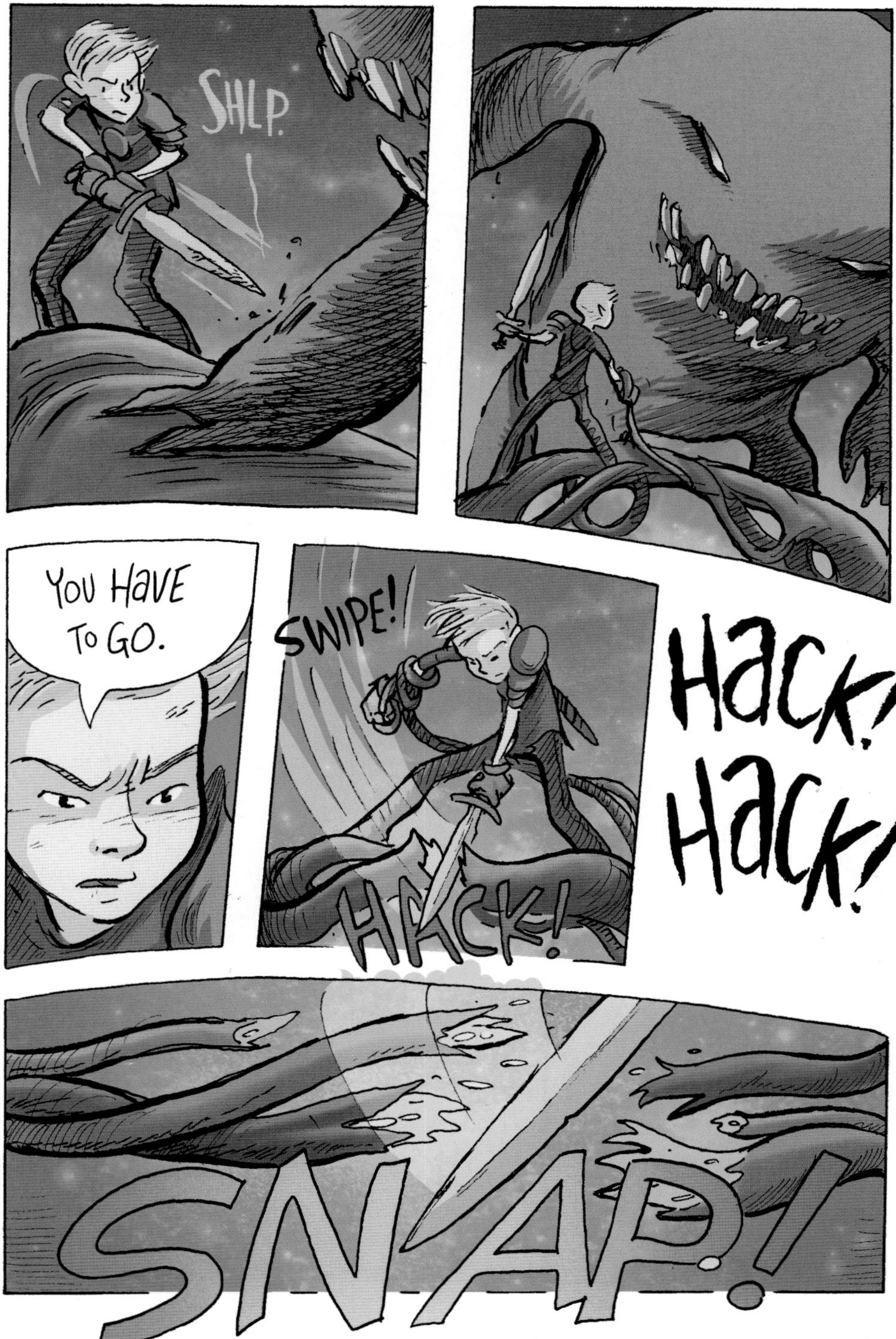
SHLP.
YOU HAVE TO GO.
SWIPE!
HACK!
HACK! HACK!
SNAP!

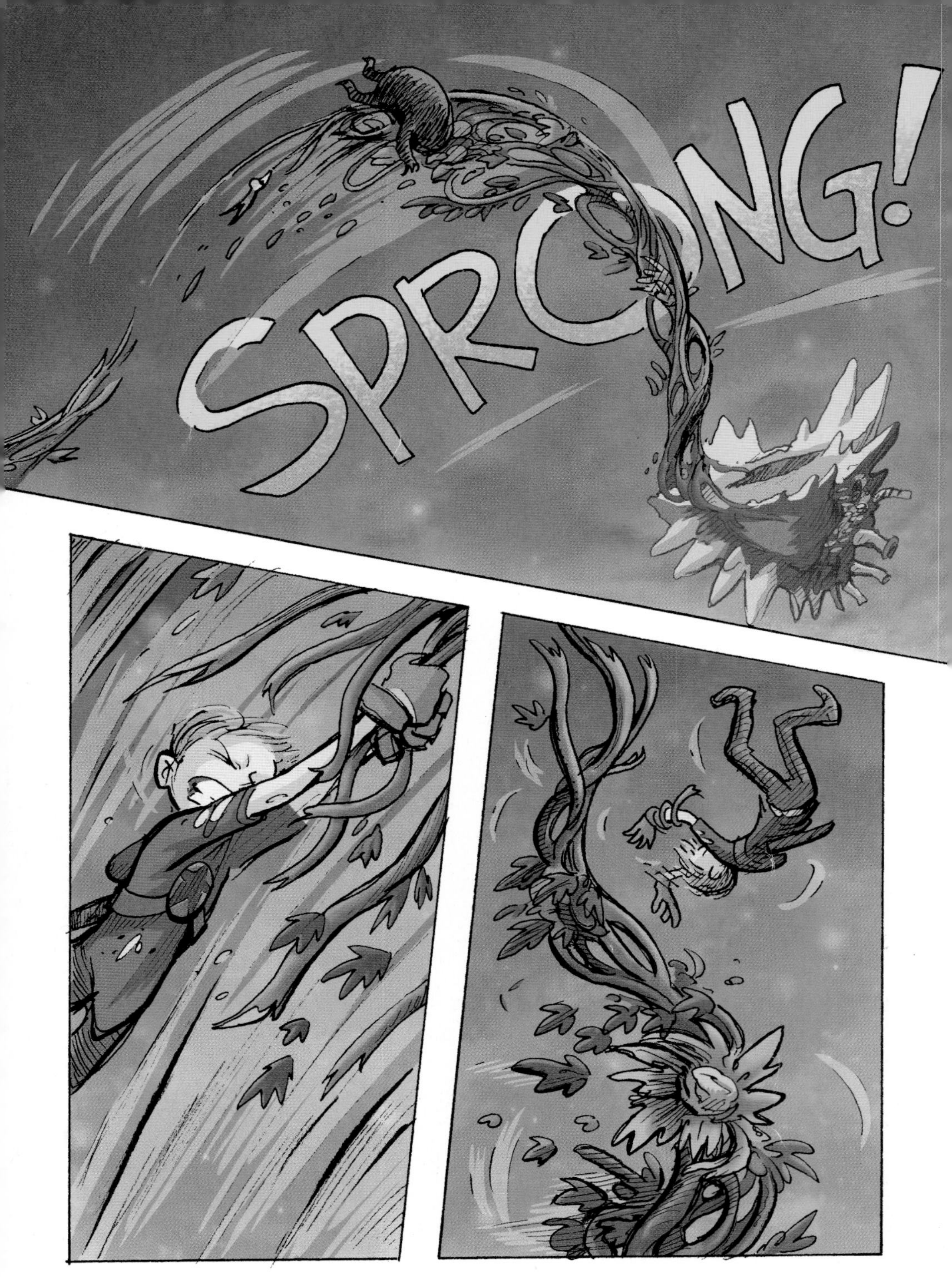
SPROONG!

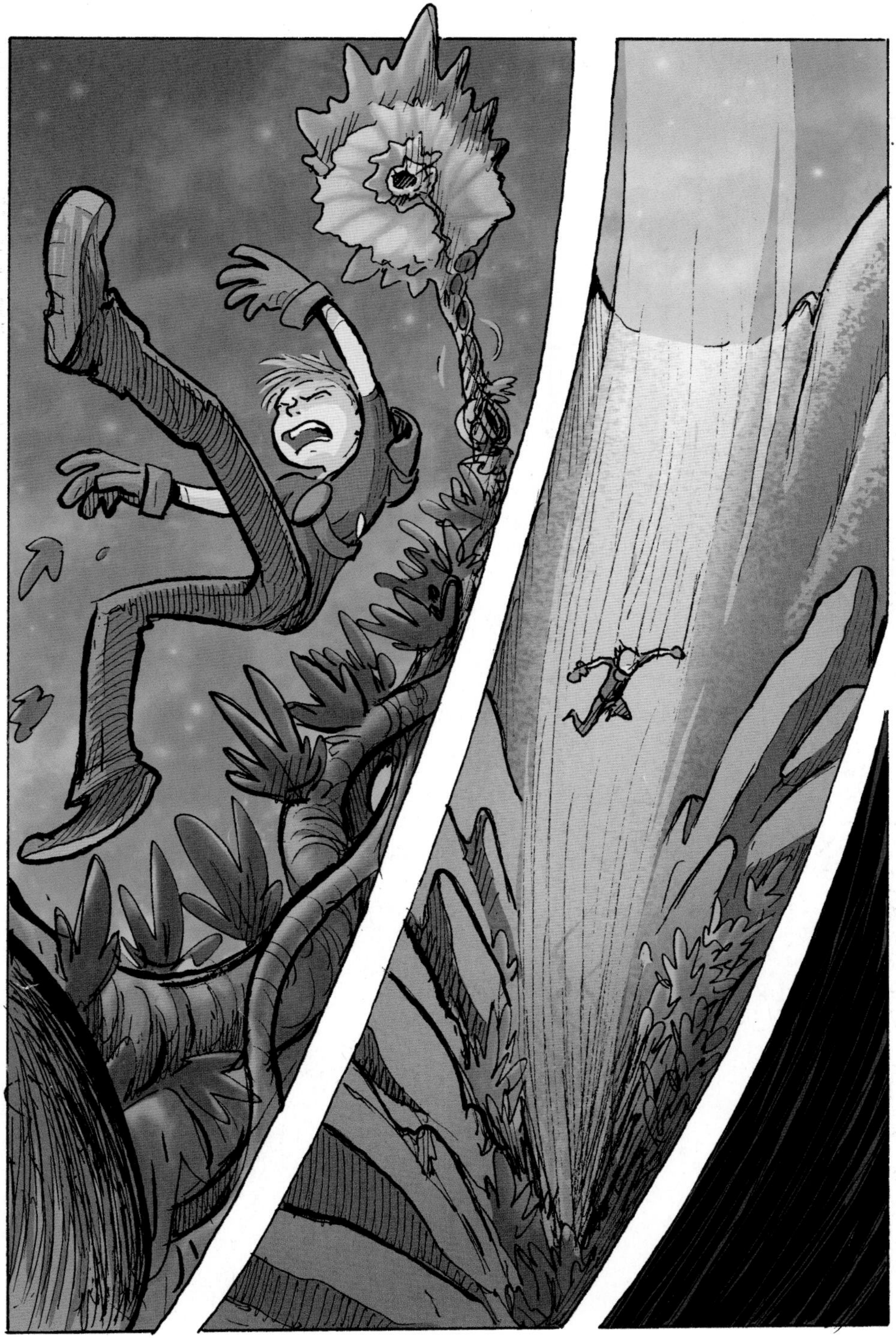

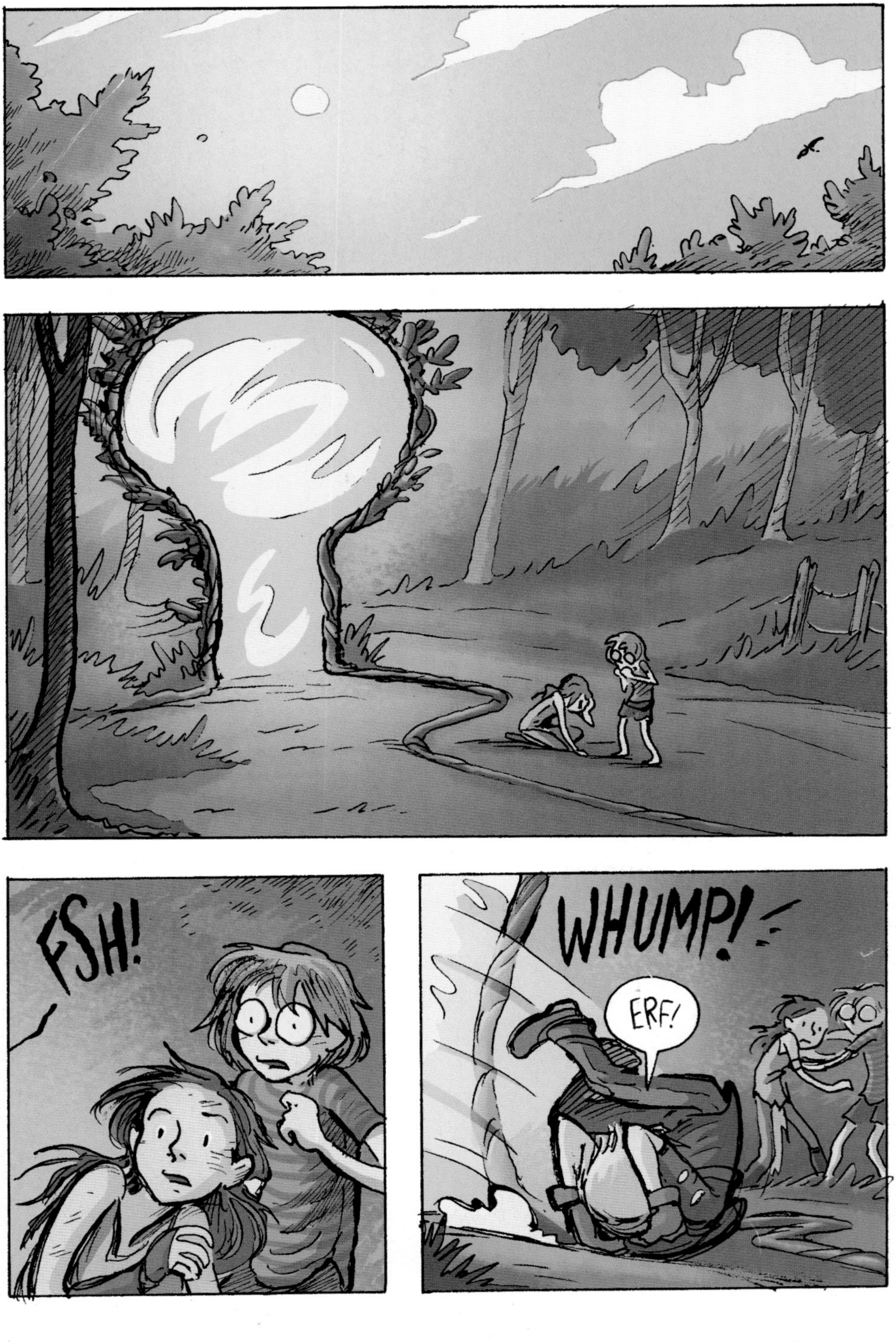
FSH!
WHUMP!
ERF!

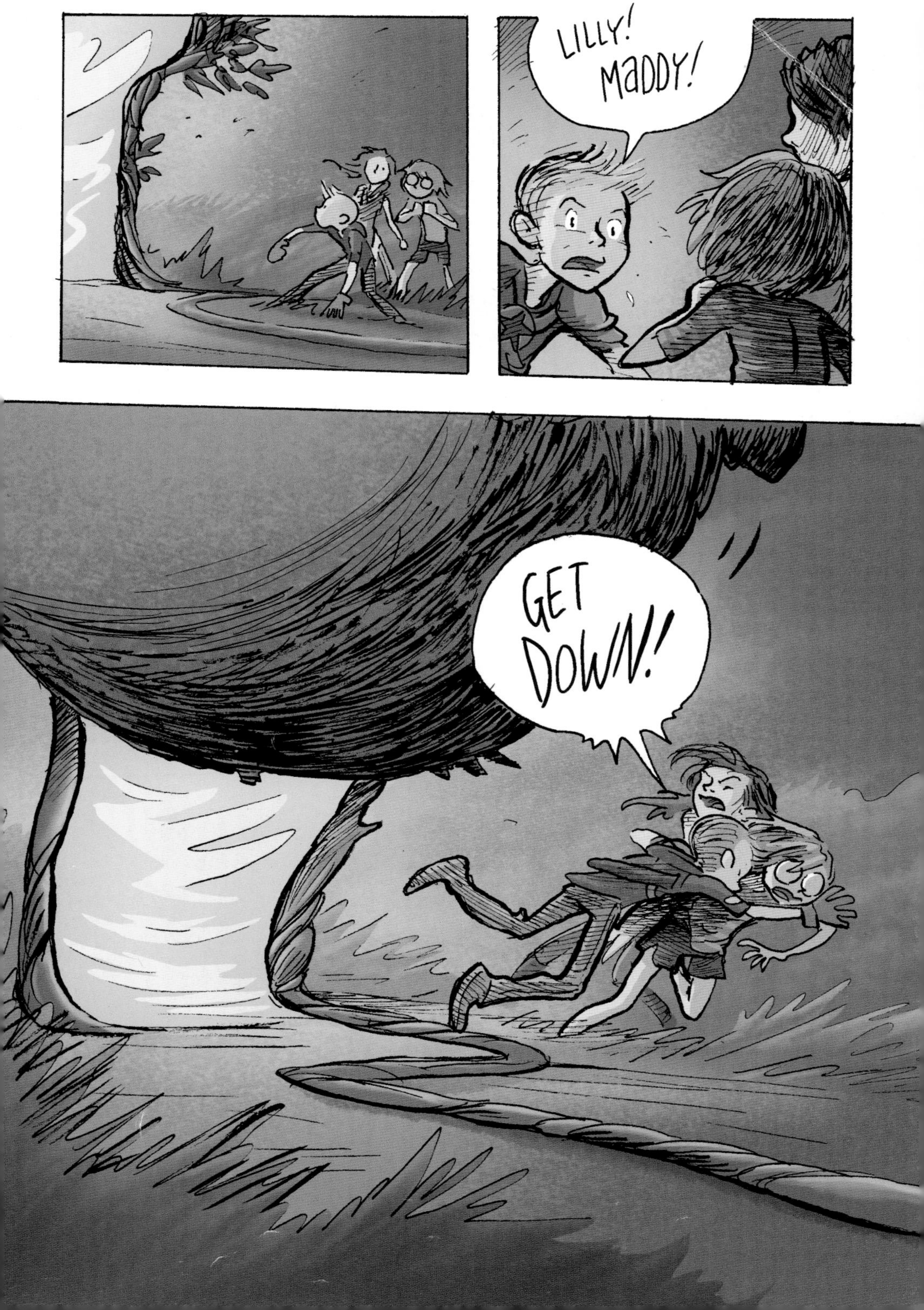
LILLY! MADDY!
GET DOWN!

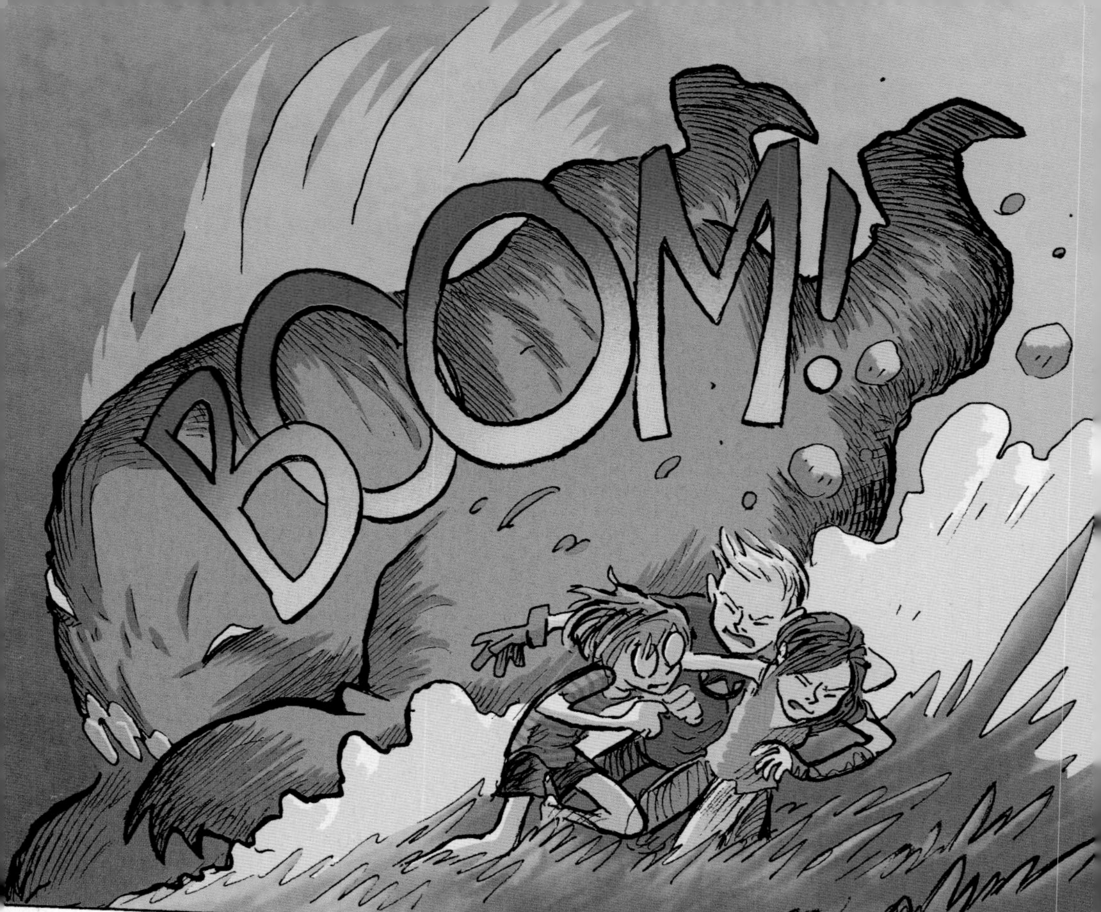
BOOM!

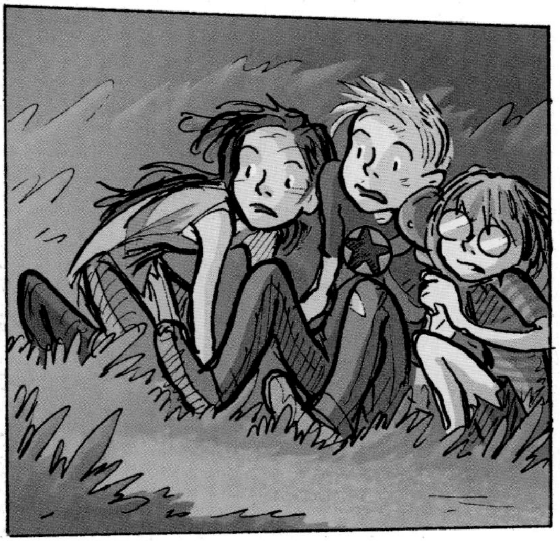

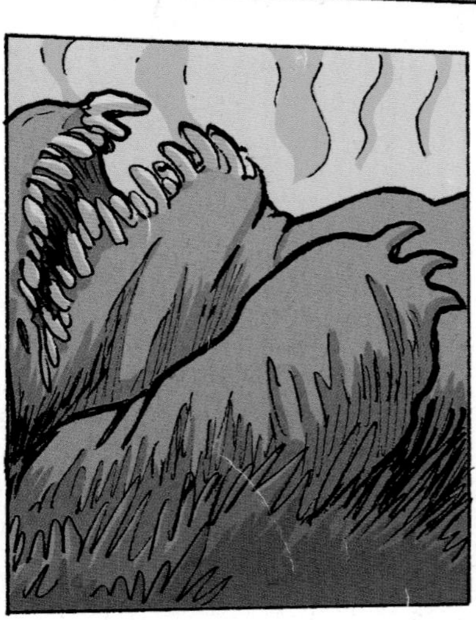

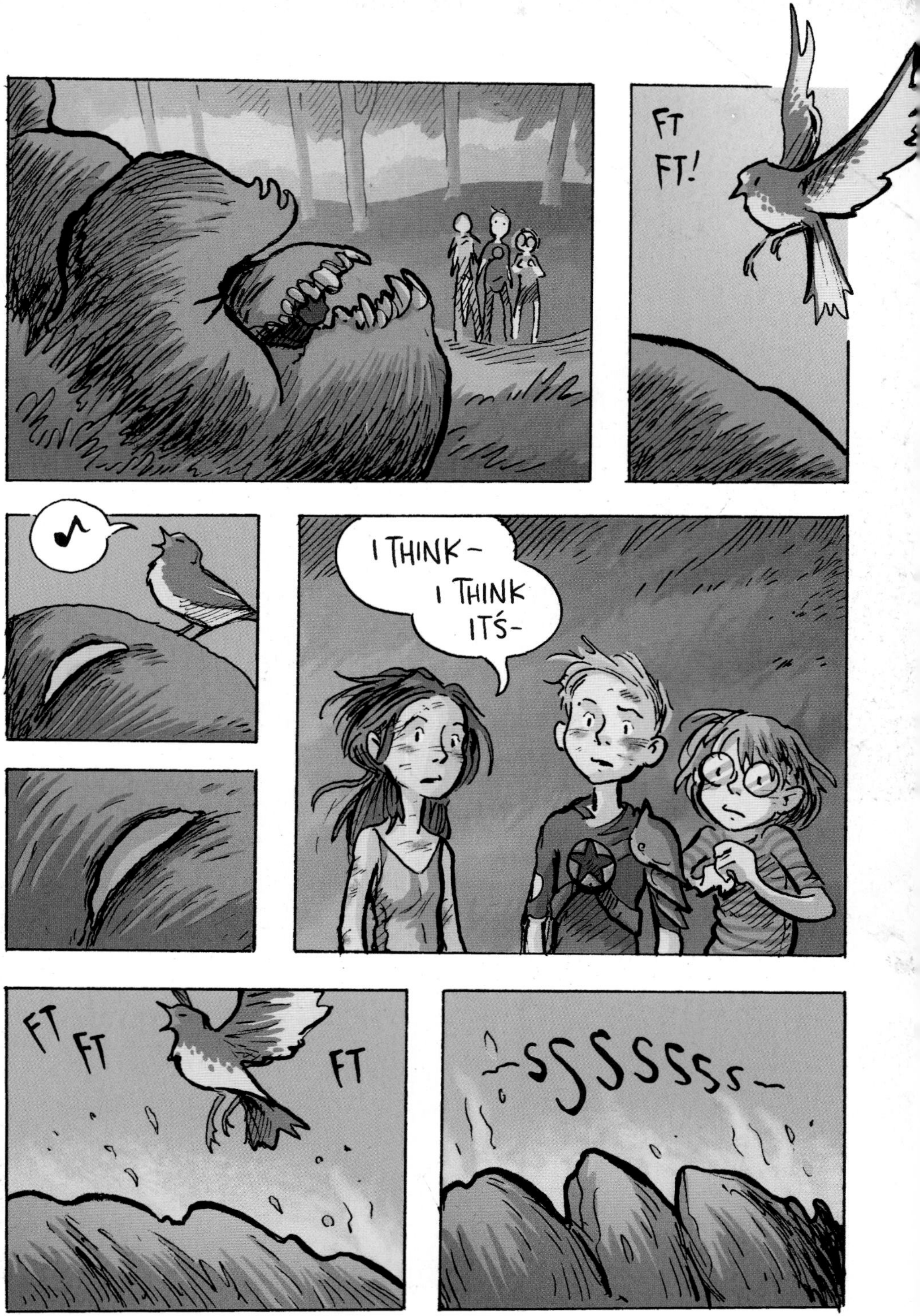
FT
FT!
I THINK-
I THINK
IT'S-
FT
FT
FT
-SSSSSSs-

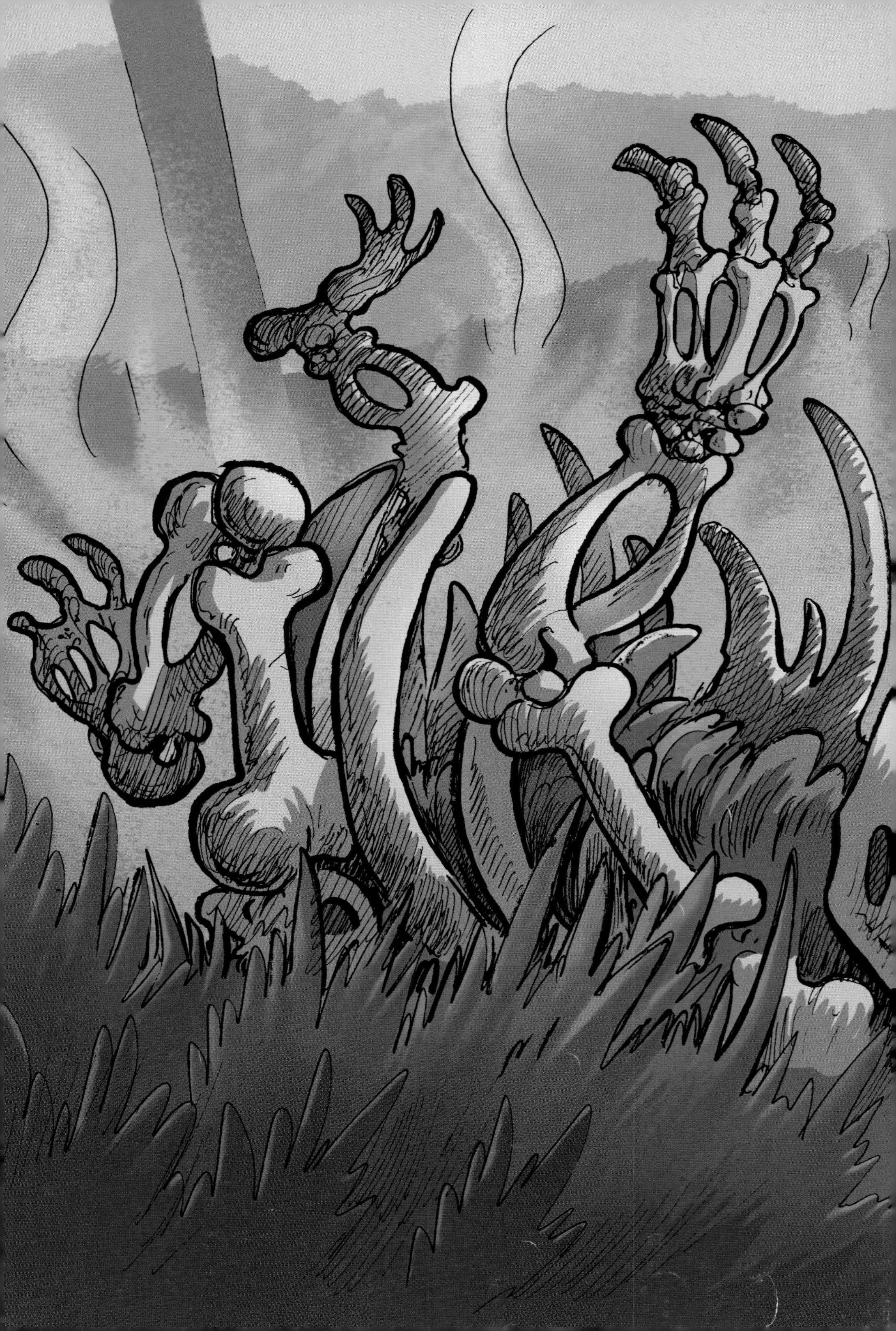

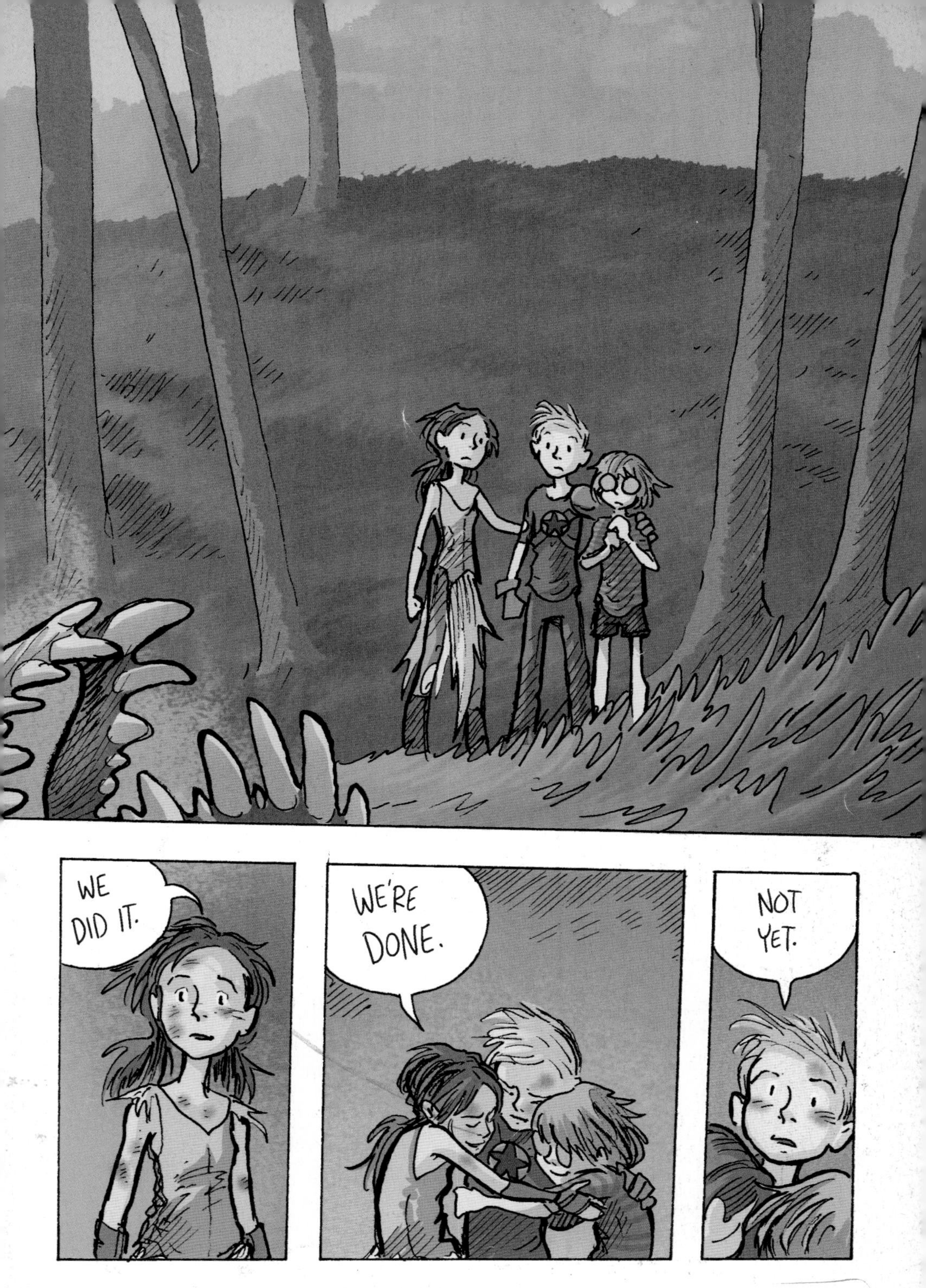
WE DID IT.
WE'RE DONE.
NOT YET.

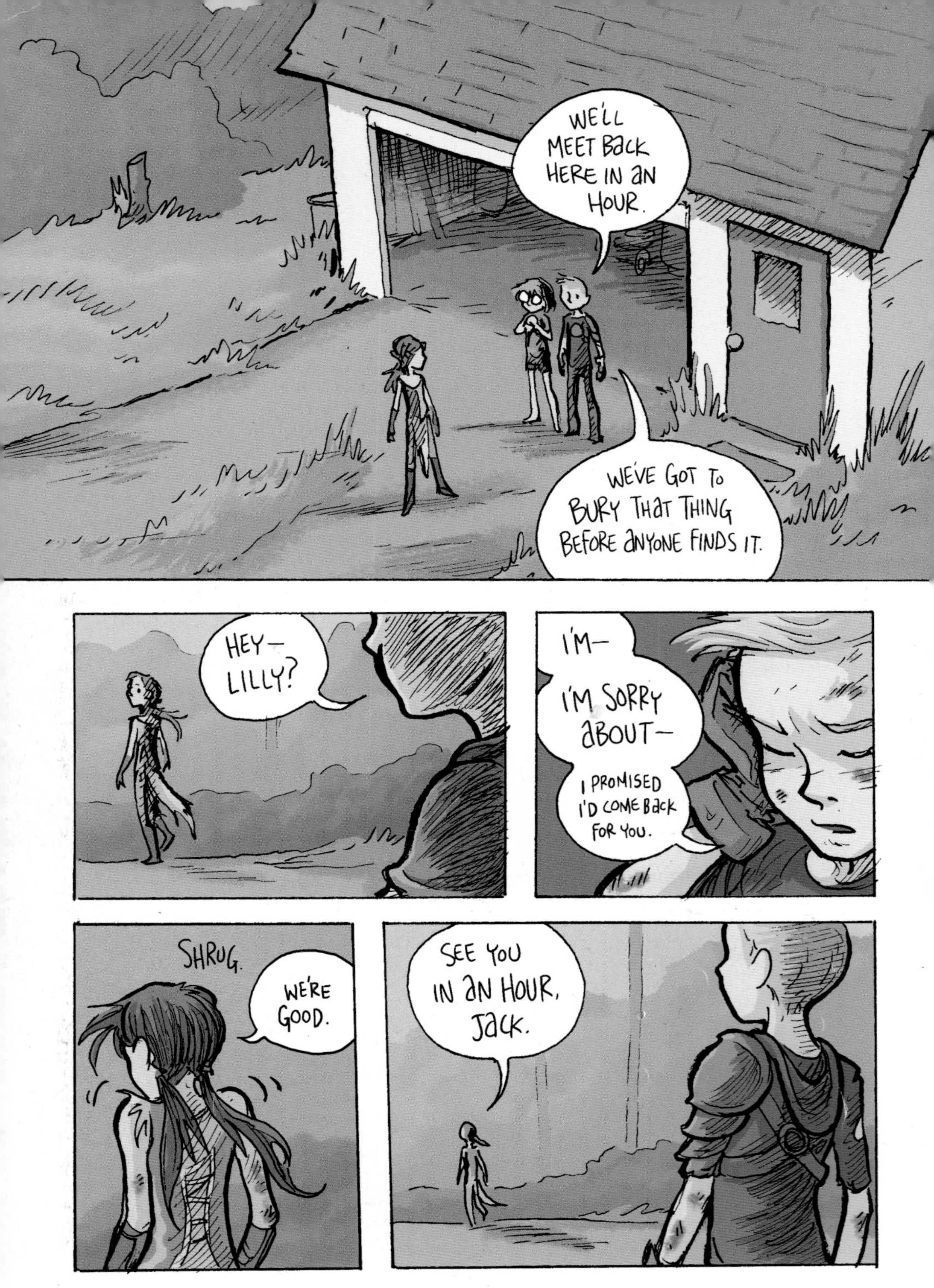
WE'LL MEET BACK HERE IN AN HOUR.
WE'VE GOT TO BURY THAT THING BEFORE ANYONE FINDS IT.
HEY— LILLY?
I'M—
I'M SORRY ABOUT—
I PROMISED I'D COME BACK FOR YOU.
SHRUG.
WE'RE GOOD.
SEE YOU IN AN HOUR, JACK.

MOM?

HUH.

SHE'S STILL AT WORK.

THAT'S WEIRD.

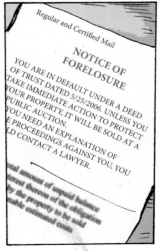

Regular and Certified Mail

NOTICE OF FORECLOSURE

YOU ARE IN DEFAULT UNDER A DEED OF TRUST DATED 5/25/2006. UNLESS YOU TAKE IMMEDIATE ACTION TO PROTECT YOUR PROPERTY, IT WILL BE SOLD AT A PUBLIC AUCTION.

YOU NEED AN EXPLANATION OF THE PROCEEDINGS AGAINST YOU, YOU SHOULD CONTACT A LAWYER.

...tal amount of unpaid balance
...erest thereon of the obligation
...by the property to be sold
...able estimated costs

C'MON MADDY, WE'VE STILL GOT A LOT OF WORK TO DO.

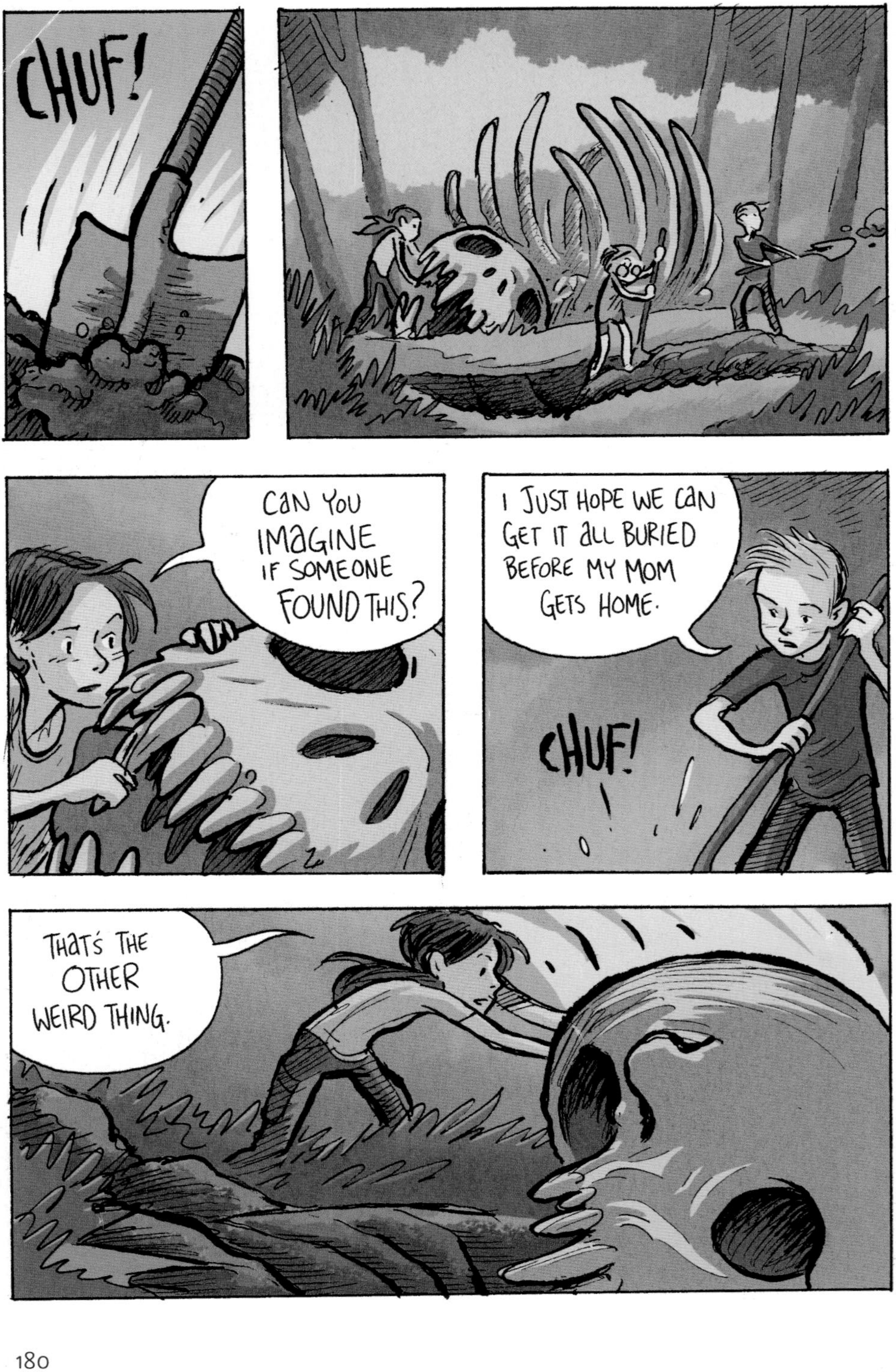
CHUF!
CAN YOU IMAGINE IF SOMEONE FOUND THIS?
I JUST HOPE WE CAN GET IT ALL BURIED BEFORE MY MOM GETS HOME.
CHUF!
THAT'S THE OTHER WEIRD THING.

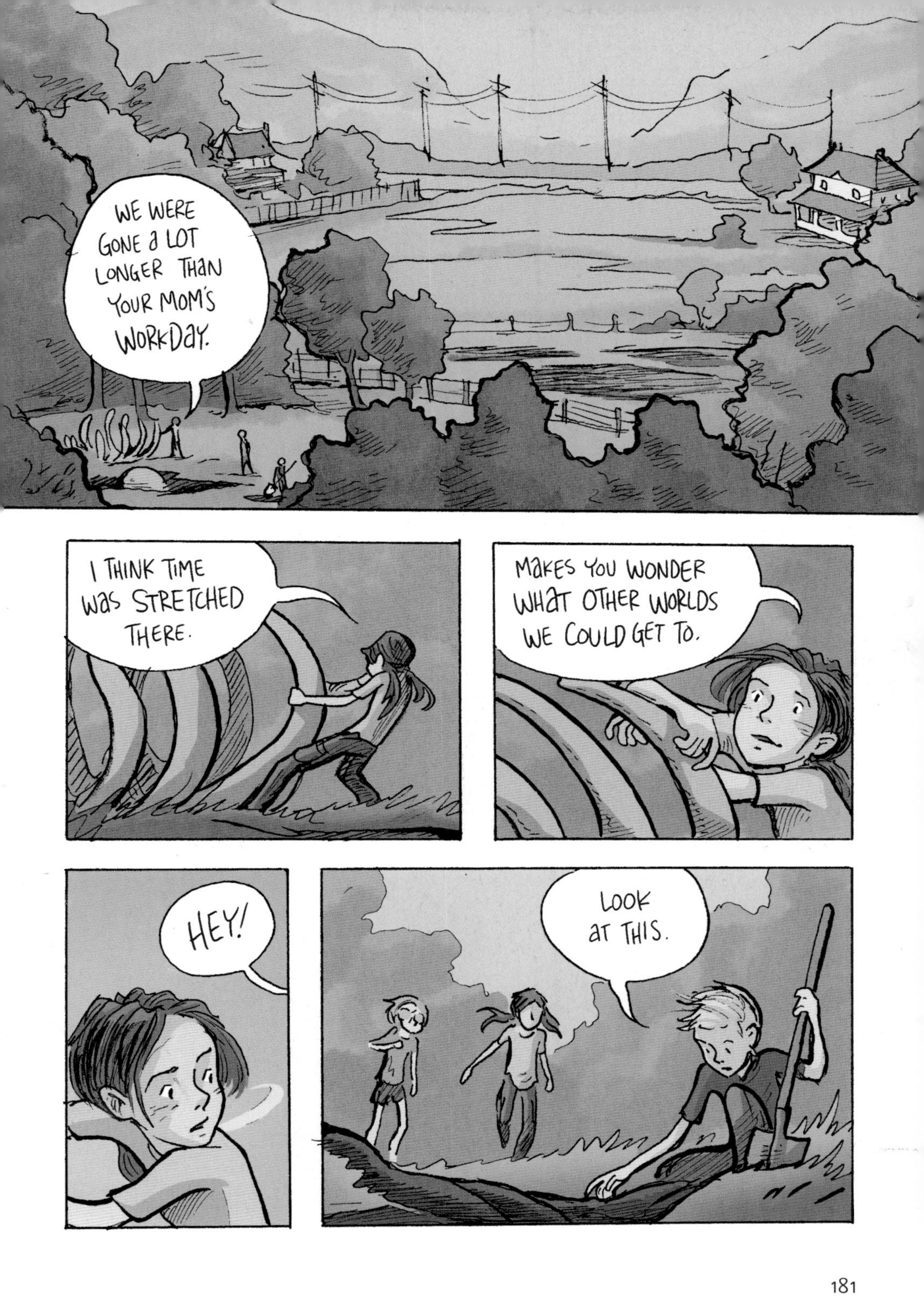
WE WERE GONE A LOT LONGER THAN YOUR MOM'S WORKDAY.
I THINK TIME WAS STRETCHED THERE.
MAKES YOU WONDER WHAT OTHER WORLDS WE COULD GET TO.
HEY!
LOOK AT THIS.

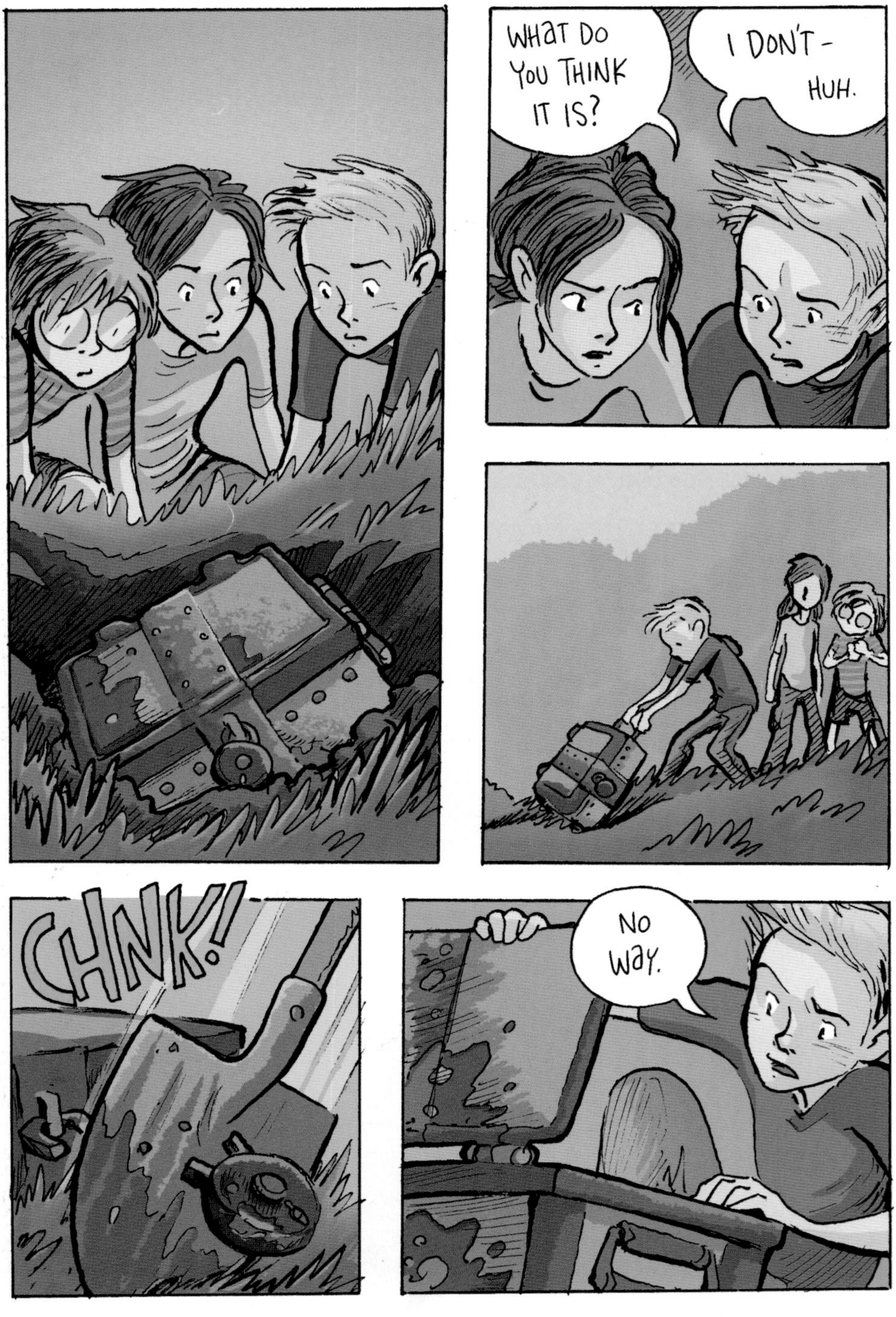
WHAT DO YOU THINK IT IS?
I DON'T -
HUH.
CHNK!
No way.

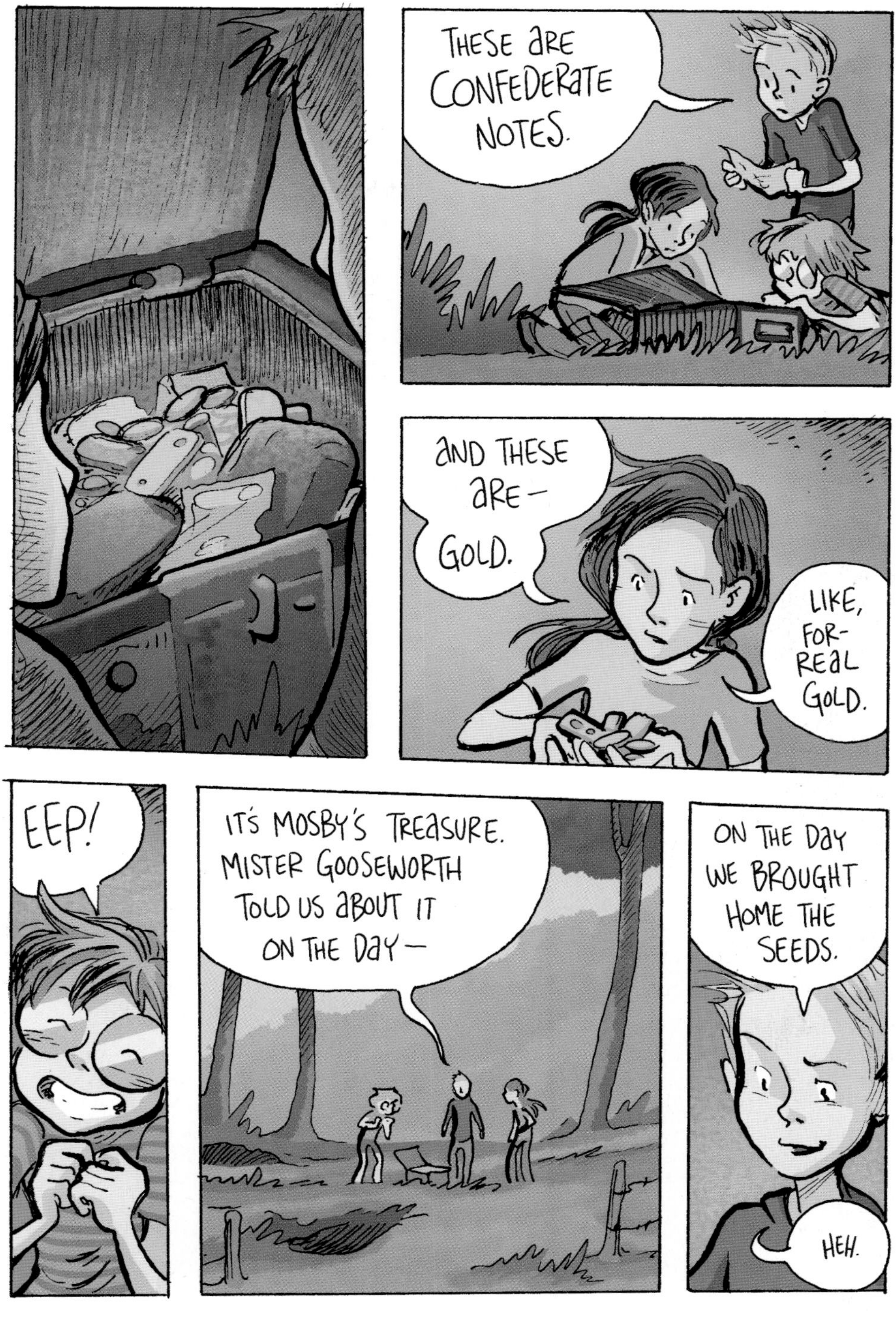

THESE ARE CONFEDERATE NOTES.
AND THESE ARE—
GOLD.
LIKE, FOR-REAL GOLD.
EEP!
IT'S MOSBY'S TREASURE. MISTER GOOSEWORTH TOLD US ABOUT IT ON THE DAY—
ON THE DAY WE BROUGHT HOME THE SEEDS.
HEH.

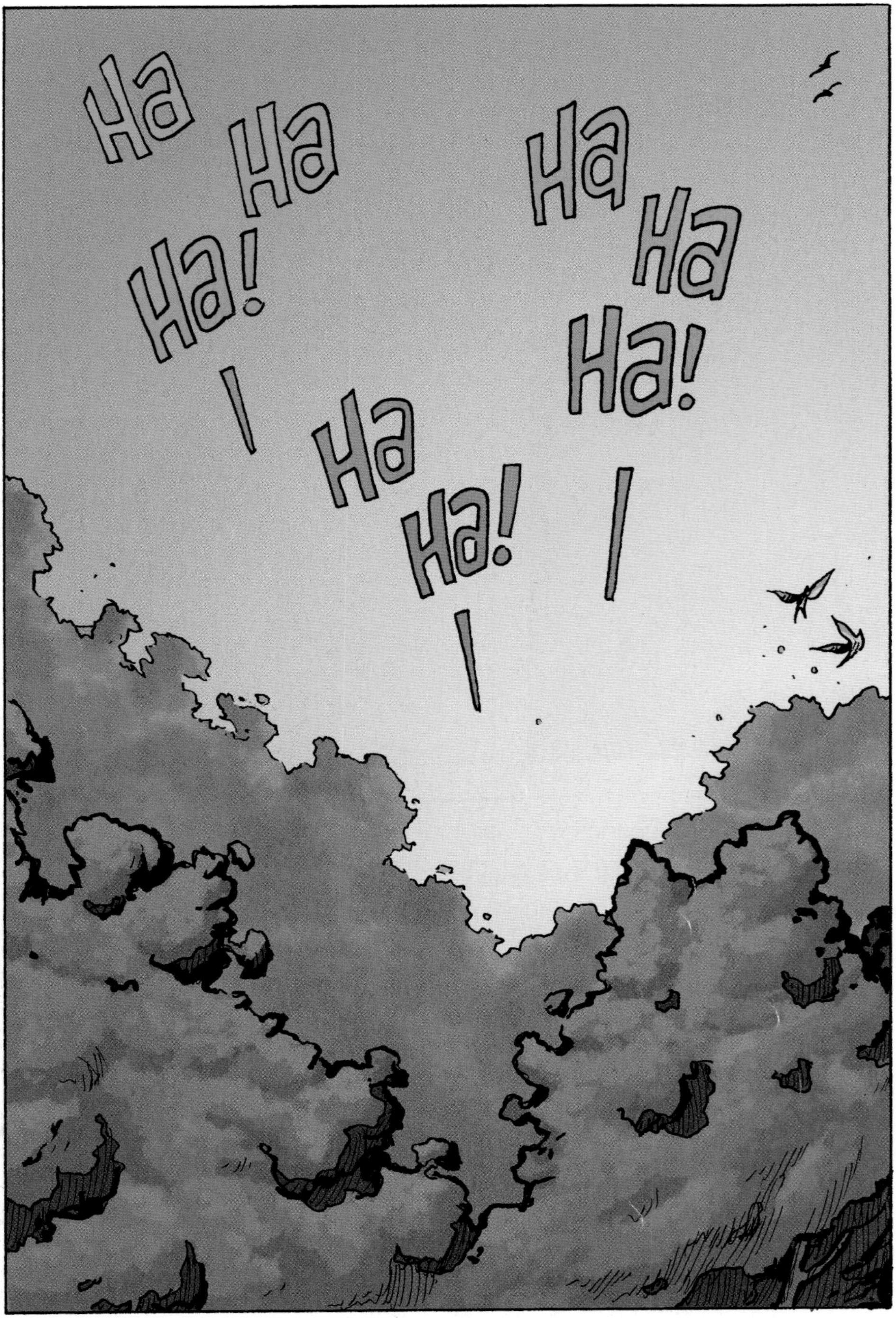
Ha Ha Ha!!
Ha Ha!!
Ha Ha Ha!!

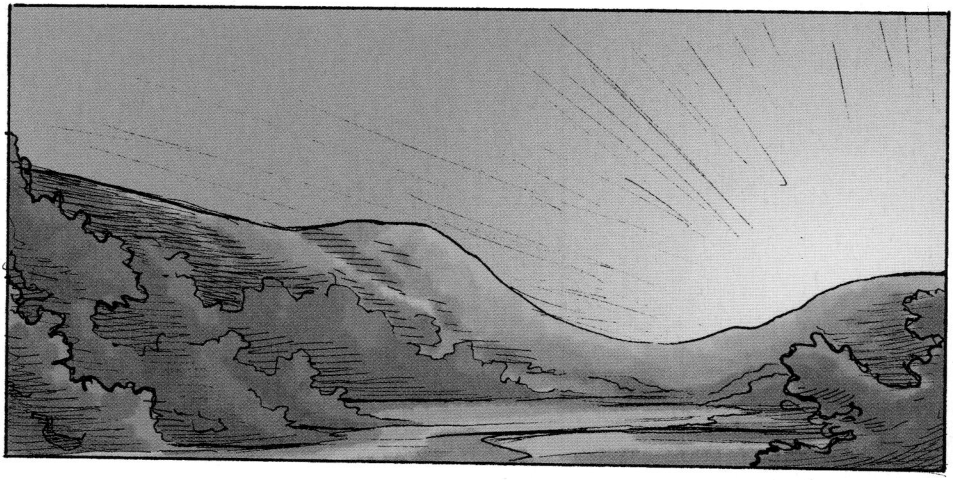

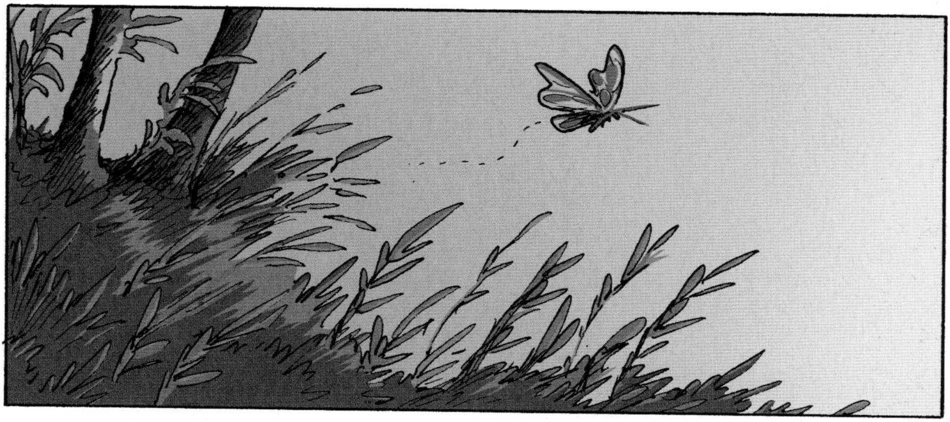

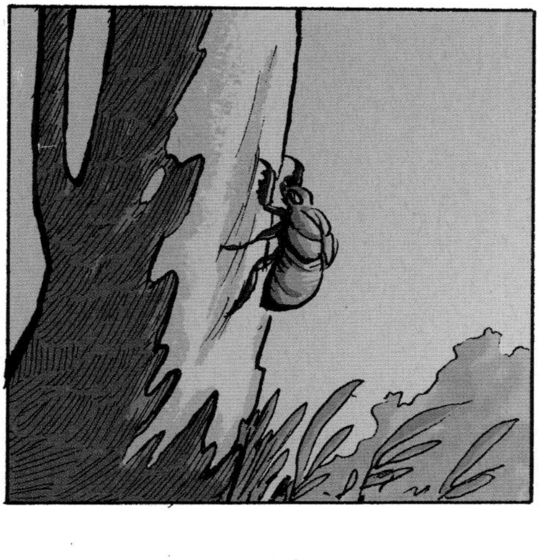

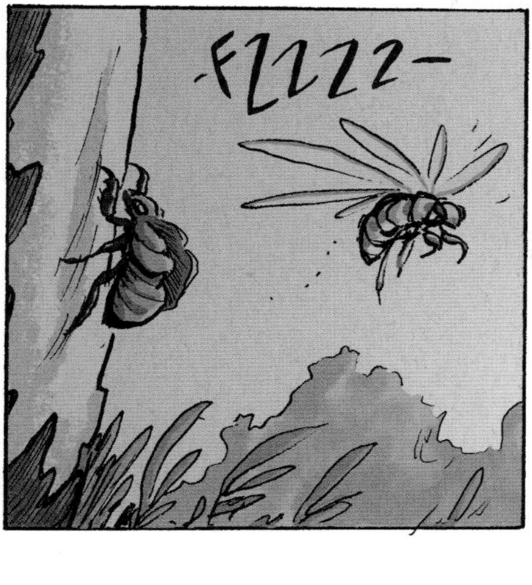
-FZZZZ-

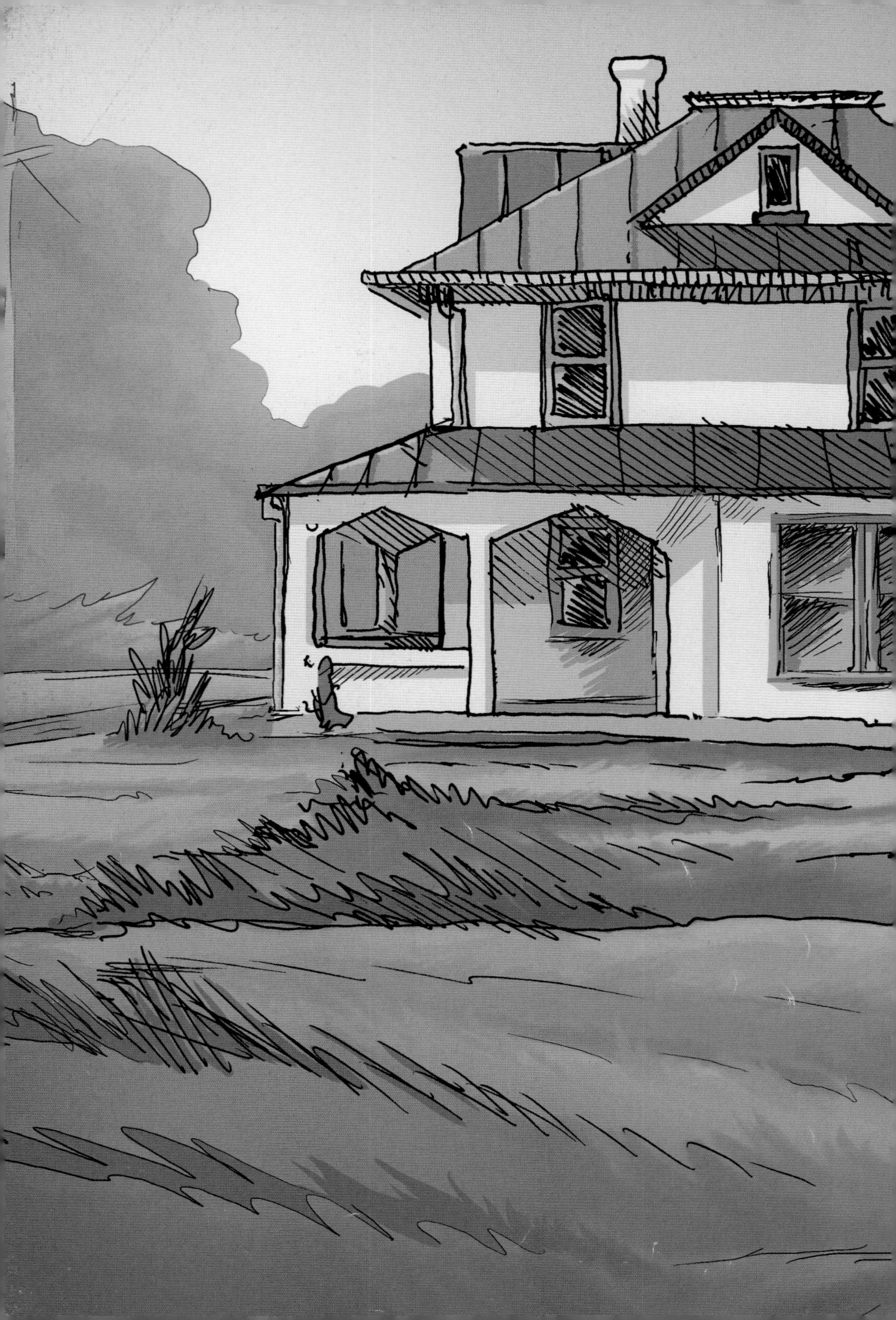

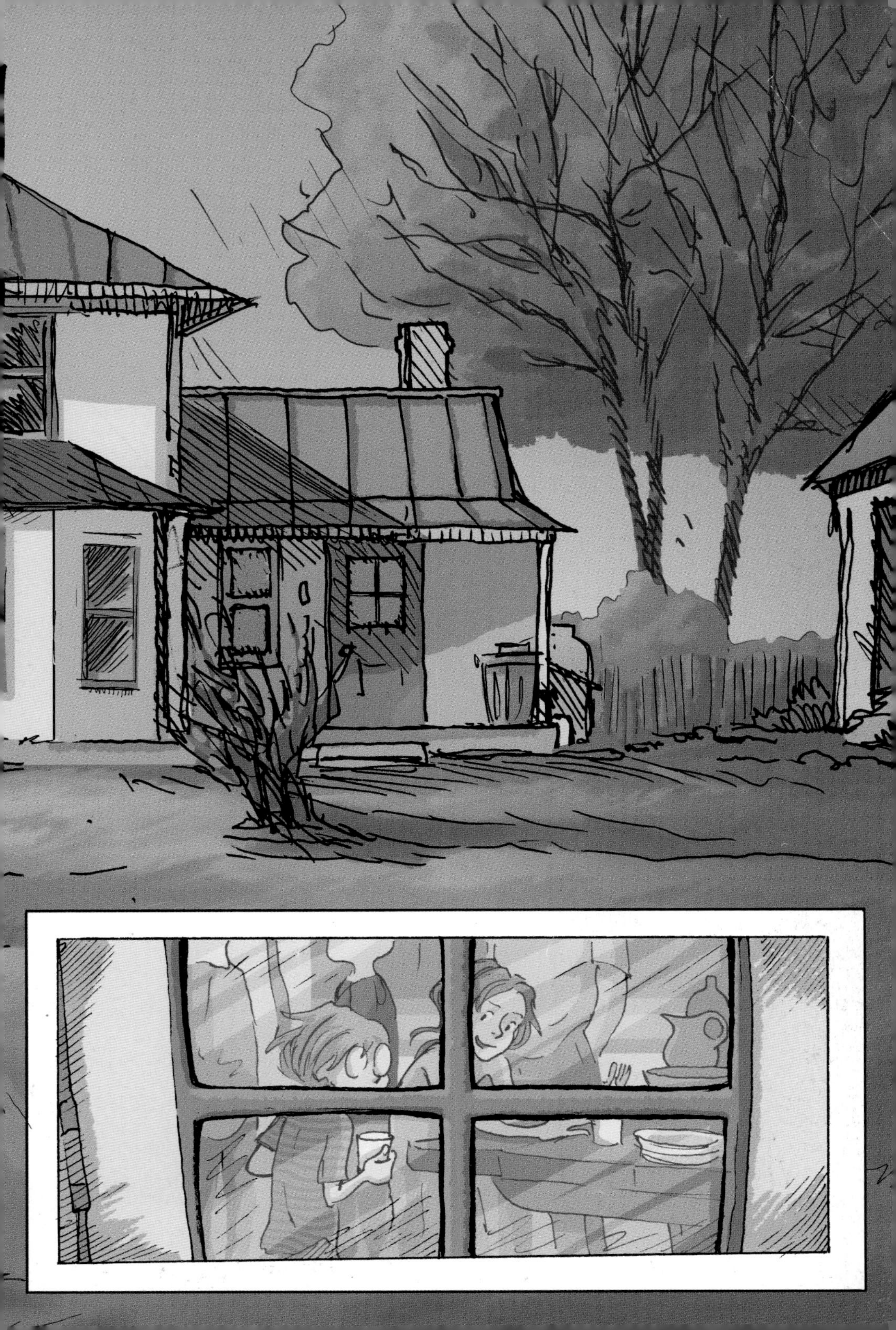

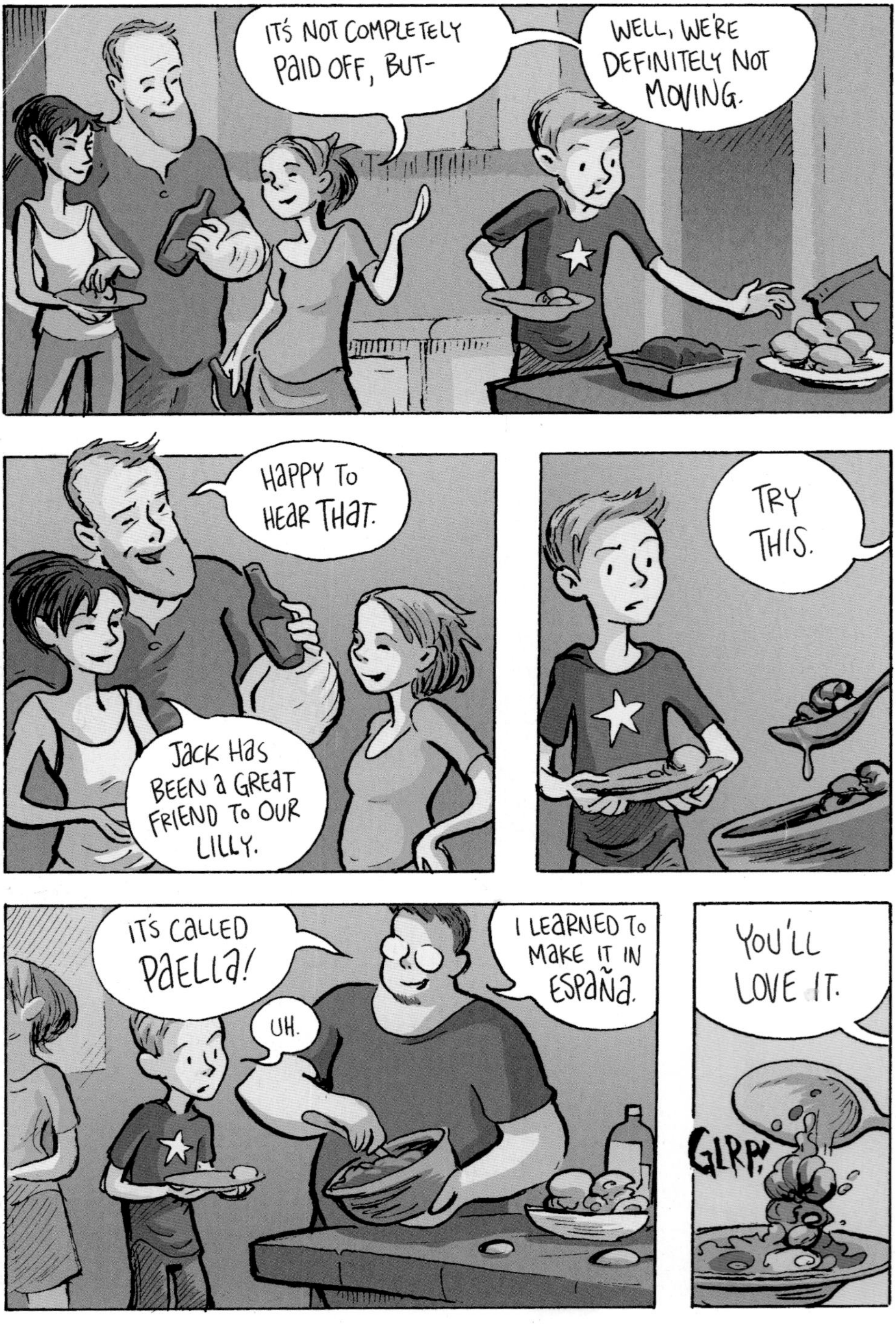
IT'S NOT COMPLETELY PAID OFF, BUT-
WELL, WE'RE DEFINITELY NOT MOVING.
HAPPY TO HEAR THAT.
JACK HAS BEEN A GREAT FRIEND TO OUR LILLY.
TRY THIS.
IT'S CALLED PAELLA!
UH.
I LEARNED TO MAKE IT IN ESPAÑA.
YOU'LL LOVE IT.
GLRP!

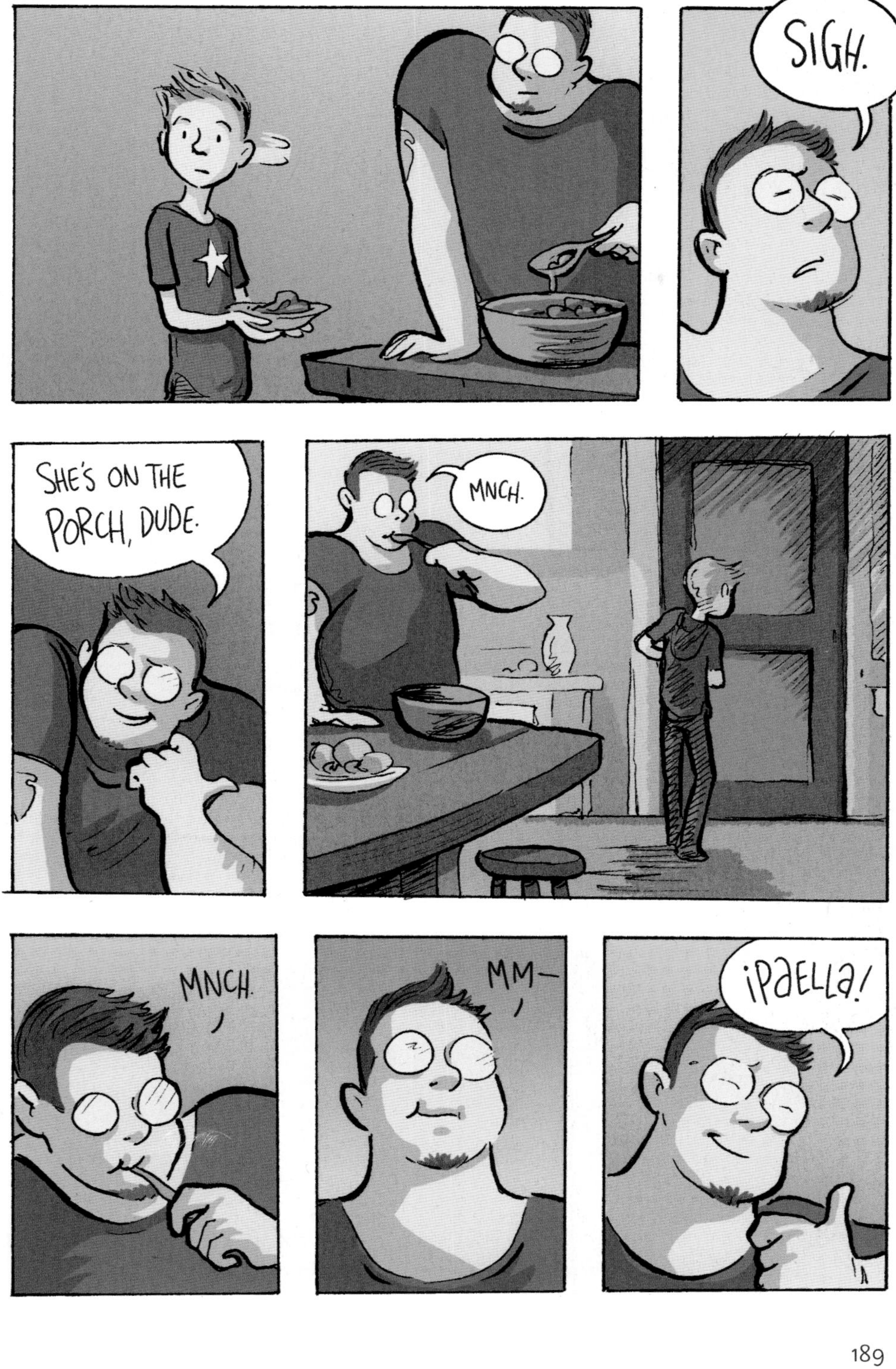
SIGH.
SHE'S ON THE PORCH, DUDE.
MNCH.
MNCH.
MM—
¡PAELLA!

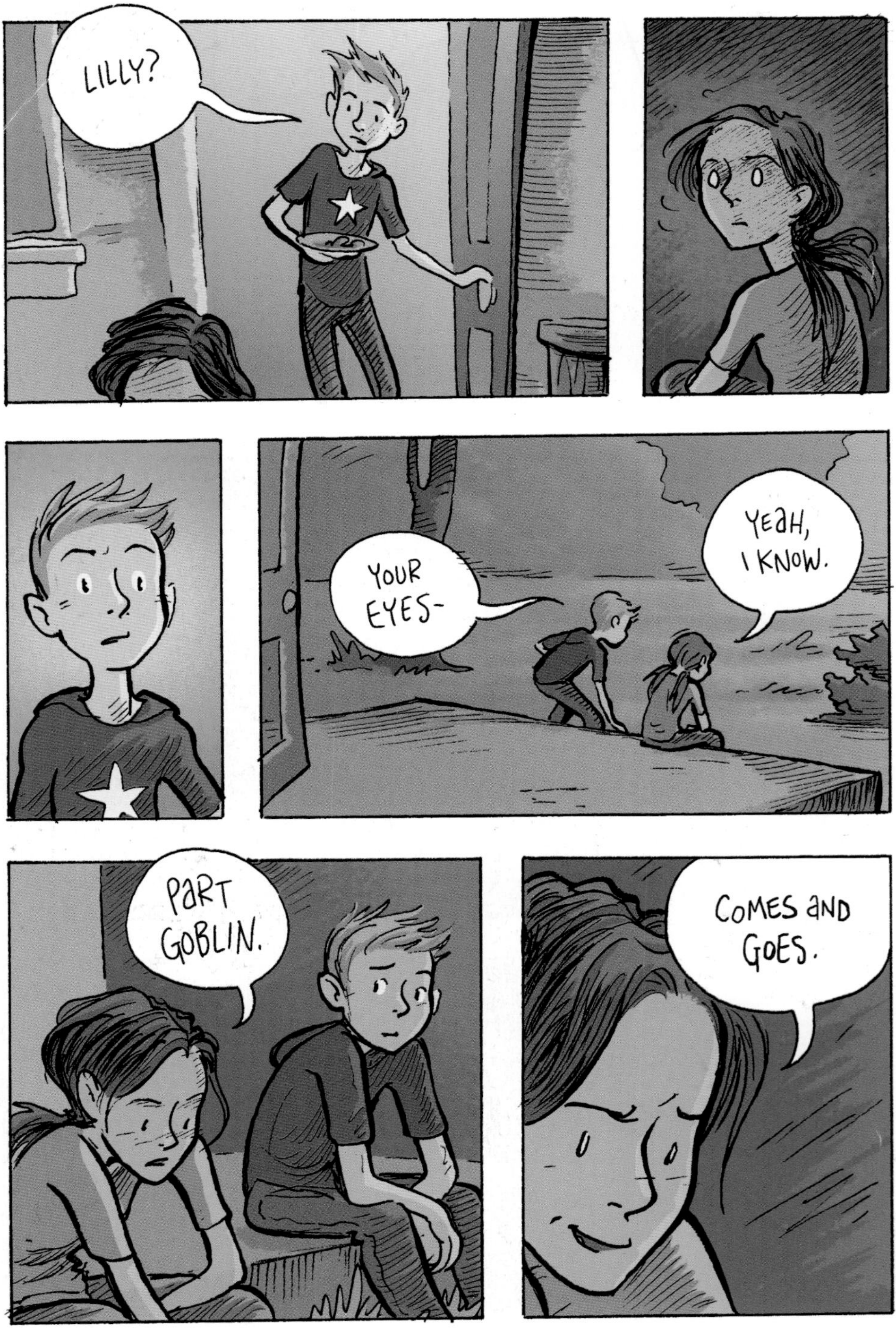
LILLY?
YOUR EYES-
YEAH, I KNOW.
PART GOBLIN.
COMES AND GOES.

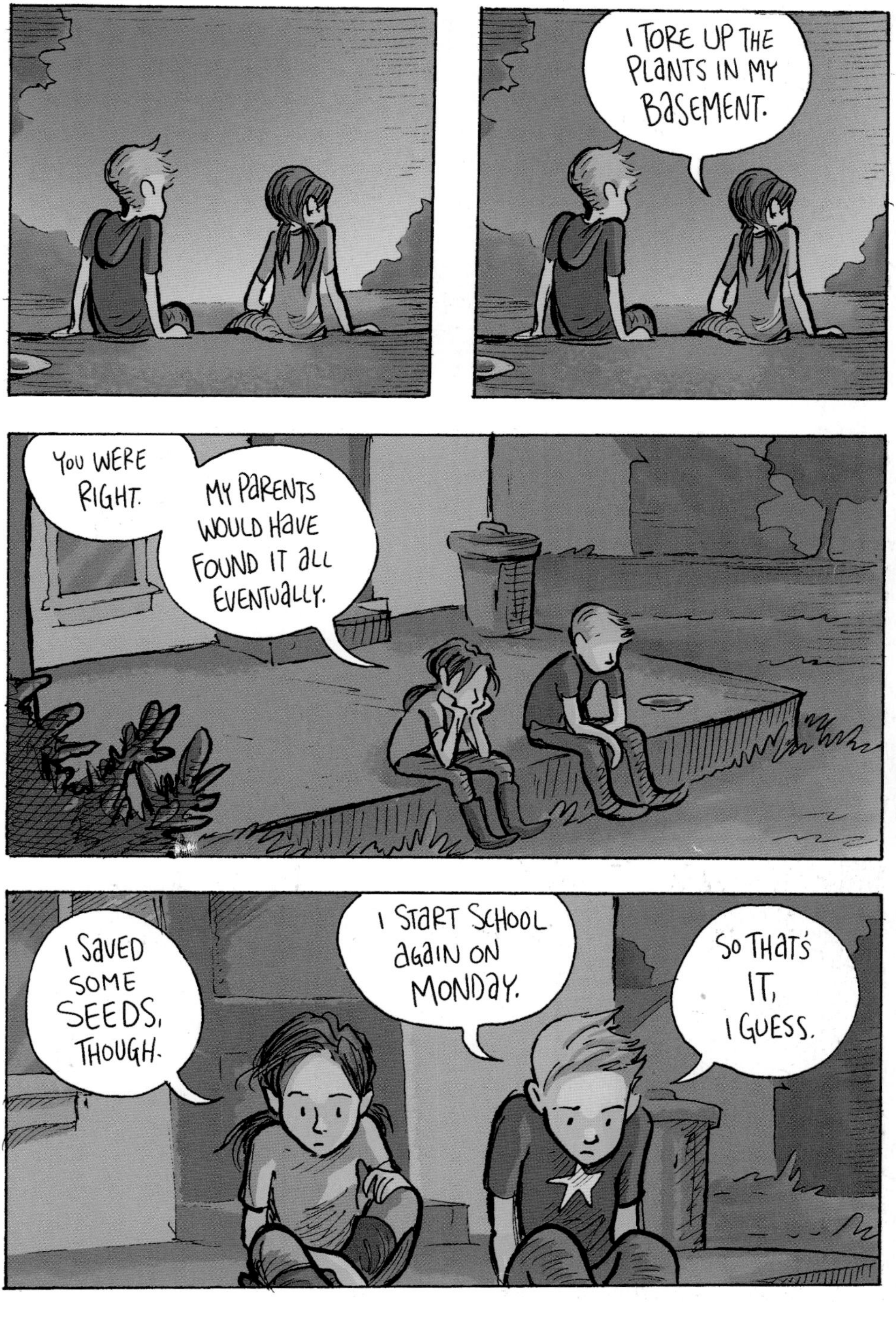
I TORE UP THE PLANTS IN MY BASEMENT.
YOU WERE RIGHT.
MY PARENTS WOULD HAVE FOUND IT ALL EVENTUALLY.
I SAVED SOME SEEDS, THOUGH.
I START SCHOOL AGAIN ON MONDAY.
SO THAT'S IT, I GUESS.

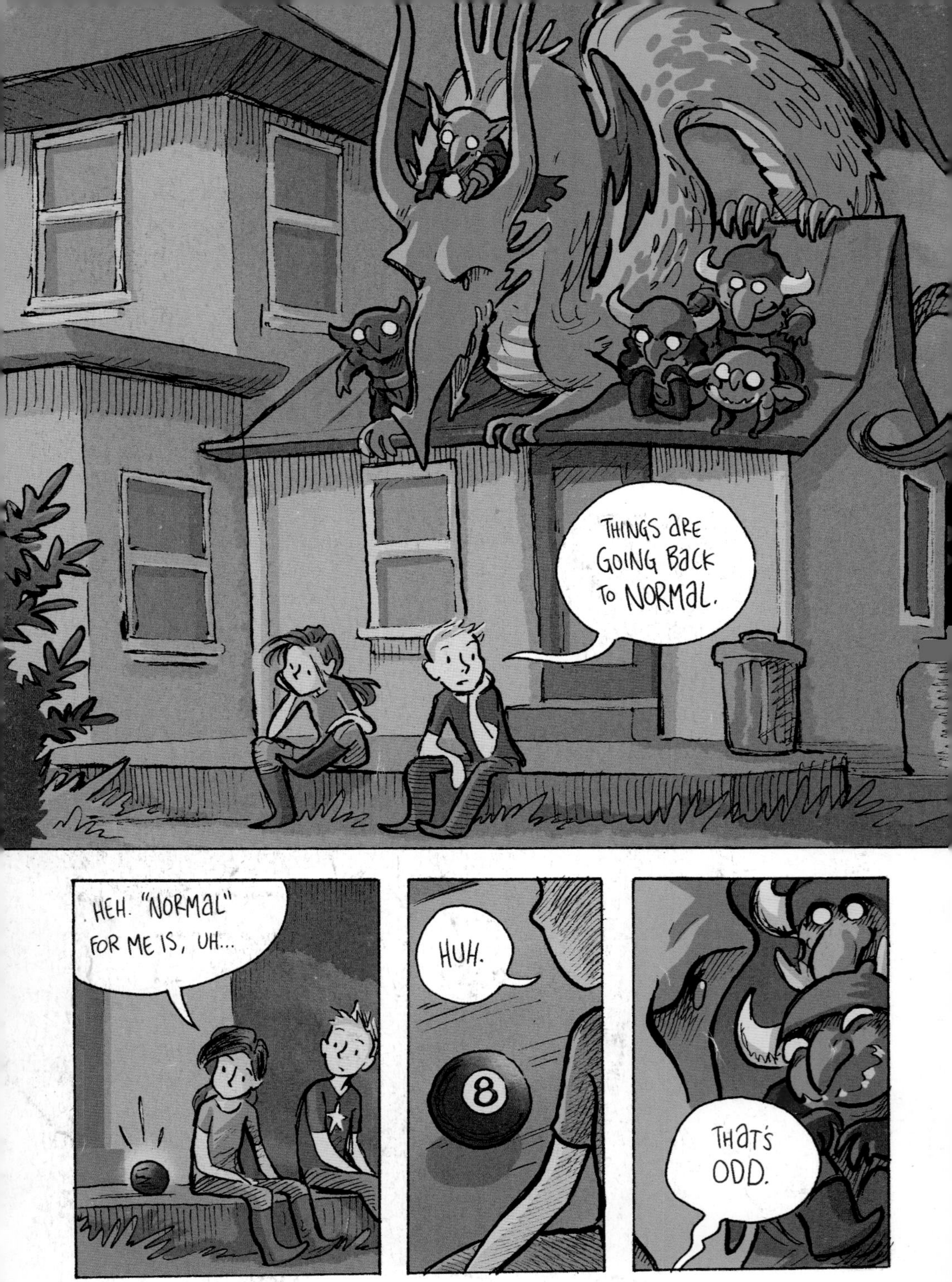
THINGS ARE GOING BACK TO NORMAL.
HEH. "NORMAL" FOR ME IS, UH...
8
HUH.
THAT'S ODD.

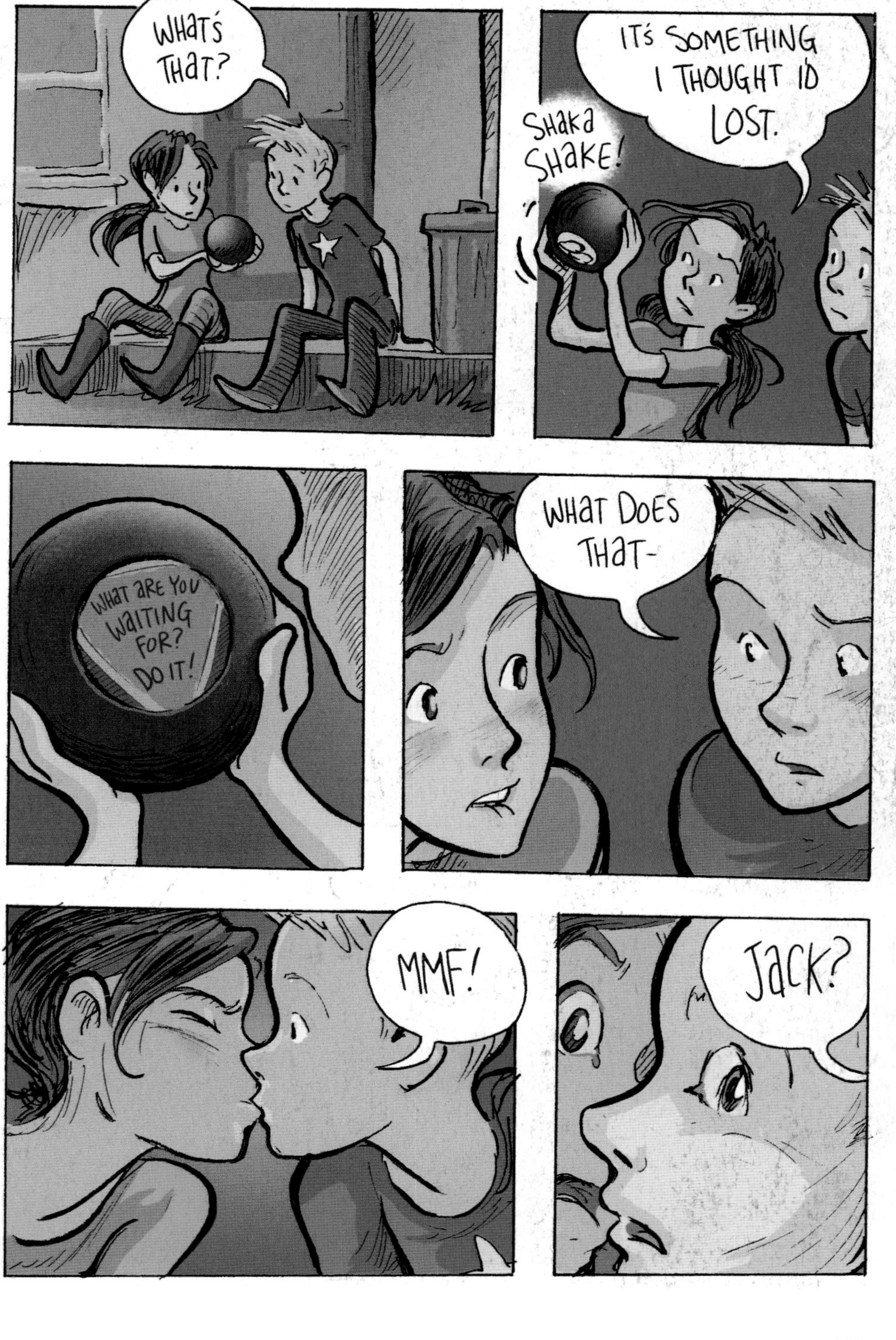
WHAT'S THAT?
IT'S SOMETHING I THOUGHT I'D LOST.
SHAKA SHAKE!
WHAT ARE YOU WAITING FOR? DO IT!
WHAT DOES THAT-
MMF!
JACK?

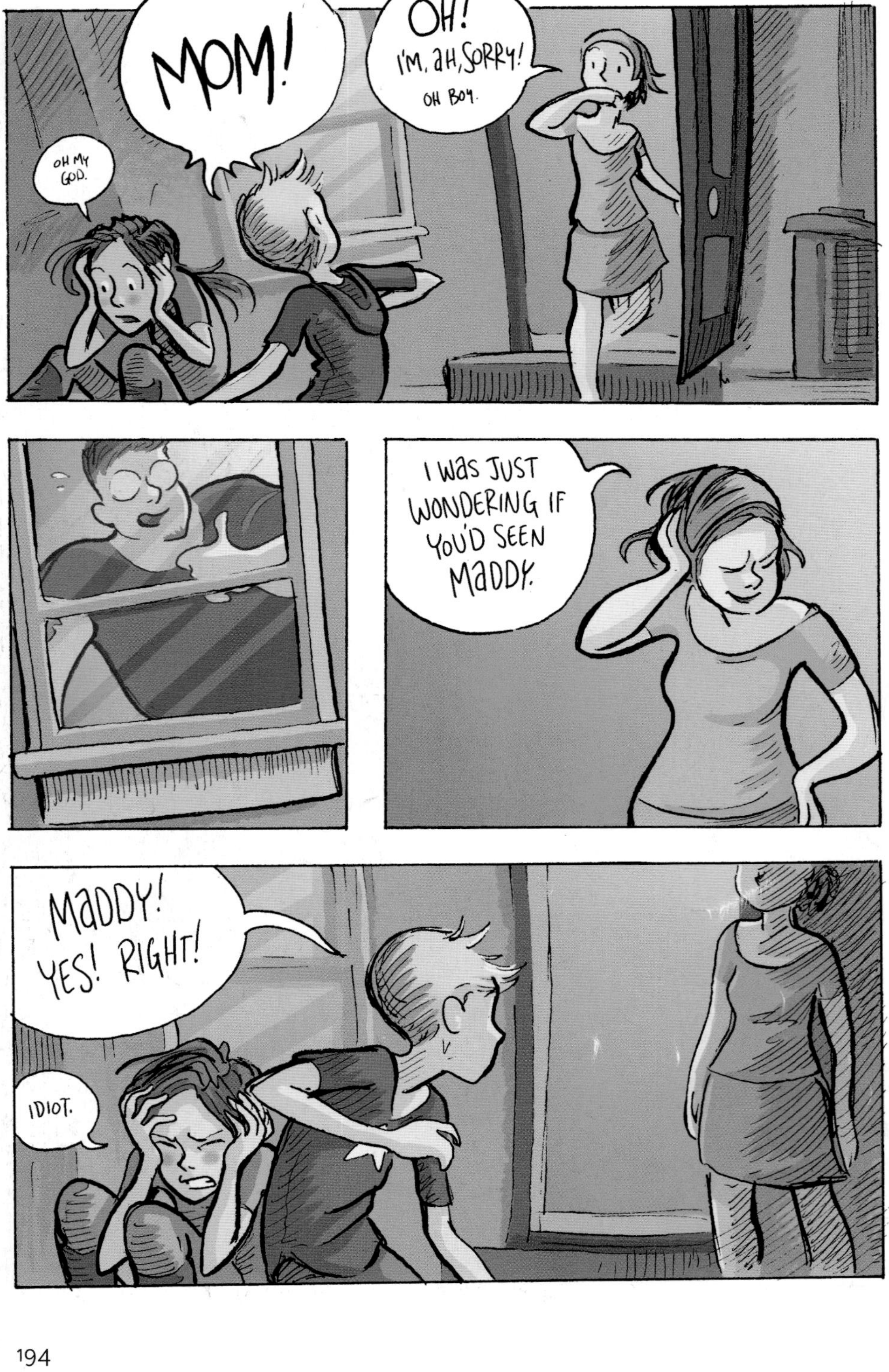
MOM!
OH! I'M, AH, SORRY! OH BOY.
OH MY GOD.
I WAS JUST WONDERING IF YOU'D SEEN MADDY.
MADDY! YES! RIGHT!
IDIOT.

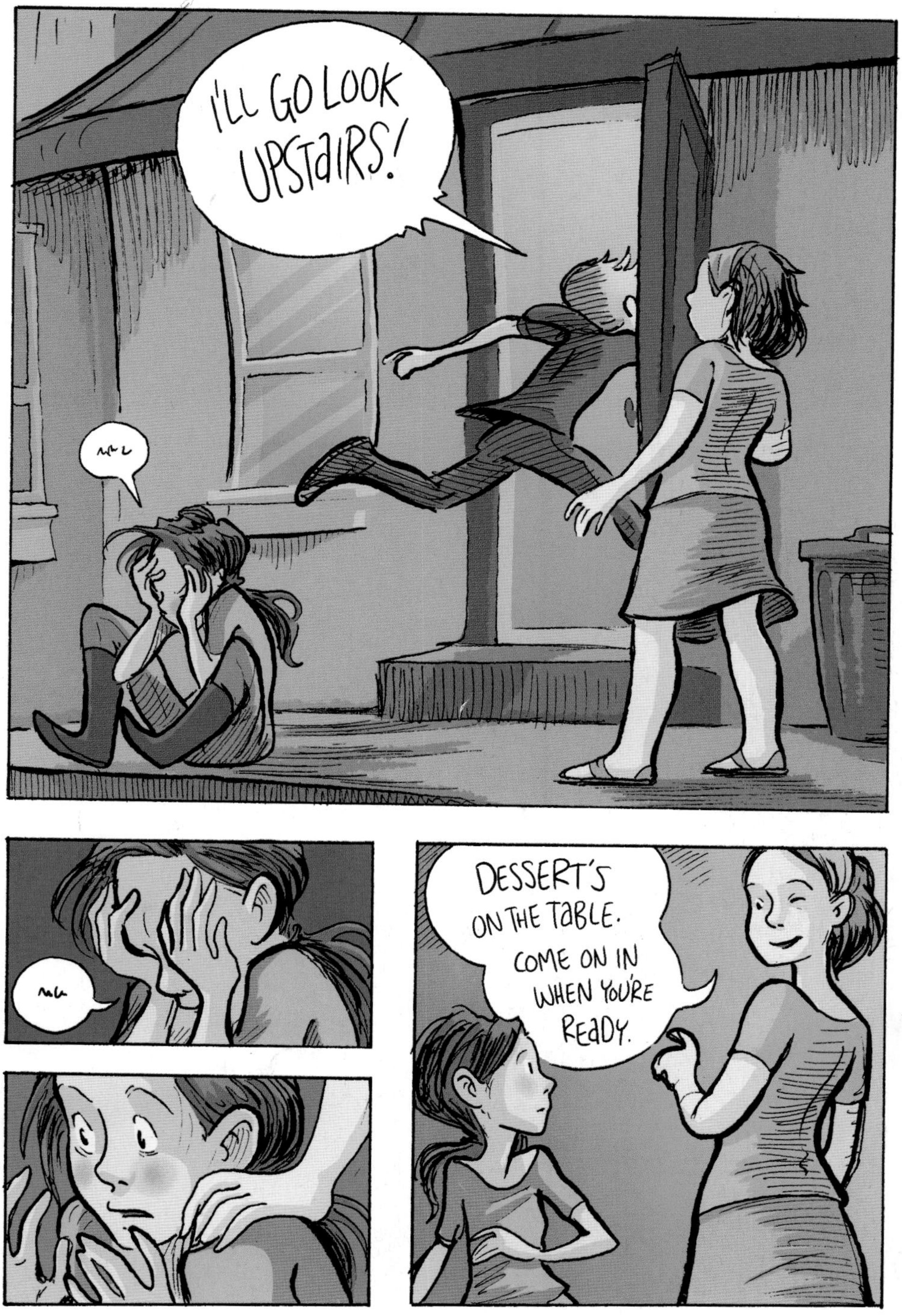
I'LL GO LOOK UPSTAIRS!
DESSERT'S ON THE TABLE.
COME ON IN WHEN YOU'RE READY.

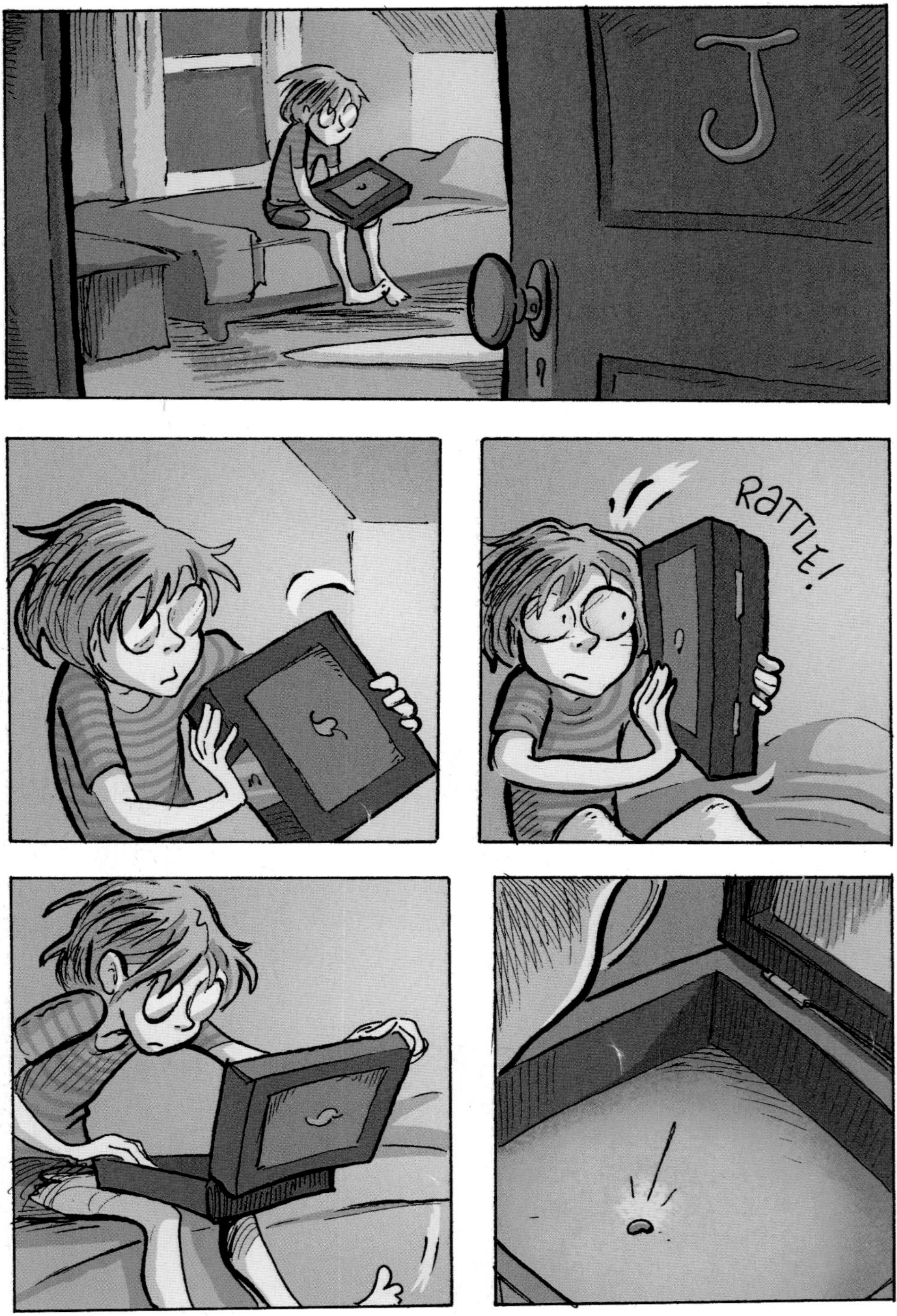
RATTLE!

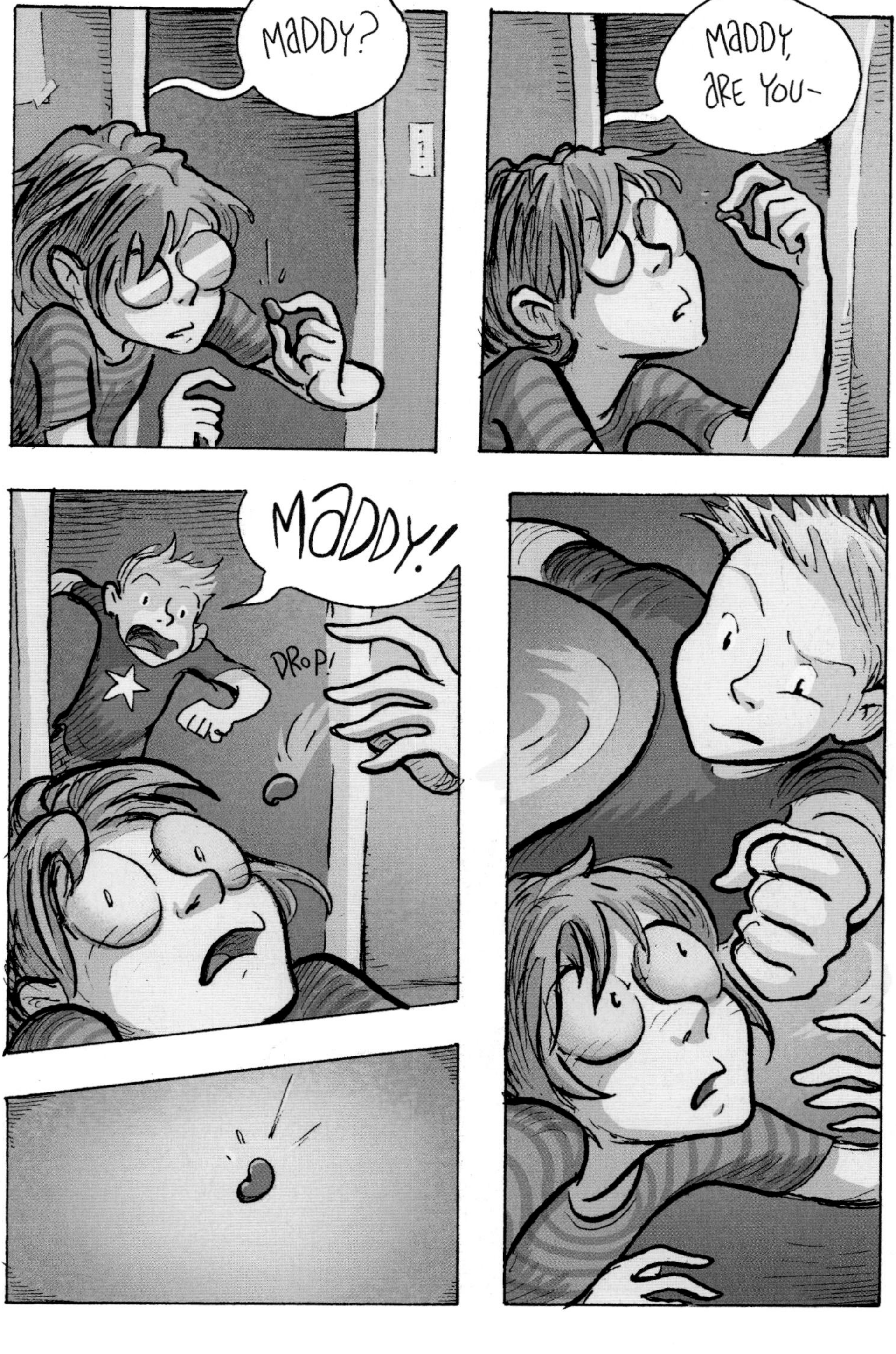
MADDY?
MADDY, ARE YOU-
MADDY!
DROP!

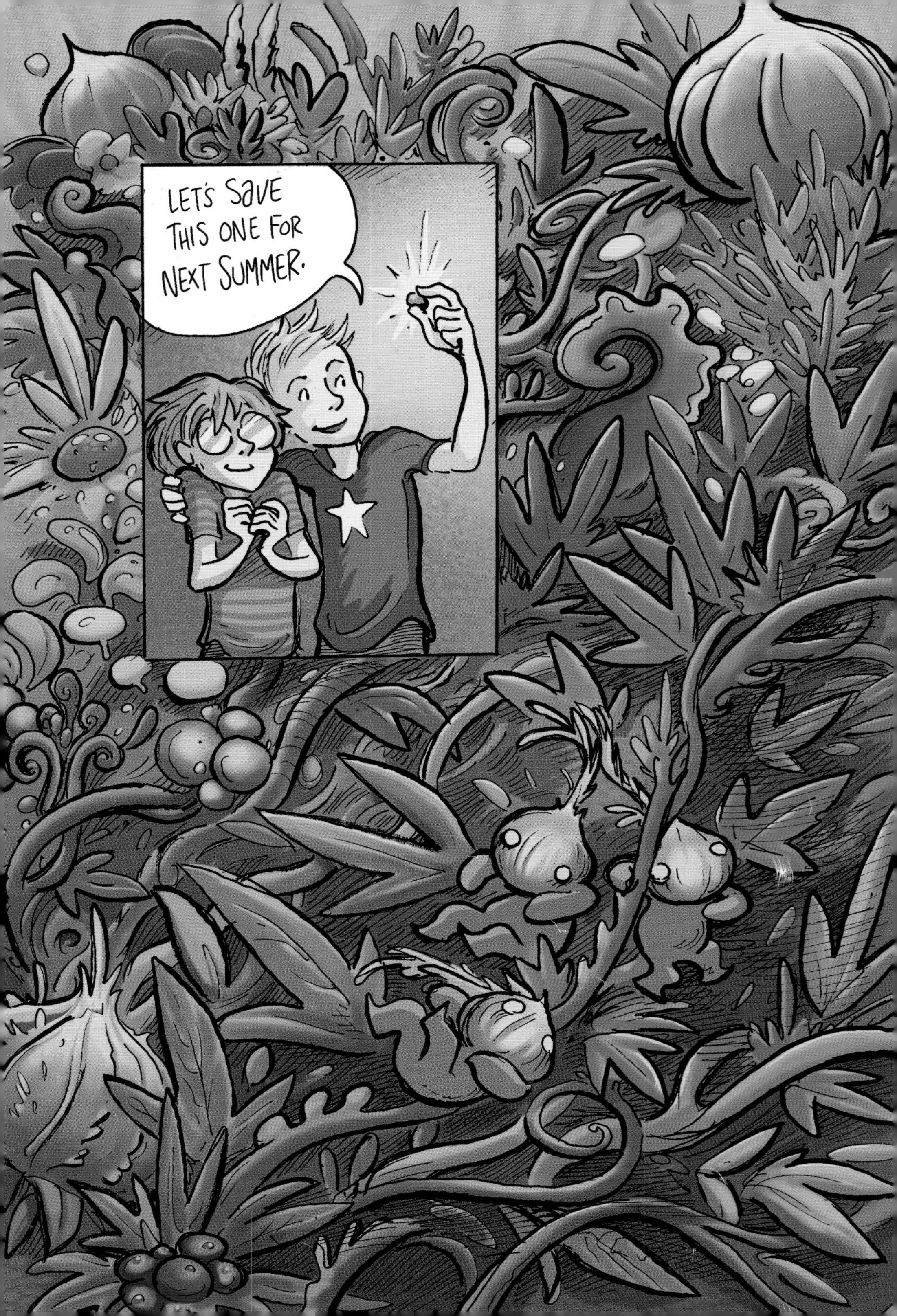
LET'S SAVE THIS ONE FOR NEXT SUMMER.

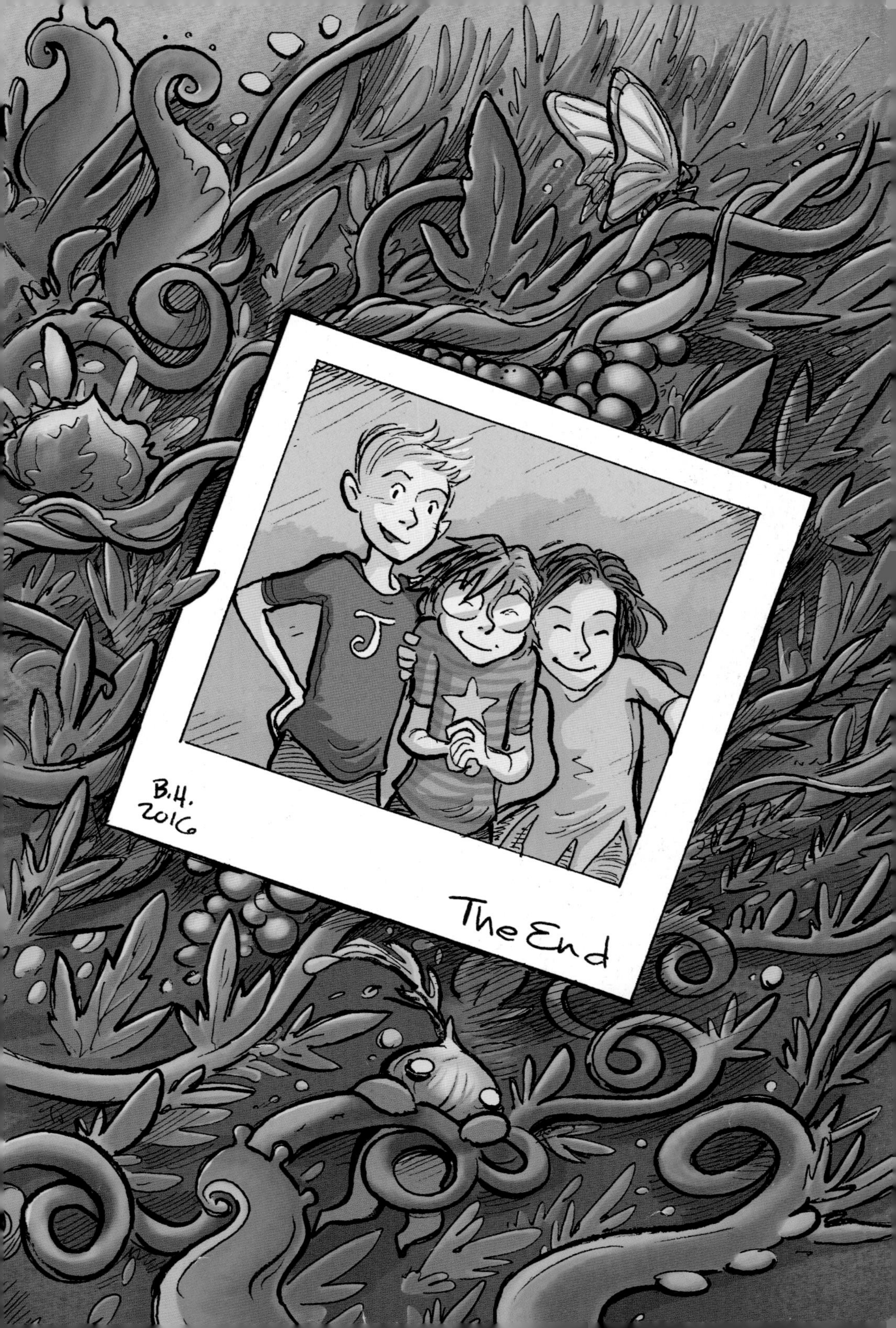
J
B.H.
2016
The End

EPILOGUE

THREE MONTHS LATER...

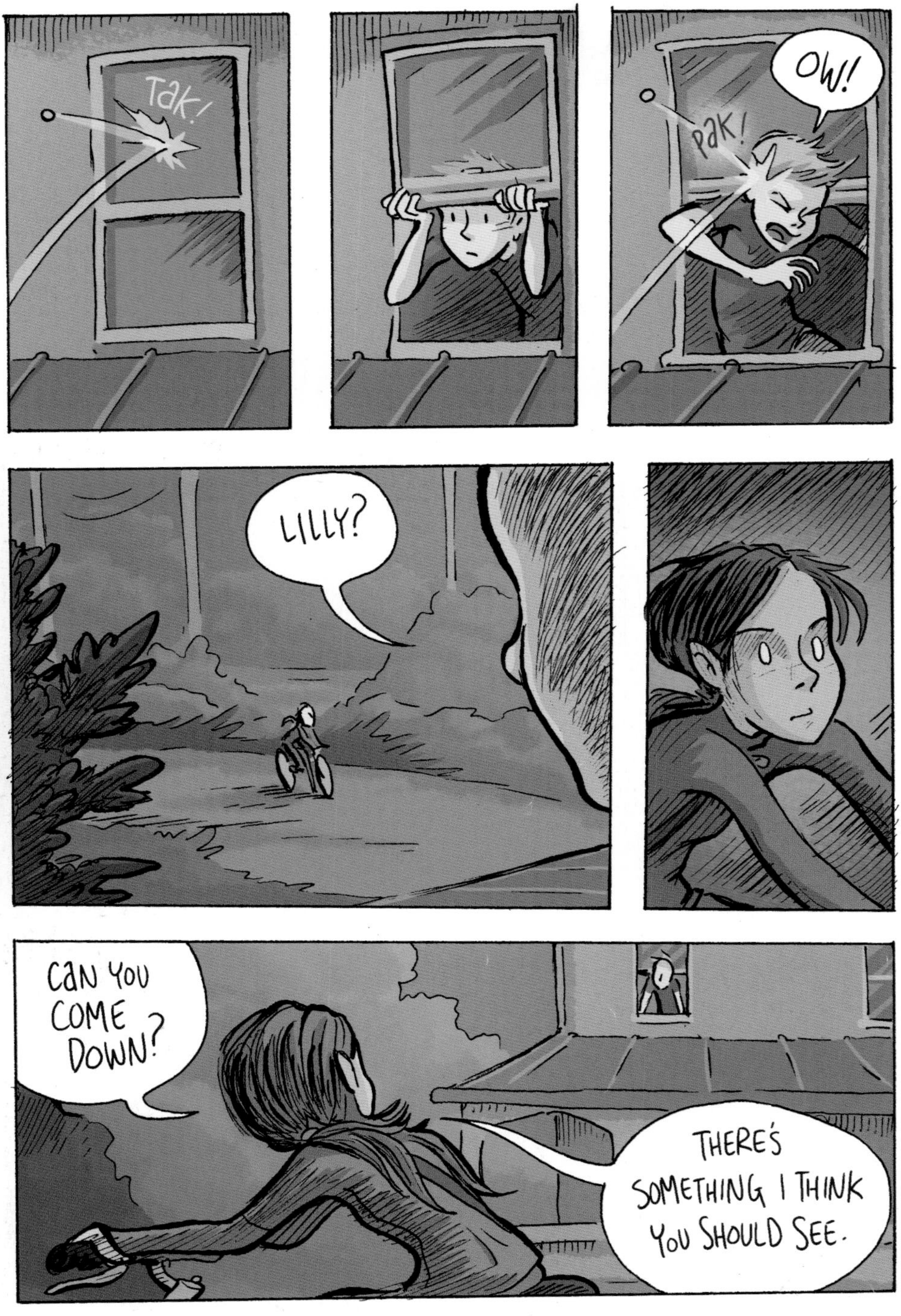
TAK!
PAK!
OW!
LILLY?
CAN YOU COME DOWN?
THERE'S SOMETHING I THINK YOU SHOULD SEE.

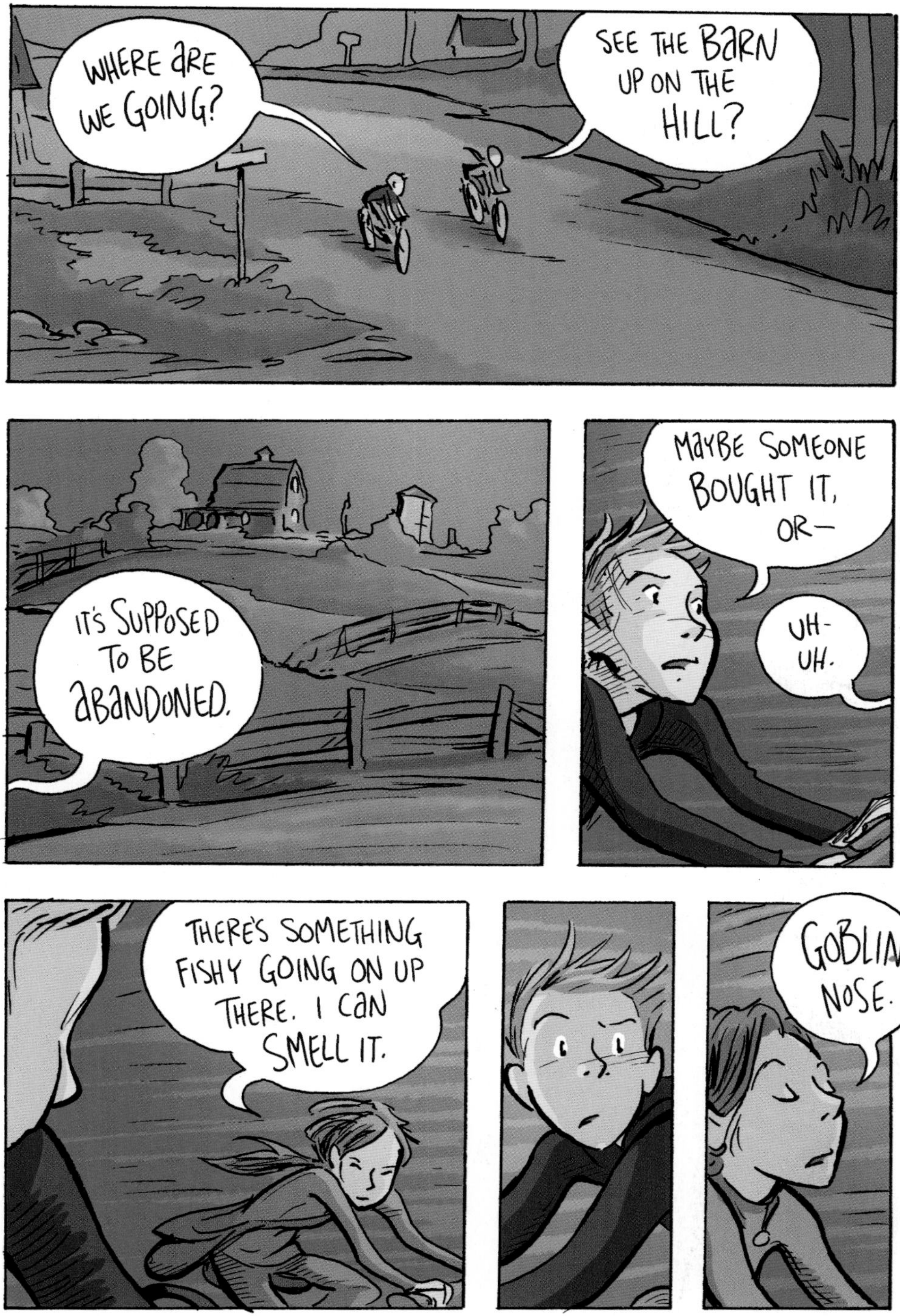
WHERE ARE WE GOING?
SEE THE BARN UP ON THE HILL?
IT'S SUPPOSED TO BE ABANDONED.
MAYBE SOMEONE BOUGHT IT, OR—
UH-UH.
THERE'S SOMETHING FISHY GOING ON UP THERE. I CAN SMELL IT.
GOBLIN NOSE.

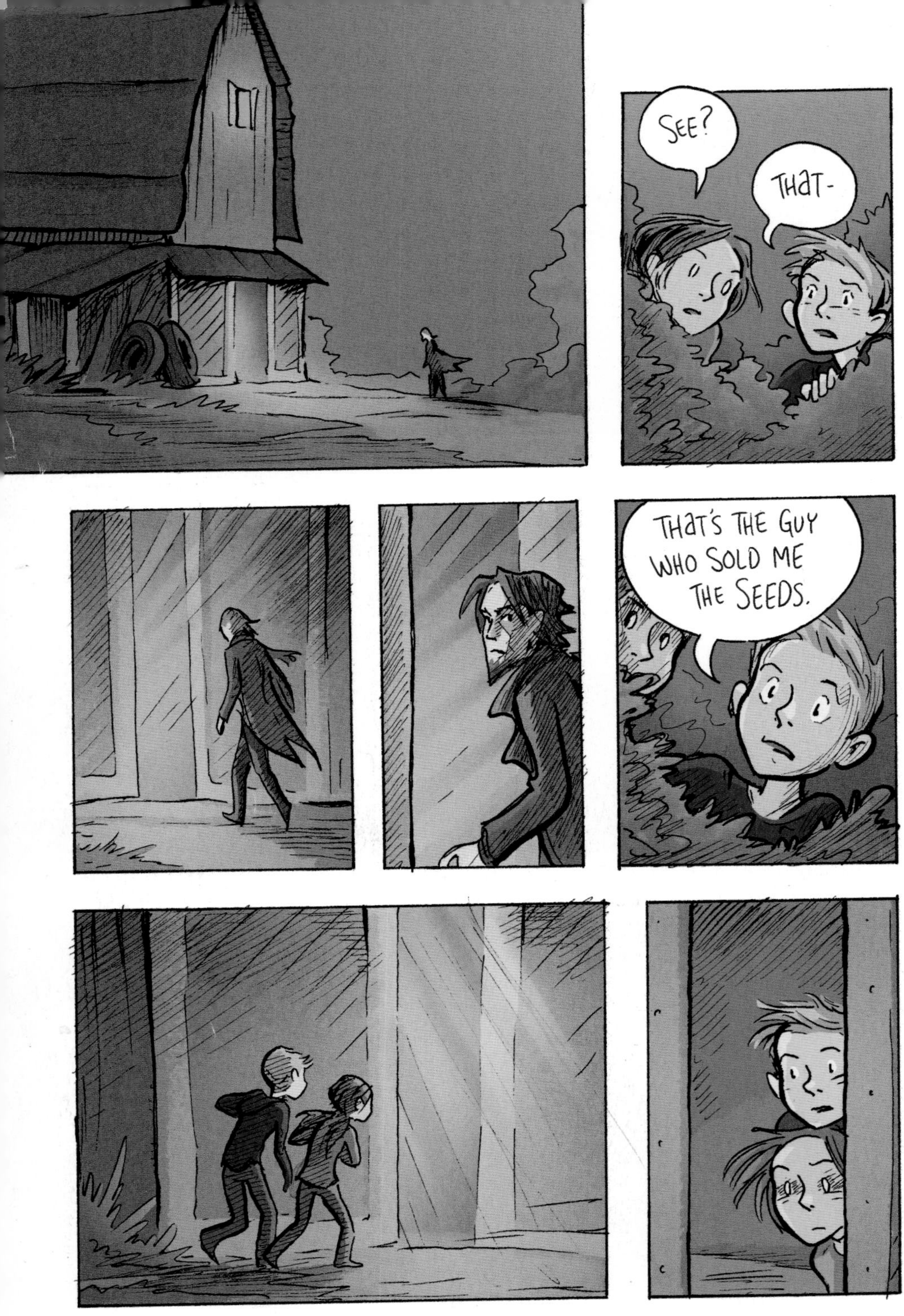
SEE?
THAT-
THAT'S THE GUY WHO SOLD ME THE SEEDS.

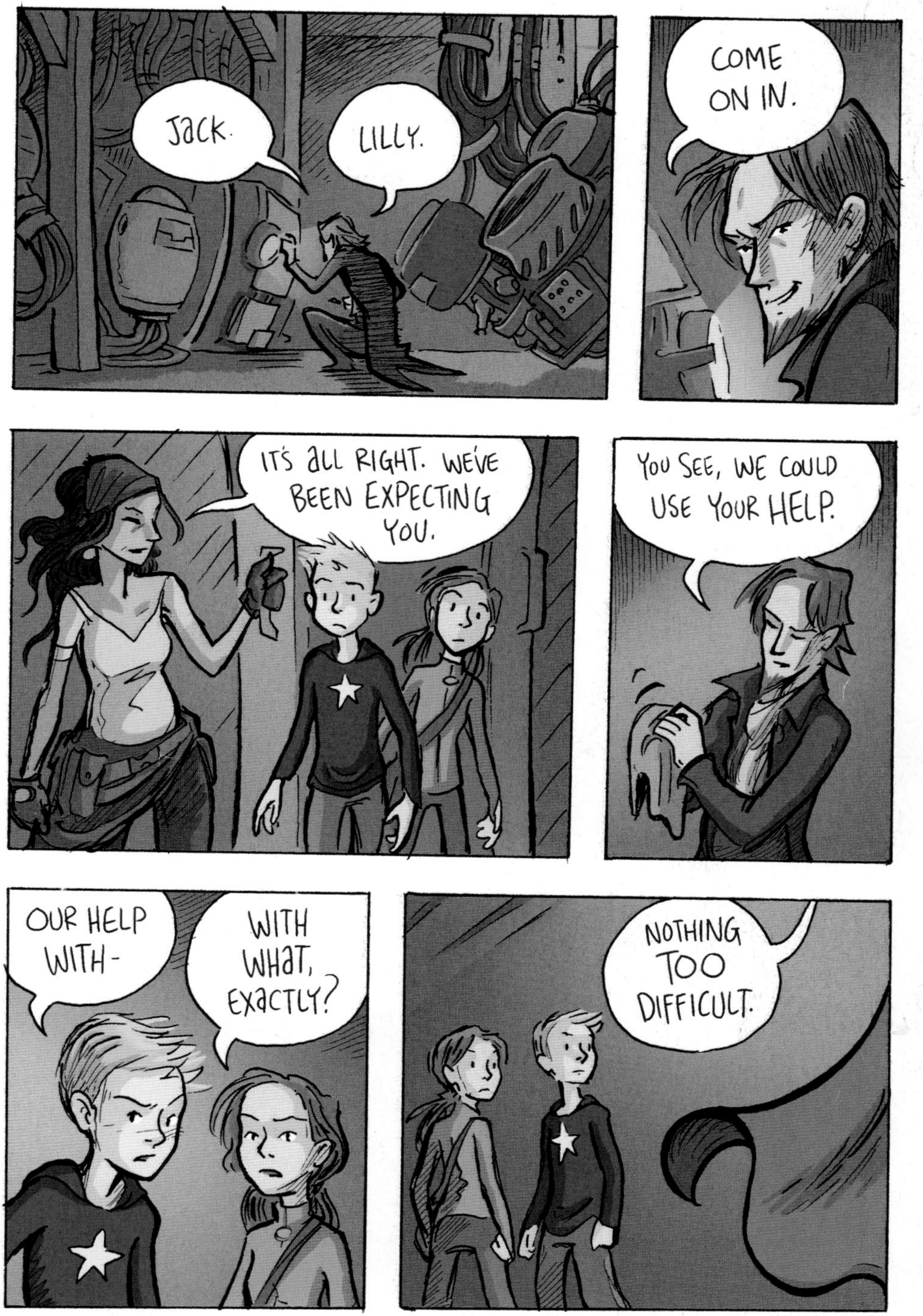
JACK.
LILLY.
COME ON IN.
IT'S ALL RIGHT. WE'VE BEEN EXPECTING YOU.
YOU SEE, WE COULD USE YOUR HELP.
OUR HELP WITH-
WITH WHAT, EXACTLY?
NOTHING TOO DIFFICULT.

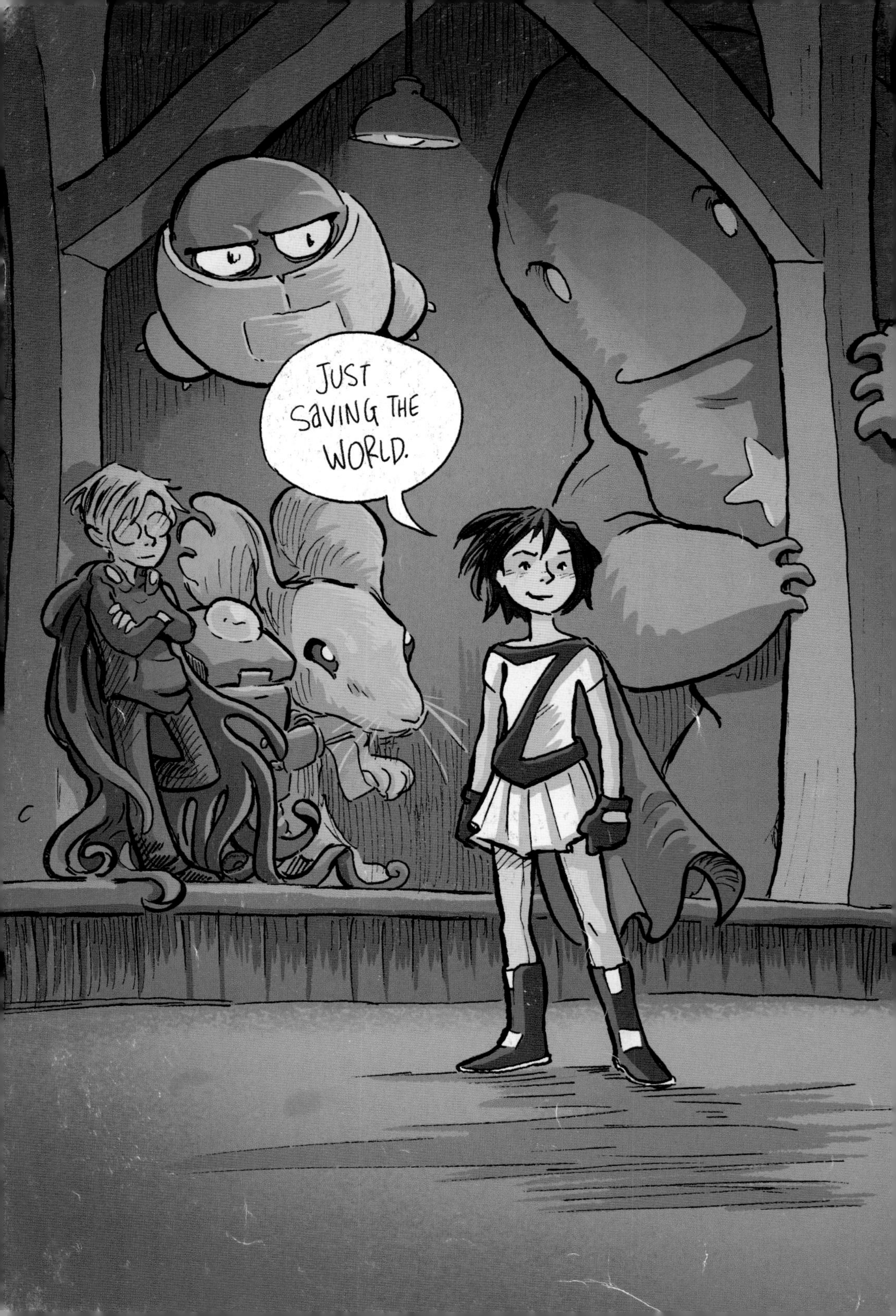
JUST SAVING THE WORLD.

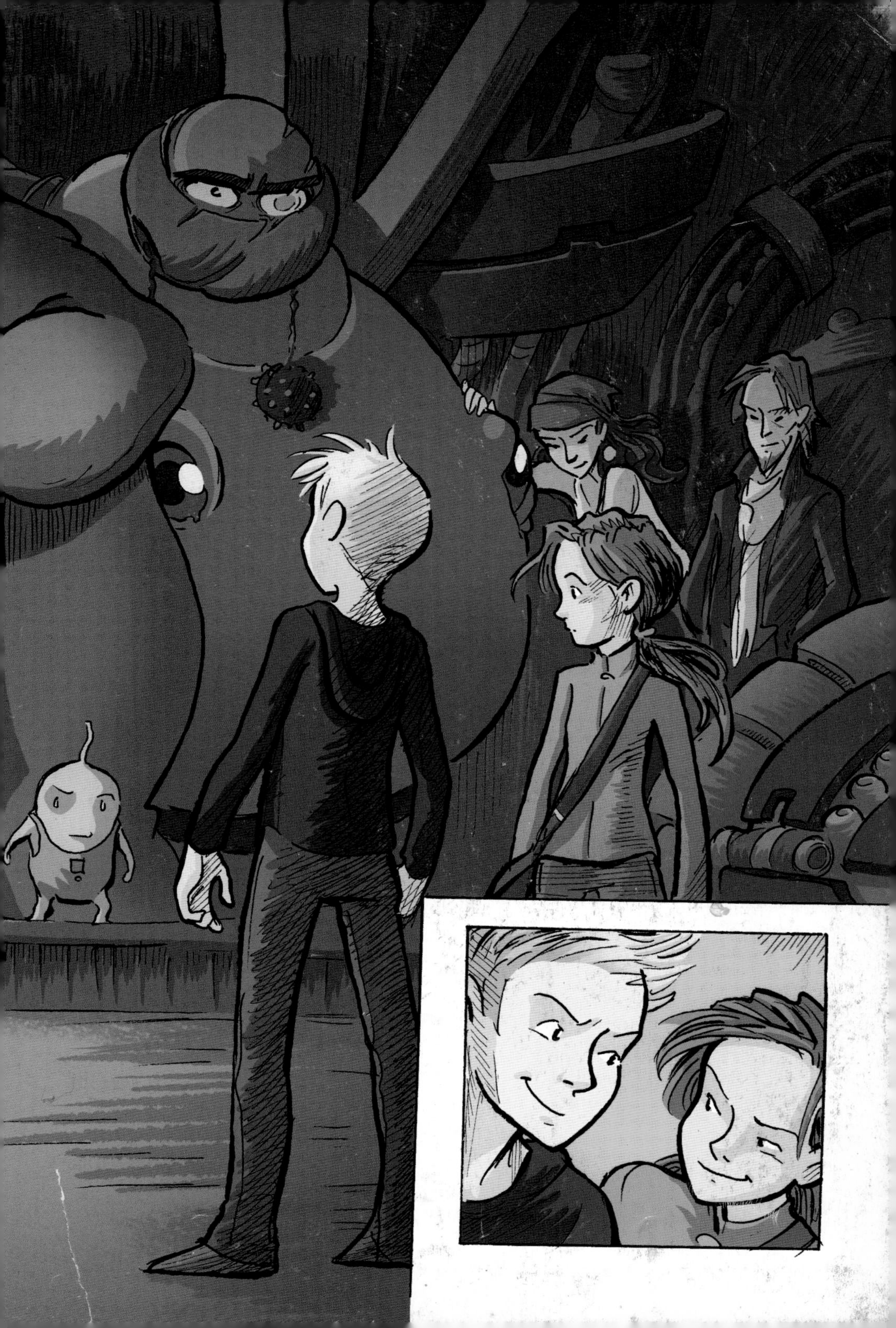

Copyright © 2017 by Ben Hatke
Published by First Second
First Second is an imprint of Roaring Brook Press,
a division of Holtzbrinck Publishing Holdings Limited Partnership
175 Fifth Avenue, New York, New York 10010

Library of Congress Control Number: 2016961549

Hardcover ISBN: 978-1-62672-267-5
Paperback ISBN: 978-1-62672-266-8

Our books may be purchased in bulk for promotional, educational, or
business use. Please contact your local bookseller or the Macmillan Corporate
and Premium Sales Department at (800) 221-7945 ext. 5442 or by e-mail
at MacmillanSpecialMarkets@macmillan.com.

The art for this book was drawn on laser printer paper with Sakura Pigma
Micron pens (sizes 005, 01, 05, and 08) over light colored pencil. Colors were
accomplished digitally using Photoshop.

First edition 2017
Book design by Joyana McDiarmid
Colors by Alex Campbell and Hilary Sycamore of Sky Blue Ink
Printed in China by Toppan Leefung Printing Ltd.,
Dongguan City, Guangdong Province

Hardcover: 10 9 8 7 6 5 4 3 2 1
Paperback: 10 9 8 7 6 5 4 3 2 1